GATSBY'S RIVAL

— A NOVEL —

RICHARD GUIMOND

First paperback edition July 2024

Book design by Duane Stapp
Cover image Shutterstock

ISBN 979-8-9909362-0-1

To my wife, Carol,
whose intelligence and loving kindness have greatly enriched my life,
and to my three remarkable daughters, whose determined and perceptive
minds have consistently guided me forward..

~~~~~~

A Special thanks to Editor Crystal Sershen, for her keen eyes and continued support,
and especially her love for the characters throughout the entire process. Also, a Thank you,
to Duane Stapp for his great work on the cover and the internals of the manuscript.

CHAPTER ONE

Early Autumn, 1922–West Egg, Long Island

JAY GATSBY SAT AT HIS LARGE FORMAL DESK, his cheerful pink suit in stark contrast to his forlorn expression and empty heart. His breakfast with Nick, his one true confidant and friend, had provided him little solace. While Nick's kind parting comment had momentarily uplifted him, it was time for that deep, honest reflection that one can only achieve alone.

Daisy had not called and his hidden vigil outside of her home had not produced any clue to what was going on in the Buchanan household. Sighing, he reached into his desk drawer and pulled out a small photo. Gently touching it, he realized it had only been six months since his grandfather's passing. Gatsby's heart pounded as his mind drifted back to the New York Brightman Hospital. He envisioned himself standing over the bed, moving closer to the man he found late in life, who had become more important to him than his own father. On that day, for the first time, Gatsby stood face to face with a different kind of death.

A middle-aged nurse sat in the private room. As Gatsby entered, a throaty moan permeated the air. She glanced up at Gatsby with a sad expression.

1

He moved closer to the bed, stared down at his grandfather, then turned to the nurse, who just shook her head.

Suddenly, the old man's eyes blinked a few times, then opened slowly. As Gatsby approached his bed, small tears slid down his pallid cheeks. In a raspy voice, "Son, you're about to see what death looks like. Now, pay attention."

Gatsby dragged a chair closer to the bed. Pa waved him even closer, then motioned the nurse away. She left the room and closed the door.

"I always do, Pa. You know...I love you...more than my own..." Tears blurred his vision. Nelson's breathing continued to labor.

"Don't try to talk, Pa."

Nelson waved away that request.

"I'm relieved you're here...seeing that your father doesn't have the balls to watch me die..."

Gatsby appeared tilted by this harsh reality. He hesitated for a moment. "I'm sorry for that, Pa."

That truth clutched at Gatsby's chest like a heart attack. He took a slow, deep breath, which did nothing to ease the pain and sorrow inside of him.

Nelson's voice intensified. "Don't be sorry. Never be sorry. He's a weak man. Always was. But you...you're my boy. You're strong, smart...and I want you to do something for me."

"Of course, Pa."

Nelson pointed to some pillows on a chair. "If you love me, I want you to use one...end my misery."

Gatsby hesitated for some time. His grandfather's eyes were partially closed, waiting. He clutched the pillow with both hands, slowly raised it over Nelson's head. Took a deep breath.

Suddenly, Nelson's hand grabbed Gatsby's wrist. "No, son. I wanted to see if you would do it. Besides, I'd never allow this to be on your conscience."

Gulping deep breaths of relief, Gatsby said, "I was only doing it as an act of love, Pa."

"I know that. Now, I need to give you some advice before it's too late."

"I'm listening, Pa."

"Your weakness for her will ruin you…" He tried to take a deep breath. "For a long time, I've watched you…pining away…"

"I've been a complete fool." Gatsby hung his head. It took a few moments before his grandfather spoke again.

"James, you can't cling to past memories. I've watched it eat away at you, like…like this disease I'm dying from. Do you understand what I'm saying?"

Gatsby nodded. "Of course, Pa. I've always respected your wisdom."

"Well…not always wise." The old man managed half a grin. "But James…she'll never be yours…" His whisper was barely audible. "Not in any real sense. She's no longer the girl of your youth."

Gatsby tried to form a reassuring sentence to Pa, but as the words struggled to drop from his lips, death washed over his grandfather's face.

Gatsby stood up from his desk, still holding the photo. "You were right, Pa. It is time to move on, I am going to—"

A tap on the open window ended his one-way conversation with the dead man. He turned to see the gardener.

"I am sorry to bother you, sir," said the gardener. "As requested, the pool is ready for your swim."

~~~~~~

Fall 1920–New Bedford, Massachusetts

Gatsby hadn't spoken since he entered the dimly lit room. Not so much as a nod to the waiting men. He gave the presence of a waterman with his dirty-blond beard and the clothes he wore—a working sailor, a fisherman, even—not the well-bred socialite familiar to the residents of The Gold Coast of Chicago, the city he had recently fled.

He glanced around at the hodgepodge of characters—each of them a walking crime, as best he could describe, easily just escaped from prison. Though he wasn't intimidated, his heart thumped like a Liberty engine—the same converted aircraft engines powering his recently constructed rum boat. If everything went according to his calculations, he'd be exactly where he wanted to be in a few months' time.

As the men waited in silence to meet him, Gatsby turned to Paul Moran—heavyset and balding, first cousin to the crooked mayor of Providence, Rhode Island, a career lawyer. Moran liked the good life: money, fine food, cigars, liquor. For some reason, women hadn't made the list.

Gatsby always marveled about Moran's role in his life and how his former mentor, the now-deceased Dan Cody, had brought them together in a most unexpected and astounding way. Prior to Gatsby meeting him, Cody had made a fortune in the Far West and Alaska. Silver mines in the Sierra Nevada mountains, copper in Montana and gold from the Yukon added to his immense wealth.

After the fateful day that Gatsby saved Cody's yacht, the *Tuolomee*, from an impending storm, Cody immediately employed the man and the pair spent five years sailing the continent together. Cody introduced Gatsby to the richness of the world and Gatsby's many roles included trying to keep the heavy drinker sober. Cody passed away in Boston days after his conniving mistress, Ella Kaye, unexpectedly boarded the yacht. After Cody's death, Kaye had found a way to legally take control of Cody's fortune, including the tidy sum left to Gatsby, and absconded with the money quickly, never looking back.

Moran, a trusted cohort of Cody's, had the delayed but distinct pleasure of informing Jay Gatsby that Dan Cody had secretly provided for him outside his will and had transferred his beloved *Tuolomee* to Gatsby's name before he died.

Moran had dutifully saw to the safekeeping of the yacht as it had taken years and a tip from one of Meyer Wolfsheim's associates for

Moran to track down the elusive Gatsby. Along with the vessel, Moran produced a confusing handwritten note from Cody to Gatsby: *"Dear Jay, Whenever you stash Tuolomee's sails in the forepeak, thank her for providing a safe voyage in rugged weather. And always give her an appreciative pat on her tight galley walls. In stormy seas, those walls will always protect you—now and well into the future. Yours, Dan"*

It was not until Gatsby encountered a hellish nor'easter sailing the boat to Newport, Rhode Island, that he discovered the note was not one of Cody's drunken ramblings but a carefully worded puzzle pointing him to investigate behind the stiff galley inside walls, where his benefactor had left him thirty-three hefty bags of gold dust and bright yellow nuggets.

Gatsby's financial future was secured. From thence on, Moran was used by Gatsby for anything legal…or illegal.

What Jay Gatsby and most politicians figured—Prohibition would last a few more years, possibly longer. Gatsby had to get out of Chicago, and his association with Paul Moran provided the perfect entrée to his next venture. He wanted to capitalize on that relationship and earn himself a bigger fortune in the bargain. A fortune worthy of Daisy and even more so than the wealth of Tom Buchanan. However, moving his operation to New England and taking control of the Rhode Island waters and the liquor trade upon them—wasn't a simple one.

A self-made waterman stood in his way: Tiverton fisherman-turned-rum-runner Joseph Bucolo—known as Foggy Joe—a name bestowed upon him by various crewmen and other captains for his skill in extreme foggy conditions, first, as an oyster pirate; second, for locating supply ships from the Canadian French islands of Miquelon and Saint Pierre.

Moran removed a gold toothpick from his mouth, pointed it at the men. "These six are the best watermen in Rhode Island, outside of Bucolo's crew."

Gatsby gave him a nod.

Moran continued, "Men who know the ocean the way Bucolo

does—especially the Narragansett Bay and Seaconnet River—and who can captain boats that stand a chance of outrunning and outsmarting the Coast Guard."

Gatsby slowly shook his head. "From what I've heard, this Foggy Joe doesn't seem to have any problem outfoxing the Coast Guard."

Moran nodded in agreement, as did a few of the men—now listening eagerly to the conversation.

One of them mumbled, "Bucolo's smart, tough, and he know-a the waters like Maggie Jackson's pussy... Been outplayin' the law since-a becoming a young oyster pirate." Kanky "Portagee" DeSouza was a mean-looking, big-nosed hulk of a man whose bear-like posture bore a forward hunch. The likeness was reinforced by small, deep-set eyes and enormous hands and arms. A thick black mustache swallowed his top lip. His complexion was dark—from years working the water and an ancestral mix of Cape Verdean and Portuguese blood. Kanky's people emigrated from the Azores in 1890, settling in Bristol, Rhode Island, and turned to farming and raising beef cattle.

That wasn't the life for Kanky. He bounced from port to port, finally landing in Tiverton, earning his living by the dark of the moon, raiding oyster beds and doing seasonal trap-fishing at Seaconnet Point, working for Max Bucolo and his adopted son, Joe. After a few years, Kanky and Max had a serious falling-out. Kanky left Tiverton with a warning from Max never to come back.

A few days before this meeting, Moran told Gatsby that Kanky had inside stories on Joe Bucolo and his men. Kanky could provide muscle to do the unpleasant work, keeping the crews and any others in line. If Gatsby was going to take a shot at rum-running and go up against Bucolo, Kanky was his man.

By Kanky's side, smoking a cigarette, was Narcisse "Collector" Jolivet. He had a square jaw, with a full head of blondish hair and eyes the color of a calm sea—a farmer's mix of French and Swedish blood. Born in the Midwest, he left home at the age of twenty. He had no interest in growing corn and—inspired by the novel *Captains*

Courageous—he'd always wanted to become a fisherman.

One of Collector's vices or attributes was the habit of stealing a memento from wherever he happened to be—thus the nickname. Not the remorseful type, he told everyone to call him Collector. But the quality he was prouder of was his facility with words—to strike up a rhyme extempore, as Shakespeare would have put it. He also told everyone he was a poet at heart and that poetry was his only true passion.

Gatsby's eyes gauged the men. "What's Bucolo's background?"

Kanky said, "First off, Joe was a runaway orphan. Max Bucolo took him in…gave Joe the Bucolo name. Over the years, all of Max's men sorta became his father, too. Joe learned a lot from Max and the other fishermen. Won't be an easy man to beat…he's had their stubborn Swamp Yankee blood drummed into him."

Gatsby thought about that—the life of an orphan—no roots, no real identity to frame you. Maybe we're alike. No real father to call Dad. Then again, Bucolo had real men around him to help. He took a deep breath and exhaled. "So, what kind of men does Bucolo have working for him? Does he have their loyalty? Will they run from a fight? What can we expect?"

Kanky motioned to Collector. In his coarse voice, said, "Tell him 'bout Hunker."

Collector nodded to Gatsby and said, "He's an unusual specimen in Bucolo's gang."

Gatsby understood the "unusual specimen" comment—linking it, and Hunker, to these men seated around him—these men he was looking to hire.

Collector's words were firm and deliberate. "In my view, Bucolo's gang is a horde of dug-in Swamp Yankees…all hatched and raised on the eastern banks of the Seaconnet River." There was a certain rhythm to his description, accented by his facial expressions. "People claimed their mothers were swamp beepers…and their pops were swamp trolls…or what the Indians called *Matchee*. I became acquainted with the one called Hunker…and that was enough for me."

Gatsby seemed spellbound. Moran watched him with curiosity.

Gatsby asked, "What drives a man like Hunker? This 'Swamp Yankee'…?"

Collector shrugged. "Mister Gatsby, frankly, for what I know of him…I…I think the devil has eaten his soul… They say he's dumber than a crate of rocks. I actually believe he's not stupid at all. He's a man to fear…through and through a Swamper…right down to the marrow in his bones…"

Gatsby, who stood by the door, appeared enthralled, possibly troubled, by Collector's depiction.

Kanky added, "I wouldn't overlook Pearly Thurston, either. He's 'nother hard-nosed Swamper, and kinda second-in-command. Thurston is-a stubborn-smart, too, and he has a pretty daughter that every man in Tiverton wants…especially the chief of police…who hates Joe Bucolo with a passion."

Gatsby asked, "Who's this chief?"

"Name's Henry Grover. Father owns a big menhaden company with a dozen seine vessels."

"Why does he hate Bucolo?"

"Chief Grover's afraid Bucolo will-a steal away the Thurston girl…like he has some of the other girls in town…and fuck her."

Gatsby grimaced his distaste for Kanky's language. "I suppose that's one way of putting it…"

A few of the men glanced at each other, on the verge of laughter, but they didn't. Kanky and Collector ignored him and chuckled anyway. Gatsby took note.

"Sorry, Mister Gatsby," Paul Moran quickly said, and shot a look of warning to the men.

Gatsby removed a cigarette from his silver case. Tamped it on the cover, engraved in gold: **JG**. It caught Collector's attention, like the eye of a covetous crow sparkling at the shiny container.

"How much do you know about Bucolo?" Gatsby asked Collector, though the timbre of his voice made it sound as if he were hesitant to know the answer.

Collector, in sing-song, replied, "Foggy Joe's a river ghost...and to this very day he makes the law look like burnt toast. And when his appendage is at high tide...most bluenose girls go and hide...yet some are still looking for his dangle... All the girls claim he's a real pro...but ya won't hear that from Joe's lips...while most agree he has a busy dick..."

Gatsby chuckled while the other men laughed. "Thank you. That was both profound and poetic."

He looked at Moran. "These men will do fine. Okay, boys, get yourself a drink."

While his new crew moved eagerly towards their nourishments, Gatsby turned to Paul Moran. "How are things progressing here?"

"Herman the German is hard to deal with. But he wants out since his son died on Rum Row."

"What about those Little Compton wharves?"

"No luck there. Those Swampers drive a hard bargain...besides, they all love Bucolo. We may have to settle on Oakland Beach and New Bedford."

"Fine, but I want a jump on the weather. As soon as it starts to break, Rum Row will be coming alive again. I want everything ready to go. Supply ships from Miquelon and Saint Pierre will be on their way here by the second week of February."

Moran asked, "Is Wolfsheim certain Prohibition isn't going to be repealed?"

Gatsby said, "He's had extensive talks with Congressman Andrew Volstead from Minnesota, who guaranteed him that it remains the law of the land!"

"Whatever you say, Mister Gatsby."

"Now, this Tiverton girl that Kanky and you mentioned—Maggie Jackson?" Gatsby paused. "Are you certain about her relationship with Bucolo?"

"She's been in his bed, on and off, for some time."

"Good... So...?"

"As it happens, Miss Jackson is a little loose, quite attractive... and I believe I can set up a meeting. I do have some dangerous rumors about her mother's past. I think it will be an incentive for her to help you."

"Dangerous! Really? Either way, for the moment, I don't need to know, until she agrees to the meeting."

"I doubt Miss Jackson will object to whatever you want."

"Good. Set it up, but not here. Providence...pick a place."

"Frankie-the-Bone's. I'll arrange it. I might add, again, she's not like those Chicago butterflies. She's rather..." Moran searched for the word, "steely."

Gatsby didn't respond. From the candle's reflection on his features, he was clearly pondering something. Finally, he said softly, "I'm sure I can handle Miss Jackson."

Moran, appearing slightly puzzled at Gatsby's intentions, stared at him for a long moment.

"Rest easy, Paul! Opportunity is coming! There's plenty of money to be made in rum-running. My intent is to control the trade at the main source. Premium booze right off those Canadian boats."

"If anyone can achieve that, Mister Gatsby, it's you. But keep in mind, you heard it tonight: Foggy Joe and his Swamp Yankees... It could turn into bullets for booze."

"That is why we need to keep our plans quiet as the grave for as long as we can. Not a whisper."

"Not going to be easy, but we can try. People love to talk."

Sensing Gatsby's annoyance Moran thought it best to take his leave and made for the door.

Gatsby quickly added, "I have decided on the boat's name. Get it done before the boat's pending sea trials."

Moran turned around, curious. "Yes, sir... What will the name be?"

"Diamond Daisy!"

CHAPTER TWO

April 10th, 1921—Atlantic Ocean

WEST OF THE SEACONNET LIGHTHOUSE, where the river and the ocean merge, a muffled sound—like building thunder—approached with clarity until the foggy air shattered with the screech of metallic engine power.

Then, the startling boom of cannon fire.

Another shell, even closer, exploded, spraying a sheet of white water over the small windshield of the *Black Duck*, soaking the deck loaded with contraband.

Manning the helm was Joseph "Foggy Joe" Bucolo, his good looks tempered by sea-weathered features, a wiry body conditioned from the hard work of a lifelong fisherman. At a certain angle, the soft lights of the instrument panel highlighted the scar on his right cheek.

Sammy Turner's ears never left the cadence of the boat's engines. His wrinkled face, wet eyes, and head of thinning silver hair standing straight up bestowed on him the suggestion of an eccentric. He moaned as a shell exploded in the water thirty feet ahead.

Sammy's anxious eyes darted from the instrument panel to his captain: "That fucking cannon!"

"I can see, Sammy, I can hear!"

"Jesus H. Christ!" Sammy screamed. "I'm getting too old for this shit! You hear?"

Joe yelled, "Hell! You're not that old!"

At the mouth of the Seaconnet, a few frightened sea ducks took flight, their shrill quacks prompting an entire flock to take to the air—the chain reaction echoing down the river.

The first blush of dawn peeked over the horizon, setting a thin, low-hanging layer of fog aflame in orange and red. The calm river steamed like a sheet of melting ice, piercing the jagged Rhode Island coastline deep into its sleeping interior.

Rooster tails of white water arched high from the sterns of three sixty-foot rum boats. They were shallow draft, with sharp bows and low-profile pilot houses—their rakish mahogany hulls painted black, no running lights. Burlap-wrapped sacks of liquor piled high on their open decks.

They roared up the long Seaconnet River in V-formation, led by the *Black Duck*. Just yards astern of the three boats, another explosion blew a column of bubbles into the air. Another geyser spouted, then another—each disrupting the wakes of the speeding boats.

"They're closing in, Joe! Damnit! They're closing in!"

Five miles north, at Sandy Point Shoals, pole-fish traps strung with cork and leaded twine were set, waiting for the first spring run of roe-filled herring. The anchored funnel nets resisted the strong outgoing current, rippling the otherwise glass-smooth surface of the Seaconnet River as it flowed between the highlands of Tiverton and the desolate eastern shoreline of Little Compton.

As though of one mind, the three vessels veered slightly east with perfect precision. The lead boat crossed over the bow of the port-side boat, cutting along the westerly edge of the river, hugging the Aquidneck Island shoreline.

~~~~~~

In pursuit, the gray, seventy-five-foot Coast Guard vessel also changed course. CG-483, a prototype, had a top speed of thirty knots and was faster than any of her sister ships. Her stripped-down hull cut effortlessly through the draining tide, slowly gaining on the heavily laden rum-runners. On her foredeck, guardsmen again readied their one-pound cannon.

~~~~~~

The lights from the instrument panel made Joe's fingers look like skeleton bones. Sammy watched as Joe's eyes darted like an osprey hunting fish, straining to see through the pilot house windows—looking for the small flag that would guide him through the shoals.

Joe turned and shouted, "Big guns have a way of making your balls tighten, eh, Sammy?"

Sammy Turner could only nod. He felt an ache in his wrist as he gripped the teak railing that ran the length of the instrument panel console. He turned towards the Coast Guard vessel. "She's faster than the others, Joe."

"So I've noticed!"

"We missed it, Joe. I'm afraid we missed it." Sammy heard a nervous squeak in his voice—like he was some snot-nosed kid. He hoped his captain hadn't heard it.

Joe yelled, "See anything?"

"Not yet!"

The engines roared on. Sammy continued to study Joe's face for signs of doom or doubt—but he saw only concentration and for that, he was thankful. If Joe missed that marker pole, they would all be in serious trouble, especially with daylight approaching. There would be no place to hide, no place to unload. And Sammy knew Joe would never toss this jag of liquor overboard. No way in hell.

"Sandy Point! Get ready!"

Sammy flicked on the engine room lights and dropped to his knees. He lifted the hatch, carefully setting it right-side up alongside the opening. He wasn't about to be visited with the bad luck that came with turning over a hatch, especially at a time like this. The pilot house filled with the deafening roar of the converted twin four-hundred-horsepower aircraft engines.

He climbed down into the brightly lit compartment, sniffing for odors and feeling for heat. Crawling between the two massive, water-cooled Liberties, he checked the gauges, scanned the stuffing boxes and the spinning shafts. Scurrying to the rear bulkhead, oblivious to the intensity of the Liberties' screams, he rested his hand on the control valve and waited for Joe's signal.

"There's the marker!" Joe yelled. "Do it now! Make the smoke! Now!"

Sammy's grease-stained claw hung on the green valve until finally the lights blinked. He turned the valve, releasing a mixture of fuel oil, drain oil, kerosene, and pyrene into the four copper tubes that ran to the front of the exhaust manifolds, where it all quickly permeated the inside chambers of the hot exhausts. He climbed out of the engine room and closed the hatch, pressed his hands against his throbbing, burning ears.

Sammy turned and looked out the rear windows over the pyramid of liquor. The *Black Duck*'s wet exhausts were vomiting a cloud of midnight smoke so thick, it swallowed the fog and everything behind it. Within moments, the *Mallard* and *Wood Duck* pierced the *Black Duck*'s wall of deception, each ejecting their own trails of murky clouds.

Joe nodded to his engineer. Sammy just shook his head, his attention riveted on the billowing wall of the rum boats' tar-black diversion. He knew the hot exhausts would burn the oil at an astonishing rate, and he was wishing he had installed holding tanks with more capacity.

They passed that first row of fish-trap poles, now slightly visible in the first light, and the color of the river changed. With the shallow shoals to port, the three rum-runners banked sharply to starboard, heading east.

~~~~~~

Coxswain Norbert tightened his life jacket as the rum boats disappeared into their billowing subterfuge. Next to him, the white-faced lieutenant slammed the compass's steel compensating ball. The needle jumped twenty degrees and clicked back and forth like a metronome.

"Fire!" the lieutenant shouted into the klaxon. The erupting bow gun shook the pilot house, rattling its windows.

The shell exploded somewhere in the black clouds ahead, just as the thick wall of blindness engulfed the patrol vessel.

The nervous coxswain cleared his throat. He turned to the lieutenant and spoke softly. "Course...Lieutenant Wallace, sir!"

"As she goes, Norbert."

"Aye-aye, sir." Coxswain Norbert glanced at the chart to his right. He could see the red warning marking the shoals.

"Those fucking Swamp Yankee fishermen!" screamed the lieutenant.

"Yes, sir," said Coxswain Norbert. "And Sandy Point Shoals... close by...maybe even dead ahead, sir."

"Continue course!"

"Aye-aye, sir," he whispered to nobody. The young coxswain tightened his grip on the steering wheel, set his feet hard, bent his knees, and waited as they steamed on through the smoke, blacker than night fog. Zero visibility. Zero perception.

And so, patrol vessel CG-483, on a more westerly course than the boats it chased, crossed directly over the fish-trap pole from which flew a red, well-weathered, second-place 4-H ribbon that Joe Bucolo won for growing tulips back in the winter of 1906 when he attended the fourth grade at Tiverton's Fort Barton School.

Just as she ran over the fish-trap pole, the patrol vessel fetched up on the first sand bank of Sandy Point. The lightened hull lurched violently upward, slamming to a halt, her waterline rising four feet out of the river. One guardsman scraped across the deck, burning off his chin and his nose, while another flipped head over heels, hitting his head on the forward deck's bulwark.

Everything in the pilot house that wasn't secured catapulted, and the air filled with ashtrays, charts, blankets, and coffee cups. The lieutenant was thrown forward, ramming his head hard on the console.

Coxswain Norbert kept his balance and adjusted his glasses while the engines revved wildly. The propellers continued spinning, blasting sand against the freshly painted hull and across the flickering shoals.

"My God!" screamed the lieutenant as he stared at his palms—dripping with the blood he had wiped from his hemorrhaging forehead. "Oh, my God!" he repeated.

Coxswain Norbert reached for the kill cord to the engines. He pulled it and silence ensued. To avoid the wrath of the lieutenant, Coxswain Norbert immediately left the pilot house to help the bleeding guardsmen.

~~~~~~

Joe Bucolo flexed his cramped fingers and motioned for another cigarette. Sammy obliged and, with shaking hands, lit two with one match, catching a slight twitch in Joe's fingers. He saw the look on his captain's face return to normal as Joe rubbed the back of his neck, tilting his head from side to side.

"Say, I'll bet they're high and dry about now."

Sammy slapped Joe's shoulder, his heart finally calming down. "Aw, shit. That ain't a bet. You know they're high and dry."

"Hope no one got hurt."

Sammy glanced at him and looked puzzled. "They sure as hell weren't thinking that when they were tossing those one-pounders at *us*."

Joe shook his head. "That's for sure."

The *Black Duck* stayed its course through the evaporating mist. Gradually, the first signs of the blood-washed sky became clear.

"Red sky in the morning," Sammy said. "Rummies take warning."

Joe grabbed Sammy's shoulder. "And this morning the handwriting was almost on the wall. Wasn't it?"

Good engineers always worried about something, and Sammy knew there was no denying that big guns had a way of making everyone's balls tighten. Jesus, he thought, some way to make a buck.

The two old friends looked at each other, smiling, smoking, and shaking their heads.

"Yeah," Sammy added, "I kept seeing white stones in a net. Good thing I didn't turn that hatch over."

Joe's cigarette waved between his clenched teeth as he smiled. "Yeah, I noticed...good thing. You were pretty excited there, Sammy."

"Could've been really bad," Sammy replied. "Could've been really bad."

Joe nodded. "We were lucky."

"Ain't nobody that could pull that off, Joe, 'cept you." As Sammy spoke, tobacco smoke circled his face. He drew on the cigarette again. "Course, I knew you'd pull us through, Joe." He glanced out the rear windows, half expecting to see the Coast Guard behind them.

Joe motioned for Sammy to take the wheel. On deck, he looked back at the *Mallard* and the *Wood Duck* following behind. In the middle of the river, the remains of the large black smoke bank slowly began to disperse.

Joe returned to the pilot house. "Betcha it's going to storm."

"Aw, shit. That ain't a bet. Call me when you get some real news." Sammy lifted the hatch and jumped into the engine room.

"While you're down there, close the valve to the oil tank!" Joe screamed over the sound of the engines.

"What the hell do you think I'm doing?" Sammy yelled with irritation in his voice.

"You're music to my ears, old man." Joe opened the pilot house door and secured the latch. He flicked his cigarette out the door. "Music to my ears."

With the Coast Guard's cannon silent, and a nor'easter's low pressure approaching, stillness lay over the Tiverton Basin. Only the tide moved, whirling with awesome force through the Basin's trestle bridge, past Ghoul Island and down the Seaconnet River towards the Atlantic.

Mayfield's Wharf, six miles south of Tiverton on the eastern shore of the Seaconnet, protruded just north of Fogland Point. The wharf was built over many years by the farming Mayfield family using plowed-up stone and was long enough to accommodate all three boats.

Tommy Walsh was a stout, red-headed Irishman, a plumber and well-digger by trade. He ran Joe's "shore crew" like the sergeant he was during the Great War. The shore crew's job was simple—unload the boats as quickly as possible onto the half-dozen or so waiting trucks.

Tommy used local labor and paid them well to do a good job and keep their mouths shut. Many a Tiverton father recommended his son to Tommy to work the gang's shore crew for an extra buck.

Depending on the season, for most of the boys, either farming or fishing occupied their days. For some, it might even be high school. The crew worked quickly and methodically. Neither drinking nor talking was permitted.

Joe paid Elmer Mayfield twenty cents a case plus two bottles of King William for the use of his facility. For that, Elmer would keep his Main Road gate locked and, if the need arose, he would store liquor—for a price. Elmer always had plenty of liquor to pass around, usually more than what Joe or Tommy handed out. When Joe wanted to take Elmer to task, Tommy just said, "It's better to know the thief a little than not to know him at all." That tickled Joe.

Beneath the dumbstruck but excited eyes of the shore crew, the *Black Duck* maneuvered into position.

Sammy Turner threw a line to Tommy.

"Heard the cannon fire," Tommy said matter-of-factly.

Sammy's nodding head jerked to a stop and tilted sort of bird-like at Tommy. "Course you heard it, you damn fool. They were shooting right at us. You hear?"

"Glad they missed, Sammy," Tommy said, chuckling.

The shore crew's operation took twenty minutes. When it was over, the workers, the trucks, and the booze were gone; all except Tommy Walsh.

"When we heard the cannon fire...I sure had a hard time keeping my boys quiet."

Joe Bucolo removed a cap from his back pocket. "We had just enough luck, Tommy, just enough." Joe set his cap at a jaunty angle.

"Don't let 'im kid you," Sammy said. "Luck ain't got anything to do with it."

Tommy Walsh grabbed the old man's chin and turned his head to the side. "Your ears are bleeding, Sammy. That's no joke, old man. You better see Doc Peckham."

Sammy glanced sternly at Tommy Walsh. "Don't call me old man! You hear?"

Tommy Walsh laughed and handed Joe the inventory—by boat and sacks unloaded. He prided himself on accuracy.

"Glad you're okay, Joe," said Tommy.

"Yeah, I know. What would you do without me, eh, Tommy?" Joe backed the *Black Duck* away from Mayfield's Wharf and turned north, following behind the *Mallard* and the *Wood Duck*.

Tommy Walsh stood on the wharf's edge, hands in his pockets, watching them idle away. "What would I do without you, Joe? That's a good question, a very good question."

~~~~~~

Leaving Mayfield's Wharf, Joe felt a familiar gladness in his chest. Even now, as exhausted and tense as he was, with his hand on the helm of the *Black Duck*, he felt that wondrous connection between the early-morning river and his feelings within. Nonetheless, something was bothering him. He decided to wait until they were back in the clubhouse to discuss it, and wondered if any of the crew had the same concerns.

Chapter Three

ACCORDING TO FISHERMEN IN THE KNOW, Foggy Joe had, at one point or another, discovered every dip, curve, and embankment of the Seaconnet River. The soft mud, the hard ground, the sugar sand, and the barnacle-encrusted rocks along that ten-mile waterway from Max's Wharf to the Atlantic Ocean was his backyard.

He knew the secret spots where fish and lobsters tried to hide. He knew where a certain spat of oysters liked to settle in, thinking they'd found a safe home, only to be disrupted every Christmas by Joe's tongs or scallop dredge. Notably, for some time, he was also in the crosshairs of oyster companies that had leases within Narragansett Bay. However, their patrols could never catch him in the fog.

Like always, Joe studied the approaching, mysterious, gossip-haunted Ghoul Island—the sentinel of the Tiverton Basin. Since the beginning of his life on the river, that island stood as a visceral reminder of the reality behind the superstitions most fishermen wrestled with on a daily basis. The island was home, some said, only to rats, terns, cormorants, and seagulls. Others whispered about things there that were not quite of this world. Local fishermen seldom ventured near the island, blaming tricky currents that surrounded the brooding mass. Those deep waters were not fit to fish, they would claim, quickly moving on to other subjects. As he got older, it represented a miniature Rock of Gibraltar, defending the entire northern end of the river.

A quarter mile away from the island, the river flowed into the entrance of the Tiverton Basin—an oblong-shaped tidal bowl of churning tides. Currents with no rhyme or reason that conjured wild, circular eddies—a difficult stretch to travel either way, and, at times, even to berth vessels.

A steel trestle bridge spanned the narrows at the north end of the Basin, providing the only train and automobile link with Aquidneck Island and the city of Newport.

With Ghoul Island now behind them, the fog lifted and through the remaining mist, the shaft of a brilliant red sun shot up from behind the "Heights" of Tiverton. For an instant, the pilot-house windows turned into an optical prism. As the three rum boats idled in their approach, the glow of first light broke over the beautiful seaside community that Joe and his gang called home.

Joe placed his hand on Sammy's shoulder and rested it there affectionately. "This nor'easter is gonna be slow coming and slow ending…with plenty of wet between." He nodded. "I'll bet it's sure gonna raise hell with those boats offshore."

"No bet, Joe."

~~~~~~

Max's Wharf lay south of the Tiverton Basin. An L-shaped, rock-filled wharf with a gravel cap stretched over two hundred feet long, its bulkhead constructed of thick oaken planks dipped in tar set. At the south end, a jutting finger pier provided protection from the strong summer sou'westers.

As was the tradition, the *Mallard* and the *Wood Duck* waited for the *Black Duck* to tie-up first. Joe and Sammy would each take their place, on the bow and stern, and help the sister boats tie up. When all were secured, they climbed the ladder and waited for the others.

About a hundred feet back from the wharf stood a long, peak-roofed building, running parallel to the building. It was painted gray and trimmed in dull yellow, with a tarpaper roof now practically whitewashed from seagull droppings.

Joe leaned against a piling and took out a package of Wings. He offered one to Sammy.

Sammy took one and nodded. "Nice to feel dry land…"

Joe glanced down at the *Black Duck*, now secure in the morning quiet, none the worse for her latest run.

"You have that look again, Joe. I can tell. You're looking at her just like you would a lady with all hell between her legs…"

Joe nodded. "She's a beautiful boat."

Yes, he loved boats, any kind—and yes, he loved the *Black Duck*. And yes, this morning they had been lucky that she didn't act like a dangerous, spiteful bitch. So many things could've gone wrong: a shell hit, an engine failure, or a missed 4-H ribbon. "Well, Sammy, I hope she'll be just like a beautiful woman—always under me, and hopefully no big gun will ever disrupt my love affair. Okay?"

"Fine by me, Joe, fine by me. You hear?"

In the beginning, especially after his first successful runs, there was no man happier about Prohibition than Joe Bucolo.

Pearly Thurston cleared the wharf's ladder. He was a tall, pot-bellied man with a perpetually flushed complexion framed by a closely clipped, salt-and-pepper beard. To most folks, Pearly resembled an immoral Kris Kringle, always checking the women out of the corners of his eyes, always twice, always jolly.

Pearly cocked his thumb at Joe. "Jesus, I wish I could've seen their faces."

Joe returned the thumb gesture vigorously, knowing if he didn't, it would spoil the after-battle fun. He had a hunch Pearly would still notice his lack of enthusiasm.

Joe said, "If we did, we'd be in the iron coop tonight, for sure…or maybe even worse."

"Bullshit, Joseph! Pure bullshit!" boomed the voice of Benjamin "Hunker" Moore, captain of the *Wood Duck*. The massive Swamp

Yankee cleared the ladder, rising up like some hairy sea creature. Hunker's pumpkin-sized head sat on a pair of wide, powerful shoulders, giving him the appearance of having no neck. He was a fish barrel of a man, solid despite his age. Viewed sideways, Hunker's nose and high cheekbones hinted of some lost Wampanoag ancestry.

"They would've never caught us. Besides, they'll be stuck on that sand bar till mean high tide." Hunker gave Pearly a long-arm hug. "Yeah, just like a beached whale, all cuz we're smarter."

Sammy interrupted. "Aw, shit, Hunker, what you really mean is that Joe was able to salt that 75's tail because he knows every nook and cranny, every hang-up on this here Seaconnet River."

Hunker removed his crooked stogie and pointed it. "Yeah, Sammy, I guess ya right. Joseph got seagull blood alright. He might even be cousin to a flounder."

Joe laughed with all of them. It tickled him the way Hunker called him "Joseph." Hunker had his ways about him, his own vision of the world.

"I need a drink," Pearly said.

"Yeah," Hunker added.

Joe looked at Sammy. "Coffee would be nice, Sammy."

Pearly snapped, "I meant a real drink."

"Coming right up." With that, the boys, except for Joe, started walking towards the building, talking amongst themselves, glad the run was over.

Joe leaned over the wharf and yelled to the Bancock boys, who were huddled together on the *Mallard*. "When you boys are through down there, you know where to find us." They waved back and returned to their jobs, cleaning the boats from bow to stern.

As Joe caught up with the men, Pearly approached him. "Something's bothering me, Joe...we need to discuss...okay?"

Hunker was right behind Pearly. "My brain has an ache, Joseph. I'm sensing some bad things were in the works this morning."

"We'll chew on it later, boys, after we settle down."

Joe entered the clubhouse, with Pearly and Hunker right behind him. By habit, his eyes scanned a framed newspaper article nailed to the wall. The main headline stated: **EXTRA! January 1920, VOLSTEAD ACT IS LAW. LIQUOR ILLEGAL TO BUY, SELL OR DRINK!** Some of the lettering is peppered by countless bullet holes.

Without a word, Sammy ritually approached his workbench, opened a drawer, and removed a .38 "Colt Special". He took out the last bullet from the box, loaded it, and handed the gun to Joe. Everyone watched him cock the pistol, and fire a round into Volstead. Now, the V letter is almost gone. "Gonna need more bullets, Sammy." Joe laughed along with his boys.

Hunker asked, "Let me use my cannon?" He then pointed to the other newspaper accounts on the wall: **New Jersey Citizen Newspaper, March 2nd, 1920: Rum boat, Solitary Man, rammed by Patrol Vessel. Two men rescued.**

March 15th, 1920, Boston Herald: Coast Guard arrests three men and a woman, on the one-hundred-foot-schooner, Panther. One rum-runner seriously injured, after a shoot-out.

March 26th, 1920, Providence Journal: Fishermen engage in the lawless trade of rum-running. Officials claim rum-runners risk their lives in the pursuit of illegal alcohol.

Joe shook his head and handed the pistol back to Sammy.

~~~~~~

The corners of the room were crowded with spare Liberty engines and used electrical systems with wires hanging from them like seaweed. There were odd-sized propellers, stacks of fish netting—and to most fishermen, a lot of other useful junk. Rusting clam rakes, oyster tongs, shackles, and vessel hardware accumulated over many years of working the water hung from hooks.

The building's interior smelled of oil, tobacco, and crackling fire-wood. Sometimes, as now, the scent of men and the sea overpowered anything else.

Off to one side sat Max's old gun cabinet, home to various horse pistols, shotguns, shell belts, ammunition boxes, and gun-cleaning equipment. There were even two long-barreled eight-gauge punt guns, once used for market hunting. The heavy, wild-fowl cannons belonged to Hunker. Circling the room on shelves were mounted geese, ducks, and pheasants.

Mounted on an overhead beam was the stuffed head of a large, rather happy-looking pig. Stuck in the left corner of its mouth was a crooked stogie.

"Where the hell is my whiskey?" Pearly asked.

"Even without the smokescreens," Hunker said, "they would've never caught us. They're stupid. We're here drinking safe and cozy cuz we're smart. That's all."

"It ain't you that's smart, Hunker! It's Joe!" And with that, Sammy slammed Pearly's whiskey glass on the workbench a little too hard, splashing him.

"Well, well," said Pearly. "I should have kept my oils on, you old weasel."

"I ain't an old weasel!"

Pearly winked at Joe. "Were you running wide open, Hunker?"

"Fuck no! I'm half-open and that 'six-bitter' thought he was gaining on me."

"Liar!" snapped Sammy.

Hunker belched and farted at the same time, which made everyone laugh. "'Course I was wide open!"

Pearly gave Sammy a victory nod of sorts.

Hunker pointed his stogie at Sammy. "Say, just before we passed the sandbars, my port engine started grunting like a sick bull. Only for a few seconds…but it kinda got me twitching inside. Ya better monkey with it, Sammy, and get it fixed."

"That's right, Sammy," said Joe. "Today...fix it!"

Sammy looked nervous. "Sounds like the magneto. But...but I don't have any spares..."

"Damn it, why not?"

"Just slipped my mind, Joe. I don't know."

A knife-like stillness made everyone uncomfortable. At the same time, the Bancock boys—after putting the boats to bed—entered the clubhouse. They glanced around at the unusual quiet. Bobby said, "What's going on?"

No one replied.

Looking at Sammy, Joe said, "Later, take my car and get one...get a few spares. You know the rules about spare equipment."

Sammy's eyes dropped slightly, like a youngster being punished.

Joe lowered his voice. "Suppose I wanted to make another trip tonight...huh, suppose?"

Sammy nodded. "Sorry, Joe."

Pearly said, "Can we discuss now? Something fishy, I think."

Hunker added, "Took the words out of my mouth."

Sammy seemed confused. "What did I do now? Did I screw up again?"

Joe said, "No, Sammy, but we're thinking here that the cutter appeared to be waiting for us on the Mussel Ridge. They've never done that before. Especially when we usually go more to the west..."

"Yeah, I did think that was strange...but I forgot about it as soon as they started chasing...and *shooting* at us..."

Bobby Bancock nodded. "I thought the same thing myself."

Hunker snapped, "Ya fucking right. They've never done that before. Maybe someone is squealing on us."

"Impossible," Sammy yelled. "Impossible! Nobody would do that, Joe!"

"Maybe you should get some sleep, Sammy. Get those parts tomorrow."

"Thanks, Joe. I am a little tired."

Joe glanced around at his crew. "Any of you boys talking outside this clubhouse?"

Everyone shook their heads.

Joe snapped, "Well, how the fuck did the Coast Guard know we were going to cross over the Mussel Ridge? *How*?"

Pearly said, "Maybe they just got lucky."

~~~~~~

On the noon high tide, the Coast Guard buoy tender *King Philip*— from Bristol, Rhode Island—attempted to free the grounded boat from the shoals. Its hawser parted three times without so much as nudging the patrol vessel. CG-483 was cemented to the sandy bottom. It took the extreme high tide of the approaching storm and two Navy tugs from New London to finally free the patrol vessel.

In her pilot house, Lieutenant Wallace stared silently at the departing Navy tugs, his thoughts drifting between rage and revenge. The patrol boat did not steam north through Tiverton, but instead went south, down the Seaconnet—away from knowing eyes, towards its base in New London, Connecticut.

Without looking at the coxswain, Lieutenant Wallace said, "Mark my words, I'm going to be poison to those Swamp Yankee rummies… mark my words…they're going to pay!"

Coxswain Norbert dared not look in the lieutenant's direction.

~~~~~~

By early evening, Tiverton, Rhode Island, was being mauled by a wild nor'easter—the "Beast from the East," as Narragansett Bay fishermen called it. Moored fishing boats in the Tiverton Basin bucked the weather in unrelenting rain and wind. All night, their cable riggings hummed an eerie tune.

Most of Tiverton was nestled on the high eastern hills bordering the Basin's harborage. The Seaconnet River—her bloodline. Everything revolved pretty much around the fishing seasons. By late 1920, this riverside community was finally entering a period of prosperity that had been missing since the end of the Great War. Things were looking up. In certain quarters, it was said that Prohibition had not hurt the local economy one bit. North and south of the Tiverton Basin, along the water's edge, shanties and wood-framed fishermen's cottages peppered the shoreline for miles in both directions.

The center of the town wasn't a church or a grassy common; it was Peabody's Wharf, the main commercial wharf used by the Providence Shipping Line, among others. Steamers *Awashonks*, *Queen City*, and *Islander* made their daily scheduled stops at Peabody's for passengers and cargo; warehouses shared the wharf with a small ship's chandlery and the Almy Ice House.

For a half-mile or so around the wharf, the shoreline was jammed with squat, cedar-shake commercial buildings that stocked everything from boat hardware to French ticklers for the fishing companies and the men who worked the sea.

The ass ends of seasonal fish markets hung precariously over the water's edge, their back doors leading to the water where the daily catch was landed by day boats and sold immediately. Not much more than shacks, the crusty riverside operations served the local housewives and restaurants from Providence and Fall River, to as far south as Little Compton, and east to Westport and Dartmouth.

A few hundred feet south of Peabody's Wharf, Wilcox's boatyard hauled out boats, painted hulls, and made engine repairs—everything to keep a vessel floating and working. Cory Wilcox also served as the local boat broker. On the ways, the *Flo*, a fishing dragger, suffered under the stinging sheets of rain and lashing wind of the nor'easter. She was presently being overhauled and painted by Wilcox. A *For Sale* sign was nailed to her pilot house.

Throughout the night, the wind and rain were unrelenting in their fury. The residents went into hibernation. Electricity was lost about midnight, and when dawn broke, little had changed.

Main Road was deserted, except for an occasional dog and Doc

Peckham heading for his morning coffee. No businesses bothered to open, except Mary's Diner. The White Horse Inn served coffee and buttermilk biscuits to the two overnight guests from Boston. They didn't even bother to light a fire in the dining room. They sat them right down in the warm kitchen.

CHAPTER FOUR

THE FOLLOWING DAY, Tiverton remained in the grip of the storm. When everyone returned to the clubhouse, the Bancock boys were still talking about the patrol boat and their close call. They went on and on like hungry crows, annoying Hunker to the point of serious irritation. For the tenth time, Billy Bancock double-tapped his whiskey bottle on the oak workbench and slurred, "I just don't know. It was damn risky."

Joe, whose annoyance registered on his face, looked over at Billy, but he didn't follow up on it.

The Bancock brothers weren't twins, but they certainly could have been. And they sort of dressed alike, were both fair-haired and in their early twenties, and were happy with their lot in life. For some reason, Bobby had better luck with girls than Billy. The brothers shared their own small cottage, left to them by their grandfather. However, Bobby preferred living at home, enjoying his mother's cooking.

For years, the Bancock women took in laundry for certain bachelors and widowers. Max Bucolo, with not so much as asking, dropped off three bags of fishermen's clothes the Saturday after his wife suddenly passed away in their fish-smoking shed.

The clothes were washed and folded neatly and remained on the corner of the Bancock porch for a week. The following Saturday,

31

Grandmother Irving and Mrs. Annie Bancock were waiting to negotiate when Max arrived with two more bags of laundry.

Grandmother Irving pointed her cane as Max prepared to leave. "Hold it there, Max Bucolo."

For fifteen minutes, discussions between the two women and Max took place, the fruit of which was to last until the elder two passed away. From that day forward, Max took Joe to the Bancocks' for dinner and a bath every Saturday night. This allowed Max to go out on the town, whatever that really meant.

The boys got their hair cut once a month, and twice a year Grandmother Irving and Mrs. Annie Bancock took them to Fall River for a new set of clothes, outfits the Bancock women kept clean and mended on a regular basis.

But one hand always washes the other in Tiverton. For twenty-eight years—until the day Max fell into the fireplace—the Bancock clan ate the best seafood the Seaconnet gave up. And there was more. One winter, Max Bucolo rebuilt the Bancocks' stone walls. Another time, he cleaned out their back forty, cutting and stacking seventy cord of firewood, which Mrs. Annie Bancock eventually sold off.

When Max bought his first motor truck, he ordered it from Joel Bancock, brother to Annie. In 1915, when Max received the news that Rex Bancock had been killed in France, without even being asked he sent Tommy Walsh, Sr. over to drop a new tub into the Bancock bathroom.

When Joe Bucolo took over Max's business and needed two new hands, he called Mrs. Bancock about the boys. Strong and not prone to seasickness, though none too bright, Billy and Bobby proved to be eager and interchangeable engineers for Pearly Thurston and Hunker Moore. Sammy taught them what they needed to know. In fact, Sammy said the Bancocks could be pretty good mechanics, if they had a mind to pay a little more attention.

"I don't know," said Billy Bancock. "I just don't know."

The potbellied stove crackled. Joe Bucolo's voice grew louder.

"After this last run, there's no doubt 'bout it, the fun's all gone—and this early in the game. Maybe someone's tryin' to muscle in on us."

Joe turned and opened the door to the stove. Orange flames reflected across his face and highlighted the scar on his right cheek. He tossed a log into the fire and slammed the iron door.

Pearly and Hunker sat on cut-down mackerel barrels, their bodies hunched forward. Each had a bottle of Overholt Rye at his feet.

"Did you hear what I said? I think someone is trying to take over our territory. I think that goddamn Kanky is toying with us—trying to muscle in. The game could get dangerous… But Kanky couldn't do it himself—he's too stupid. Whoever he's working for—could be a big problem for us."

"Like hell," Hunker snapped. "Nobody is gonna take over Narragansett Bay, or take the Seaconnet River from us. That'll be the fucking day…"

"I agree with Hunker," Bobby Bancock said.

Joe shook his head. "None of this is worth bloodshed."

Annoyed, Pearly rubbed his hand vigorously over his beard. "Speak for yourself. Didn't we make a good month's wages in ten hours?"

"Well," Joe said, "like it or not, you better realize there may be a bad shift in the wind. It could get dangerous."

"Of course that's true!" Hunker snapped. "But it's still a matter of knowing the waters and how to use her."

"Speaking of knowing the river," Pearly said, "wonder how the Coast Guard's taking that grounding on Sandy Point."

Hunker slapped his knee. "God, that was beautiful."

"Don't worry!" Joe added. "They ain't gonna let us forget it!" Joe wondered how drunk he was, thinking he might want to check himself. He pulled out his pocket watch. "Sammy left a few hours ago… ain't back yet."

Pearly said, "He just likes driving your machine. Maybe he stopped off in Pawtucket for a little jollying."

"Hey, good luck to him," Joe said.

"Yeah," Hunker added, "anyone that skinny needs all the luck he can get. Say, let's play some pinochle."

Joe fingered a pile of fish netting. "Ya know, I've been living by my hooks ever since Max died. I got a feeling our luck could be running short." He dropped the netting and, without looking at Pearly or Hunker, said, "Might wanna think about going back fishing."

Pearly shook his head. "You mean starvation! That's the only word for the fishing trade."

Joe's expression tightened. They had dragged this net before. Pearly's wisdom, like a heavy anchor dropping into the river, always hooked the same ground: fishing was a lot of work for little money.

Joe cocked his thumb. "I'm telling you, getting killed or getting thrown into the iron coop is something to ponder. We've been running liquor now for well over a year, now. I think the handwriting is on that wall." He pointed to the newspaper articles on the wall. "We don't want to be part of that collection."

The Bancock brothers nodded their heads vigorously, much too vigorously for Hunker, who gave them a look that sent them out of the clubhouse immediately. They didn't even say goodbye.

With the slam of the door, Hunker grunted. "Don't need to listen to those snot-noses anymore. Fuck no! The Kaiser's guns didn't stop this body and no fucking Coast Guard is gonna stop me either! It's just a matter of using our heads."

Pearly stood up. "Hunker's right! This is Rhode Island. And don't forget if we do quit, what will we do? Go back fishing? Raise turkeys? None of us want that."

Joe's eyes flashed. "If you don't believe that our luck could run out, then fuck off!"

Pearly raised his hands as though to ward off Joe's anger.

Hunker added his own thoughts. "Hey, Joseph, we're only talking here."

"That's right," Pearly added.

"We're talking," Joe said, "but you're not listening." His voice softened. "I know fishing's hard, but the money's good most of the time… and it's who I am. And it's you boys, too. And you both know it."

Pearly said, "Look, even with the problems, you love it. Hell, yesterday's chase, even as close as it was, it was still fun beating them. Admit it, Joe, it was a great feeling."

Joe remembered Sammy's face and said, "Well, those one-pounders were closer to us than you, so you might want to ask Sammy about that. Shit, Sammy was even seeing white stones in our fishing nets…"

Pearly and Hunker's smiles dropped.

Hunker said, "Don't talk 'bout tombstones, white stones, bad luck, and all that shit—aches my brain."

Joe and Pearly squelched their laughter, but it hovered there, ready to roar.

Pearly nodded. "Superstitions or not, Sammy's still like us. He loves the game."

Joe said, "He doesn't want to die for it or end up in the iron coop for a long time though. And neither do I."

Hunker nodded. "Ya speaks for me on that count. No coop for me."

"And another thing," Pearly said, "you've got a new boat to pay off."

"Yeah, I know." Joe picked up Pearly's bottle and took a short swig. "It sure seemed like a good idea at the time."

Pearly mumbled, "Doesn't it always…"

"Don't worry," Hunker added, "that new rummy is gonna pay off quick. She'll be able to work in real dirty weather…carry bigger loads…"

Joe replied, "I should've put the money in a fishing boat instead."

Annoyed with the conversation, Hunker stood and scratched the chin of the mounted pig's head. He chuckled and, after a moment, turned back to Joe.

"Christ's sake, Joe, will ya forget all this serious shit for a spell…"

He took another swig of his Overholt and smacked his lips in relish. "Some men find love through their stomachs, but for you, Joseph, it's always been boats and ya prick."

"I only know one thing," Pearly said, "the girls are nothing like they were when I was younger. Jesus, in the old days, you were lucky to get yourself a sniff. And that was only with ya fingers…"

"Ain't that surely the truth," Hunker added. "Anyway, I gotta go home now and eat supper. I don't wanna get my Gertie mad at me."

Pearly asked, "Why?"

"Cuz she's beginning to force me to use my wingless flies more and more…"

Joe said, "You and your wingless flies…" He laid a cigarette across the back of his hand, flipped it in the air, and tried to catch it in his mouth, without success.

"Yeah, my Gertie's just interested in soul-saving and baking pies. I can't figure her out. Been sleeping separate for quite a spell now. Ever since her pet pig…of course, her sacred friendship with the minister…" For a moment, he was silent. "She was baking pies today."

"Maybe you should go to church with her," Joe said. "You might find religion."

He took another swig. "Gertie's still stealing my booze. She's supplying the holy minister. I'm thinking that he's drinking more than me."

"That's not possible," Pearly said.

"The holy man seems to prefer vodka, the phony. Been keeping a running check on my decoy bottles, and Gertie's stealing more and more. I don't believe Gertie's doing the drinking, though I wish she would."

"Why don't you just take it up with her?" Pearly asked.

"Naw, I'd rather let her play her little game. I like having some secret on Gertie. Might hafta use it someday."

Joe and Pearly just nodded their heads, doing their best not to laugh.

"Truth is, I've been wondering lately if there's more going on between the minister and Gertie than just my booze and her pies. 'Course, in that regard, I gotta wish the minister the best of luck. Cuz he's gonna need it."

Hunker grunted again. They just waited.

Glancing affectionately at the mounted pig's head, Hunker continued, "'Course, Gertie thought it was the work of the devil, eating her pet pig and then having its head stuffed. I can't figure out what's wrong with her."

Joe said, "It ain't her, Hunker, it's you and your barnyard habits."

"What's wrong with my habits?"

Smiling, Pearly asked, "Yeah, what's wrong with Hunker's habits?"

Joe shook his head. "Nothing…if you live in a barnyard with the animals."

"Well, speak for ya self," Hunker added. He stood up and approached Joe. He lifted his bottle and said, "Joe…we both knows it's booze and broads…and in that order."

Joe smiled, knowing well that his friend was again about to belt out his favorite troopship song. On the way over to fight the war, when everyone else was seasick, heaving their guts up, Hunker would stoke his stogie and sing and—in a way—gave the green-gill landlubber soldiers something to smile about.

"Oh, give me beans when I'm hungry,
Whiskey when I'm dry,
A tight pussy for my stiff cock,
And old heaven when I die…
When I die…"

Like always, he roared with laughter. Then Joe and Pearly joined in, singing the song again.

When they finished, Hunker did a little jig. "Yessiree, a tight pussy for my stiff cock…that's all I ask. And if I don't have that, wingless flies."

Pearly shifted forward on the barrel. "What in Christ do you do exactly with those goddamn wingless flies?"

Hunker just grinned.

For a long time, they were silent, listening to the storm and the rain outside, knowing it was churning up the ocean out on Rum Row. Every seaman respected a nor'easter—this no-mercy, get-even wind that, at times, even made some men hate the sea.

After a few moments, Joe stretched and walked over to a window that faced the channel. He lifted a canvas covering and, for a second, saw his reflection in the glass. The river and sky had darkened almost to the color of coal dust.

Joe raised his hand. "I hear something."

"Keep playing," Hunker mumbled, picking up his cards.

The wind suddenly blew the door open. Sawdust whirled from the floorboards, and a canvas tarp flapped noisily. One lantern went out.

Sammy Turner, his bony body no match for the pounding nor'easter, stumbled through the big door. The jolt of cold air added life to the stove, and the fire popped and crackled loudly.

Hunker jumped up and closed the door. Sammy leaned against the wall. His face was caked with blood. He could barely stand.

"Jesus H. Christ!" Hunker snapped, his voice bordering on surprise and anger. "What the hell happened to you?"

"Kanky and his mugs worked me over…I was getting the magneto, and he must've seen your machine—maybe they thought it was you, Joe. Anyway, they cornered me at Zeke's."

Pearly shouted, "The prick! That prick is back! After we warned him, but good."

Joe felt like he was broaching in a following sea, wondering if his boat would behave or if the unforgiving wave would swallow her up. "Wait a minute," Joe said. "Kanky might fuck with our territory, but he wouldn't do this on his own. Someone's definitely paying him… giving the orders…"

"Kanky never did anything for free," Pearly added with a shake of his head.

"Finish, Sammy," Joe said, "tell us what happened."

Sammy sat down and motioned for a drink. Pearly uncorked his bottle and handed it to Sammy.

"Like I said, Kanky came in with a couple of his mugs. In no time, I was dancing with that big-nose Portagee." Sammy took a swig and looked up at Joe. "Well, they gave me a couple here and there. And Kanky threatened you, Joe. But he said it in a weird way that didn't really sound like a threat. You know, he kind of talks funny...gotta listen close."

"What did he say?" Hunker growled. "What'd he say?"

Sammy took another drink. "Said...said..." Anger twisted Sammy's wrinkled face as he stared into Joe's eyes. He was frightened and embarrassed, and they were all angered by what they saw.

"Come on!" Hunker snapped. "What the hell did Kanky say?"

Sammy swallowed hard, making his Adam's apple jump. "I think he said he's gonna hang Joe's balls up on the chandelier of his boss's gin mill." Sammy shot up from his seat and started pacing.

Joe smiled. "Well, that's original...but it wouldn't be pleasant."

Pearly glanced at Hunker. "There's that new joint in Oakland Beach. People say the owner is from Chicago...or someplace around there."

"That bastard!" Sammy snapped.

Joe banged his hand against a ceiling stanchion. Hunker grabbed Sammy as he was about to slide down the wall. They helped him back to his seat and sat him down.

Sammy turned back to Joe. "Ah shit, Joe, if I weren't so skinny, I'd have taken care of them." His voice trailed off apologetically. "I just didn't stand a dead mackerel whore's chance of licking those bums. Not alone anyway. Wish I had a gun with me, I'd kill them deader'n mackerel."

"Yeah, sure," Pearly said, "and it would've been you ending up dead. When Kanky worked down at Seaconnet Point on the trap boats, he was always getting into fights with other crewmen. He had a nasty temper. He was capable of anything…for sure."

Hunker added, "I didn't like him, and he didn't like me. I don't know why."

The boys laughed. "Beats me," Joe said.

Hunker continued, "He had a friend that hung around with him. I remember he had a strange name…Collector…he called himself…" Hunker licked his lips.

Pearly said, "Well, Kanky beats Sammy up and next he wants to hang ya balls in his boss's speakeasy. Jesus Christ! Maybe he lost his rudder?"

Joe slowly shook his head as he tended Sammy's bruised face.

Hunker's chest heaved. "At some point, maybe I should just jam my goose gun up Kanky's ass…maybe even his boss's…whoever he is! Ya knows what I mean? I speak the truth. I'd sooner jam my goose gun up an enemy's ass than talk to him."

For a moment, except for the storm and crackling fire, there was silence. Pearly and Hunker occasioned a glance at one another. Joe touched Sammy's chin and moved it gently to get a better look. "We better get you over to Doc Peckham's."

"No, no, not that drunken sawbones. I'll be okay."

Sammy's face was badly bruised and his large, hooked nose appeared broken. Dried blood caked the corners of his mouth, and one eye was swollen shut. Sammy looked like a suffering, plucked chicken—his right arm hanging limp against his body like a broken wing. Sammy sniffed hard, then cleared his throat, like he was having trouble breathing.

"Are you sure you don't wanna see the doc?" Joe asked.

Sammy hesitated for a moment. "Maybe I oughta. My nose sure feels awful funny."

"Damn thing sure looks different," Hunker said. "Might even be an improvement."

Sammy found a smile.

Hunker looked at Joe. "I'll drive him over to Doc Peckham's." Without even asking, Hunker lifted Sammy easily under one arm.

"Hey, put me down, I can walk."

"Shut ya mouth," Hunker said. "Besides, ya don't weigh nothin'. Christ Almighty, ya sure are bony! I feel like I'm carrying a bundle of sticks. Ya knows, Sammy, if you don't put some meat on your bones pretty soon, I'll be pissin' on ya grave."

"Hey, put me down, you horse's ass! Put me down!"

Hunker gave Sammy a slight shake. "Maybe I should bring ya home with me. Give ya to my Gertie as a pet. She might be able to fatten ya up, just like her pet pig."

Sammy was genuinely insulted by the invite. "Put me down, you horse's ass!"

"Hey, I'm the best friend ya ever had. Remember that."

"Maybe," Sammy said, "but you're still a horse's ass. Pissin' on my grave…"

Hunker headed out with Sammy into the miserable weather.

~~~~~~

When the door slammed shut, Pearly glanced at Joe, who had his elbows on his knees, head in his hands, staring at his boots. "What's Kanky trying to prove? He knows we won't stand for this kind of shit."

Joe said, "Kanky never got over being tossed out of Tiverton by Max."

Pearly exploded with impatience. "Remember, he was a thief! Besides, I always thought he was rocky in the head—maybe even nuts. Someday he's gonna hurt you bad, maybe even all of us. You're gonna have to face whoever this new competition is, Joe, sooner or later."

"I will, Pearly, I will… First things first. We need to find out who's behind Kanky."

"If you don't stop him, they'll take over the Seaconnet quicker than a rat after a dead fish."

Pearly placed his weight behind the door and unlocked it. "Let's check the boats. I want to go home."

They dressed into their oilskins and went out into the storm.

Above, the rain and gale-force winds whipped through the empty trees. Holding a lantern, Joe climbed down the wharf's ladder and boarded the *Black Duck*. The *Mallard* and *Wood Duck* lay hard against the pilings.

Between the hulls and the wharf, water slapped against the mahogany planking. The hulls jerked, then rebounded gently from the taut spring lines. Their manila bow ropes strained, creaking at the power of the wind-driven tide and the turbulent black waters.

Joe danced from boat to boat like a nimble water sprite, tightening lines and checking the heavy manila bumpers. By habit, his eyes swept over the hatch covers, making sure they were snug and tight. He tied off the rudder arm on the *Mallard* so it wouldn't bang around, then secured a deck bucket rolling around on the *Wood Duck*.

Despite the weather, Joe loved this exercise—being on a boat in a storm in the dark, a fisherman and his vessel, completely reliant on each other.

To escape the storm, Pearly had retreated to the comfort of Joe's Buick. He turned on the headlights and began honking the horn.

A few minutes later, when Joe slid behind the wheel, he said, "I'm glad I didn't fall into the water."

Pearly said, "Hell yeah, good thing. You're not the best swimmer. This damned weather is not for me. It makes my bones ache. Take me home."

═══ Chapter Five ═══

BILLY BANCOCK'S SMALL COTTAGE was located two cornfields due east of Maggie Jackson's house. For over an hour now, he'd been waiting for that anticipated soft knock.

He paced his small living room while he constantly glanced at the door. On the wall, a clock read ten-thirty. Again, he mumbled out loud. "Where the fuck is she?"

Annoyed, in his stretched underwear, he now waited on the edge of his bed. Staring through his bedroom door at the clock, his legs nervously beat against the floor like an engine piston. It read eleven-fifteen. He was ready to explode as he rehashed Maggie's words from this past winter: "Billy, I'm a woman who requires lovemaking on a regular basis. I want a lover, and I'd like you to be that man."

"I'd like to believe that, Maggie, but if Joe finds out, he'll whip my ass. But still…seeing to your lovemaking needs on a regular basis might just be worth it… I might be willing to give us another chance."

"You won't regret it," she said. "Just remember those early days in the pine grove."

"How could I forget…that's where I fell in love with you."

"Mmmm. So sweet, Billy. That's why I wanted us to get back together again. I think deep down, I felt the same way."

Of course, he was never sure about Maggie. She was a mercurial

43

girl—and for his money, one of the prettiest girls in Tiverton. Either way, she did get him worked up.

Billy, at around twelve years of age, and Maggie, at fourteen, frequently played together in a pine grove not far from Maggie's house; they would hug, kiss, even touch each other's privates, which—under Maggie's guidance, with her oversexed body and knowing hands—led to all kinds of pleasures, except one. Maggie wouldn't allow Billy to penetrate her. She was deadly afraid of her mother and didn't want to become pregnant. Pleasing each other manually worked for a long time. As they got older, they drifted apart; that was until this past February, when Maggie ran into him and wished him a happy birthday.

She told him she wanted to get reacquainted. Billy was thrilled. He had found it hard to get any Tiverton girls interested in him; most of them looked down on fishermen and farmers. Those girls all wanted to travel to the big cities, where successful men had money, dressed nice, and treated women the way they should be treated—or at least how they thought they should.

But there was a big problem. Maggie and Joe Bucolo were well-known bedfellows—and spending time with her was sure to buy Billy a whole new level of trouble he didn't want any part of. But Maggie told Billy that Foggy Joe was too busy and was no longer paying any attention to her. Billy rehashed her words for the hundredth time.

The soft knock on the door broke his train of thought. He took a deep breath, then cautiously opened it.

"Hi, Billy...sorry. I was waiting for the rain to stop. I'm soaked," Maggie said softly.

Maggie stripped off her wet clothes and slipped into bed. Billy moved over, while his hands and fingers quickly went to work. "Take it easy, Billy. That's a delicate area."

"Sorry, Maggie. I'm just so..."

For some time, they kissed and kissed. To her surprise, Maggie discovered Billy had become a good kisser. He knew how to use his mouth and lips. He finally took Maggie's hand and placed it on his erection. She chuckled. "Boy, are you ready. I guess you've been thinking about my promise to love-up your monkey."

"I've been ready since my big woody this morning. I was even tempted to play with myself…but I wanted to save it for you."

Maggie laughed. "Sometimes I have that same problem. I have to do what we did when we were in the pine grove."

"I hate that we have to keep it a secret. You're my girl now…" Billy leaned over and kissed her hard nipples.

"Let me remind you again, Billy, this renewed love relationship has to be a deep secret."

"You don't have to remind me."

"So, let's just go easy and have fun…it has to be hush-hush."

"Of course! If he ever found out we were together, we could end up as lobster bait. Joe's pretty worked up, especially after having cannonballs fired at us!"

"I know, don't worry." Maggie took a long moment. Finally, she asked, "Are you gonna quit rum running?"

"Not yet…the money's good but I'm not looking forward to facing those big guns again."

"Billy, when's your next run?"

"Joe's keeping us in the dark on that, but he's changing our location for unloading the booze. Best I can figure, it has to be Booker's Wharf…Common Fence Point."

Now finally, she thought—that's real news.

"Promise me you'll stay safe Billy."

"I just love you, Maggie. I'll do anything for you."

Maggie stared at him in the semi-darkness of the room. His eyes were full of emotion. It tugged at her. In those moments, she felt truly bad for manipulating him. What could she do? She had no choice. She was their pawn, being manipulated herself. She thought back to the day it had started, and wished she had never met Paul Moran.

CHAPTER SIX

Four Months Earlier, Providence, Rhode Island

MAGGIE JACKSON SAT in Paul Moran's Packard, waiting for Jay Gatsby. He was to arrive at four o'clock, on the corner of Dean and Westminster Streets. Light snow blanketed the hood of the car and clung to the windows.

A month away from her twenty-third birthday—with killer, hungry green eyes that could hitch a man's breath—it wasn't hard to imagine why Maggie Jackson, next to Janie Thurston, was considered one of the prettiest girls in Tiverton. She wore an emerald-green, curve-hugging evening dress with a bold confidence that was reinforced by her mother's compliments when she dazzled her way out the door an hour before.

Moran had been enthusiastic in brokering the blind date—so much so, he purchased the dress for her, then handed her his calling card—*J. Paul Moran, Esquire*—hinting that he knew someone who would appreciate her beauty. The shop clerk—a slight, well-kempt woman of middle age, with pale skin and dark hair—half-smiled and nodded, her elegant fingers whispering along the satiny tissue paper as she swaddled the silk and tucked it delicately into a golden shopping bag. When she came around the counter and placed the treasure in

Maggie's hand, she squeezed it—almost imperceptibly—as if to portend the omen sure to come with the acceptance of such generosity.

"I must say, Miss Jackson, you look wonderful."

"Thank you. I love this dress… It was a nice gesture."

"Purchased by your date. I was just the go-between…"

Reflections of colorful Christmas lights from the nearby stores glowed through the car's frosted windows. Maggie rubbed the condensation from the side window to see more of the decorations: hanging tinsel, ornaments in festive shapes, cutouts of Saint Nick adorning windows and doorways. "Christmas is always such a nice time of the year," she whispered, her voice nostalgic. "How will I get back to Tiverton tonight?"

Not looking at her, Moran instead checked his watch. "It probably will be more like tomorrow, Miss Jackson. You will be staying tonight at the Providence Imperial Hotel. It's quite lavish—"

"Really?" Maggie's tone turned edgy. "We'll see about that, Mister Moran. I decide where I'll sleep. I have since I was born." She turned back to the Christmas lights.

It was then that Moran leaned over and whispered in her ear. He sat back and stared at her intently.

Maggie's body quaked, as if she had been bitten by a rattlesnake. In an effort to calm her, he grabbed her cold hand and patted it. He quickly added, "Your mother's secret is very safe with me. Even your date tonight knows nothing about it. It's ours to keep and, more importantly, keep it from the law."

Maggie appeared desperate to find the right response. It was impossible. She swallowed hard while the red Christmas lights reflected, almost sinister-like, in her eyes.

"How do I know that?"

"I don't lie, Miss Jackson. Besides, your date doesn't appreciate complications. My advice would be to keep your personality intact… it's rather endearing."

She whispered, "Thank you."

Maggie asked softly, "He's not dangerous, is he, Mister Moran?" He missed the real concern in her eyes.

Before he could answer, Gatsby's Packard pulled up. Moran was out of his seat in an instant, crossing around the rear of the car, opening the door for Maggie to alight. She stepped carefully out of Moran's Packard and onto the snow-encrusted street. The rear door of Gatsby's car opened like a cavernous maw, and Maggie slid in. She turned slightly and mumbled, "Thank you, Mister Moran."

Maggie fixed her dress, adjusted herself in the seat, turned to Gatsby, but didn't speak. She just waited on him, still stunned by the cryptic threat Moran had whispered.

Gatsby seemed at a loss. "Nice…nice to meet you, Miss Jackson. I'm Jay Gatsby."

"Please, just call me Maggie, Mister Gatsby. Nobody is that polite where I'm from…"

"Okay, Maggie. I like your honesty, makes me more relaxed…"

She smiled and fixed her eyes on the back of the chauffeur's cap.

In that moment, Gatsby's eyes turned cat-like, scoping his prey: a genuine small-town girl—so different from what he was accustomed to in Chicago.

Maggie didn't need to see any part of him to realize he was taking her measure.

~~~~~~

Just southwest of Brown University, Frankie-the-Bone's Hideaway was one of the most popular night spots in Providence. Located in the cellar of the Caisson Flatiron Building, the private club was well-visited by Brown's faculty and wealthier college students. A large hat factory and a bread company occupied the four floors above it.

Gatsby, with Maggie on his arm, entered the outer hallway, which faced the club's entrance. A man in a suit and tie smiled as they approached. "Good evening, sir. Welcome to Frankie's."

Gatsby palmed a bill to the doorman.

"Thank you, sir…a pleasant evening to you both."

He led them into a dimly lit lounge filled with patrons enjoying the freedom that only money can buy. The faint sound of machinery and the aroma of baking bread were the only signs that this private club existed in Providence—at times known for its patrons indulging in certain bacchanal delights. Gatsby motioned for Maggie to precede him up the narrow stairway, watching her climb the short flight and appreciating the swing of her pleasant, very snug ass.

The stairway opened onto a balcony of booths with high rosewood walls that provided maximum privacy. The main room below was jammed with tables, each with a candle shimmering inside a red bowl. In the far corner, just beyond the dance floor, a five-piece band played. A few people danced while the majority mingled, cocktails in hand, greeting old friends and making new acquaintances. It was still early, and Gatsby imagined the evening wearing on, when drinks would spill, friends would become lovers, and acquaintanceships would take a turn towards passion or enmity—all thanks to the booze that fueled the soul's deepest desires.

Maggie was caught up in the excitement, so much so that she kept walking around the perimeter of the room, taking in the ambiance. Photographs and paintings adorned the high walls—their subjects a testament to this new decade: celebrities, movie stars, even politicians.

Gatsby enjoyed her reactions and relished the idea of using the young beauty reputed to be Foggy Joe's lover—at least according to Paul Moran. He wondered if Foggy Joe had the same weakness for Maggie as he had for Daisy.

"Where would you like to sit?" he asked.

Maggie nodded towards a small table by the railing, overlooking the action below.

Gatsby smiled. "Good choice. I like to watch too. Do you like to watch, Maggie?"

She nodded shyly and let him guide her to the table.

Seeing Maggie seated comfortably, he took his own chair and surveyed the room below—a smattering of old money, college professors puffing their chests and entertaining university patrons, and college kids riding on their families' names or the coattails of those they came with. Gatsby slowly glanced around the lower room, and some looked up at him. Maggie realized he had a way of silently drawing attention—as if his gaze ignited sensation as he scrutinized people, speculating on their thoughts.

For the first time, Maggie took in Gatsby's profile and realized he was quite good-looking. "This is exciting," she said softly. "Never been to a place like this."

He turned back to her. "Well, I'm sure it won't be your last." Gatsby smiled, exposing fine, white teeth. Almost too white, Maggie thought.

As they waited for a server, Gatsby's hand tilted her head up, straight into his line of vision. "Your eyes are as stunning as the color of your dress. You, my dear, are what they call the bee's knees."

Maggie scrunched her face in confusion.

"Means beautiful."

"Ah. Thank you."

Gatsby lit a cigarette and offered one to Maggie. She shook her head. "So, Maggie, tell me about yourself."

"Well…" Maggie shifted in her seat. "I tend to keep private—until I'm really comfortable with someone." Her voice was so pleasant, it was clear she meant no offense. "So, Mister Gatsby, you will only know what I allow you to know."

Gatsby half smiled. "Well, Miss Jackson—excuse me, Maggie—I happen to be a very private person myself, so I can certainly understand that. Although, I have to say, I don't meet many women who won't jump at the opportunity to talk about themselves…even if their doing so is rather trite and boring." His half-smile turned full.

She smiled. "I'm not your usual woman."

"That is becoming clear." About to continue, Gatsby noticed Maggie looking past him.

Frankie-the-Bone climbed the balcony stairs two at a time. A tall, gaunt man—with wide-spaced buck teeth and black hair parted in the middle and slicked down hard—Frankie looked like he belonged at a funeral parlor, except that he had a perpetual smile—like he knew some important secret that you didn't, and to him it was funny.

"Sir, you honor my club. Your first time?"

"Yes, actually. You have a nice place here."

"I'm honored." Frankie glanced towards Maggie. "But I'm afraid the décor pales in the beauty of your companion. Good evening, and welcome. My friends call me Frankie. Please do so."

Maggie beamed as she stared up into Frankie's face. For her, it was a face that had a way of mesmerizing or scaring you, depending on the circumstances.

Gatsby said, "Frankie, this is Shannon McGuire."

Maggie gave Gatsby a puzzled look, but said nothing.

Frankie nodded. "And you, sir?"

"James Gatz."

Frankie removed the white cigarette holder from between his lips with his left hand and extended his right. "Pleased to meet you, Mister Gatz."

Maggie smiled. "My first time here as well."

"I hope this evening will be one you'll not forget."

Frankie signaled a waiter and, with a graceful nod, returned to the main floor.

Gatsby smiled and looked at Maggie. "I shall do my best to make it memorable."

"It is already—you and I have new names."

Gatsby smiled. "I'll explain later. Trust me, there's a reason."

"I already have a pretty good idea."

"Really? And what would that be?"

"Something illegal, I suspect."

He nodded, surprised but appreciative that Maggie was turning out to be more astute than he'd assumed her to be. "Of course, this is strictly between you and me."

"I don't blabber, Mister Gatsby, I profit."

Gatsby chuckled. "Well, then, we do understand each other."

"Possibly."

He now appeared to be even more intrigued. "What about romance...love?"

"I am not fooled by love. My dear mother claims there's nothing more dangerous than a man with charm."

Gatsby had a sudden flash of Moran uttering, *She's rather...steely.*

About a half-hour later, their drinks nearly untouched, Gatsby signaled the waiter. The young man rushed over, glancing down at the full glasses. "Your gin and tonics weren't satisfactory, sir?"

"They were fine...but we have dinner reservations for eight o'clock." Gatsby paid the check, handing a few extra bills to the waiter. "Tell Frankie we'll be seeing him again."

Smiling with appreciation, the waiter nodded and left.

"I gather you're not a drinker, Shannon?"

"Not the fancy stuff. We are basic in my neck of the woods."

Intrigued, Gatsby replied, "You should have told me."

CHAPTER SEVEN

THE PROVIDENCE IMPERIAL HOTEL was, at the moment, the finest hotel in the area. It would soon have major competition from the Biltmore, now in the early stages of construction. At the reception desk, two bellhops stood by as Gatsby—carrying only a small satchel and Maggie on his arm—approached.

Maggie became unsettled, checking into a hotel with no luggage. She was certain the manager and bellhops would figure her for a whore—and the coming evening was quickly losing its allure. Leaning into Gatsby, she gave him a stern look and whispered, "I have a feeling they think I'm a harlot."

Gatsby led her away from the desk to a couch in the lobby. "Would you rather I take you home?"

Maggie looked around at the expensive surroundings. "Well, at least let's have supper. I am hungry, *Jay*."

He nodded. "Let's use our real names when we're alone."

"I do prefer honesty, Mister Gatsby, in all things."

He forced a weak smile. "That's become obvious, Maggie."

As Gatsby and Maggie stood and approached the desk, the rather plump but distinguished-looking manager smiled warmly. "Mister Gatz, madame, it's our honor to have you. We've taken the liberty of providing your suite with a hospitality package—which should contain anything you and your associate may need, following your dinner."

Maggie was ill at ease but smiled anyway. Gatsby held on to the satchel, but still tipped the two bellhops.

~~~~~~

The Bacchante dining room was luxurious yet intimate, with dimmed lights and smoky, mirrored walls. Many of the diners' eyes drifted to Gatsby—mysterious in his dark suit and white tie—as he and Maggie followed the hostess to their table. They crossed through the cocktail bar, with its glass floor under-lit with a luminescent pink—a feature that showcased the attendants' shapely legs beneath the translucent skirts of their fashionable uniforms.

Maggie voiced her awe, whispering into Gatsby's ear, "This ain't Mary's Diner, for sure."

He smiled. "I'm glad you like it, Maggie. I was getting worried."

The hostess stopped before a private banquette. Waiting for them to settle in, she motioned to a service button that would alert an attendant to their needs.

As she stepped away, a waiter appeared in her place. "May I provide you with a cocktail before dinner?"

Gatsby looked at Maggie. She said, "I'll have what you're having."

"Two shots of Wild Turkey…and two glasses of your best beer."

Maggie appeared surprised, but smiled at the order, as did the waiter. "Yes, sir. Right on it, sir."

"Interesting choice," Maggie said. "Reminds me of the White Horse Inn in Tiverton."

"So, maybe I have a chance of redeeming myself?"

She said, "I may have been a little too hasty."

Gatsby watched the waiter give the order to the bartender, who turned towards them and gave him a smiling nod. Gatsby whispered, "Another world, for sure."

Maggie politely ignored the comment.

After the waiter delivered their round, Gatsby and Maggie saluted each other with the hotel's elegant shot glasses. They both downed the whiskey, then took a sip of beer.

Allowing them ample time to finish their drinks, the waiter returned for their dinner order. "Tonight, our menu offers thyme-scented standing rib roast with Yorkshire pudding and roasted garlic pods, glazed butter carrots, and to start, a watercress salad with maple walnuts."

Maggie said, "Sounds wonderful. Make mine rare."

"Same here. And we'd like two more shots, please."

Even with one shot and a little beer, Maggie began to feel the glow. She glanced around the room, her face slightly flushed, relishing the exotic environment.

The meal arrived in the hands of two beautiful attendants. A waiter followed. "Sir, this dinner suggests pairing with a lovely French red…"

Maggie whispered, "Really, French wine?"

The waiter said, "Yes."

"Sounds like a fine choice," Gatsby said.

After their roast beef dinner, and two bottles of wine, Maggie was clearly feeling no pain. She tried to gain some semblance of being sober. She glanced again at the sign over the bar. It read: *Welcome to the Bacchante Lounge, where friends get lost in time.*

She turned back to Gatsby. "I need to look up what that means."

Gatsby laughed. "A drunken female reveler of Bacchus."

"Who is Bacchus?"

"In ancient Greece, he was a god of wine, giver of ecstasy…also in Rome…a popular, fun god…"

She laughed softly. "I'm beginning to feel like the drunken reveler…and I think you might be Bacchus."

"You could be right, Maggie. We'll have to see how our night goes."

"Now…tell me the real reason why I'm here."

"I want you to listen carefully."

"Of course, Jay."

He continued, "I'm about to embark on a major enterprise. I intend to take over and control the smuggling of liquor into Rhode Island waters."

Maggie's expression quickly turned troubled. He watched her reaction closely. "Like...like...Joe, err...like Joey's been doing?" Realizing Gatsby's eyes were on her, "I've heard whispers about his success... It's all quite secretive..." Her words sounded like a confession. For the first time, she lost some of the self-assurance in her demeanor.

Gatsby nodded. "Yes, Maggie, I want to know about those secrets...those whispers. They will help me in my endeavor. I'm after a prize that my success in the rum trade will get me closer to winning..."

Maggie seems momentarily confused. "The prize...meaning money?"

He shakes his head, develops a thoughtful look.

She's intrigued "Then what is it?"

"Some other time."

"Why do I believe it's a woman?"

Gatsby's surprised. "What gives you that notion?"

She smiles, leans in towards him. "Simple, you haven't made a play for me."

"I must say, Maggie, you are astute. Certainly, beautiful and desirable."

Maggie shakes off his comeback.

"Will anyone get hurt?"

He caught the twitch in her body. He stood up, an attempt to exhibit power. "No, but I do need to be kept informed on what your friend Mister Bucolo is doing...what his rum-running strategy will be. Things of that nature. Of course, it has to be done in a very quiet, secretive way. I intend to be on top, Maggie. *Need* to be on top. Mister Moran implied you would be able to help us."

He waited for her reply as Maggie thought about who she needed to protect her—her mother—and who she would have to betray—Joe, her town—and tried to calculate the lesser of all these evils. Finally, she silently nodded.

Her response took so long that Gatsby released a stored breath. "That's great, Maggie. Now I won't have to kill you…"

Maggie's eyes widened. She thought, "How did I let myself be taken in for a satin dress and a prime rib dinner? She knew Jessica was no angel but what the hell had her mother done to bring about such a serious threat from Moran? She forced an insecure smile. He saw that she was clearly afraid, so he took hold of her hand, and Maggie didn't object. He added, "You know I'm only kidding…"

"Of course, Jay."

"Now, is there anyone close to Mister Bucolo you can work with?"

Hesitantly, she said, "I'll give it some thought."

"I'd like you to get going soon. The next few weeks or so. Plenty of time to work on…" he smiled, "your accomplice."

Around eleven o'clock that night, Gatsby walked Maggie from the restaurant to the lobby, where a surprised Paul Moran was waiting to take her home.

He gave Maggie a hug and kissed her cheek. "Maggie, Paul will see you home. I'm sure he has the car nice and warm. Remember everything we discussed. Just contact Moran about anything. This is very important to me."

"Yes, Jay."

She turned and headed towards the lobby doors, where a smiling doorman waited.

Her eyes locked onto the glass panel with the Imperial's gold-leaf insignia. As she left, Maggie felt there was real danger coming her way.

Gatsby's and Moran's eyes followed her. Gatsby said, "'Steely' was a bit weak, Paul."

Moran nodded as they watched Maggie get into the Packard. He turned to Gatsby. "Kanky and his men are getting impatient. Kanky has his own beef with Bucolo."

Gatsby took out a cigarette and lit it. "What exactly does Kanky want to do?"

"Start giving Bucolo aggravations. Nothing major yet… Give him and his boys some issues to ponder. Might make it easier for you to take over the operation."

"What does he have in mind?"

Moran said, "Squeeze Bucolo. See how he responds. Kanky feels that a little fear goes a long way."

Gatsby said, "Kanky's awfully sure of himself, but nothing violent. No one knows what's inside another man until he's pushed to the limit. Anyway, nothing wrong with testing the opposition…do it!"

Chapter Eight

GERTIE MOORE DARKENED Minister Bottomley's doorway. Gertie usually visited the minister when Hunker was sleeping off a drunk or down at the clubhouse with the boys.

The minister stood there in his robe, looking like a large duck egg—certainly not like a man of the cloth, she reasoned...but not for long. He was, after all, a minister, sent mysteriously to rescue Tiverton, which he referred to as a "valley of sin."

His belly swelled from his chest, his legs were white and hairless. He had a vein-webbed nose and spaces between his teeth. When he talked, his full lips appeared to bounce.

Even still, beyond being a minister, Gertie thought Bottomley was a handsome man. He was pure of heart. Of course, he liked his drink now and then, but it was mostly from the chill one could get living on the river's edge. She raided Hunker's hooch, pinching a little here, a little there, storing the booze in mason jars until the minister asked for more.

"Gertrude! What are you doing out on a night like this?" He pulled her into the entryway, looked right into her face. Gertie dropped her eyes.

Bottomley quickly relieved her of the linen-covered basket. He peeked beneath the cover and saw the mason jar and the pies. Smiling, he said, "Oh, Gertrude, you are a sight for sore eyes."

She watched closely, wanting him to look at her—not the stolen liquor. Finally, he did. "Yes, Gertrude, come on in and sit down. We must talk."

She followed him up the stairs and into the parlor. She smelled cigar smoke—not the kind that Hunker smoked, but sweeter, cleaner, much purer. She waited until the minister sat down before she took a chair. *Respect*, she reminded herself.

"I brought you an apple and a peach pie. They're from my canned preserves."

"I love your can—" Bottomley cleared his throat, "your canned fruits. You have a way with canned fruits."

"Thank you," she said softly.

"Do you mind?" he asked, lifting a mason jar.

"Do you feel the chill, dearest Minister?"

There, she finally said "dearest," and he didn't object.

He nodded. "I fear this riverside dwelling will suffer my bones. I shall need more of this."

Gertie's eyes widened. She wanted to tell him that she was beginning to worry that Hunker might be noticing the losses. "Of course, my dear Minister, of course." Bottomley then snapped down the locking wire and removed the glass cap from the mason jar.

She watched him drink. She had met the minister almost five years earlier as he made the rounds, visiting his prospective flock—as he called it, *his* congregation. He shook her hand, his rheumy eyes lingering on hers, like some sad, overfed beagle. Yet she found him interesting, especially the way he praised her cooking, her pies, her booze, her spiritual ways. And now it appeared that he'd become particularly fond of her "canning" prowess.

Bottomley gave Gertie the responsibility of being "coordinator"—an honored, demanding position. She found the minister required a lot of coordinating. She was the prime mover in persuading wealthy Francis Grover to donate this old, dilapidated oyster building for a church. Francis Grover liked Gertrude Moore, but not the man she married.

She watched the minister take another drink. He offered a smile, and she returned it. His robe opened and she saw his very white, fleshy thighs. Like big turkey drumsticks, she thought. Good enough to eat. God, she couldn't believe her thoughts. Gertie felt that rush of desire again.

He saw it on her face and raised his finger as if to make a point. "My Gertrude, the best sermons are lived, not preached."

Yes, being an overripe forty-eight-year-old, she was thankful the minister had such a pure, pure heart.

He took another sip from the mason jar. The storm howled. Bottomley's point was well taken. Gertie went to her knees and moved closer to the minister.

"Oh, Gertie, you are such a fine, fine woman… You make me so, so happy."

"Amen," she whispered.

CHAPTER NINE

ON FEBRUARY 22, 1919, while celebrating Joe's thirtieth birthday at the White Horse Inn, Max Bucolo tripped backwards into the colonial walk-in fireplace during a raging knife fight with an irate husband who accused Max of seducing his wife. Max's body lay there until the smell of burning flesh finally drew attention, where-upon Pearly Thurston, Sammy Turner, and Hunker Moore removed Max's charcoaled remains.

Joe pursued the furious husband, who slashed his cheek. The boys turned the man over to the police, who refused to press charges be-cause Chief Grover said Max Bucolo was a marriage wrecker and deserved just what he got.

Come to find out later, Max was part owner of the White Horse Inn. Soon after the incident and Max's demise, Pat Morris gave the place a facelift. The food improved, the dining room was enlarged, and the second-floor party suites and bed-and-breakfast rooms were fixed up. In the east cellar, drinks were still available to locals and special customers; but the White Horse Inn, as Tiverton's "wets" be-moaned, was not going to be the future speakeasy it would have been, had Max not been a homewrecker and fallen into the fireplace.

A rare, thick prime rib, with plenty of au jus, was the only thing on Joe's mind when he charged up the steps of the inn. The nor'easter had lost its grip, and he knew by late tomorrow Tiverton would be enjoying spring weather. He opened the door and was greeted by the muffled sounds of conversation and the mouth-watering smell of food.

Moments later, Henry Grover stepped out of his police car and glanced over at Bucolo's white Buick. Annoyed, he shook his head. Avoiding the puddles in his shiny new boots, he ran to the front entrance of the inn.

Earlier that same night, Henry Grover wore his new navy-blue uniform to the inn for the first time. It was recently issued by Governor Pothier to each of the police chiefs in Rhode Island, and he was anxious to show it off—similar as it was in every detail (except color) to the gray uniform worn by Colonel Everett Chaffee, superintendent of the recently established Rhode Island State Police. The only thing missing was his revolver.

Henry Grover felt proud and connected as he walked slowly down the shiny wood floor of the inn's empty hallway. He stopped for a moment and gazed into the mirror on the wall. Satisfied, he continued to the double doorway of the dining room, where he stood at parade-rest, looking over the busy tables filled with Tivertonians, most of whom he knew.

The inn was a clean, well-run place, with white linens, fine dishware, and candles. Henry Grover was proud to have at least this one substantial business in his town. Pat Morris sure knew how to make a place cozy—that was for sure—how to create an atmosphere, Henry Grover observed to himself. He admired old Pat.

Maggie Jackson was leaning over with her butt in the air, whispering into the ear of a man in a suit who looked to be a salesman. When she saw Grover at the door, she waved, which made her dinner partner frown. Henry gave Maggie Jackson his best grin.

Janie Thurston was with her Newport swell and another odd-looking Swamp Yankee couple from Little Compton. Henry wondered what they were doing here in this Tiverton establishment. He remembered what his father said once: always drink upstream from the herd. Maybe, he thought, I need to pass a town ordinance.

George Potter, the town clerk, entertained his mother and his wife's family. Mrs. Mary Snellman, head librarian at the town's Essex Hall, was getting up from her table.

"How they hangin', Henry?" Joe Bucolo's voice startled him, and he jumped nervously.

"And how are you, Bucolo?" Grover could tell that Joe was giving his uniform the once-over. He wasn't sure if he should take off his broad-brimmed trooper's hat while inside a building or not.

"I'm hungry, that's how I am," Joe answered. "Why don't you arrest somebody so I can get a table?"

"Seems to me to you'd be more comfortable in a speakeasy, Joe," Henry quipped, proud of himself for the quick comeback.

"Hello, Joe," said Mrs. Snellman. She patted his arm as she passed them.

"Oh, Mrs. Snellman?" Henry Grover asked. "Are you and your party about to leave?"

"No, Henry, I'm going to the powder room, if that's alright with you. Take off your hat, Henry, and relax."

"Yes, ma'am." Henry removed his hat.

Joe chuckled. "You sure have a way with the women, Henry."

"I get what I want, Bucolo." Henry's eyes locked onto Janie Thurston's table. Under his breath, "What does Janie see in that pimple-faced asshole?"

Joe's ears captured the whisper. "I don't know, but I can ask." Before Grover could say anything, Joe walked across the dining room to Janie's table. As he approached, Janie said something that made everybody laugh, including Joe. Janie's friend stood and shook Joe's hand. It appeared to Henry Grover that Joe was being introduced to the other couple too.

Joe leaned over between Janie and her friend, and everybody at the table turned in their chairs to look at Henry standing in the doorway. Somebody said something, and everyone began to howl with laughter.

Janie looked pleased with herself, and Henry was quick to notice. The men kept laughing and slapping their knees and the tabletop. The other woman hugged Janie. When Joe returned to where Henry was standing, he said, "The girls think you look great in that new uniform, Henry."

"Really?"

Joe shook his head. "No, not really. They said you look like a million dollars and a pocket full of French ticklers."

Henry felt his back turn hot. He gritted his teeth at Joe and glared at Janie Thurston's table. All four waved, but unlike the others, Janie wasn't smiling anymore. She suddenly seemed a tad worried, which suited Henry's mood just fine. Right then, he knew she realized he could make her suffer for taking part of this blatant embarrassment. After all, her father was a rum-runner, a lawbreaker.

"You, too, will pay for that one, Bucolo," Henry Grover softly said, smiling and waving back at Janie's table.

"I pay for everything, Henry, one way or another. You know that."

Mike McGreavy started to warm up the piano. He fingered a soft, slow melody. Some of the old-timers began to dance. Henry watched Janie and her friend get up. His eyes followed Janie's tall, lithe body moving over the dance floor.

Joe turned to Henry. "Dancing…something I never learned."

"You'll dance soon enough, you Eye-talian low-life." Henry's words hissed with vengeance into Joe Bucolo's shocked face. "You'll dance for the death of that poor Coast Guard sailor, I'll tell you. You think you're going to get away with that? You'll dance for your sins soon enough, Bucolo."

Sick to his stomach, Joe rushed into the kitchen. He felt as though he needed a drink. He needed to calm down. Now! Joe knew Willy always kept a bottle of Overholt beneath his sink. He knew because every so often, he brought him one.

Surprised to see Joe in the kitchen, Pat Morris approached him and asked, "Everything okay, Joe?"

"No, Pat, everything has gone to shit."

"Anything I can do?" Pat asked.

Joe's only response was to pour a double shot into a cup.

Pat shrugged. "Listen, party upstairs, Sunday afternoon. Should be fun. How about if I invite Janie Thurston?"

Joe refilled his cup, not really paying attention.

Surprised and puzzled, Pat Morris nodded his head. "Okay," he said and walked out of the kitchen.

Willy watched Joe continue to gulp down his precious booze.

"Willy," Joe said, "go into the dining room; tell Maggie Jackson I want to see her tonight."

"Sure thing, Joe. Tell her you want to see her tonight."

Willy, however, just stood there, as though he were waiting for further instructions.

"What the hell's wrong, Willy?"

"Where do you want to see her tonight?"

Joe threw the empty bottle into the rubbish barrel. "Have Maggie meet me right here, Willy. Right here, right now!"

"Okay, Joe, now I got it."

Willy left the kitchen while Joe tried to shake the terrible feeling growing inside him. Christ! A dead sailor!

~~~~~~

Kanky saw Joe Bucolo in the kitchen of the White Horse Inn, pouring himself whiskey. He wondered, What in hell is eating him? Foggy Joe actually looked upset. It warmed Kanky's small heart.

Earlier, through another window, Kanky had also watched Joe sneak up behind Henry Grover in the hall, who jumped when Joe said something to the chief.

Kanky had to laugh at that. He had a feeling Joe could probably pimp Henry better than anyone. It's good to have some warm feelings about your enemy, Kanky thought.

Kanky had hailed his mugs. They came running and stood on the steps, waiting, looking annoyed.

"Come up-a here. Stand along the railing, look-a pissed off." He glanced at Collector. "There's a police car in the lot. Don't do-a anything to it except cut a wire or two." Kanky laughed. "Grover will-a blame Bucolo." Kanky relished the cleverness of his idea. "Go, go," he said. Collector headed towards the parking lot.

When Kanky returned to the window, he caught Joe and Henry having words. Henry looked really angry, and Joe didn't seem too happy either. Kanky was warmed. Whatever the hell Henry said, it made Joe run to the kitchen and gulp whiskey.

Kanky laughed out loud. All in all, he was enjoying himself, spying on his enemy. The smell of food now made him hungry as he watched that juicy little tramp, Maggie Jackson, walk into the kitchen in a tight, white polka-dot dress. She talked to Joe, and they headed towards the back door.

Kanky whistled. Collector and three men approached. "Block-a the steps…don't let-a him get by. I wanna talk to Foggy Joe."

They manned the stairs, their fedoras pulled down tight. "Look-a pissed off," he told them.

"I *am* pissed off," Collector mumbled. "Do you want me to sing Bucolo a little ditty?"

Kanky laughed, stepped back, and leaned against the porch railing. He ran a comb through his hair, adjusted his tie, and waited for Joe and Maggie, who just came through the door.

Beneath the dull light, Joe's eyes met Kanky's face—a face that broke into a large grin.

"Are you being-a chased out the back door, Joe?"

"What do you want, Kanky?"

"Want a say hello, Joe."

"For beating up Sammy, I suppose?"

"I didn't beat up-a Sammy. Why would-a I do that?"

"You're a fucking liar!!"

"You-a right on that count, Joe."

Kanky cautiously checked the position of Joe's right arm. He moved closer. He wanted Joe to feel his heat and smell his cigarette breath.

"Seeing that you *did* beat him up, what now?"

"Maybe you better-a sleep with one eye open."

"I always do."

"Are you-a interested in selling out?"

Joe spit over the railing and said, "Fuck you! And fuck whoever you're working for! Make sure you tell him, too."

Maggie's mouth dropped open. She was certain a fight was brewing. "Joe, let's leave now. Please!"

Joe ignored Maggie.

Kanky observed Joe buttoning up his worn leather jacket. It had belonged to Max, made by a New York saddler. He wondered if Joe was getting ready for a fight. He quickly stepped back, refocusing on his enemy. Normally he'd be in a rage, having some asshole talk to him like that. It just went to show—like he told Gatsby—Bucolo wasn't going to be an easy target.

Kanky tried to relax his own shoulders, ease his voice. "Why don't you-a take the chip off your shoulder?" He moved closer and spoke low. "Just wanna be friendly, Joe, like-a old times, like when I worked for Max...your phony daddy...remember?"

Maggie saw Joe's fist tighten. She pleaded again, "Joe, please, let's leave."

Kanky glanced at Maggie as if she had just arrived. He made a soft sucking sound through his lips and the spaces in his teeth. "Hello, Maggie. Damn! You look-a great."

Joe took her arm and started walking towards the steps at the other end of the long porch.

"God," whispered Maggie, "with that mustache...Kanky looks like an old photo of my father."

Joe asked, "Is it possible he's your father?"

"I'd scream if I even thought so... Don't say that, Joe. Besides, my mother said my father died at sea."

Joe gave her a questionable look and nodded. "I won't say that again. I promise."

Kanky walked rapidly after them. He yanked Joe's shoulder, spinning him face to face. "Listen! I gotta talk with-a you...I ain't-a kidding." Kanky grabbed Maggie's arms and moved her back on the steps between his mugs. "Stay!" he shouted. "Stay!"

Maggie's eyes were big and lively. "I'm not a dog, Kanky!" But she didn't move, standing between the men with her polka-dot dress clinging nicely to her hips.

Kanky sucked his teeth again: what a body. "How's-a your mother, Maggie?"

Alone with Joe, Kanky caught his mugs out of the corner of his eye, ready to move, but he didn't call them. What he did say, he thought, sounded pretty good: "My phony friend, you'll be outta business sooner than-a you think."

Without another word, Kanky walked silently away. As he passed Maggie, he pinched her ass. "Felt-a just like your mother's, Maggie..."

She actually laughed, the dumb pussy. Joe was about to go after him, but she grabbed his arm and shook her head. "No big deal," she whispered. "It's my ass."

Joe said, "What's with you and asses?"

Maggie laughed. "Oh, Joey."

They watched Kanky get into the back seat of his black Packard, with Collector driving. The other men got into their own cars, and they all drove up Main Road out of Tiverton.

~~~~~~

After the doctor examined him, Sammy returned to the clubhouse with his chest wrapped. His nose was broken, but it'd mend. Doc said he was lucky. Sammy supposed so. Hunker helped him inside, stoked up the fire, and left him alone, sitting on his cot.

Sammy had a few drinks. He truly enjoyed being in his cups or—as Hunker would say—happy as a muddy pig in the sunshine. He glanced around the familiar building and listened to the wind.

Inside his sore head, Sammy worked out a vital lesson. From now on, he wouldn't go to East Providence for parts. Yet, truth be known, he only went there because he figured on stopping by Rosella's.

"Yessiree, Turner, 'bout time you stop acting like a striped-assed, horny monkey…" His voice was thin and weak to his own ears, but he knew he'd be okay. He released a low, happy cackle—he'd be visiting Rosella's as long as the old pecker had some life to it.

"Yessiree, quite a turn of events. Boys didn't say much, but they were thinking: Sammy, you're getting old. Yessiree, too fucking old! Forgetting about all those important engine parts…" He took another drink and rolled the bottle between his hands while his head throbbed along with his private rambling. "Kinda felt like a hero, being beat up and all. Hell, it was great that the boys and Doc gave me all that attention."

He took off his trousers and then his shirt. His union suit was frayed and spotted with ancient oil stains. But it was clean. He lay back on the pillow and his eyes roamed over the ceiling. They stopped momentarily on the mounted pig's smiling head. While Sammy's eyes focused on the bent stogie in the pig's mouth, he said, "Night, Hunker, sleep tight."

CHAPTER TEN

AS THAT SAME NIGHT WORE ON, weakening laughter filled Janie Thurston's evening with Pierre Nadeau at the White Horse Inn. Evenings with Pierre were very amusing; "amusing" being one of his favorite words. Such-and-such was amusing, he'd say, and he'd go on and on, telling such funny stories, but after an hour or so, she began to find him boring.

Pierre's humor wasn't vulgar or ethnic, just sort of silly, happy-go-lucky. Janie marveled at how his mind could jump, how his various accents played with tones, the way his eyes and hands moved, how his blond mustache lifted when he smiled and his slicked-down hair was so, so classy. And now they were parked in his car just off Riverside Drive, not far from the Thurston home. Pierre, it seemed, felt it was time for Janie to pay the fiddler, for they had been going out together over six months.

Pierre unbuttoned his pants and said hopefully, "I have a French prophylactic."

"Dream on," she answered.

He shifted his hips as if to say, skip the chatter and let's get on with it. Realizing she was annoyed, he moved to kiss her, but she turned away from him.

Pierre said, "Wait a minute here. I have strong feelings for you, Janie."

Without looking at him, she said, "You're only looking for fun, Pierre, but I'm looking for something else. I don't blame you for going after what you want. In the beginning, I thought we had a consensus, but I'm not ready to make a commitment to us." She sighed, shook her head, and waited.

"Is this because you think your proposal for some new fishing plant down in Virginia is gonna get you out of Tiverton?" Pierre sounded bitter.

"I told you that was a secret—you don't know anything about it! Anyway, it doesn't matter. It'll never happen." Janie slumped and looked out the window.

"Well…maybe you got an eye for that fellow Bucolo?"

"Don't be ridiculous."

"Then maybe that police chief?"

Janie opened the car door. "Goodbye, Pierre." It bothered her slightly that he didn't give her much of an argument as she walked alone to the door of the little shingled cottage her grandfather Cory Thurston had built so many years ago. It pulled at her heart just to think about it. After all, she had been born there twenty-two years ago. Right now, it felt like a lifetime.

Pearly Thurston was lying on the sun porch, too tired, drunk, or both to climb up the stairs to his bedroom.

"Everything okay?"

"Sure, Daddy. What's the weather for tomorrow?"

"Joe figures by morning it'll be nice. Gonna get cool tonight. Northwest wind coming."

"Good. I'm going to Providence with Maggie on the ten-o-five."

In the bathroom, she washed her face and brushed her teeth. She looked in the mirror again. "Well, Janie, you're free as a bird now. And Pierre didn't get what he wanted."

Pearly knocked on the door. "What?" he asked. "What did you say? I didn't hear you."

"Nothing, Daddy. Good night."

~~~~~~

After peeking through the window and finding Sammy asleep, Joe made a quick check of the boats. Back in the car with Maggie, he headed north on Main Road.

"Say, did you have any trouble unloading your friend?" Joe asked.

"Nope." Maggie lifted the blanket off her head and shoulders. "Say, Henry Grover looked sharp in his new uniform."

"Yeah, great, like a million bucks."

Maggie resembled a praying nun draped in black. He placed his arm around her neck. She was shivering. Maggie kissed his neck. "Forget about Kanky, will you?"

"Sure, if you forget about Henry Grover."

She was surprised by his comment. She waited for him to say something more, but he was silent. She didn't follow up, only because she didn't want to spoil tonight's lovemaking.

He swung east onto South Avenue, and his Buick struggled slowly up the steep road. At the top, he took a right and headed south down Highland Road.

Joe's cottage was originally Max's, set on the highest lay of the land, next to a bubbling freshwater stream called Sin and Flesh Brook—a name some said matched the persona of Max and Joe Bucolo. The brook flowed into Nanaquaket Pond, emptying and filling into the Seaconnet River on the tides of each day.

Max built the house himself between 1886 and 1888, over a full stone basement, on a twelve-acre parcel at the south end of Highland Road, one of the highest and prettiest spots in town.

He used the best wood, heavy horseshoe nails, and oaken dowels throughout. The interior woodwork was hand-wrought and had wide-plank floors and mahogany doors, with ten-foot ceilings. The west windows gave a nice view of Nanaquaket Pond and the Sea-connet River.

When Max Bucolo died, Tiverton's town solicitor, a bony, hairless lawyer from Newport named Sheffield, told Joe Bucolo that if he didn't feel comfortable living up on Highland Road, he'd find a buyer for his father's shack. "Shack," Sheffield had called it.

"No, thanks," Joe quickly said. In his mind, the thing about the shack was its perfect isolation, its construction, and the fact it once belonged to Max, whom he loved. Joe didn't get to know Nora Bucolo, as she had hung herself in the smoking shed before Joe became part of Max's life.

To the bluebloods living on the "Heights," the most amazing thing about the shack was that it had been built on a piece of property that Max Bucolo, an otherwise obscure fisherman and oyster pirate, came to inherit from the estate of one Perry Lewis, Tiverton's chief of police from 1874 to 1886. When that news got around, no one could ever figure out that relationship.

Maggie ran up onto the porch. Joe unlocked the door and flicked on a light.

"God, Joey, when are you gonna get rid of Max's stuff?"

"Never," he said.

She gave him a repentant look. "Sorry." Maggie kicked off her shoes and headed for the bedroom. "Hurry, Joey, I'm horny and cold."

Joe whispered, "You're always horny."

He walked to the kitchen and checked the barometer. Holding steady now, a clear harbinger of better weather approaching. Down the hallway, he stopped at Max's bedroom and opened the door. Here was a neat room, bed made perfectly, smelling of cedar from the large clothes closets Max had built. For Max, everything in its place. That's the way he ran his life. Orderly. Very orderly, especially as he got older.

Joe whispered, "Had a close one, Max. Maybe you saw it. I thank you every day for what I know. And you're probably thinking I should've stayed fishing."

Maggie's voice broke his reverie.

He returned to the kitchen and made a couple of whiskies and water.

Maggie Jackson didn't waste much time with formalities. She was undressed and in bed, trying to get warm and doing her best to control herself. When she heard him walking down the hall, she began panting like a rabbit hound.

He entered the room and walked slowly over to the bed. She tossed off her blanket. His eyes roamed over her, and she felt his appreciation. Maggie took the glass from Joe and put it on the table.

"Come on, Joey…hurry up."

When it came to sex with Joe, Maggie had no reservations at all. She relished his naked body. She loved the way he slouched, as though he were listening intently to a conversation. He was familiar, friendly. She liked the hardness of his chest, his hairy legs, muscular and tight from his years as a fisherman. She even liked his scar, the one an irate husband gave him. Joe told her once that, in a way, the scar was a memento from Max Bucolo.

When he entered her, she whispered, "Oh, Joey, you're like my best friend."

She wished he kissed her more, but he didn't. At times, he would. They would kiss and kiss, sucking each other's tongues, each other's lips, for a long time. But not tonight; it's only a small complaint, she thought.

She grabbed his arms and sort of held him off. "I love it when you're right there. Just go slow, Joey…real slow."

Maggie's hands slowly squeezed his buttocks. "I love your ass, Joey."

"You talk like the boys, Maggie."

"Do the boys like your ass, too?"

In a slightly flustered voice, Joe asked, "Maggie, what the hell is this thing…never mind."

She shifted her hips. "I'm just a bad…bad girl, Joey." She pulled him in hard and her body sizzled. For a moment, he froze while she felt herself continue to rise.

"Move, Joey, move!" Maggie wished that she was a quiet lover, but it was impossible. She loved to hear his breathing build. "Oh, Ja… Joey, you're so good to me." She almost said *Jay*.

"You talk too much."

Be quiet, she told herself. He's like a horse, she thought, wild and strong. She knew his timing. His starts and stops. His control was everything.

He stopped. She pursed her lips in pure contentment. She gazed up at him. She arched her back and she made some small appreciative noises, and he started again and she pumped her hips in cadence with his. She knew if Joey kept his mind off her, he could make love forever. With Joey, she was always rewarded—sometimes more than once. She thought he was an incredible man, but tonight he was angry.

Yet she still let herself go and soared like a storm petrel into the wind where her moaning was miles away. "Oh, that was beautiful, Joey…so, so good. Thank you."

Before falling asleep, she gently took hold of him, and for what seemed a long time, she listened to his breathing and the dying storm outside. Soon she found herself thinking about Jay Gatsby—the betrayal he had forced upon her. She was afraid of him and now she had to be afraid for Joe. How long would the sins of her mother haunt her?

CHAPTER ELEVEN

MAGGIE WAS PALE ON THIS GRAY MORNING. She had no make-up and her lips were puffy. Her eyelashes flickered. She looked out the window as though deep in thought. "My eye keeps watering," she said.

He nodded his head slightly as though acknowledging her words, yet not really wanting to pursue them. He said, "I'm sorry that I was angry last night."

"It's okay," she said softly. "Kanky isn't a nice man."

"Say, aren't you going to Providence today?"

"Me and Janie, we're supposed to catch the ten o'clock boat."

"I hope you have a nice time."

Maggie glanced at Joe, sadness in her eyes. "It'd be better if you were with me, Joey."

~~~~~~

They passed Peabody's Ferry Wharf, where Main Road curved towards the Basin. On the east side, businesses lined a wooden sidewalk: a clothing store, bakery, barber shop, post office, and the town hall, which also housed the police station. Joe parked in front of Brown's Provender, a combination grocery, feed, and hardware store. Maggie lived with her mother in an apartment on the second floor.

Across the street from Brown's Provender stood the First Riverside House of Worship. About ten years prior, it was the Mount Hope Bay Oyster Company. It was a looming three-story building with a huge wet-storage cellar for keeping oysters fresh, and on the river's side, a long, timber-built unloading dock. There was a banked, crushed-shell driveway on the north side of the structure, where oyster boats would unload their catch right into market-bound trucks.

But now, the first floor was the Sunday meeting place for the congregation, while the second served as living quarters for Minister Isaac Bottomley, the goofiest-looking man Joe ever saw. The minister made Joe smile just thinking about him.

Maggie looked miserable. Her fingers played with the door handle. Joe knew she was again going to break their rules. Finally, she did. "When will I see you?"

He shrugged and glanced towards Brown's. "How's your mother?"

"Jessica's doing okay, I guess. She's lonely. We still fight a lot." Her voice softened.

"No men friends?" Joe wondered how many times he had asked this question.

Maggie shook her head. "She still goes out on her Sunday afternoons, but she never tells me where she goes or with who. Of course, she's been doing that for as long as I can remember."

He took a deep breath, reached into his pocket, took out some money. "Here, buy her something pretty. Be nice to her."

Maggie took the bills and gripped them in a fist. She leaned over and kissed him on the cheek.

"Bye, Joey."

"I'll see you around."

"When?" she asked softly.

"It's a small town. We know where to find each other."

He made a U-turn and headed back towards Mary's Diner, wondering if Maggie would actually buy something for her mother.

He watched her through the rearview mirror as she went to wave, but didn't.

~~~~~~

From his hiding place in the church, Minister Bottomley watched Maggie Jackson step out of Joe Bucolo's car.

The Jackson women seldom made a move the minister didn't know about. He shook his head as he chewed on his worn thumbnail. He loved the sway of Maggie's ass. What delicious thoughts raced through his mind. He wondered what that rum-runner sinner had done last night. It made his imagination run wild.

Living right across the street, Maggie and Jessica Jackson made it really interesting for him. Although fresh youth had its appeal, it wasn't Maggie he had his sights on, but her mother, Jessica. Besides Gertrude Moore, he needed another woman, a woman with a bad reputation. A woman who would open her legs, something Gertie just wouldn't do. Yes, she would drop to her knees, which was delightful, but he wanted the conjugal bed.

Of late, he'd been contemplating offering the heavenly kingdom to Maggie's mother in return for some earthly satisfaction. However, he suspected Jessica might turn into a gossiping granny.

With difficulty, he leaned over and picked up a basket holding Gertrude's peach pie. "Time to be a good neighbor," he said softly. "Besides, if you're going to grow some corn, you have to sow some seeds."

Chapter Twelve

TIVERTON WAS FINALLY COMING ALIVE as Joe drove back up towards Highland Road. Traffic on Main Road had picked up. Exhaust puffs were visible on a number of fishing boats, their captains anxious to make up the lost money and time due to the recent storm.

Many of Joe's neighbors, some of the oldest families and earliest settlers, lived on the Heights. Unlike the Grovers, most of them tended to their own business. The homes were well-kept Colonials, and most of the lots were enclosed with hand-built stone walls. It was an old neighborhood, heavily treed with large, spreading oaks.

The largest home on the Heights belonged to Barnabus Simmons, who made his money in lumber in the family-owned commercial waterfront property south of the trestle bridge, where schooners from all over arrived, carrying lumber.

One time, Barnabus purchased an entire boatload of Pacific redwood that had to sail over thousands of miles around Cape Horn. That was pretty good doing.

The Simmons had four sons who, like their grim and silent father, had wild, bushy beards. When they turned of age, they all worked for their father. At the age of fifty-eight, Barnabus shot himself with his black-powder pistol, leaving practically no head on his shoulders. He left a note saying that families should never be in business together.

Another neighbor, the Grinnells, who, in the old days, had a horse and livery stable, switched to selling automobiles; the Grinnells had three dealerships in Rhode Island, where they sold Buicks. Joe bought his car from Paul Grinnell and had it painted white. As far as anybody knew, it was the only white Buick in Rhode Island.

The Brownells and the Tompkins, whose ancestors came over on the *Mayflower* and sold hardware, and the Palmers, whose son ran the town's barber shop, and of course the Widow Bancock, whose whiskey-soaked sons often slept off their drunks with Hunker in his Swamp Yankee barn overlooking Seapowet Marsh—most were all friends to Joe.

~~~~~~

The white Buick stopped abruptly at the top of South Avenue. Joe took in a very gray but panoramic view of the Tiverton Basin. Here, at this very spot, Max showed a young orphan where he would live and earn his living. Thinking of Max, Joe subconsciously ran his finger over his scar. He taught me so much. Fewer trees then, but so much has changed in my life.

The Seaconnet was still awash with the storm's runoff. Fresh winds, sun, and a few tide changes would take care of that. He knew the herring could be detoured by the murky water for a few days.

In past seasons, just as now, they often set their fish traps off Seaconnet Point and Sandy Point Shoals; long fences of anchored netting would direct, confuse, and eventually trap tons of herring, butterfish, scup, and striped bass.

As a boy, Joe could hardly swallow his excitement. He'd pull the loaded nets, hear the water bubbling, and see the flashing silver bodies thrashing in their jeweled foam.

Laughing and shouting orders, Max's voice filled the air. They would pull, tighten, roll, and gradually shape the catch into a perfect bowl that they'd scoop out onto the waiting vessel's deck. The slippery arm of Max's rain slicker would clutch Joe's neck in a gentle hammer-lock, dragging him from bow to stern to show him the bulging net frothing with dying fish or to see the twine-whacked, bleeding fingers of some greenhorn deckhand. Yanking Joe's head in every direction, Max would scream like a carnival barker. "She can drive good men nuts, the river. Nuts! Look around, Joe, these fishermen are nuts. Look at their faces; see their eyes as they haul in the fish. Do you see it? The madness!"

Other times, Max would clamp Joe's arms and lift him off the deck, Joe's face lying right against the bowl of Max's pipe, so close he could feel the heat. Through clenched, yellow teeth Max would shout, "You'll never go hungry by this river, Joe. Not much money, but you eat like a king." Max would let go and Joe would fall into the mountain of fish, always smiling and always happy.

Joe grew up gauging the seasons by the fish he caught. Herring and scup for the spring, lobsters for the summer, and codfish for the winter. Fall and its early darkness was reserved for night raids on Rhode Island companies that had leased-ground oyster beds.

He listened to the wisdom and the lies of the older, experienced fishermen, the ones with the crazy eyes. Their exaggerated stories of the sea, the Seaconnet, the women—always the women—filled their talk. The first time he touched a woman's pussy and put his fingers to his nose, he was disappointed not to smell the dead herring he was often told he would smell while growing up on the Seaconnet.

"Joe, the Seaconnet River and the ocean is our mother. Treat her nice...but respect her, too."

Through the morning's cool haze, he surveyed the Basin, picking out various fishing vessels, knowing each by name, each by colors, their riggings, their masts and booms, even the shapes of their pilot houses. They were, in some ways, human, all with different characteristics and quirks. Like humans, some boats were stiff, some rolled too much, some were very wet, some were exceptional, and some were not.

At the bottom of Newhill Avenue, Main Road was deserted, except for a lone coal truck that rumbled noisily by. Two dogs snapped at the truck's big, solid rubber tires as Joe pulled into Mary's Diner.

~~~~~~

A robust Mary Standish looked at herself in the mirror. Her hair was tied neatly in a bun. Her cheeks were pink. Wide-shouldered, she had an appealing, durable stature that tickled a man's imagination. A widow of ten years, she continually longed for the arms of a man.

The aromas of coffee and bacon gave Mary's Diner a homey atmosphere. Under glass covers, home-baked pies and fresh sweet rolls waited. On a blackboard, facing the customers as they came in the door, were Mary's today's specials: *Fish Stew or Boston Baked Beans and Ham.*

Along the wall that Saturday morning, all the booths and tables, covered in red-and-white checkered tablecloths, were occupied. Cousins Ray and Pete Almy, partners in a local turkey farm, drank their coffee black. In the next booth sat George Pontes, a cutthroat fish dealer from Seaconnet Point, who never left a tip. Manny and Jake Pavao, partners in a landscape business, appreciated a good kale soup with chunks of sourdough bread in the morning and for lunch.

The Bancock brothers, as handsome as any two boys Mary ever knew (except possibly for Joe Bucolo), ate silently today with nervous expressions on their faces. Doc Peckham sat alone, reading the paper, farting off the preceding night's whiskey and beer chasers.

This morning, the usual jovial chatter at the diner was silent as cold winter fog. Mary wondered if the arrival of Joe Bucolo would change things.

Joe sat down and picked up the *Providence Journal* and read the glaring headlines: COAST GUARDSMAN KILLED IN RUMMY CHASE! She saw his eyes blink. She glanced around the diner and noticed the Bancock brothers were also watching Joe. They looked like they were about to jump out of their coveralls. In fact, everyone was staring at Joe except the two strangers in business suits at the end of the counter. They were looking out the back windows, towards the Seaconnet.

Joe folded the paper and placed it back on the counter.

"Morning, Joe," Mary said quickly, cheerfully.

"Morning, Mary. Gonna be a fine day."

"Good for business, I hope," she said, looking outside. "Why, I haven't seen a boat leave the Basin yet."

"It's gonna take most of the day for the seas to calm down. With this northwest wind, that'll cut the seas down...sunny and cool tomorrow."

Mary always enjoyed Joe's weather report.

Ray Almy nodded pleasantly and he motioned for Joe to come over.

Joe did and leaned into Ray's booth.

Ray whispered, "Heard some strange booms the other morning, frightened my birds, Joe. Did you happen to hear it?"

Joe shook his head. "No, Ray, I was sleeping like a babe. Sorry, though, it bothered your gobblers."

"Just so you know, Joe, I've got plenty of storage space in my back barn. I can always use a few extra bucks."

"I'll remember that, Ray. Thanks." Joe touched Ray's shoulder and moved on. Ray and Pete smiled. Joe passed by George Pontes as though the man wasn't there.

He stopped at Doc Peckham's booth. Mary knew where the Doc's loyalty lay.

"Morning, Doc."

The doctor looked up over his glasses and said softly, "Morning, Joe. How's Sammy?"

Joe nodded. "He's okay. Thanks for taking a look."

Doctor Peckham said softly, "Keep that medicine coming in, boy, keep it coming." The doctor motioned towards the paper and added, "Tough break on that guardsman. But despite those Chicago gangster headlines, this country and this town needs booze."

"We're only fishermen at heart, Doc." Joe returned to his seat at the counter, and Mary brought him a cup of coffee. "Bacon, eggs, Jonnycakes, Joe?" And then whispered, "Check out the two guys at the far end."

Joe said, "Sounds good, Mary." One of the men dressed in suits glanced at Joe and nodded to whatever his partner was saying.

Mary worked for Joe. From her living quarters above the diner, she operated a shortwave radio. To the vessels anchored on Rum Row, she was known as "Sparky." Whenever possible, Mary would receive from various "outside vessels" their location, cargo, arrival time, sometimes even the weather. It could be very helpful.

Last fall, Pearly designed the new code, which gave Sparky and the offshore rummies the ability to exchange reports on any potential "six-bitters" or "four-stackers" patrolling the area. With the radio antenna hidden inside her attic, Mary just opened a south dormer window that gave her a clear path for transmitting right down the Seaconnet River. Mary enjoyed the action, and it gave her extra money to spend in Boston when she visited the Old Howard Nightclub, a good place to meet older men looking for love, away from the busybodies of Tiverton.

Usually, Mary talked nonstop in the morning, shrewdly extracting gossip from anyone who would give it. But today she felt bad about news of the dead sailor. She also knew that it would be bothering Joe. She brought over his breakfast without a word.

Finally, Mary and the rest of the silent patrons watched as the two men in suits paid their check and left. As the door closed behind them, the diner snapped to life. "Have you ever seen them before?" Mary asked.

The Bancock brothers left the booth and came over. Billy quickly said, "We think they were the law."

"He's right, Joe," Bobby Bancock added. "I kept watching them. They were talking low and they kept looking out towards the river… like they were scheming something."

Mary nodded. "They clearly were studying the river."

Joe glanced outside. "It'll take more than sitting here, drinking your good coffee and looking through your windows, to learn about the Seaconnet."

"Joe's right, those swells got a lot to learn," Bobby Bancock said.

Joe nodded towards the paper and said, "Probably federal agents. They're snooping because of what's happened."

"Yeah," Billy Bancock added, "plotting revenge for that dead sailor."

Joe poked Billy's arm. "And you better not let Hunker hear you talking like that."

Bobby hit Billy on the shoulder, paid their check, and the two left, whispering between themselves.

Mary and Joe watched them go out the door. "Can't blame them for being excited," Mary said. "It's not your fault. The Seaconnet River made Sandy Point Shoals, not you."

Joe stared at Mary. "I love you, Mary. But in this case, you're wrong."

She shrugged and filled Joe's cup again.

Mary poured herself a cup of coffee, walked around the counter, and sat next to Joe. "Pearly's been avoiding this place like it was church."

Joe smiled and slowly shook his head.

"I wish you luck, Mary. Pearly Thurston would be lucky to get you, but I think he's too far gone."

"I wonder," she said. "I really wonder."

A bedraggled-looking man entered. Mary and Joe glanced at him. She said, "Now here's one crewman, probably from down south; clearly a little too early for the menhaden season."

"No bet."

The man certainly looked down on his luck. He took a seat a few stools from Joe. He nodded and eyed Joe, who returned the greeting. Mary asked, "What can I get you, stranger?"

The man shrugged and placed a coin on the counter. He said, "Whatever this will get me."

Mary stood, glanced at Joe, then back to the man. "I think it'll buy you a good breakfast."

Surprised, the man smiled. "Thank you, ma'am."

He rubbed his hands together, almost as though he were cold. Joe took a dollar from his pocket and slid it over to him. In a bit of disbelief, the man glanced at the money and then back to Joe. Mary made like she didn't see it and continued to work her grill. She didn't even turn around when Joe said goodbye. But through the mirror, she saw the stranger's head turn to follow Joe out the door.

~~~~~~

When the cloudy skies finally cleared out, the Seaconnet River, almost like magic, turned a lavender blue. Sammy, despite his beating, was at the job early.

Below, in the engine room of the *Black Duck*, he had just finished changing the oil on the two engines. When he heard Joe's car, he stuck his head up through the deck hatch and watched Joe stop at Max's cat boat, which they used to use for dredging oysters. It was set on blocks, near a pile of old, empty oyster baskets. Sammy lost track of the nights he had helped Max and Joe cull oysters by the dark of the moon after a raid.

As Joe walked towards the rum boats, Sammy's memories began to fade. Even now, after three years, Sammy felt a void in his daily routine without Max. He was sure he missed Max just about as much as anybody, especially Joe.

Joe climbed down the ladder. "Morning, Sammy. How's that face?"

He could barely see Joe through the slit of his purple-black eye. His nose was swollen. Hunker said it was an improvement. And after examining it in the mirror, Sammy secretly had to agree with his close friend.

Sammy watched Joe move around the *Black Duck*. He and Joe were of the same mind working around boats—it made them feel good. They both loved the mixed smells of wood and varnish, oil and gas. There was nothing more natural than feeling the fluid movement of the hull, like an unborn baby floating safely in the womb.

Joe's love of boats had nothing to do with business or money. Even now, he could hear Max preaching to him. *Son, a boat is like a beautiful woman, needs constant attention. And because she is beautiful, she expects you to kiss her ass every day. But because she's truly detached from this earth, she makes you think you're in heaven. If you have a good boat, you really don't need a wife...*

"I said good morning, Sammy."

"Sorry, Joe, I was drifting a bit."

Joe nodded. "How do you feel?"

"Little sore, and my damn eye won't stop watering." Sammy stood and wiped his hands. "I've just finished changing the *Duck*'s oils."

Joe nodded and glanced out towards Ghoul Island.

Sammy added, "Sorry 'bout yesterday, Joe. But I've been thinking, don't you trust Kanky at all."

"I don't, Sammy, and I won't."

"I know it's crazy, but it's uncanny how he reminds me of Max. When I first went to work for Max, he was about Kanky's age now. I remember how Max looked."

The hairs on Joe's neck tickled him.

"For a moment there," Sammy added, "I thought I was looking at Max's ghost. It must be the mustache."

Joe placed his hand on Sammy's shoulder. "Mustache or no mustache, there's only one Max, Sammy, and he's gone."

"I know, Joe, I know."

"You might as well know—a sailor died in that grounding on Sandy Point."

"Jesus Christ! No kidding?" Sammy shook his head as it began to throb with pain. He pressed his hands over his ears. "Goddamn!

Never thought anything like that would happen to us. No kidding, huh, Joe?"

Joe shook his head. "Nothing to kid 'bout there."

"Can't blame yourself, Joe, you can't. Could've been us blown apart with a cannonball." Sammy waited for Joe's response, but none came.

After a long moment of silence, Sammy said, "By the way, I got another magneto from New Bedford. Hunker gave me a ride over early this morning."

"Good."

"Got a couple of spares, too."

Joe nodded and climbed up the ladder. On the wharf, he leaned against a piling and spoke in a low voice down to Sammy. "You slow down, Sammy. You've been hurt."

Sammy waved him off and descended back into the heart of the *Black Duck*.

CHAPTER THIRTEEN

SHAPED LIKE A HORSE'S HEAD, Oakland Beach was bordered on three sides by salt water. Shallow coves etched the shore east and west of the community, while the beach itself faced Warwick Bay. By automobile or speedboat, it was perhaps twenty-five minutes from Providence. The jagged beach was famous for its ragtag shoreline of gaudy summer shanties and dilapidated piers. For the most part, every tilted porch facing the water hung the lusty Rhode Island symbols of having a real good time: empty liquor bottles and women's underwear.

Like beach tar that wouldn't wash away with the next tide, Walter Hill followed Gatsby when he left Chicago. Walter came from a well-to-do family. Unlike Gatsby, he had no mystery about him. Tall and wiry, Walter had soft, clean-cut features and thick brown hair. He was happy that Gatsby had given him a job, and he intended on toughening up his soft side working alongside Kanky, where he saw a potential partnership, promised by Gatsby. Both men seized on the opportunity and were turning the place into quite an establishment. Given free rein, the two had spawned a much darker underworld with a more varied menu of both booze and women. Anything illegal was for sale, including, but not limited to, simple hobnobbing, opium smoking, porno parties, oiling, lamb rentals (often patrons heard the sounds of *BAAAH* coming from a back room). On special occasions, cock fighting and even Oriental slave trading took place.

Aggressively celebrating its intemperance on major holidays, residents of the Beach flew three sheets in the wind from the *White Witch*, an old, wrecked schooner grounded in the gale of 1894, the former seafaring temptress now serving as hostess to revelers. Kanky and Walter even began to charge fees for booze parties and cookouts aboard her deck.

Despite its notoriety, the Beach was immune from the local police force. This blatant blind eye cast by law enforcers turned the tide in the General Assembly, which mandated the organization of a new independent Rhode Island State Police—sure to be a threat to the darker and extremely lucrative goings-on in Oakland Beach if any of the cops proved to be worth their mettle.

Smack in the center of this heady mishmash of smells, sounds, and night lights stood Gatsby's two-story speakeasy and whorehouse: *Tumble Inn, Tumble Out*. Gatsby was making more money here than he had on any of his falsely advertised "drug stores" in New York City or even Chicago. These medicinal stores were fronts for selling illegal booze, but came with problems from gangsters trying to muscle in on the profits. However, Oakland Beach operated without the violence or threats from what he called "wannabe hoodlums with no brains."

Painted yellow with black shutters, the establishment perched over the rickety bungalows of its unfortunate neighbors. As business grew, and with Gatsby's total permission, Kanky and Walter, in an attempt to keep up with their booming business, had additions built in every direction, turning the one-time beach club into a speakeasy hotel.

Most of the first floor of the Tumble Inn was a huge lounge, set up like an open living room. Floor lamps flanked twenty or so couches with low-slung cocktail tables on which patrons would place their feet, their drinks, their cigarettes...or anything else they wished, if they had the money. Along the back wall was a long mahogany bar with a brass footrail. The perimeter of the room was lined with heavy draperies, between which hung giant, gold-framed paintings of naked women, landscapes, and street maps of Paris. The local consensus had it pegged: What a joint.

In their speakeasy office, after relaying his scheme to trap Foggy Joe, Kanky stared at Gatsby, waiting for his response.

Finally, Gatsby said, "If it works, you're in for a nice bonus."

"Thanks, Boss. It oughta work…long as the law get-a the right information."

Gatsby thought about it for a moment. "So, how do we set this in motion?"

"I think we give it to that asshole, Chief Grover, as a present. Let him bring it to the Federal men and the Coast Guard."

Gatsby started to laugh. "I love it. But how?"

"Well, he'd definitely recognize my voice. We can't take that chance."

Gatsby nodded. "Good thinking. Get Walter in here. We'll rehearse him…"

After Kanky spelled out the plan, even writing down notes to prompt Walter when he made the phone call, Walter cracked up in laughter halfway through his first practice run, causing Gatsby and Kanky to break up as well.

Gatsby said, "All right. Sober up—time to get serious—make the call, Walter…"

~~~~~~

Henry Grover sat at his desk, glancing through the *New Yorker* magazine, when the phone rang. He lifted up the earpiece. "Hello."

"Is this the Tiverton police chief?"

"Yes, it is. Who's calling?"

"Never mind. But I know it's my duty to inform and help the law with rum-runners."

Grover said, "Of course…that's called being a good citizen—performing your civic duty, as it were."

"Listen close, Chief. If you have a pencil and paper, you may want to take down some notes."

For some time, Henry Grover made notes with painstaking attention. The longer the conversation went on, the more excited his expression became.

"I hope you will act on this information."

Grover said, "I certainly will! Don't you know who I am?"

The phone remained silent.

"I'm happy you shared this information. Tell me, what made you call?"

"Joseph Bucolo. He fucked my girlfriend and he'll fuck yours."

"Who is this?"

The phone went dead. Grover stared at the receiver momentarily, finally releasing a weird smile as he envisioned himself as the famous lawman who ended the career of Foggy Joe Bucolo.

Chapter Fourteen

AT THE STROKE OF NINE, Edmund Palmer unlatched the door to his barber shop. Palmer wasn't too thin or too bald to be a proper-looking gentleman. He had a pencil-thin mustache and puffy bags under his eyes, just like his dad. May he rest in peace, the penny-pinching bastard.

Edmund was happy to see Joe's car stop out front. He took a deep breath and wondered how he should handle the dead guardsman. Say nothing, he thought. Of course, if it's mentioned, say something smart, but what?

Edmund said, "How are you this morning, Mister Bucolo?"

"Fine, Ed. You?"

Edmund gestured towards the empty chair. Whenever someone was getting ready to sit, Edmund stood stiff as a soldier, with a white towel draped over his arm, just like his dad used to do.

Joe sat and Edmund spun the chair around to face the mirror. The barber flapped the towel out, and pinned it carefully around Joe's neck.

Edmund asked, "What will it be?"

"Shave and a clip."

While he trimmed Joe's thick head of hair, Tommy Walsh came in. "Morning, Mister Walsh."

Tommy nodded. "Hi, Ed. Hey, Joe, some bad storm, huh…?"

"Good for your business, Tommy?"

Tommy laughed. "A plumber's dream, indeed." He took a seat and picked up the morning paper. "Jesus! A dead sailor on Sandy Point! Damn!"

"I hear you there," Joe said, a hint of sadness in his voice.

Edmund snipped away. "Boys, life in general is filled with risks."

From outside, the loud cracking exhaust of a motorcycle revving finally quieted. Edmund glanced into the mirror at Joe and then at Tommy Walsh, who was absorbed in the paper, but still shook his head. They both knew who was coming, as there was only one motorcycle in town.

"Times like this, I wish there was another barber in town," Edmund said.

Joe looked at Edmund and said, "Relax, Henry Grover doesn't bother me."

But Edmund Palmer couldn't. He knew the Grover family had no use for Joe Bucolo.

Henry Grover's tall frame filled the doorway. His boyish features still seemed out of place in his new uniform. He had leather gloves in one hand and a newspaper in the other. He was wearing brown, high-laced riding boots and a gun on his hip with a braided cord drooping from its grip to his belt, similar to the Canadian Mounties. Henry sat down.

Edmund Palmer snipped away. "Good morning, Chief. How are you today?"

"Not bad, Edmund, not bad at all." Grover's aloof blue eyes glanced into the mirror, searching. "Hello, boys."

"Fine-looking outfit you have there, Chief." Edmund surveyed the new uniform. "Is that what the Town Council allocated that money for?"

"That's right, Edmund. Same as the new State Police uniforms, only theirs are gray." Henry's hand smoothed down the shirt. "It takes a little getting used to."

Edmund had to stifle his laugh.

Returning to trimming Joe's hair, he kept glancing nervously into the mirror, waiting for something to happen. He watched as Grover opened the *Providence Journal*. Then, just as Edmund was lathering up Joe's face, he saw Grover and Joe staring at each other in the mirror like angry bulldogs. Joe didn't turn away, nor did Grover.

Grover's voice broke the quiet. "Say, Joe, did you read the *Providence Journal* yet this morning?"

Edmund slowly sharpened his razor on the chair's leather strap. Joe replied softly, "No, I haven't had the chance." Edmund nervously began to shave Joe.

Grover continued, "Coast Guard is going to be hotter than the devil in hell. Gonna be looking to settle the score, I'd say. With whomever is responsible. Don't suspect it'll be hard to find out who."

The barber figured something bad was coming, but he wasn't sure what. Feeling his own nervousness in his hands, he removed the straight razor from Joe's neck.

"I'd sure hate to be the object of their revenge. I wonder if they even knew who they were chasing. Evidently, there were three rummies. And they blew a wall of smoke out their exhausts, engulfing the Coast Guard boat, which subsequently ran aground on Sandy Point. The boy lost his face and his head was split by a rail. They claimed his head appeared to be chopped by a long-handled axe. Lord, oh Lord. It was a sad moment on the Seaconnet."

Joe continued to stare in the mirror. With his face still lathered, he said, "Are you trying to make a point, Henry?"

Grover stood up. "As I told you last night, my only point is that those responsible are going to dance. I don't like to see the bad guys kill the good guys."

"Anything else you don't like?" Joe asked.

Edmund Palmer felt his heart begin to pick up speed. His hands began to sweat. Nothing like this had ever happened in his shop before, or in his dad's shop either, he imagined. He didn't know what to do. Yet, there was something exhilarating about it. Edmund said nervously, "I say, gentlemen, I don't like ill-wind in my shop."

Henry Grover ignored Edmund. "For the record, Bucolo, there are some people who don't like the idea of Tiverton being used as a rum-running port."

"Give me a name, Henry."

"And there are a lot of people who don't like your cock aimed at every good-looking woman in Tiverton either. And I'm warning you: keep your lousy eyes and your lousy intentions off Janie Thurston."

Edmund swore he could hear Joe's heart thumping, for the veins on his forehead were pulsing like night crawlers. He couldn't remember ever seeing Joe this angry.

"Well, now we're getting down to the real issues," Joe said. "Nothing to do with a dead sailor." Then a half-smile broke through the lather around the corners of Joe's mouth. "Last time I looked, Janie was a grown woman, and I believe she's quite capable of making her own decisions."

"I have honorable intentions towards Janie Thurston, something you wouldn't understand."

"Well now, Chief Hard-on," interrupted Tommy. "If you're going to be wearing a uniform, walking around, and telling us who we can fuck or not fuck, you've got a personal problem. And frankly, you're out of order, mister."

"Keep your nose out of it, Tommy Walsh, or I'll be pulling your trucks over five times a day."

"Tell me, Henry," Joe asked, "did you clear your honorable intentions with Janie? What would she think if she knew you were threatening me not to wave my cock in her face?"

For a moment, Henry was taken aback by the questions.

Joe leaned back in the chair and looked at Palmer. "You can finish shaving me, Ed."

Edmund Palmer nodded nervously.

Grover started to leave, but not before gazing angrily back at the chair.

When the door slammed, Tommy Walsh said, "Why, that two-faced sonofabitch. Jesus, a dead guardsman! Tough break, Joe, but that's the rum trade. Their cannon fire could've killed you, too."

They all listened to Grover's Harley-Davidson leave in a hurry.

Joe lifted his head and looked at Tommy through the mirror. "Well, at least we know where Grover stands."

"Jeez, Grover's eyes were burning like a blacksmith's iron," Tommy said. "That asshole sure has it in for you."

Before he knew it, Edmund Palmer popped out his own thoughts. "I say, I think Chief Grover doesn't want you stealing Janie Thurston away from him. More importantly, the Grover family never liked Max Bucolo. And to them, even though he's dead, you're Max Bucolo's legacy."

Tommy Walsh started to grin, almost breaking into laughter. "What Edmund is saying, Joe, sure makes a lot of sense. Course, I kind of liked that thing about your cock being a gun. I thought it rang true, didn't you?"

Joe said, "Good thing I like you, Tommy, or I'd shoot you right this minute. No one's safe in Tiverton when Bucolo's gun is loaded. Yessiree, it's a good thing you're an excellent plumber."

Tommy continued his wide grin. He enjoyed the compliment. "Hey, Joe, except for the Grovers and their band of Bible-banging fundamentalists, I ain't heard anyone complaining about your business...or your jollying."

Edmund Palmer unfastened the towel from around Joe's neck and held out a small mirror. Joe pushed it away and got out of the chair. "You always do a good job, Ed, thank you."

They all heard the hoots of the *Queen City* arriving at Peabody's Wharf. By habit, everyone glanced up at the barber's clock.

"The only woman that's ever on time," Edmund Palmer quipped.

Standing in the shop's doorway, Joe looked north and watched the *Queen City* steam through the open span of the trestle bridge. The white hull trimmed in red, against the blue water and bright sky, lit up the Basin. She was a little ahead of her schedule as she swung wide to the east towards Peabody's Wharf, again hooting her horn.

Tommy asked, "Where you heading, Joe?"

"Going over to Wilcox's boatyard…I want to check out a fishing dragger."

Tommy said, "Don't you have enough boats?"

Joe laughed.

~~~~~~

As stately as Joe Bucolo's home appeared outside, inside it was cluttered—understandable for a bachelor. In one corner, a small table fit snugly beneath a round, leaded, stained-glass window. Here, Max carved his boat models out of pine. The table, the cutting knives, chisels, small hammers, even old shavings were in a bucket beneath his chair.

Joe moved the chair slightly and the light revealed a perfectly formed, ancient cobweb, thick with dust, strung between the chair and the wall. Yes, Joe thought, just like a fish trap.

There were fourteen models around the house, replicas of famous clipper ships; the *Sovereign*, known as the longest, sharpest, most beautiful ship in the world, had a special place in the parlor where all could see. She had been Max's pride.

Another was the *America*, a favorite of shipping merchants because of her fast passages. The *Stag Hound*, one of the first "extreme" clippers, a sailing ship designed for speed. The *Wild Pigeon*, one of the smallest and sharpest "extreme" clippers ever made. One after another, perfect in detail, but all dusty.

Joe telephoned Pearly. Janie answered.

He smiled, hearing the twang in her voice. "Say, aren't you catching the ferry?" he asked.

"I have plenty of time."

"Okay, have fun." He waited for a response; none came. In the background, he heard Pearly saying goodbye.

Then Pearly took over the phone and asked, "Hey Joe, do you hear the wind whispering?"

Joe said, "Yes, I surely do."

Pearly's voice brightened. "Good, I'll call Hunker and the others. Say, did Sammy replace the magneto?"

"He's been busy."

~~~~~~

Henry Grover was at Peabody's Wharf at nine forty-five, watching George Pontes' fish truck back up to the cargo ramp of the *Queen City*. On the boxes, it read: *FRESH FISH*. Henry smirked. He knew that the fish were caught before the storm. George Pontes kept them iced, knowing the bad weather would drive prices up. Grover whispered, "Pontes is a thief." He wasn't there to check on fish, but Maggie had mentioned she was taking the ferry to Providence with Janie.

Maggie Jackson stood alone on the ferry gangway. As he walked towards her, Grover adjusted his hat and brushed his right shoulder. This blue uniform is going to be a pain, he thought.

"Morning, Chief!" Maggie said loudly.

"Call me Henry, Maggie. We're friends." Henry didn't take his hat off, not wanting to disturb his dandruff.

He said, "Going to the big city, huh?"

Maggie nodded. "I like your new uniform, Henry. You look good in blue."

She flicked her fingers across his shoulder. "Try Dandrene for dandruff; works for me."

He made a slight face. "Thought I was being made a fool of at the White Horse last night. By Bucolo for one."

"Not by me, Henry."

"What about Bucolo?"

"Joey's not bad," Maggie said. "He treats—"

"I'm not interested in how he treats you!" Henry snapped. "And why do you call him Joey?"

"Well, I'm sorry, Chief, but you brought him up. It's just a nickname from our Fort Barton School days. Stop being so sensitive, you are a police officer. Don't worry about Joey."

Henry noticed, as he had on several occasions when they were alone, how Maggie's every move was different, in an interesting way, towards him. Luscious body, he continually thought.

"That new uniform is very stimulating, Henry." She moved slightly closer, and he took a step forward. He thought he detected more than true friendship in Maggie's voice.

Grover's attention shifted to Janie Thurston's Ford splashing through a puddle in the lot. She quickly got out of the car and waved.

Henry yanked off his hat as Janie approached. The breeze pressed her cotton dress, with its twill bottom, against her body. No tits, compared to Maggie, he thought, but he loved Janie's legs.

"Morning, Henry…Maggie…"

Before he could respond, Janie glanced towards the ferry and began walking. "We're late."

Just then, another Pontes' fish truck pulled in. Henry motioned to the fish truck. "Plenty of time, they've got another truck to unload."

Both women nodded, but clearly annoyed, they stood side by side, hands on their hips. Maggie was a woman alright, Grover was thinking, but Janie is a wife. If she'd only have me…I could make her so happy. Then his thought turned nasty. She will have me, one way or another.

— = Chapter Fifteen = —

A FEW HUNDRED FEET SOUTH of Peabody's Wharf, Wilcox's boatyard hauled boats, painted hulls, and made engine repairs—everything to keep a vessel floating and working. Cory Wilcox also served as the local boat-broker. On the railway, the *Flo*, a sixty-foot fishing dragger, was presently being overhauled and painted. A *For Sale* sign was nailed to her pilot house.

Like a flashy summer suit at a funeral wake, Joe's white Buick entered the wharf's loading area of crushed oyster shells, adjacent to the boatyard.

Shifting their gaze from the *Queen City*, Grover, Janie, and Maggie turned towards the Buick. He shut off the engine and just sat there for a moment, looking at them.

Grover whispered, "See, Bucolo just doesn't want to face me."

Janie and Maggie looked at each other and almost laughed.

In the next moment, Joe got out of his Buick and headed right for the trio.

Maggie glanced at Janie. "Your cheeks are blushing. Wonder what that means?"

"Usually means I'm angry."

Maggie smiled. "Don't think so."

For some reason, Janie's hand went to her face, and as she was about to turn away, she saw Joe smile at her, and she knew it was only for her. She knew, and Maggie, hurt by it, knew it too because then Joe said, "Hi, Maggie, going for a boat ride?" Joe simply ignored Chief Grover.

Grover asked, "Why are you here, Bucolo? You going for a boat ride, too?"

Joe pointed over to the *Flo*. "I'm going back fishing."

Grover appeared shocked, maybe even disappointed—clearly lost for words.

Janie couldn't hide her surprise, but Maggie seemed to accept it without comment. Joe did catch her nonchalant attitude.

Joe added, "Watch out for those city men. They love small-town girls; especially girls as pretty as you gals." Joe's eyes were on Janie, who seemed to go into a deeper flush.

She started to laugh, but quickly turned away from Joe's gaze.

Maggie added, "We can't wait to see if you are right."

The ferry's horn blew and the girls twirled around and walked towards it.

Joe yelled, "Have a good time," but the horn blast drowned out his words. Janie gave him a wave and boarded the *Queen City*. Maggie walked on without a look. The ferry backed noisily out of the slip.

Joe walked past Grover towards Wilcox's boatyard. From behind, the policeman yelled, "I don't believe you're going back fishing."

Joe didn't respond, but he did have a small smile on his lips. He enjoyed annoying Henry Grover.

Henry got on his motorcycle and sat for a moment, his scalp itching. Damn! Bucolo was just like this itch he needed to scratch, but so far hadn't been able to. Of course, just as important, he feared for Janie's virtue anytime Joe was around. He also wondered what her secret thoughts were when she was looking at the rum-runner. He thought about the phone call and tried to figure out who the squealer was. If nothing else, he knew it had to be someone who wanted Joe out of the rum game.

Henry didn't share his father's dislike of Max, but he sure found it easy to dislike Max's rum-running, low-life son—adopted at that—a real bastard, that was what they called him.

Henry Grover revved his motorcycle. He said out loud, "I can't wait to smash Joey Bucolo."

~~~~~~

Janie felt almost trapped inside the cold and empty passenger lounge. The interior had recently been repainted a light blue with all the exposed pipes done in white. There was an odor from the new paint job. The gray deck beneath her feet vibrated from the chugging engine and turning shaft.

A coal cooking stove provided some welcome heat. A porter in a white jacket got ready to serve coffee, scones, and muffins. That was half the fun of going on the *Queen City*.

Janie was amused how different Tiverton looked from the river, especially with the community's high hills. In Fort Barton School, she had been taught about ice glaciers chiseling their way into Rhode Island, carving out its rivers and bays. But Janie's third-grade version imagined a prehistoric giant walking up the Seaconnet River into the Basin, scooping up earth and rocks, piling it onto the shoreline, creating the town's steep landscape and turning the river into a watery valley.

Her eyes tracked the jagged horizon from Peabody's Wharf to as far south as she could see. Tiverton was still dressed in winter brown, but spring was almost here. Actually, some trees had an ever-so-light-green hint to them. Flowers had bulbs ready to erupt. Hadn't she smelled it this morning? Hadn't she worn a spring dress, cotton slip, cotton underwear, too?

They had seated themselves by a large, starboard window. While Maggie pensively watched the passing scenery, Janie studied her friend's lightly made-up face. The two of them were really not that different. They were the prettiest girls all through grade school and high school. These memories gave Janie a sudden surge of well-being, and she took a deep breath.

Maggie turned and said, "I think Henry Grover is more serious about you than you realize, Janie."

"Really?"

"Yes, really."

Janie nodded but didn't want to pursue it. "I can see that you didn't sleep much last night." Janie's voice hinged on a question more than a comment.

Maggie bit her lip, shook her head.

After passing through the trestle bridge, the *Queen City* picked up speed and continued towards Common Fence Point. To the east and north, Francis Grover's fleet of menhaden vessels were pinned to their moorings. Each was named after one of the Twelve Apostles. The one-hundred-foot, smoke-stacked steamers—all painted black with white pilot houses—were moored in a perfect south-to-north line.

Behind them, Grover's processing building overwhelmed that eastern section of Tiverton's shoreline. At the moment, the factory's smelly cooking chimneys were dormant, waiting for the season to begin. Painted on the peaked roof, in white block letters: **GROVER**. At each corner, a religious cross was erected.

Maggie lit a cigarette, motioned towards the fish plant. "How would you like to have that for a married name?"

Janie was surprised at Maggie's directness. "I don't know. I suppose Henry's okay. But the Grovers exist in a peculiar sanctimonious world. Remember, I work for Henry's father."

"I don't know how you do it, Janie. According to my mother, he's a very strange man."

"Strange? You want strange? Every morning, Mister Grover stands before my bookkeeping table…and thanks the Lord for his success—with his bony, shaking hands, white skin, yellow teeth, and his black suit… It's a bizarre beginning to my unbearably boring days. At times, when he mumbles his prayers, his eyes will roll upward, turning white, and I have to look away."

"That's pretty scary, Janie… Not to mention slightly disgusting."

"And just how does your mother know Mister Grover is very strange?"

Maggie shrugged. "Well, even with Henry Grover's shortcomings…he will offer someone a comfortable life."

Janie glanced at Maggie. "Money is important but I want a fulfilling life also. I want to travel, I want a relationship that has romance… passion."

Maggie quickly responded, "I believe lovemaking should be part of a woman's life. It can be more than pleasurable…sometimes, it can be incredible…beyond words…you almost don't care if you live or die…"

Janie gave Maggie an exasperated look.

"Maggie…please…I don't need to hear about Joe again."

"It's really about all men," she said softly. Janie noticed that Maggie was off somewhere in hidden thoughts. She found her comment curious. In the past, Maggie was always willing to reveal everything about her love life, especially with *Joey*.

Maggie blew her cigarette smoke into the air. She nibbled at her puffy bottom lip. "I had such a night with Joey. He drives me absolutely crazy. He's like one of Tubby Brown's bulls…if you know what I mean."

Janie took a deep breath. She knew that Maggie loved to brag when it came to Joseph Bucolo, almost to the point of annoyance. She even bragged that his nickname, *Joey*, was what she whispered when they made love. Yet, deep down, Janie was glad Maggie couldn't keep secrets. For a long time, Maggie provided her with all the earthy, lusty gossip she could handle. In many ways, it was a nice little education about men. Then again, Maggie often lied—going all the way back to grade school.

"Let's forget about men for today," Janie quickly said. "We'll sit through the movie twice. Gulp popcorn, drink Strawberry Phosa in the dark. Oh, Rudolph Valentino!"

Janie liked to see Maggie laugh. She said, "I'll never marry a fisherman." As soon as the words came out, Janie wondered why she'd even said it. "Did you hear Joe…he told Grover he was going back fishing. I don't believe him."

"Oh, Janie, being a fisherman has nothing to do with it." Maggie's eyes blinked. "Last night, I was free and wild. It was just incredible."

Janie felt embarrassment for them both. She thought what a poor little girl Maggie was. At times, she wondered if Maggie was losing her mind—preoccupied with sex so much.

As they rounded Common Fence Point, the ferry turned south and entered Mount Hope Bay. Janie was relieved that the porter arrived. They each ordered coffee, and scones with whipped cream and delicious-looking preserves.

Maggie smashed out her cigarette and continued, "He does everything so good, Janie—"

"Stop!" Janie snapped.

Maggie ran her finger through the clotted cream and licked it off. Maggie was being bad, having fun.

Janie understood about clotted cream.

Maggie opened her purse and took out a silver dollar. She lifted it up into the air. "Joey is this round."

"Maggie!" Janie said with a chill. "Stop talking like that…now!"

Maggie leaned closer. "When he asks me if I took a hot bath, it's like this ferry boat tooting its horn. You know, it's for a reason. Get my drift?"

"What's the reason?" Janie blurted, louder than she intended. Her mind tried to imagine, but her tongue responded quicker than her brain. She swallowed hard. She felt her pulse zip. A rush of heat lodged in her neck.

Maggie smiled like she was living a dream. "Oh, never mind. Besides, you know…"

Janie wondered if she'd be as aroused if Maggie were talking about Rudolph Valentino. At least she would be more detached.

Maggie asked, "So tell me, you and Pierre. What is going on?"

"I've closed down with Pierre…it's over."

Janie watched Maggie's surprised expression. "But why?"

"It wasn't going anywhere. He's not for me."

"Well, that's your choice. But you take someone like Henry Grover for a ride just one night, Janie, and you'll be on easy street the rest of your life."

Janie shook her head. "Like I said, from here on in, I'm playing a different game. I'm even working on a business proposal for Mister Grover. I'm looking to improve my life."

Maggie looked stunned. "You are?" It was about the only two words she could think of at the moment. There was a long moment of silence, except the vibrating noises of the ferry and her churning propeller.

Finally, Janie said, "It could be my ticket…maybe even run this new operation in Virginia. Sort of a partnership with Grover."

Maggie was still in shock at Janie's revelation. "Tell me about it, Janie."

So, between the ferry passing through the abutments for the new Mount Hope Bridge that would connect Portsmouth with Bristol and the time they arrived at Fox Point in Providence, Janie Thurston had revealed her dreams and business proposal to her best friend.

While they waited in the lounge for the trolley to take them downtown, Maggie said, "I think Henry Grover has loftier visions than just a roll in the blanket, Janie. Like maybe marriage?"

"It would still be Tiverton," Janie said.

"What 'bout Joe?"

Janie slowly shook her head, but said nothing.

Maggie wore a serious expression and spoke with conviction. "Frankly, I love being bad, and everything else that goes with it. And now I want to get wild again. If not Joe, someone—maybe even Henry."

"Maggie, you have the morals of an alley cat."

Maggie reached over and touched her hand. She said, "You're actually my only friend."

Slightly taken aback, Janie said softly, "Earlier, I was thinking about you being my only friend as well."

Maggie leaned closer. "Can I tell you something, something real personal?"

Janie laughed at her question. "Maggie, if you get any more intimate, I just might have to be *you!*"

"You're lucky to be a virgin, Janie, really lucky."

Janie suddenly felt embarrassed. "You think so, Maggie? You really think so?"

Chapter Sixteen

IN NEW BEDFORD, the cobblestone streets were empty and slick with dew. The downtown seemed to be tucked in for the night; Prohibition had that effect on a city. Entertainment activities were mostly behind closed doors.

In the south section of New Bedford, and recently sold to Gatsby, Herman the German's base of operations was on Pino's Wharf. The sale included his warehouse, four trucks, and a long, granite-built wharf where Gatsby intended to tie-up his new rum boat, *Diamond Daisy*. The German's two converted sixty-foot yachts, *Tramp* and *Hobo*, had been moved to Oakland Beach. The death of his son, for whom he had high hopes, ended the German's rum-running venture. Desperate to sell everything, Herman was almost happy when Gatsby swooped in and pretty much stole his operation.

Moran's Packard and a large truck sat alongside the building. Blocked partially by the warehouse was the flashing beacon of the Fort Rodman Lighthouse. Except for it and two corner lights, the vicinity was dark. Waves splashed against the wharf in a constant rhythm.

Most of the fishing fleet berthed north, in the center of the harbor close to the auction companies. Here, wholesalers operated their fillet houses, with cod and haddock their primary cutting fish.

Inside the warehouse's office, Gatsby laid down the newspaper he'd been reading, looking up at Paul Moran as he walked in.

"What did you find out?"

Moran looked pleased. "This morning, Miss Jackson stopped by the office in Bristol. She asked about you."

"What did you tell her?"

"You were away on business. Anyway, Miss Jackson's been busy," he smiled. "She had some intriguing news: Bucolo is changing his location for unloading his next run."

"Interesting. Where?"

"Booker's Wharf...on Common Fence Point."

Gatsby stood and approached a marine chart of Narragansett Bay on the wall. He ran his finger over it until he found Common Fence Point. He nodded. "They'll be coming in through the East Passage. Interesting. I'll let Kanky and the boys know..."

Moran smiled. He liked providing good news. "Also, Maggie heard that Miss Janie Thurston has a proposal for Grover about establishing a menhaden plant in Virginia—which could prove to be very profitable."

"Who's Miss Thurston?"

"Works for Francis Grover...daughter to that Swamp Yankee, Pearly Thurston, who runs booze with Joe Bucolo. According to Kanky, he's 'kinda second-in-command.'"

Gatsby smirked. "Ah, yes. Now I remember. Interesting," he said softly. "What do you know about Miss Thurston's personal life?"

"Not much, except Maggie says she's the most beautiful girl in Tiverton."

"I think Miss Jackson must be exaggerating. Anyway, let's see if Maggie can get confirmation from Miss Thurston. Then make an appointment for me with Mister Grover. Sooner the better."

"I already did. Day after tomorrow, eleven o'clock."

Gatsby smiled. "You're clearly getting to know how I think."

CHAPTER SEVENTEEN

TWO DAYS LATER, FRANCIS GROVER, in his habitual black suit, stared at the man sitting in front of him. It took him a moment to speak. "How much did you say you're willing to invest?"

"As much as needed."

Grover's eyes couldn't hide his enthusiasm. "Miss Thurston has worked on this proposal for some time. She should arrive soon."

The man nodded.

Grover added, "Her proposal appears to have the ability to make a great deal of money."

"That's what I like to hear, Mister Grover. I don't invest in failures."

"I couldn't agree with you more," Grover offered, trying to decipher his potential investor. "It's the very reason I've been so successful with my menhaden factory. And there is still much opportunity."

Just then Janie strolled in.

"Here she is." Grover got up and went to the glass separator, pointed to her white folder, and beckoned her inside.

Janie entered, carrying the folder. "Miss Thurston, this is James Gatz. Mister Gatz has interest in investing in your proposal."

The man turned and stood up. Janie seemed surprised by the gesture. Grover had already sat down.

Gatsby remained standing, extended his hand. "Pleased to meet you, Miss Thurston. I understand you have an intriguing business idea."

Still taken aback, Janie managed, "Thank you. I appreciate the opportunity." She gave Grover a quick glance. "May I ask how you found out about it?"

Gatsby said, "I have other interests in vessels that are in the fishing trade. I was involved in a salmon fishery on the Great Lakes for a time. My representative is always on the lookout for new investments. He contacted Mister Grover and…here I am."

Francis Grover appeared to be getting impatient. "Miss Thurston, would you proceed with your presentation."

Janie said, "I believe by expanding Mister Grover's fish-rendering operation in the Mid-Atlantic region, his fleet could unload there… and continue to fish…instead of making the long trip back to Tiverton. This company only makes money if the seiners are catching product."

"That's very true. An astute observation, Miss Thurston. Do you have a location in mind?"

"Norfolk, Virginia… It has great harborage and plenty of cheap waterfront land. I have all the projections here, including the cost of building another menhaden-rendering plant." Janie handed him the paperwork. Gatsby gave it a quick scan as she watched proudly. Even Grover beamed at Janie.

"At first glance, it appears to be a very thorough proposal, Miss Thurston."

Grover looked at Gatsby. "Miss Thurston is a bright bloom in my garden of weeds." Then, almost self-consciously, he added, "If only my son had business insight… Instead…"

Gatsby picked up on the comment. "Your son isn't in the fishing business?"

"No, unfortunately…" Grover looked past them, through the glass partition, into the outer office. "Here he is now…Tiverton's own police chief." Francis waved him into the office.

Gatsby said, "Isn't that interesting."

Henry entered. "Is this a bad time, Father?" He turned to Janie. "Hello, Janie."

She was about to develop an annoyed frown, but quickly shifted it into a nod and smiled.

"Son, this is James Gatz."

Henry offered a weak handshake, then asked, "Are you in the fishing business, sir?"

"In a roundabout way, you could say that."

"Son, Mister Gatz here may be interested in our Virginia expansion plan."

"What is that, Father?" Henry sputtered, surprised something of that nature existed of which he was unaware.

Janie and Gatsby took notice. Francis Grover appeared embarrassed.

"Miss Thurston has worked very hard on it, Son. I'm quite proud of her. I...thought I'd told you about it."

Janie glanced at Francis Grover and forced a smile. "Thank you, Mister Grover. I appreciate that." She stood taller than ever.

"Indeed?" Henry said, sounding somehow prejudiced...or simply ignorant.

Gatsby looked to Janie for a reaction. Seeing none, he followed up. "Well, I have to say Miss Thurston has sold me on this project." He turned to Janie and said, "I'm in. The only stipulation is that I take Miss Thurston to lunch so we can discuss her breakdown of the finances...future blueprints, if you will."

Janie's height seemed to increase by another inch, but she was too stunned to speak.

Henry was mortified.

Grover smiled widely. "Why naturally, Mister Gatz." He glanced at Janie with an agreeable expression, making the decision for her.

"Certainly, Mister Gatz. I'd like that."

Gatsby fingered the crest of his hat. "Do you have a preference for a restaurant in Fall River?"

"Yes, I do." Janie was glowing now as she turned on her heel towards the door.

Henry looked on in silent displeasure as he watched Gatz follow Janie out of the office. As Gatz closed the office door, he turned towards Henry, tipped his hat, and proffered a look that simultaneously pitied Henry's paralysis and quietly noted that he, Gatsby, had just hooked the catch of the day.

Turning to his father, his face beet red, Henry blurted, "I felt like a fool...me...the chief of police! Why didn't you tell me about Janie's proposal?"

Francis Grover was a shade redder than his son. "You settle down now, Henry! First off, I had no intention of giving any credit to a hired woman...and a Thurston at that! Telling Francis Grover how to run his fishing business. That'll be the day!"

Henry's voice strengthened. "I intend to make Janie my wife, Father. I love her."

Francis Grover stood up, leaned slightly forward, and hammered his knuckles on his desk. "Can't you find some other woman? God Almighty, Son, Pearly Thurston as your father-in-law is my idea of Satan himself. Besides, you should associate with a better class of people than the Thurston family, the thirsty Thurstons—always thirsty for more—never satisfied. I've watched it for a lifetime—Janie Thurston is no better."

"That's not true, Father. She could be a real wife. Not to mention her beauty."

Francis Grover shook his head. "Pearly Thurston works for Bucolo, who's the Devil-in-Chief!"

"Not for long, Father."

Grover eyeballed his son's uniform. "If you're so damned determined to wear that uniform, then I suggest you make use of it."

Henry stiffened; a flush of real anger crept up his neck.

Francis added, "Our waterfront…our community is turning into a valley of sin…thanks to Joe Bucolo, Pearly Thurston…and that crazy Swamper, Hunker Moore."

Grover pointed a bony finger at the closed door and an invisible Janie Thurston. "If you are determined to marry that girl, then you need to destroy Bucolo and his cohorts. I will not have my grandchildren's legacy stained with the vile records of the thirsty Thurstons. It's your job to see that Joe Bucolo is apprehended…and dispensed with."

"Don't worry, Father. I'll get him."

Henry left the office.

Francis got up from his desk and went to a window that overlooked his prize possessions—and it wasn't his son, Henry. With no wind, his enterprise loomed quietly over the falling tide whirling south in bubbling eddies. North of the railroad trestle, on their moorings, straining against the flowing tide, the menhaden fleet hung in a tight north-south direction. They were an impressive sight, and as always, Francis Grover silently counted his floating assets. Even though he didn't particularly like the river or boats or fishing, what floated out there represented a lifetime of work. Someday, all this would be Henry's. Time goes by so fast, he thought, and I taught the boy so little.

Francis watched his son heading towards his patrol car. He also saw some of the help looking on as he dodged around the puddles in his new boots. Henry didn't see the workers laughing at him, but Francis did.

~~~~~~

The Lakeside Restaurant was busy for Wednesday's lunch. It was their day for half-priced meals. The menu included choices of roasted meats, oysters, steamers, and lobster. Most were priced at two dollars, and that included coffee and dessert.

Gatsby and Janie sat near a window that overlooked the Fall River

Reservoir, which supplied drinking water for the city. It was one of the most pristine lakes in the region.

A waitress approached and handed them a menu. Gatsby nodded. He looked at Janie. "Do you indulge in the hard spirits?"

She smiled. "It's illegal."

"Good answer. So, Miss Thurston, tell me a little bit about yourself. It's unusual that a woman is interested in the fishing trade."

"Well, it was either that, or become deckhand on a boat."

Gatsby laughed. "Well, if I were looking for one, I'd hire you."

He gave her a look with plenty of thought behind it. "Would you consider me very forward if I asked you to call me James? And I called you Janie?"

"Not at all."

"Good…now, shall we order, Janie?"

~~~~~~

On the drive back to Tiverton, Janie noticed a marine book against the firewall on the floor of Gatsby's car. She leaned over, read the title. "*Sea-Going Navigation*? Interesting reading, James." She picked up the book, noticing a page marker, opened to it. A chapter title read: "How a captain should navigate in the fog, utilizing the tides, wind direction, and a timepiece." Janie looked at him in silence for a moment.

"That surprises you?"

"You don't strike me as a sailor."

"Really?" Gatsby seemed almost annoyed. "I want to be prepared when I get my own yacht. Maybe even travel the seven seas. Does that appeal to you, Janie?"

She stared at him, not sure if he was serious. "It does sound interesting. There is an appeal to traveling the world… And I certainly do find the thought of leaving Tiverton exciting."

"I must confess, I find it very invigorating, what you are attempting to do. In these times, most women I've encountered leave this type of business…well…to men."

"What type of women, Mister Gatz?"

Gatsby shrugged. "Are you committed to anyone, Janie?"

"Are you committed yourself?" Her retort came out like a bullet leaving a gun.

He laughed. "You're quite direct, Janie. The answer is: I hope to be one day."

Janie's eyes stayed on him. "Tell me more."

Gatsby looked straight ahead. "It might just be better if we didn't… delve in." On the last two words, he tilted his head in Janie's direction, his gaze absorbing the outline of her, his thoughts still on some distant horizon.

Janie looked down at her hands in her lap. "That seems reasonable."

"Frankly, I'm quite curious about *you*."

"Curious? I'll take that as a compliment."

Gatsby smiled. "Yes, it is a compliment. So, Janie, may I ask you out to dinner sometime?"

She took a few moments. "Of course."

— Chapter Eighteen —

BY THE 1920S, MOST MODES of transportation merged at Grand Central Station. Located at 42nd Street and Park Avenue, it had become the irrefutable core of New York, transporting not only city dwellers but also affluent suburbanites, taking the train to and from the upper reaches of the state, Connecticut, and New Jersey, and the increasingly popular Long Island.

A Tiffany clock—monument to the grace, power, and frisson at once present in New York City—graced the entrance to the station. The statue adorning her was named *Transportation* in honor of the virtues of the railroad—the train's speed embodied by Mercury, its intellect by Minerva, its strength by Hercules. Another, more modest clock—perched upon the central ticket booth of Grand Central's interior, a sentinel that glowed quietly amidst the chaos of travelers and commuters bustling to and fro—became the official meeting place where thousands of people would connect, choosing to "meet at the clock."

It currently read twelve-fifteen. Daisy Faye Buchanan was wearing a light-blue dress whose hue emphasized the habitual melancholy of her face, yet to her credit, her eyes were quite lively, with hidden secrets (worthless or not) ready to share with the right person, or anyone whom she thought might be interested or worthy of such. On the right side of Daisy's mouth was a small, dark mole that emphasized the pallor of her complexion. Her golden hair was curly and disrupted from the blustery wind that barreled forcefully through the chasms of the city's tall buildings.

Daisy and Jordan Baker sat opposite each other in the Top Hat Restaurant, two blocks north of the recently constructed Strand Theatre. Daisy had selected this meeting spot as she knew that they catered to many women who enjoyed or required a little more than tea with their noon repast.

Jordan, like Daisy, was a little on the thin side, with small breasts. Yet there was something alluring about her slender build; maybe it was the way she carried herself? Clearly, her body reacted in a positive way to all of her tennis playing and horseback riding—her veins jutting from her arms, thanks to years of astute racket handling. With her outdoor activities, Jordan had developed a fine tan. She seldom spent any time in the cold Northeast, opting for sunny climates as soon as the weather began to turn.

Both women were quiet as the waiter filled their water glasses. Finally, Daisy smiled as she tried to fix her hair. "How long has it been, Jordan? It seems…oh…oh, so like an eternity."

Jordan managed a slight shrug and, in an almost snooty way, raised her chin slightly, as if to emphasize her comment. "It's been a long time, I suppose, you marrying Tom and becoming a mother while I am adrift. I just dumped another man from my bed. An experience I would rather forget."

Daisy stared at Jordan, realizing not much had changed for her friend. Not able to find fitting words, she said, "You're so beautiful and talented, Jordan. The world is your oyster, you know that."

"If that is true, I certainly have been getting more sand than pearls," Jordan said, a little cooly. "Order us some drinks, please."

Daisy signaled the waiter, who nearly ran over to the women. "Two *very* dry martinis…with extra olives, please."

He took off with as much speed as he'd arrived. The waiter

brought over their cocktails, setting the earthenware down very carefully. His eyes reminded Daisy of the four olives on toothpicks. She turned away. Jordan acknowledged his good deed with the slight cock of her head and a small smile.

"Why was it an experience you would rather forget…" It had taken Daisy that long before that paramount sexual question made a complete circle in her brain. She really wanted to know. "Why was it so bad—in bed with your latest?"

Jordan stared at her and quickly drained her glass. "A perfect martini," she whispered. "But I prefer the original cocktail glass, thank you."

Daisy tried not to get annoyed. She was more interested about the man than the drink. But she also knew Jordan had a way of leaving someone hanging on comments or parts thereof…usually on purpose.

"Honestly, he was about as passionate as a bowl of cold noodles." She hesitated, glancing at a couple who just walked into the restaurant. "He couldn't find his way around a woman's body with a map and a compass."

"I am sorry Jordan. I think that calls for another cocktail," Daisy whispered, "this time, a Gin Rickey. Then after that, I have something very important to ask you."

"I knew you were not here in New York to shop, so how important?"

"Very."

"I'm waiting," Jordan said.

Daisy leaned forward. "I want you to do something for me …."

Jordan listened intently to Daisy. When her friend was finished speaking, Jordan released a deep sigh. With a pronounced nod, she said, "Well, I'm really impressed."

CHAPTER NINETEEN

LIKE ALWAYS, PEARLY HAD BEEN UP EARLY, sitting on the enclosed sunporch. He made the coffee and used the bathroom before Janie got up for work. The Tiverton Basin was calm, with swirls of mist dissipating over the west shore of Portsmouth.

Many mornings, seagulls or cormorants were alarm clocks for the waterfront residents. At the moment, a half-dozen swans were drifting with the outgoing tide. In the middle of their train, three cygnets swam along with them, well-protected by their parents.

Janie walked onto the sunporch with her coffee. "Morning, Daddy."

He looked up and smiled. "Morning…"

Janie sat down. "Did you just get home?"

She knew he would avoid her question. Lately, generally, anything pertaining to going out with Joe or the boys pretty much went unanswered. Pearly asked, "So, tell me how your proposal went with Mister Grover."

She smiled. "Not until you tell me how Joe is handling that poor sailor's death."

"Of course, it's really bothering Joe…me…all the boys."

"Not enough to give up rum-running?"

Pearly stifled his flustered expression. "Frankly, the captain of that patrol boat was reckless and stupid. He apparently didn't bother to look at the navigation chart…ran his damn boat up onto Sandy Point shoals. He should have given up on the chase."

Janie's expression appeared to mellow slightly. "Men and their dangerous games." Her words came out slowly. Pearly made like he didn't hear them.

She decided then not to discuss Grover and her proposal, and wondered if her reticence was more about Mister Gatz than about the proposal itself. It was both; suddenly her existence had taken an interesting turn. Yes, deep down, she was very excited.

Pearly stood up. "I'll be gone most of the day, don't bother about me for supper."

"Should I ask where you'll be?"

"New Bedford and Schmitz's boatyard. Gotta help Sammy in the engine room of Joe's new boat. Not sure when I'll be home."

"I've heard enough, Daddy. Be careful."

"Always am."

As soon as Pearly left, she knew there was something she had to act on. She picked up the receiver and called Joe.

"Hello." Joe yawned through the greeting.

Janie pulled a slight face. "Morning, Joe, did I wake you?"

At first, he didn't recognize her voice. When he did, he assumed something was wrong with Pearly. "Janie…everything okay?"

"Everything is fine," she said. "How about coming over and having lunch with me?"

"Lunch with you?"

"Yes, why not?"

"At your house?" Joe asked.

"Why not? Pearly's in New Bedford, as if you didn't know."

There was a short, hesitant pause. "Are you sure…at your house?"

She laughed. "Yes, Joe, my house."

Joe asked, "What time?"

"Twelve o'clock."

~~~~~~

Noon was a little early in the day to be wearing his best, but after a quick shave at Palmer's and with his hair under control, Joe almost felt civilized, almost handsome on a sunny afternoon going to visit a young girl. He unbuttoned his jacket and knocked gently on the screen door. A strange feeling rumbled through his stomach at the thought of invading Pearly's household. The door opened, with Janie smiling. The flash of her teeth caught his attention.

"Hi!" Her eyes, soft and commanding, were trained steadily on him. He wondered if it was because her father wasn't around.

She closed the door behind him and said, "It's such a lovely day, we'll have lunch on the sunporch." She chuckled uneasily. "Overlooking the beautiful Seaconnet River, home port to fishermen and rum-runners alike." She walked ahead, out onto the porch. She was wearing a simple cotton dress. It suited her and she looked good. As Joe followed, his eyes lingered over her shapely transom.

On the sunporch, a table was impressively set. "I'm not used to this."

Janie said, "You stay here. I've got to check on the food."

"Need some help?"

She shook her head. "I can handle it." For a moment she stood there, almost awkwardly.

He said softly, "You look very nice."

"Thank you." She nodded towards a cabinet and added, "If you want, make yourself a drink. You know how to pour an illegal whiskey, don't you, Joe?" She chuckled warmly, teasingly.

Joe smiled and laughed lightly. "I can try…"

He glanced around. The porch was bright and warm. The windows were clean and sparkled. He wondered if they were washed for him, but thought not.

He opened the door to the liquor cabinet and took out a bottle of King William. He pondered briefly on what Pearly would say if he saw him now. He took a hard gulp, replaced the cork, and returned the bottle. No need to get drunk.

From the kitchen, Janie called, "How long will Pearly be gone?"

He felt warmer. Was it the intimacy of her question spoken aloud, or was it the King William? "Whenever they go to New Bedford, it's usually most of the day."

She returned, carrying two bowls of clam chowder. "Fresh quahogs from Bridgeport Seafood. I hope you're hungry."

He stared at her. "You bet."

"I meant food."

"I know what you meant."

She almost smiled. After the chowder, she brought pork chops, fried onions, and applesauce. She looked awkward and motioned to his plate. "No mashed potatoes, but plenty of bread and butter."

"You know what I don't eat?"

"Of course. Pearly tells me everything. He's my father."

She set the plates down and said, "Hope you like it."

"I will. I will."

Little was said as they ate.

Compliments from Joe and some uneasy glances were about all they managed. Janie served herself small portions and what she had, she just moved around with her fork.

When he was finished, she looked at his empty plate. "Guess it wasn't half bad?"

"The best I've had in a long time," he said.

She cleared the table. Joe studied her as he slowly took out a pack of Wings. She said, "I'll make some coffee. How does apple pie sound?"

"Great." He lit a cigarette. "No wonder Pearly's thick around the middle."

From the other room, she said, "He's thick in the head, too."

Joe nodded firmly. "You won't get any argument on that."

They sat quietly through their coffee. Joe had two pieces of pie, on her insistence. Finally, he looked her straight in the eyes. "I'm trying to figure out why I'm here?"

"I wanted to talk about Pearly."

"That's too bad; I thought you might have other things in mind."
He hoped that it didn't sound too forward.

"I've been having bad dreams. I keep seeing Pearly dead and maybe other people. Maybe even you. I mean, I'm not really superstitious
or anything like that…"

"Of course not," Joe said. This wasn't exactly what he wanted to
talk about.

She said, "Nobody can continue to fight the law and expect to
win. Eventually, they're going to blow you out of the water."

"You don't have to be so damn direct," he said.

"Cannonballs have a way of being direct," she answered.

"Pearly's a big boy, and he's capable of making his own decisions."

"That's not good enough. You're the leader of the gang. You're
responsible for what happens."

"Jesus Christ! What do you want to happen, Janie?"

"First, I don't want my father to die. I love him very much, despite
his naughty ways. I think he's either going to have a heart attack, or
get a bullet, or drown."

"I see." Joe was irritated, and he thought she recognized it.

She added quickly, "Of course, I'm still trying to sort some other
things out."

"What kind of things?"

She hesitated slightly. "Well, for a long time, you've been in the
background of my life. You know, seeing you around, hearing things
from my father. Joe did this, we did that. You were almost like one of
the family, especially after Max died."

"I know, and I'll always appreciate that, Janie. It's something I'll
never forget."

"You sound like it's all gone."

He shook his head. "It's just not the same anymore…" He looked
at her sitting there with her knees together, hands folded in her lap
like Mrs. Snellman, her head cocked slightly, intently, listening to

his response. Janie's playful expression of moments before was gone. "Truth is, I'm more alone now than I've ever been," he added.

She nodded almost incomprehensibly at his remark. "Joe, there's people around you all the time."

"Sure, friends, good friends, but it's not the same as family. Tell me, where's my future with these friends? Sammy, your father, Hunker—they're older, they already have families. The Bancocks...well, it's just not the same."

Janie stared at him in silence.

There was a long pause and then he continued, "And this thing with Kanky hasn't been easy, believe me."

"Kanky! Some nerve..." Her eyes flickered anger for a moment. Joe noted her reaction. Interesting, he thought.

"My father's convinced Kanky will hurt you, him, the boys, if you're not careful."

"Maybe he will, maybe he won't. But now we really believe he's working for someone else. Someone who could be a bigger problem."

"More reason for you and my father to quit rum-running."

Joe glanced out the sunporch windows. His eyes caught sight of a fish breaching the surface. Probably a striped bass, he thought. He turned back to Janie. "Pearly grew up in this house, safe as a fiddler crab in its tunnel. Kanky won't hurt him, or anyone. So don't worry about your father. Okay?"

They shared an uncomfortable silence for a few moments. Janie seemed ready to say something a couple of times, but didn't. Whatever it was, she was having a difficult time getting it out.

"Seeing that you and I are being honest," she said, "I'd like to tell you something about families."

"I'm listening."

"My father subtly tries to keep me away from you."

"I know."

She continued, "Well, simply put, my father still wants to stay part of your gang. He wants you to be his friend. You are his youth. You are his youthful, whoring friend." She nodded slightly. "Your fun is Pearly's fun. And Pearly doesn't want me to rain on his parade. Get my drift? He wants to chase young girls and drink with the boys down on Max's Wharf until the day he dies."

Joe smiled. "A noble ambition—any waterman will tell you that." Seeing Janie's frown, he added, "But I think there's a little more to it than that. Pearly also wants the best for you."

"True, but he doesn't realize that I want my own life, and I want to make my own decisions."

"It sounds like you've already started. Pearly told me about your proposal with Grover…and there's even an investor interested."

"I suppose. It almost seems too good to be true."

"Who's the investor?"

"Mister James Gatz."

Joe silently nodded. Finally, he got back on track. "Listen, your father believes that I'm not the right man for you. Actually, he thinks I'm 'too bad for you,' whatever that means." He smiled but noticed that she didn't find the statement amusing.

"That's because he's a daddy." She said it with a very firm voice. "My father may have my interest at heart, but in truth, Pearly only thinks of the four F's: find 'em, feel 'em, fuck 'em, forget 'em. I know what boys do, or want to do."

Joe was slightly shocked by her bluntness.

Janie asked, rather seriously, "Question is, do *you* think that you'd be bad for me?"

"Look, you're a kid. I'm three years older than you. When I was in sixth grade, you were in fourth grade. Jesus! Look at your bubs; they're still in fourth grade."

She cocked her head and laughed. "Is that how you gauge the women you go out with?"

He chuckled. "Not hardly."

"Tell me, Joseph Bucolo, are you bad for women?"

"They never complain," he said. For some reason he felt as if she were asking some unfair questions, and feeling a bit annoyed, he said, "I guess you'd have to ask whoever."

She laughed. "I wouldn't know where to start. So, I'm asking you." She stood up and began to clear off the table.

Joe said, "Why does it matter? You're not every woman. You're Janie Thurston. Pearly's little sweet thing."

"Oh, Joey, he's just trying to protect me."

"Joey?"

Janie's face flushed and she became tongue-tied. She waited for him to comment on her use of *Joey*, but he didn't. She appreciated that and returned to the table. She carried the remaining dishes into the kitchen.

He followed her. Beneath his feet the kitchen linoleum made a light crackling sound. The room still smelled of cooking. It looked and felt comfortable, far different from his home. He liked it. Here was a woman in the kitchen. It smelled good and she looked good.

Since Max died, Joe realized no woman had ever really lived in his house. Sure, he had Maggie in his bed occasionally, but she certainly didn't make for a home. Here in Pearly's house, it had Janie's fragrance, and that touch of softness. He knew that Pearly was lucky.

Janie was at the sink, her back to him, placing the dishes into a wash pan.

"Someday I'd like to show you the new boat. Would you be interested?"

"Sure, someday…but I can wait." She just stood there, hands in the dishwater.

"I think you'd enjoy seeing this boat. It's sorta like a newborn… ready to be launched."

Janie turned around and puckered her lips slightly. "Now, really?"

"That's the truth. There's a saying about how a boat grows with you and becomes a beautiful woman that is always—"

"Don't give me that bullshit!" Janie held her hand in front of her eyes as if protecting herself from a blinding light. "I was born into a fisherman's family, on the shore of the beautiful Seaconnet. It's that boat bullshit that kept us living hand to mouth. I was a little girl when…it killed my mother, and it keeps my father playing a boy's game."

"I just saw an expression on you that I remember from Fort Barton School," he said. "Why, you're still a little girl."

She looked at him with a strange, questioning face. It really wasn't an insult, more like a compliment, like they were back in Fort Barton School.

"Now that you fed me a fine lunch," he said, "I'd like to return the favor and take you out later. Okay?"

She turned around. The tips of her fingers stuck to her right cheek like she was witnessing some awe-inspiring wonder. "Yes, Joe, in some ways, I am still a goddamn little girl, especially around you. Seeing that I don't need to make supper for Pearly, why not."

He started for the screen door. "See you later."

She followed him.

He turned around. She was standing closer to him than she had ever been. Up close with a small smile, she looked incredibly fresh. Fresh—that was the word that came to his mind. It tilted him for just a moment.

Janie let the screen close in front of her face. "What time, later?" she asked.

He kept moving across the sparse lawn. "I'll pick you up at four o'clock." He was smiling as he got into the Buick.

Driving off, he wondered why he hadn't attempted to kiss her. "Damn, I've always felt good around her," he said aloud. He burped up onions and lit a cigarette. "She's one fine girl, no doubt 'bout that."

Chapter Twenty

AT FOUR O'CLOCK THAT AFTERNOON, Joe Bucolo drove up to the Thurston waterfront cottage and tapped his horn twice. It sounded like a northern goose calling for his mate on Furtado's potato fields.

Janie was sitting at the kitchen table, waiting. She ran to the bathroom to check her face and her hair. She grabbed her purse, locked the kitchen door, and ran up the walk to the passenger's side of the white Buick. Joe leaned over and opened the door for her. His silent reaction to her outfit made her nervous. She said, "You don't like it?"

Joe's eyes skirted her nervously. "Well, you do look different."

"That means you don't like it?"

"You look like someone else."

"You mean I don't look like a little girl?"

Joe seemed confused. "Well, certainly not a little girl."

"Well, I suppose that's a start towards an honest friendship." Despite her bravado, Janie's voice shook and she felt upset. Joe certainly wasn't making it easy. If there had been a place to hide, she might have used it.

She asked, "Where we going?"

"To a nice nightclub."

"You mean a place they call a speakeasy?" Again, her voice revealed her nervousness. She couldn't stop her eyes from watering. Turning to him, she asked, "Why, because I look like a lady of the night?"

Joe dropped his head to the steering wheel in exasperation. "Of course not. You'll like Frankie-the-Bone's…it's on the east side of Providence near Brown University. Full of college kids just your age. You'll be the prettiest one there. Besides, I got business with the owner."

~~~~~~

They headed through Fall River at dusk. The Slade's Ferry Bridge was open, so they had to wait for ten minutes, looking over the dark Taunton River.

Joe pointed north. "Not long ago, I sold a load of booze up there for Micky Thompson."

She nodded. "Have you decided on a name for your new boat yet?"

Joe looked at her; he seemed surprised by the question. "Yes… *Whispering Winds.*"

Janie cocked her head, thinking about it. After a moment, she added, "I like it. I really do."

"Don't tell your father. I want the boys to be surprised at the christening."

Janie almost laughed. "Your secret is safe with me."

He nodded. "Good." He kept his eyes on the road, and they drove silently into the night.

When she had said, "Your secret's safe with me," she was being overly sincere, perhaps even trying to be amusing. But when he responded, "Good," she realized she was close to his core. Surprising the boys at the christening was nothing to joke about.

She watched him. He certainly looked older than anyone she had gone out with before. His hands were rough. They had seen a lot of work, in all kinds of weather. In the dark, his scar made him look dangerous. The sort of man a young girl would be told to stay away from. She said, "I've heard Pearly say the wind is whispering."

"Those words belonged to Max. It was something Max used to

say when he wanted to go oyster pirating. He'd say, 'Do you hear the winds whispering, Pearly?'"

Joe's expression softened. "At night sometimes, I listen to the wind…and do you know, depending on the direction, it always sounds different?"

Janie said nothing.

"When it's from the east, I swear I hear Max trying to talk to me."

She said, "Easterly is always a bad wind."

Joe looked over at her and nodded. "Well, that's right. But that's when I hear him. Sometimes I wonder what he's trying to tell me. Is it good or is it bad?"

"Well, it couldn't be bad. He loved you like a son."

Joe nodded but kept his eyes on the road.

She knew their conversation was now as close to his heart as she'd ever get. She wanted to touch his hand but resisted.

He shook his head with a deprecating grin. "Jeez, I can't believe I'm telling you this. I sound like Bottomley preaching about his special messages delivered on the wings of angels."

Impersonating Bottomley, Janie threw her hands up to the liner top of the Buick and shook all over. "I was on the shore of the Seaconnet River last night, and my dear friends of Jesus, I heard Max Bucolo whispering to his son, Joseph Bucolo, that instrument of Satan."

Joe's grin widened. She could tell that he enjoyed her show.

Janie laughed and suddenly her expression hardened. "I do get angry when Bottomley refers to rum-runners as the sons of Satan. Pearly's naughty, but no son of Satan."

Joe said, "Old Bottomley shouldn't be casting any stones."

Janie leaned forward in the seat and stared at him. "Are you trying to tell me something, Joseph Bucolo?"

"I ain't spreading any gossip. But someday Bottomley's skeleton will come rattling out of his pulpit. And then his flock can determine who should be…" Joe's voice rose to hysteria, "condemned to the everlasting fires of hell."

Janie shook all over and slapped her legs. "Hallelujah! Hallelujah!"

~~~~~~

Joe knocked. He was surveyed through a peephole, then the door opened. He slipped a bill to the doorman. "Thank you, Mister Bucolo."

Janie glanced at Joe. "My first speak."

They were led into a dimly lit lounge filled with people doing anything but speaking easy. Joe slowed his gait as they descended a short flight of stairs and watched Janie's eyes. The faint sound of machinery and the aroma of baking bread were ever-present in the air.

They entered a hall facing another door. The doorman said, "Good evening, Mister Bucolo. Frankie is expecting you."

On the balcony, Joe wanted to take a booth, but Janie insisted they sit at a small table for two by the railing. In the far corner, just beyond the dance floor, a five-piece band played. A few people were dancing; others just sat, enjoying the atmosphere.

As soon as Frankie saw Joe, he climbed the balcony steps. "Joe, it's good to see you so soon." He glanced at Janie. "Well, good evening."

Janie beamed, slightly off balance, staring up at Frankie's face.

"Frankie, this is Janie Thurston, Pearly's daughter."

"Pleased to meet you, Miss Thurston. Your father is a friend of mine."

Janie's smile came easy. "This is my first time here, Frankie."

"Well, in that case." He raised his hand, signaling a waiter, who rushed over. Frankie handed Janie a menu. "I recommend the lobster. Fresh this morning, from Narragansett Bay."

"Will you join us later?" Joe asked. "I've got a little something to discuss."

"Certainly, Joe, later."

The waiter took their drink order, and they watched the college crowd enjoying their Saturday night. Without looking up, Janie said again, "My first speakeasy."

"If you don't stop saying that, I'm going to feel like I'm corrupting you."

"I love it. Look at that couple dance. Wow!"

She ordered lobster and Joe had steak. After dinner, the band slowed down the music. "Would you like to dance?"

Joe was surprised. "Sure, if I knew how."

She took his hand. "It's easy, I'll show you." She led him to the dance floor.

Joe embraced her. "I've got this part down," he said.

For a long moment, they looked into each other's eyes. He pulled her closer.

"Okay, what next?"

Janie said, "I'll lead. You follow."

He followed but was quite awkward. Janie continued to lead. She was enjoying it; he just stumbled on, happy to hold her.

She laughed into his shoulder.

"What the hell's so funny?"

"Just pretend you're checking the boats and you're on your toes, jumping from one deck to the next. Be light, be nimble, and be quick, Joe jump over the candlestick. The quicker you move, the lighter you can be. Like a southwest cloud, Foggy Joe. That's it, two-left-feet. See? You can dance."

"Two-left-feet," he mumbled. Joe chuckled, a rich, throaty sound, clearly suggesting he was enjoying her banter.

She pulled back and looked at him. "What's so funny?" They now were more at a standstill and just moved back and forth. "You're going to say something about my fourth-grade chest, right?" She tapped his shoulder and said, "So I don't have big bubs like Maggie."

They practically stopped moving. "I wouldn't know," Joe said. "I've never danced with Maggie."

She tapped his shoulder again. "I can't believe we're dancing and talking about Maggie Jackson," she said.

"I'll tell you one thing: You've got something Maggie doesn't have."

"What?"

"You have the longest legs in Rhode Island."

"It's a small state, Joe. Anyway, Frankie's got me beat." They stopped dancing and returned to their table.

Carrying fresh drinks, Frankie handed her a gin and tonic. He pulled up a chair. "Something you wanted to discuss, Joe?"

"Excuse me," she said. "I'm going to the powder room."

Joe watched her walk away, then turned to Frankie. "I'm working on a big shipment. If it actually happens, I may need your money upfront."

Frankie nodded agreeably. "I trust you, Joe, but business is business…if I advance the cash, I want at least fifty percent of what you land."

"Agreed. And Frankie, it's gonna be a lot of booze." Joe tested him again. "I'm talking a real big load. Also, you need to send extra men with your trucks to help with the unloading. This operation has to move very, very fast."

"I can handle that. When the time comes, just tell me how much money you need." Frankie raised his coffee cup. "Good luck to both of us."

"Thanks, Frankie. Remember, not a word to anyone."

"No problem." They shook and Frankie left.

Janie was cheerful when she sat down. "It seems to me," she said immediately, as though she had thought about it in the ladies' room, "lovely legs are important, but bubs—that's something a man can put his hands on. Don't you agree, Foggy Joe?"

He wondered why she liked to needle him. Yet sometimes she didn't know when to stop chatting. Her mouth moved like a hummingbird's wings, and he realized then that she couldn't hold her liquor, either.

He asked, "Are you ready to go?"

"Yes."

~~~~~~

Joe pulled up in front of the house and shut off the engine.

"Pearly isn't home yet," she observed.

"New Bedford has a way of doing that to you."

She said, "I had a nice time today, especially tonight."

"Me too, and look how early it is."

They sat quietly for a while. He lit a cigarette and rolled down his window. They could hear the gentle slapping of water against the Basin's shoreline.

"Curiosity, Janie. Why do you allow Henry Grover to squire you around?" Joe might have been asking out of curiosity, but he sounded like it made his stomach ache.

She thought for a bit. "Henry Grover's a nice enough guy. I pretty much know where he stands. I mean, he treats me nice. Granted, I'm not crazy about his attitude towards Prohibition...but at least he's not bothering you or Daddy." Janie tapped him on the arm. "Henry is considered a pretty good catch by most of the local girls. Maggie thinks he's interesting."

Joe's eyes danced amusingly. "Who am I to argue with Maggie's opinion?"

She tried to get a better look at him, to see what his eyes were saying about Maggie, but in the dark, trying to read his weathered face was like trying to breathe underwater.

"Maggie's just a friend, Janie...nothing more."

"It's really none of my business," she said softly. She waited for his reply, but nothing came.

"What's the latest on this investor? Pearly said he took you to lunch."

Janie smiled. "Business. Nothing more. Why do you ask?"

He silently shrugged. A long moment passed, and she moved slightly closer while Joe leaned into her. They looked into each other's face for a moment.

He whispered, "Curiosity, Janie. Can I kiss you goodnight?"

"Of course, for curiosity's sake."

The kiss was long, gentle, controlled.

She thought he had the lips and the scent of a real man. She was surprised when he broke away first.

She opened the car door. "I'm glad tonight happened."

"Me too."

She swung the door shut and cut across the dewy grass. She turned and waved. He tapped the horn and drove off.

CHAPTER TWENTY-ONE

THE ONCE ELEGANT GREEK REVIVAL had, of late, shown signs of needing maintenance, especially for a Lake Shore Drive mansion in Chicago. The Buchanans had only taken up residence recently, but issues persisted across the once-verdant property. A scraggly mongrel was darting across the burnt lawn and running in and out of the overgrown gardens, pursuing what looked like a mink that had just left the water. It had a shiny black mussel in its mouth. The small animal headed towards the Buchanans' lily pond, which appeared to have flooded out into a mishmash of weeds and leaves. There was a sense about the property that money and landscape care had dried up.

A few hundred feet off the shore of Lake Michigan, a speedboat that belonged to the master of the house, Tom Buchanan, rolled and bucked against a moon tide and the southerly wind. With each roll, dirty seagrass clung like an unruly neighbor to the boat's faded-red bottom.

At nine o'clock, the Buchanan household was barely awake. Daisy, unable to find the cook, had just stumbled through making a pot of coffee, and for a moment, she watched the Empco's glass top bubble and perk. She leaned over the pot and sniffed the aroma. She then glanced out the kitchen window. "My, the lawn looks rather unkempt," she said aloud. "How is it I've never noticed it before?"

She walked into the bedroom and began to noisily rifle through some drawers.

Tom was still in bed, but slowly stirring. He snarled, "Do you have to make so much fucking noise?" By the tenor of his voice, he clearly had awakened in a nasty mood.

She shook her head. "Such language, and so early in the day. What are you going to do when dearest baby is old enough to understand those vulgar words?"

He didn't respond. Daisy continued to rummage through various drawers.

"I can't find my pearls. The ones my grandmother gave me. I'm beside myself. Have you seen them?" Daisy's expression turned to real worry.

Tom again didn't respond.

"Is it possible the cook or nanny stole them?"

Finally, through gritted teeth, he said, "Nobody stole them. I had to pawn them."

It took a moment to sink in for Daisy. "What are you saying?"

He sat up, brushed down his hair with both hands. "Listen, you spoiled princess, we are living on tight money. By the way, there isn't any help as of today, so it's time for you to start taking care of me and acting like a wife."

"I've always been your wife."

"Sure…when it's convenient."

"We know you haven't always been a wonderful husband. Have you?"

Tom didn't answer. He got out of bed, stood motionless for a few seconds, then vigorously scratched his balls, maneuvering them from side to side as though making sure they were still there. Naked, he seemed twice his size—like a tall mountain gorilla without hair. His hand-scratching gave him a slight morning boner; for his build, it seemed rather inadequate.

Daisy, with a shake of her head, turned away from his manly exercise. "Tight money?" She had a long pause of reflection. "What are we going to do?"

Tom Buchanan seemed prepared for the question. "I'm happy you used the word 'we.' I want you to figure it out. You come from money. I can't go to my people this time. That well has dried up, at least for now."

Tom pulled up a pair of wrinkled trousers without putting on any underwear.

Daisy shook her head. "I can't believe I'm even hearing this. For the sake of our family, I guess I will throw myself at my parents' mercy, or at someone…"

"I knew you would."

Chapter Twenty-Two

GATSBY AND PAUL MORAN WERE SITTING alone in a private coach, heading for New York—Moran with a brown folder on his lap, Gatsby with a large valise between his legs. Gatsby was dressed again in his waterman's clothes and wore a Greek mariner's cap.

For a moment, and he wasn't sure why, he thought of Ella Kay and smiled to himself. How would that woman react if she knew she had been fooled from the grave? She may have kept him from what Dan had bequeathed him in his will, but the secret fortune Dan had visited on him, although delayed, had given him the freedom to be whomever he desired.

Moran said, "I got this telegram just before we boarded this morning…when you arrive in Canada, the boat will be ready for sea trials. *Diamond Daisy* is already on the stern. George Cramp loved the name. Said it's good advertisement for his boat-building business."

Gatsby chuckled. "Long as we don't get blown out of the water."

Moran just stared at Gatsby but didn't respond.

Moran nodded towards the valise. "You sure you don't want me to go with you…or have Kanky accompany you?"

Gatsby unbuttoned his coat; Moran eyeballed a pistol in a shoulder holster. "I'll be fine."

Moran opened his folder, removed a handbill and some tickets. "You're taking the S.S. *Prince Edward* out of Boston for Yarmouth. The ferry leaves at two this afternoon. The shipyard will pick you up in Yarmouth, take you to the yard. Cramp reserved a room for you at the Hotel Oceanside."

Gatsby nodded. "In a couple of days, send Kanky and Collector to the shipyard. By then, the sea trials should be over...as long as Cramp did a good job."

"He's the best boat builder in Canada."

Gatsby nodded. "The three of us will run the boat back to New Bedford."

"Cramp is sending his engineer with you on her maiden voyage home...part of the contract."

"Good. Where will the crews stay in New Bedford?"

"You now own a boardinghouse near the wharf. Right across the street from the warehouse. Also, a cook for the men. Not too far from your residence."

~~~~~

After three days of successful sea trials, the beamy seventy-foot *Diamond Daisy* left the George Cramp shipyard. At that time, she had to be the finest rum boat floating on the East Coast. Painted black, she had three converted Liberty aircraft engines, a bulletproof wheelhouse, side panels of steel plating protecting the engine room, a smoke diversion setup, as well as the latest radio and navigation equipment. However, with her wide beam, she did tend to broach in heavy, following seas. Cramp immediately hauled out the boat and added more diameter to the dual rudders. That helped, but the shipbuilder determined that when loading the boat, more weight needed to be placed in the stern. That did solve most of the problem.

Before leaving Nova Scotia, Gatsby outdid himself with a christening party for the shipyard workers and their families.

~~~~~~

Kanky and Collector continually told Gatsby, on the trip back to New Bedford, there was no other boat, whether Coast Guard or rum-runner, that could match Diamond Daisy.

Unbeknownst to Gatsby and his men, Joe Bucolo's new boat was resting in a cradle at Heinrich Schmitz boatyard on the banks of the Acushnet River in Fairhaven, Massachusetts. She was only a few weeks away from being launched. According to the German boat builder, at eighty-feet in length and with four Liberty engines, she would be the fastest rum boat ever built.

Gatsby wanted to arrive in New Bedford under cover of darkness. His new base of operation, formerly a huge warehouse, provided almost complete privacy from land traffic. The fewer people who knew about *Diamond Daisy*, the better. When tied-up at the wharf, Gatsby devised a fake camouflage of a phony two-masted schooner covered with a tent-like structure, making it appear that the vessel was being refitted.

CHAPTER TWENTY-THREE

TONIGHT, THERE WASN'T A RIPPLE on the water. To the south and west, thin ocean fog reflected the city lights of New Bedford. From the Fairhaven Bridge north, a car bounced along the dirt road that ran parallel to the Acushnet.

Forty yards up the river's embankment, behind the huge boat-shed, Nina Schmitz's cottage was built into the side of a small hill. A narrow, rickety porch, attached to the east side of the shanty, was hidden from the river by ailing evergreens twisted by the wind. Inside, Nina Schmitz sat by candlelight, reciting the philosopher Frenchman Émile Coué's words: "*Tous les jours à tous points de vue, je vais de mieux en mieux.*" ("Day by day in every way, I am getting better and better.")

She sat erect, hands on her knees, palms up, with Coué's open book resting between her legs. A belt of rope held her hand-sewn canvas shorts tight to her waist. The night air cooled her bare torso and buoyant breasts. A paint-splattered work shirt hung by the door, next to a picture of the great Rudolph Valentino starring in *The Sheik*.

She heard a car approaching. Clearly in a big hurry, she thought. Reflections from the headlights danced against the still trees as the automobile approached. Nina blew out the candle and slipped on the shirt. She heard the surplus generator in the boat shed being fired up by her father.

By the time the driver got out of his car, Nina had reached the boat shed. As Joe approached the office door, she entered the building through a loft window. She moved cat-like along the rafters until she stood ten feet above the drawing table where her white-haired father—a bespectacled, humorless man—sat in front of his hand-drawn blueprints, sucking on a handmade pipe.

There was a knock at the shed door. Heinrich Schmitz glanced up at Nina and shook his head. "Please be quiet, Nina."

Joe followed the old man into his office, which overlooked the massive shed. "Sorry I'm late, Mister Schmitz."

"You're not late, Joseph. You are early." Heinrich shook Joe Bucolo's hand. "Eight o'clock is a little past my bedtime, but I don't mind staying up occasionally. Did you bring my gelt?"

Joe touched his stomach. "Of course." He walked behind the drawing table and dropped his pants. With some difficulty, he untied the money belt.

Joe pulled up his pants and buckled his belt. Methodically, he counted out thirty-five one-hundred-dollar bills, laying them out on top of Heinrich's drafting table, all with Benjamin Franklin's face up.

Heinrich wrote a receipt, which Bucolo read slowly, then tucked it into his shirt pocket.

On the rafters above, Nina thought to herself, *This guy is either not too bright or he can't read.*

"Can we look at her?" Joe asked.

"It's a little late, but…" Heinrich turned on a string of bulbs draped along the rafters. It lit up the boat, resting in her cradle.

Joe looked down through the glass partition into the shed. "By Jesus, will you look at that?" Heinrich had windows between his office and the construction area so he could keep an eye on his workers.

The mahogany-planked vessel commandeered the entire shed. The hull, recently painted, revealed the skill of a master boat builder. Without taking his eyes off the boat, Joe said, "Heinrich, if I didn't want this beauty now, what could I get for her as she sits tonight?"

"Hard to tell." Heinrich scratched his mutton-chop sideburns, as was his habit when he didn't like something.

"Let's take a look at her, Heinrich."

The shipwright made no move to negotiate the ladder leading down into the work area. He stood there, gazing at his craftmanship through the office window. "When I look at her, I see her finished, fitted out, perfect." He paused. "She is perhaps the finest boat I've ever built."

"I won't argue that, Heinrich. Come show me your work."

"No, my boy. You go down; it's much too late for me tonight. My bed is waiting." Heinrich shook Joe's hand. "Don't worry about the lights, Joseph. My daughter will shut them off when you're done."

Joe slowly climbed down the ladder to the floor of the boat shed. Heinrich said, as if to himself, on the way out the door, "I'm sure your brother will be interested to learn how Mister Bucolo's business is doing."

Nina walked along the rafters directly over the vessel, where Joe was inspecting the hull thirty feet below. He circled the boat, rubbing his hand over the smooth sides. Aloud, he said, "Like a baby's ass."

He sat on a sawhorse and lit a cigarette.

He smokes with great exhaustion, Nina thought; something is wrong. He puffs in and out like an engine.

Softly, but clear enough for Nina to understand, he said aloud, "What the hell am I doing, Max?"

Nina grabbed the ropes of a block and tackle and let herself down alongside the hull. She thought she'd surprise him, but he must have seen the fallen dust because he asked nonchalantly, "How long you been up there, blondie?"

"Well," she said, holding herself extremely erect, imagining, as she enjoyed imagining, that her body was connected to some invisible string hanging from heaven, "I saw you drop your pants and take off your money belt. Are you a Portagee?"

Joe did not answer.

Finally, he said softly, "I suppose that's possible. I'm an orphan, so I can't say."

She was surprised at this unexpected admission. "Well, I love your skin, and that scar, your blue eyes. You have an olive Portuguese face. Your name, Bucolo, is Italian. But your accent is almost French. So," she said matter-of-factly, releasing her body from the ropes, jumping down onto the dirt floor of the shed, "I'm confused." She stood squarely in front of him in her best posture. "Got a smoke, Joe?"

He held out his package of Wings.

Nina unbuttoned her shirt, revealing portions of her breasts. She reached for a cigarette. "Max? Who is he?" she asked. "And you said, 'What the hell am I doing, Max?'"

"Max was my father," he answered, his eyes locked on her breasts.

"Really," she said, lighting a match, "and I thought you were an orphan?"

"Are you as crazy as they say?"

"Crazy? Are you not the bad boy of Tiverton who fucks all the girls in town? Are you not the one bringing in boatloads of booze? Are you not the one the Coast Guard would like to drown or throw in jail? Look who speaks about crazy!"

She could see he was surprised by her comments and her knowledge of him. "You just hurt my father's feelings. Why do you want to sell this fine boat, when it's not even finished?"

"It's a she!" Joe said quickly.

"Is it really?" She laughed and pirouetted on the spot. "Do they really say I'm crazy, Bucolo?"

"They say you're one lovely fräulein."

From a bucket, she scooped a dripping handful of green slop and held it out under his nose, which made him recoil. "Do you know what this is?" she asked.

"No."

"My father uses it on every boat he builds. It's magic. It protects the newborn boat. It protects your 'she' from the *Nocnitsa,* the sea hag that sinks boats and eats their crew."

She watched Joe's eyes widen. This one's superstitious, she thought. Good. "My father puts this grease between the bow stem and the stern frame, before the planking is fastened. It keeps the bad spirits away."

"What is that stuff?" he asked quietly.

"Pressed goat testicles mixed with…other things I cannot reveal."

"You like to kid, don't you, fräulein?"

"Kid?" she said. Nina flicked her cigarette into the dirt and blew a thin trail of smoke in his face.

She placed her hand on her throat and slowly spread the green goop along her torso. Joe's eyes widened. Her hand moved around and under her breasts and down the valley between them, careful not to allow any grease to color her erect nipples.

She shifted her left shoulder in his direction. "Help me here, or-phan. Cover my tits."

She grabbed his hands and clamped them on her breasts.

"Easy!" she said. "Just rub them gently, orphan." She made a pleasurable moan, watching for his reaction. Joe became more atten-tive and moved slower. I've got this fisherman hooked, she told herself as she shifted sensually under his touch.

"I'm no crazy fräulein, Bucolo. I'm the most exciting woman you'll ever meet." Their eyes locked. She pushed her breasts harder into his hands, regaining his attention. "I'm no dried Yankee fruit, I'll tell you. And I'm not crazy… Germans are not crazy…" She shud-dered, as though she were cold. "I'm just different. I come from a different place, and so do you, orphan boy."

Joe grabbed the waist of her canvas shorts.

"No, no, Bucolo! Are you stupid, Italian? Tonight is bad…buck like you fuck me tonight, I'd have twins tomorrow." She placed the palm of her hand on his chest. "But," she added in a lower voice, "in a few days…"

Joe slowly released her.

She nodded. "Good night, Bucolo."

"Good night, fräulein."

The night air was still cool. Nina lit her candle in her shack, heated a pan of warm water, took a cloth and a bar of soap, and gently washed the *Nocnitsa* grease from her body.

She thought of Bucolo, smoking cigarettes, driving back to Tiverton, probably very confused and smelling that god-awful grease. Nina started to chuckle, the sound resonating inside the naughty cauldron of her chest, and quickly erupted into outright laughter.

~~~~~

Joe could hear the phone ringing as he unlocked his door.

He grabbed the telephone receiver.

"Joe, it's Frankie-the-Bone…"

"What's up?"

"Something you should know. Kanky came by, trying to get my business. I told him I was happy dealing with Foggy Joe, but he said he'll be back in a couple of weeks—in case I 'change my mind.' Joe, what's he trying to tell me? You still there?"

"Yes, Frankie, I appreciate the word."

"There's more." Frankie's tone changed to one of real seriousness. "Listen carefully, Joe, this is very important."

After a minute or so of listening, Joe said, "Chicago…gangsters… If that doesn't yank your balls, I don't know what does. Thanks, Frankie."

Joe hung up the receiver and shook his head.

Feeling uneasy, he repacked his money belt for the night's run and left the house.

~~~~~

At the wharf, all the boys were there, waiting. As soon as Joe walked in, they knew something had happened. Something bad.

Pearly spoke first. "Let's hear it, Joe."

Joe said, "I've got some news we all need to pay attention to. Some future decisions are gonna be needed."

Hunker said, "Let's hear it, Joseph."

"Before I left the house, I got a call from Frankie-the-Bone. He said Kanky's boss is a guy named Jay Gatsby…"

"Who the hell is he?"

"Gangster…run out of Chicago. Frankie said he intends to take over all of Rhode Island's booze activity."

"Where did Frankie hear this?"

"Mayor of Providence was at his club. Got pretty drunk…spilled the beans. Appears his cousin, a lawyer named Paul Moran, works for this Gatsby, who owns the Oakland Beach speakeasy. It's operating pretty much in the open. Plenty of payoffs going on. A friend… Walter somebody, also from Chicago…is running the club… Gatsby is keeping two of his rum boats there, formerly owned by Herman the German… Sounds like Gatsby took advantage of his grief and bought out the German's operation in New Bedford after his son died."

"Jesus!" Pearly shook his head. "*Hobo* and *Tramp*! Sonofabitch! This guy sounds big… Two operations. 'Magine a city slicker havin' the stones to think he can kick us off our own river!"

Joe said, "Now, Pearly," his eyes swept over his crew, "we all know that's not going to happen."

Hunker, like always, pushed the issue. "I think we should take our asses right over to Oakland Beach…maybe finish him off. At least break his knees and strip him."

Pearly gave Hunker a hard stare.

No one commented until Joe said, "First things first… Seeing that we have a late start, we'll only use two boats tonight. Sammy, you're staying here. You and the *Wood Duck* have the night off." Joe tried to see Sammy's face but he turned quickly away, trying to hide the disappointment as well as the swelling that had closed his eye.

For a long moment, they were silent. Finally, Sammy began to

softly hem and haw, rearranging the tools on the work table. "But…
but Joe, I gotta go," he said, waving the wrench in his hand. "Bad luck
to change your crew… You hear?!"

"Shut up, with your bad luck!" Joe quickly raised his hand.
"That's the end of it. Your eye is still closed and you know what that
can mean. Answer's no! And I don't want any bad-luck talk."

Sammy tossed the wrench onto his workbench, spilling an oil can.
Cursing, he started to mop up the mess.

Joe turned to Hunker. "You'll come with me. Bancocks with Pearly."

Hunker puffed on his stogie. He didn't appear that happy.

Pearly said, "Maybe we should forget tonight's run?"

Joe did a double-take. "That's a strange fucking sound coming
from you, Pearly."

"Maybe, but we *are* running behind. It's gonna put more pressure
on us."

"From here on in, if we're gonna run liquor, we're gonna have to
eat pressure." Joe was adamant, offering no room for discussion. "Besides, maybe it'll help us remember how easy fishing was."

The boys managed a weak chuckle, but it was their eyes, especially Pearly's, that reflected a begrudging acceptance of the new reality.

"With only two boats, we'll make up lost time loading and at the
drop. Besides…" Joe tapped his top pocket, "Sparky made contact
with the *Maria Morso*. Captain Durall is waiting, and I've got his position." He straightened up and shifted the money belt around his
waist. "Sparky says Durall's carrying top-grade goods. Johnny Walker, Old Parr, Golden Wedding."

Everyone made appreciative sounds. "Guess you're right," said
Pearly. "Kinda hard to pass up such fine booze."

"We still unloading at Booker's Wharf?" Hunker asked. There
was a hint of concern in his voice, just a hint.

Billy Bancock turned towards Hunker while his ears stayed perked.

Joe nodded. "Charlie Piermount is gonna take this entire trip."

"So, we're coming home through the East Passage?" Pearly asked.

"We're better off in the East Passage," Hunker added, "at least there's more room to run. Especially if there's a chase."

Joe said, "There's gonna be fogbanks offshore, so we have got to be prepared."

"Are ya sure?" Hunker asked.

Joe made like he didn't hear the question. "Pearly, you keep on my portside at all times. At least I'll know where you are. Okay?"

Pearly nodded. "No problem."

Hunker and the Bancock brothers headed for the door. Joe called out, "Hey, Hunker, no smoking stogies in my pilot house. And no farts in the fo'c'sle."

Without turning, Hunker grunted, "Ya sound like my Gertie." Had he turned around, he would've seen Joe and Pearly smiling. Sammy, landlocked, had nothing to be happy about.

Chapter Twenty-Four

OVERHEAD, THE SKY WAS DEVELOPING thin streaks of fog, and with a damp southwest wind, it had the makings for a cool, clammy night. Joe knew for certain that the warm breeze would soon clash with the colder waters of the ocean and they would be running through pea-soup fog. It would be broken—one moment clear, the next socked in tighter than a lamb's ass.

The boys, especially Sammy, feared fog more than sin, especially running out to Rum Row, traveling through the east-westbound shipping lanes. Besides steamers and freighters, the shipping lanes were used by smaller vessels, most notably fishing trawlers and small-time rummies who had no idea what they were doing in the fog. It could be a mess.

Like ghosts, the two shadows moved quickly down the Seaconnet. Occasionally, shore lights from Tiverton and Aquidneck Island reflected erratically across the river. The farther they traveled south, the darker it became. After Fogland Point, both shorelines lost all signs of civilization.

The big Liberties reached proper temperature, and Joe pushed the throttles ahead. The *Black Duck* lurched forward with Pearly following in the *Mallard*. From the middle of the river, with drifting fog building, it was hard to tell where the water ended and the land began.

154

"Fuckin' fog!" Hunker said. "Ya sure called it right, Joseph."

Joe didn't respond. Hunker sucked his unlit cigar and wondered what Joseph had on his mind. Yes, a lot to wonder. Beneath his feet, the twin engines hummed and the mahogany hull vibrated slightly. Joe flicked the panel lights. Hunker leaned over to read the gauges. Everything was functioning properly. To their portside, Pearly was running about five hundred feet astern, the *Mallard*'s bow spraying up white water.

"I hope the hell we have a quiet night," Joe said.

"Me too." Hunker gently sucked on his stogie, wishing for a match. He would light it on Rum Row when they started loading. In the semi-darkness of the pilot house, he watched Joe's eyes shifting between the compass and the window. Serious and deep in thought, Hunker reasoned, that's why Joseph is lucky, and why we've all made some good money. And I've been some help. And despite what Pearly and the others say, I keep Joseph on course.

The two boats approached High Hill and had already passed Almy's Rock, a jagged mass submerged at high water. Both vessels kept their bows west of the Seaconnet Lighthouse. Usually, the flashing beacon provided an excellent bearing. Its beam tonight was already absorbed by the spreading bank of fog.

As they approached the Atlantic, the sea swelled beneath them, a slight holdover from the recent storm. The ocean was greeting the Seaconnet River. The fog appeared to thin some.

"It's gonna take the hard chop of a northwester to knock down these seas," Joe offered, sounding to Hunker a lot like Max.

Leaving the lee of the river's west bank, they headed south by southwest, and the wind quickly became more evident. At the same time, they passed through the approaching northern wall of the fog bank.

"Fuckin' fog gives me the creeps," Hunker said, realizing that he had just exposed one of his own superstitions. He wondered if Joseph would let it go by.

"How's that?" Joe asked.

"Reminds me of the goddamn graveyard," Hunker replied softly.

"Oh, stop with the fucking graveyard."

"Christ! Then don't ask me them goddamn kind of questions. I ain't any sky pilot."

After about five minutes, long enough that Hunker forgot what he had just said, Joe mumbled, "You would've made a good preacher, Hunker. You and Minister Bottomley."

Hunker roared, drawing a wide grin from Joe.

Pearly maneuvered closer to the *Black Duck*, and Joe slowed the engines a notch. Both vessels were now on the same 190-degree heading. Joe checked the chart, his pocket watch, and made a few pencil calculations.

"What's our time?" Pearly yelled across.

"At this speed, we should reach the *Maria Morso* in about an hour and twelve minutes," Joe shouted back.

Twelve minutes, Hunker thought. Yes, Joseph, you are serious tonight.

Totally submerged in the thick fog, the large, uniform swells lifted the hulls. The southwest wind slapped against their starboard bows. They were headed about nine miles southeast of Block Island. If nothing changed since Sparky's radio contact, the *Maria Morso* would be anchored on the thirty-fathom edge of Coxe's Ledge.

Over the sounds of the sea working against the hull, Joe said, "Damn, if this ain't the life, you know, Hunker? Being on a boat, you're free of the land. Damn! What a great feeling to be free of the land."

This talk caught Hunker off guard. "Yeah, almost like my favorite song."

Joe laughed, "No, Hunker. Your song is when you're on land. This here's different."

Hunker wasn't really sure he wanted to know what Joe meant. "Why don't ya spit it out, what's bothering ya, Joseph? Ya all twisted up like a hog's pecker."

Joe nodded in silent agreement. Hunker just grinned. "I know when something is bothering ya. I ain't stupid. So, just tell me."

"Frankie's news tonight about this Gatsby fella…"

"Ya, I figured…" Hunker grabbed a sandwich out of the bag. "Damn it, Joseph, ya sure getting ya share of misery."

"Yes, in some ways," Joe softly replied.

"Bullshit, Joseph." Hunker, chewing, raised his finger and pointed to his eyes. "Kanky knows ya got a softness inside and that prick's gonna use it to his benefit."

"Maybe, maybe not," Joe added. "Kanky's like a horse with blinders. Sees what he wants to see. Does what he wants to do."

Hunker just stared at him in the semi-darkness. "By Jesus, Kanky, the shit he is, his mama popped him from her asshole. Yes, Joseph, that's a fact."

"What Kanky…and this Gatsby fella are doing ain't worth killing over."

Hunker shrugged. "Can't agree with that." He paused, as though debating something.

The pilot house windows began to hold fog-drip, beads of water so thick that it seemed like it was raining.

"Pull the wiper cord, Hunker?" He pulled on the cord, and visibility improved slightly. "Fuckin' fog!"

Joe opened a fresh pack of Wings and offered him a cigarette.

"No, thanks, too skinny! I'll probably eat it!"

Joe lit a smoke. He inhaled deeply and glanced at Hunker. "If you want to light your stogie, go 'head, but open the door and blow the mule outside."

At the doorway, Hunker puffed, allowing the southwest wind to carry the smoke away. From that angle, Joe's face reflected the red glow of the compass light. Tonight, for Hunker, Joe appeared younger than he was.

Hunker shrugged. "I need a piss."

"Don't fall over, we're running a few minutes late."

"If I do, don't stop."

"Don't worry."

The long, foggy seas played host to the *Black Duck* for another thirty minutes. The fog wouldn't give in. Hunker's eyes seldom left the soft red glow of the compass or the dripping windows.

Again and again, Joe checked his pocket watch. Then at closer intervals, until he began to slow the engines down.

"We here?" Hunker asked, marveling.

Joe shifted the *Black Duck*'s engines into neutral and let them idle. On his portside, the *Mallard* drifted into sight. In the fog's magnified deception, she appeared twice her size.

"Give an ear, Hunker?"

Hunker went out onto the deck, leaned over the gunnel, and listened. Moments later, the sound of a bell clanged eerily through the fog. He pointed his cigar. "That direction."

Joe's face turned to the compass. "South by southeast," he called and spun the *Black Duck*'s helm onto that bearing.

Hunker returned to the pilot house. He uncovered the *Duck*'s bell and cracked it at ten-second intervals. A few minutes passed when suddenly, out of the fog, an immense, almost ghostly presence took shape. A small anchor lantern burned from her centerline bridge, her stern and bow range lights glowing dimly. Worn, barely readable letters came into view. It was the *Maria Morso*.

"Foggy Joe...Foggy Joe," Hunker slowly whispered. "Surely you have seagull blood."

Joe smiled. "Thanks, Hunker."

The *Maria Morso* was over two hundred feet long and had been used as a lumber carrier until Prohibition. About five weeks back, in a light snowfall, the gang had plucked some choice labels from the *Maria*. Finer brands were easy sellers and always brought the best prices. Hunker was happy to see the *Maria* again.

Someone swung a lantern. Joe blinked his spotlight and came around to the lee of the vessel. Hunker deftly secured the *Black Duck* to a manila-bumpered platform. With the direction of the tide and the vessel's high sides, the *Maria* was lying broadside to the southwest wind and her deep draft acted like a breakwater.

The man with the lantern came down the gangway.

"That's Peter, the first mate," Joe said.

"I remember," Hunker mumbled.

He was thin with a freckled, country-bred face. "Hello, there," Peter said loudly. His voice was pleasant. He seemed to recognize Joe. "How was your trip out?"

"No problems," Joe said. By the lantern, they shook hands.

"Surprised you found us, with all this fog."

Hunker mumbled something inaudible.

After helping Pearly secure the *Mallard*, they dressed in their oilskins and went up the swaying gangway. They climbed over the gunnel and found the steel decking wet and slippery. There was a dank odor blowing across the *Maria*. She needed a good cleaning, and a fresh paint job. They stood under the ship's stern-quarters overhang, where fog-drip fell like rain every time the ship dipped and gently rolled.

"Say, how'd that nor'easter treat you?" Joe asked.

"Miserable as hell." Peter reflected for a moment and added, "This old tub sure did a lot of dancing around. We should've hoisted anchor and run with the wind."

"Why didn't you?" Hunker asked.

"Captain was too busy," Peter said. "Follow me."

They ducked into the crew's quarters. Three men were playing cards, someone was sleeping. The cabin smelled sour and of cigarette smoke. The crew greeted them with meager attention. Their real interest was in the card game and the stakes in the center of the table. The prize appeared to be a woman's red corset and a frilly red garter.

"It is what you are thinking," Peter said. "They are playing cards for a woman."

"A woman!" Hunker snapped. "Here on the *Maria*?" He picked

up the corset, brought it to his face, and sniffed deeply. A bitter smell. "I know this woman." Hunker's comment created howling, toothless grins from the card players.

"Smells to me like she's been pickled in a fish barrel." Hunker tossed the corset back onto the table, like it had a dose of the crabs.

"Where is she?" Pearly asked.

"When can I see Captain Durall?" Joe asked.

One crewman spit a hacker into a wooden box by the table. "When he's not in bed. Goddamn it!" He threw his cards on the table.

Joe winked at Peter.

Peter unfolded a piece of brown paper, which he took from his shirt pocket. "Let's see. Nine hundred cases split evenly between Absolut, Johnny Walker, Old Parr, and Highland Queen. Three hundred cases per boat. Right?"

"Glad you can read my codes," Joe said.

"Yes, I pay attention. Besides, I write it down as your Sparky gives it out."

Joe said, "There's one change. I only got two boats tonight. So, it'll be four hundred fifty per boat."

Peter wrote the order out on a ship's manifest. "You're almost cleaning us out. With this past storm, it's been a long anchor." He handed Joe the manifest. "Captain Durall will figure out the prices."

Joe glanced at the paper, then back to Peter. "How about seeing if Durall's got his pants on? Pearly, keep a check on the loading."

The fresh air was welcome. Hunker followed Joe and the first mate up onto the mid-ship bridge. The red glow of the compass served as a night light. The wheelhouse was silent as a tomb. A musty aroma of old charts and strong tobacco hung in the air. A giant but dull brass steering wheel overwhelmed the forward console. The padded captain's chair was worn and split. The captain's quarters were located in the rear of the wheelhouse. Peter knocked on the door and then left.

"Come in," a croaky voice replied.

They entered the empty cabin. A hanging light swayed slowly

from the ceiling. The portholes were painted over and closed. The air stank of cologne and liquor. Durall walked out of an adjoining cabin, buttoning his baggy red flannel union suit. "Joe Bucolo. How are you?" He nodded at Hunker, who gave Durall a little wave.

"Good, and you, Captain?"

Durall made a sluggish gesture with his eyes and hands. He appeared sweaty and fatigued. His thin, black hair hung over his forehead. His face was pale, his cheeks and lips puckered, as if his teeth were missing.

A woman shuffled out of the cabin. Not much to look at, Hunker thought. He gave her a fast survey. What the hell, out here, anything looks good.

Durall said weakly, "Louisa is my first mate." He laughed and his body seemed to rattle inside his long johns.

Hunker had a hard time keeping a straight face. Durall and his bedmate were a strange-looking pair. As Hunker thought about it, he almost blew his ears out suppressing his laugh.

"Well, let's talk." Durall nodded to Louisa, and she withdrew behind the curtain.

Hunker noticed that Louisa didn't shave under her arms, just like some of the women in Europe. He loved to tickle their armpits. But maybe not Louisa's.

Durall saw Hunker staring. He turned around to see Louisa snap the curtain shut. He leaned forward over the table. "Do you want a round with her?" he asked softly.

Joe's head jerked back in surprise.

Hunker quickly nodded.

"I don't mind," Durall added, "long as I can watch."

"No, thanks," Hunker said, noticing Joe's annoyance. "I'm a little rusty."

Durall released a sigh. "This Louisa is one of the strangest women I've ever had." He started laughing, enjoying his joke.

Hunker's eyes widened. "Why?" he asked.

Durall shook his head and tapped his chest. "I have a weakness for strange women."

Joe glanced at Hunker. "Yeah, who doesn't?"

"Sounds interesting, I'd say," Hunker offered. "Too young for me, though. But thanks anyway, Captain."

Joe flashed a don't-fuck-with-this-guy look at Hunker, then said, "Maybe you should let your poker-playing crew help you out."

"Like hell."

"What about the corset?" Hunker continued.

"A joke," Durall said. "Helps to keep them on their toes."

Hunker noticed that Durall's head kept shifting, as though he were listening to make sure no one was sneaking up to the cabin door. Hunker said, "You better watch out they don't heave you overboard."

Durall yanked a horse pistol from the holster slung over his chair. "I am still captain," he said, touching his chest with the long barrel. He returned the gun to its holster. "Come now, let us talk business. My prices are always good," Durall said, his eyes finally flashing excitement.

"You're looking forward to going home?" Joe asked.

"But of course!"

"Give us your best price then, and you can head back north."

Hunker was impressed with Joe's salesmanship. Durall still said nothing, but he did scratch his balls.

Joe asked, "When will you be back?"

The captain laughed. "Depends. Depends on many things. Saint Pierre is going crazy; I might just get knifed or shot. But I think also we should hurry before your government stops us. I worry the Coast Guard will begin to patrol offshore. That would make it very difficult for us to entertain gentlemen like you."

Hunker saw Joe lean over, as though inspecting Durall's horse pistol. "So, when will you be back?" Joe asked again.

"The closer we get to better weather, the less time I have to wait out here, so maybe two, three weeks," Durall said. "I wish there was a way to offload my cargo quicker."

Joe nodded. "That would be nice, wouldn't it? I've been thinking about that, Captain. There just might be a way."

Durall's expression came alive. "There is? How?"

"When you return," Joe said, "immediately radio my Sparky. If weather conditions are right, I may be able to unload your entire cargo all at once."

"Impossible! How could you do this?" Durall began to bounce around in his chair. He asked softly, "You have a facility large enough for the *Maria*?" The way he asked the question, he appeared slightly insane, and he actually drooled a little.

Joe hesitated and then gave him a quick nod.

Durall leaned forward, his interest trapped. He finally wiped his mouth with the flannel arm. "You do realize, Joe Bucolo, this vessel is over two hundred feet long? And you understand that the *Maria* is capable of carrying a tremendous amount of liquor; maybe fifty thousand cases. Do you have that kind of money?"

Hunker caught a slight reaction on Joe's face at the amount.

"I can do it. But I need your best price, and you'll need a full crew to speed things up. No drunken, horny men playing cards for pussy."

Hunker lit a new cigar. It tasted fine.

"May I?" Durall said, asking for a stogie. Hunker held the match while Durall sucked and blew. They all sat in silence. Then Durall said, "Explain your idea, please."

"If I do, it won't be mine anymore. You gotta wait until you return. Then I'll radio it to you, in code."

Hunker was again impressed. He nodded fatherly approval at Joe's response.

For a moment, Durall pondered Joe's reply. Then he cracked a grin. "If it doesn't happen, the only thing I'm out is the cost of a good crew, and some very angry liquor dealers back north."

Everyone laughed at that one.

Joe placed the manifest on the table. Durall picked up a carpenter's pencil and wet the tip with his tongue. Durall cut his price three dollars a case. Hunker figured a twenty-seven-hundred-dollar discount wasn't too bad for fifteen minutes of bullshit.

While Durall worked his figures, Joe double-checked them. At fifty-three dollars a case, Durall began counting out, for the second time, forty-seven thousand dollars.

Hunker closed the cabin door behind him. He pestered Joe, "Ya bullshitting about a fucking 'bang in'? Aren't you? Why?"

"Something to feather your nest before we get out of the trade."

Hunker took a deep breath, deflated. "How did I know you were going to say that?"

Chapter Twenty-Five

PEARLY AND THE BANCOCK BROTHERS had helped First Mate Peter and his weary, good-for-nothing crew set up a chute, similar to a sluice run. They slid the crates and burlap hams right down onto the decks of the rum boats. Pearly divided the cargo equally between the two boats. He insisted that half the Absolut be loaded on each boat. Half the Old Parr. Half the Johnny Walker. As a result, they had to run the chute back and forth between the *Black Duck* and the *Mallard* for each label.

The operation took about an hour and twenty minutes, mostly because of Pearly's obsession about splitting the load and keeping the boats trim and proper. Finally, First Mate Peter became so confused, Pearly was able to accomplish his goal and scuff up an additional fifty-five cases between the two boats. By two o'clock, they were ready to leave, with the loads split, well-balanced, and secure. Pearly felt that the boats would be slow, each carrying a load and a half.

He was standing on the platform joking with First Mate Peter when Captain Durall shouted from the bridge. Lifting a lantern high, Durall stumbled and jerked down the gangway. Wearing a peacoat and seamen's cap pulled over his forehead, Pearly thought he looked like the comical, silent movie star Charlie Chaplin, a favorite of his.

"I am going to take your advice," Durall said, "keep my crew happy."

Joe pushed past Pearly. "That's good," Joe said. "Else they'll be carrying you off the *Maria* in a box. We wouldn't want that...would we?"

"See you soon," Durall said.

"Remember, Captain, when you return, radio Sparky immediately."

"Do not worry."

On the *Maria*, Joe turned to Pearly. "You come with me. Hunker, you take the *Mallard*."

Hunker's shit-eating grin pissed Pearly off, but neither man said anything. The Bancock brothers, like usual, seemed confused.

Heavy in the water, the two rum boats backed away from the *Maria Morso*, their weighted sterns jammed hard into the rolling seas. Waves drenched the decks and cargo. The large scuppers worked overtime. Once clear of the *Maria*, the boats rolled lazily between the swells as their bows turned towards shore.

The *Black Duck*'s compass read three hundred fifty-five degrees. Pearly reached over and flicked the panel lights. Joe slowly pushed the throttles forward. The bow lifted quickly as she began to slice her way north by northwest through the misty black night.

No sooner had they left the *Maria*, and Pearly started to chatter. "Durall's quite a hoot. From what his crew says, they think he's screwing himself to death. Meanwhile, we pinched fifty-five cases of Johnny Walker!"

"Jesus Christ, Pearly, I'm trying to make a future deal with Durall, and you do that?"

"I didn't know. Don't worry, Durall doesn't know either."

"When the hell will you change your ways?"

Pearly said, "When I'm dead, that's when. Men don't change. Boys change. Besides, they'll never miss them. And another thing, I'm just looking out for all of us. What's the harm?"

Joe shook his head but pushed it no further. Pearly weighted down the chart for Joe to check over. "You did a damn fine job of finding Durall in this pea soup."

Joe eyed Pearly suspiciously. "Jesus, you guys are killing me with compliments."

"Feels like the breeze picked up a little," Pearly added, looking out through the spray-splattered windows.

Joe said, "It's gonna lift the fog."

A half-hour later, with the breeze continuing to freshen, the fog did lift. Through the open port door, they glanced west by northwest and saw the first dull sweeps of the Beavertail Lighthouse. To the northeast, the shore's high, black outline slowly took shape. A moment later, a few lights flickered from Newport's Ocean Drive.

Joe broke the silence. "Check on Hunker."

Pearly stuck his head out the door. After a moment, he said, "I can't see him at all. He had a good head start on us."

Pearly's breath steamed and the heat from the small coal stove in the fo'c'sle felt good. His hunger was gnawing. "I left my sandwich on the *Mallard*."

"I'm sure Hunker will save it for you."

"Oh, no doubt."

Twenty minutes later, Joe slowed the engines. "I think we'll play it cozy." The high, rocky cliffs of Jamestown marked the entrance to the East Passage. With a falling tide, the swells and wind were erratic and rough. As the *Black Duck* got closer to the mouth of the East Passage of Narragansett Bay, the ocean flattened and the narrow strait turned into swift-moving currents. The dumping tide yanked on the rudders and Joe gripped the wheel. No lights were visible in any direction. The shadows of the high ledges made everything very dark.

The rum boat was now moving along at about quarter speed. Pearly opened the pilot house door and kept a sharp eye. In the distance, Prudence Island Light beckoned. When they cleared Fort

Adams, lights from Newport made the harbor seem friendly. "So far, so good," Pearly said softly, his eyes searching.

"If they're on patrol," Joe ventured, "maybe this fog screwed them up."

"Hope so," Pearly added.

~~~~~~

Booker's Wharf, located just north of the railroad trestle on Common Fence Point, was in blackness. The seasonal deep-water wharf was only used when the southern menhaden fleet came up north in July and sold their catches to Grover's fish-processing company, and they used the wharf for laying over. It was also one of Joe's rendezvous whenever he used the East Passage.

He slowed the engines and shifted into neutral. With the freshening wind, they drifted quickly. Both men peered towards the shore. Joe figured Hunker had to be unloaded already. Suddenly, two sets of headlights drilled through the flat darkness, and the trucks' engines strained as they climbed the grade leading away from the landing.

"What the hell?" Joe asked.

"Something ain't right!" Pearly snapped.

"Maybe," Joe said softly. "Get my gun..."

Joe turned the boat about and eased her ahead slowly, towards the wharf. The outline of the *Mallard* became apparent. Joe maneuvered alongside the deserted wharf, just astern of her.

"Where the hell is everybody?" Joe whispered.

"We've been hijacked, old buddy!" Pearly handed him the twelve-gauge, grabbed the searchlight, and quickly tied off the bow.

It hit Joe solid in the stomach and about took his voice away.

"Fuck," he said softly, "you're right."

Pearly was on the wharf already, checking out the empty *Mallard*. Joe looped the stern line around a piling and pulled her snug.

"Those trucks just left with our liquor," Pearly reported back.

"Where are the boys?" Joe asked, pumping a shell into the chamber.

"Jesus," said Pearly, "you don't suppose?"

"Easy does it. Let's not get spooked."

Two of Charlie Piermount's trucks were on the wharf. He had been contracted to supply three. One for each boat. "There's a truck missing," Joe whispered. "This way."

"Are you saying they took the boys?"

"Not without a fight!" Joe said. "Besides, hijackers usually have their own trucks."

They separated by about ten yards and walked slowly across the crushed-shell-filled landing. The brisk wind worked the bushes and whistled through the stiff, budding branches of the high maples. It was noisy, dark, and a little nerve-wracking. They had moved about a hundred feet when they heard voices.

Joe pointed the barrel of his gun. "Over there!"

On the south side of a squat shed was the missing truck, parked so that the back doors couldn't be opened.

Joe jumped into the cab and pushed in the clutch and the truck rolled clear. Pearly swung the doors open and was greeted by Hunker. "'Bout fucking time!"

Pearly quickly slammed the door shut. "Nothing back here!" he yelled to Joe.

Screaming, kicking, and thumping, the Bancocks and Charlie Piermount's boys sounded more than a little hysterical.

Pearly opened the door again. He flicked on the flashlight and aimed the beam into the truck. Joe saw naked bodies back-to-back, tied in twos, looking out at him. At the end of Pearly's jerking beam of light, the stark white bodies looked like ghosts of the damned.

Hunker was the only one who was tied front to back. Hunker's bare-assed victim was Billy Bancock. Joe and Pearly, happy to have found them but shocked at their grim images, simply began to laugh.

"Jesus H. Christ!" Pearly yelled. "What a sight for sore eyes."

"Where are your clothes?" Joe asked between roars.

"Kanky's idea of a fucking joke!" Hunker yelled.

"Untie us! This minute," cried Charlie Piermount.

"Yeah, hurry up," Billy Bancock said. "I've been feeling Hunker's cock between the crack of my ass…"

"No need to hurry," Hunker said, "I think I'm falling in love." Then he pecked Billy on the side of his head. "Besides, I gotta do somethin' with this woody…"

Charlie Piermount and his drivers looked terrified. They weren't amused by any of Hunker's joking. "I thought I was a dead man," Charlie said as Joe loosened the rope from his feet. Then, glancing over at Hunker, "I think you're a sick man, Hunker. May God bless you with whatever it is you need."

"Amen," added Charlie's driver, "that goes for me, double."

"Go fuck ya selves," Hunker scowled. "Ya yellow-bellied, striped-ass monkeys. 'Fraid of ya fucking shadows."

Joe yelled, "Knock it off, Hunker!"

Still laughing, Pearly whacked Hunker on his hairy shoulder and began to untie them. "Don't know how your Gertie puts up with you."

Billy Bancock jumped away while Hunker's substantial cock sprung into the air.

Charlie was rubbing his ankles. "Isn't anything sacred with you, Hunker?"

"Hey, is it my fault Billy's warm and soft? Give my woody some slack."

Billy grabbed his clothes and jumped naked from the truck.

When they were dressed, everyone started talking at once, and it got a bit friendlier.

"When we arrived," Charlie Piermount said, "Kanky and his go-rillas were hiding in the bushes. They took us by complete surprise. Shit, it was really easy for them. We weren't thinking about a hijack."

"Yeah," Hunker added, glancing at Pearly, "we walked right into it, too. We were surprised just like Charlie. We should've known."

"In the darkness, Kanky looked like Max a little," Billy said.

"Yeah," Bobby agreed. "Now that you mention it, he sure did.

The mustache, right?"

Joe shouted, "Shut the fuck up about Max and Kanky!"

The Bancocks pulled back; they instantly knew they had said the wrong thing.

Hunker said, "He had us undress so he could rub it in your nose, Joe. I tell ya, Kanky and his men are all batty. Ya remembers a guy they called Collector. He worked at Seaconnet Point for a while…he was kinda singing a song…something about Swamp Yankees…and how we're born…"

Charlie Piermount shouted, "Like hell…born…more like hatched!"

Pearly said, "I remember him…good-looking fella…"

Billy tied his boots. "Kanky's gotten worse since Max threw him out of Tiverton."

"Yeah, Kanky said next time he won't be so generous," Charlie added. "Whatever that means to you."

"He didn't hurt us," Bobby said, "cuz you weren't with us, Joe. He said he wants us to watch when he hurts you. Said you wouldn't sell out, so Kanky decided to just take it. Isn't that something?"

Hunker, buttoning up his shirt, shouted, "By the time I get done with him, and whoever he's working for, they'll wish they killed me. And I won't bother to undress him."

Joe looked at Pearly, who seemed preoccupied, and a little too quiet.

Hunker added loudly, "Kanky's inside ya head, Joseph…and big trouble's coming to him…to us…"

"Well, I hope I'm not around to see it," Charlie Piermount said. "This is going to make some story to tell."

"Did he fuck with the *Mallard*?" Pearly asked.

"Billy, go with Pearly and check out the *Mallard*. Be sure to check the engines, Pearly." Joe turned to Charlie. "Get your boys started on my boat."

"Okay, Joe. But I gotta tell you. This is my last transaction with you. Things are dangerous enough without having to put up with you and Kanky feuding. People are going to die."

Charlie Piermount's words hung in the night air. Hunker's voice broke the silence. "We're all gonna die, Charlie, sooner or later!"

Charlie directed the unloading of the *Black Duck*. In twenty minutes, the boat was empty and the taillights on Charlie's trucks disappeared into the darkness.

Pearly ran the engines on the *Mallard*. As far as he could tell, no damage had been done.

The cost of the evening suddenly sunk in. Losing over four hundred cases put a big hole in his cushion. Almost twenty-five thousand dollars' worth of liquor stolen, plus he lost a good customer in Charlie Piermount.

Joe walked to the stern of the *Black Duck* and fired into the water, again and again. The buckshot exploded fluorescent geysers of falling water into the air, like a miniature fireworks display. He didn't stop pumping until the gun was empty.

Hunker, Pearly, and the boys watched in silence. They knew big trouble was coming, and they were all wondering: How did Gatsby and Kanky know they were going to unload at Booker's Wharf?

CHAPTER TWENTY-SIX

JANIE WAS HUMMING "AMAZING GRACE" when she stepped out of the steaming tub. She relished her bath-time solitude. She paid slow and deliberate attention to drying herself. Behind her, the drain sucked her bathwater away.

She cracked the window, then wiped the moisture off the wood-framed mirror hanging from a nail above the sink, fanned her towel to move the dewy air. She positioned herself to see her profile in the mirror. Standing back slightly, she studied her shoulders, neck, and breasts. She said, "They ain't fried eggs yet, Mama."

"Won't be long before those perky little things are flat as fried eggs," Jessica Jackson once told her. "It's just a matter of time. So, think about it. Prepare for the future. Both of you young things."

Jessica's remark disturbed Janie. Maggie's mother never corked her opinions, good or bad. They were usually something to ponder. She smiled into the mirror and said aloud, "You got great legs and Joe likes that. You got nice hips, good makings for babies, but like Mama said, I'm gonna get wide in the beam before I know it. I ain't so bad, Joey," she said even louder. She wondered why she said *Joey*.

She wiped off the mirror again, and for a long moment, she stared at her reflection. Her eyes looked devilish. She opened her mouth into a big O, making herself laugh. From her bathrobe pocket, she removed her mother's lucky silver dollar and placed it near her mouth for comparison. It was a stretch. She wondered if Maggie was just exaggerating.

She wrapped herself in her mother's worn flannel bathrobe and headed through the kitchen on her way upstairs. Pearly was sipping coffee, a bottle of King William on the kitchen table. The small door to the "hideout" beneath the stairs was open. The strongbox was on the floor next to his boots. She glanced at the box, the whiskey, then his face. "What's wrong?"

Pearly took another sip of coffee. "A really bad night, sweet thing…"

Janie wrapped her hair in a towel and sat down. She couldn't remember her father ever complaining about a bad night.

"You want some bacon and eggs?"

"Make it six," he said, "I'm hungry."

She sat there, waiting on more to unfold. She thought his voice sounded a little shaky.

"When Hunker landed at Booker's Wharf ahead of us, he got hijacked by Kanky and his mugs." He poured more whiskey into his coffee.

"Hijacked?"

"They stole our booze, 'bout twenty-five thousand dollars' worth."

"My God! How could Hunker let them do that? I mean, how did they manage to do it?"

"Took him by surprise. First time we've ever had this kind of problem."

Janie's hand went to her mouth. "Oh, Daddy! You could've been hurt, or worse!"

He shook his head, but he still appreciated her worry. He knew it made her feel better. "It's one thing to get shot at and outrun the law," he said, "but it's another thing to be hijacked by the likes of Kanky the Portagee."

"My God…Kanky… I remember him well…not a nice fella!"

She just stared at her father, an incredulous look on her face.

"Well, me and the boys figure Kanky can read Joe's mind," he said. "I really think he's capable of doing that."

Janie said, "When he worked for Max Bucolo, I remember Kanky being nothing but a huffing and puffing, disgusting man. He always undressed women with his eyes…and then he fucked them with his eyes." Immediately, she wished she hadn't said it that way.

However, Pearly didn't blink. Is he totally drunk? she wondered, tears building.

Pearly unlatched the money box and slowly opened the cover. All that green. He motioned to Janie, who came over to look in the box. "Still ain't enough in there. We gotta get it chock-filled, like a barrel full of herring, so we can't get the cover on. I gotta take care of us, sweet thing."

She dropped her mother's lucky dollar into the box. "You always have, Daddy." Janie's voice was clear and true. "You always have."

Pearly's eyes moistened. "Maybe, maybe not. But I still want this box full before…" He closed the cover. "Joe's gotta be careful, or we could be having serious trouble with Kanky. Another thing, we found out the name of the guy Kanky's working for. He's someone big, from Chicago…wants Joe's operation…"

"Chicago…he sounds very…very dangerous. What's his name?"

"Jay Gatsby…owns a speakeasy in Oakland Beach…also a warehouse in New Bedford. Two rum boats as well."

Janie's expression deepened as though she were thinking on something.

Pearly caught her look. "What's on ya mind?"

"Sounds quite serious, Daddy."

"Like I said, could be big trouble." Pearly nodded slowly. He had a disturbed expression on his face.

The sight of the bankroll and the idea of losing it filled her mind. "Well, someone had better cork Kanky's hole and his boss's hole, or nothing's gonna be safe around here."

Pearly's eyes twinkled. "I'm afraid they're going to be spoilers. Kanky is also getting revenge on Joe because of Max." He got up from the table slowly, bones cracking, and returned the strongbox to its hideout.

"I'm getting old," he said.

She laid the bacon into the hot pan, sliced the bread, and began cracking the eggs. "Another thing, Daddy, we can't have the law shooting at you." Her voice broke, sort of into a mousy squeak. "Why, I can't stand it!"

He said, "You're the image of your mother when we got married."

Later, he picked up an egg whole with his fork and slipped it into his mouth. He chewed. "I miss my Rosemary every day. Every time I reach for that screen door, I pretend she's standing at the stove, stirring the fish chowder."

"That's strange to hear, Daddy. All I ever remember is you and Mama fighting over the fishing business. Never enough money, never enough time to fix anything around the house. God, all you ever did was fight."

"That wasn't fighting, that was love in disagreements."

"Call it what you will. I'll never marry a fisherman."

Pearly's little grin irritated her. She shook her head and started back for the stairs but stopped again. Her posture stiffened and her expression seemed guarded.

"I've said it before, Daddy, but in a very short time, rum-running has become very dangerous. I wish you'd give it up."

Pearly said, "I hope I never have to give it up."

"I hope you don't mean that, Daddy." She bolted up the stairs.

Behind her, Pearly's head shook and his eyes rolled up at the ceiling. "She's just like you, Rosemary."

~~~~~~

Twenty minutes later, dressed for church, Janie Thurston cried, tears flowing like the outgoing tide. Sadness was jammed into every corner of her heart. In the kitchen, she stared at her father, wondering why she even bothered going to church, but today, there was a good enough reason. Things might be looking up in her life, but not her father's.

"Say a little prayer for your old man."

She hesitated, trying to detect sarcasm, but hearing none, said, "I always do," and gave the screen door a shove.

Chapter Twenty-Seven

BEFORE MOST OF TIVERTON got ready for the day, Minister Isaac Bottomley had already sketched out his Sunday sermon. Again, he would ponder the outrageous vices of liquor. Yesterday's telephone call from Francis Grover helped underscore the direction of Bottomley's sermon with an even sharper vengeance.

Bottomley wasn't exactly pleased to hear from Francis Grover, attempting to dictate the subject of his pontifications: the evils of drink and the ways of Prohibition. And while he was at it, he should remember that Grover's son, Tiverton's esteemed police chief, was protecting all the good people of this seaside community. Bottomley just let Francis babble on.

At eleven o'clock, Bottomley looked through a dime-sized hole in the back wall and surveyed his flock. He quickly spotted Gertrude Moore sitting blissfully in her customary pew. Bottomley rubbed his crotch and considered their last visit. Henry Grover escorted Janie Thurston down the aisle. What a confluence of family trees that union would graft. He knew Janie Thurston worked for Francis Grover, something he always thought odd. The elder Grover explained it as an act of charity, if you will. Such self-serving attributions from Francis Grover always had a way of reminding him what side his bread was buttered on, and by whom. Bottomley hated Francis Grover—the self-righteous son of a bitch.

Slicking his thinning hair, he adjusted his black smock. He removed a silver flask from the back of his sideboard, took a quick slug, smacked his lips.

From the very beginning of Prohibition, he quickly learned that nothing generated a larger Sunday collection from the Tiverton "drys" than his fiery outbursts against the demon rum. He fully anticipated that any late rum-running news would help add to his collection plate.

He pondered behind the curtain a moment, took a deep breath, and walked to the pulpit. The congregation stood.

"Good morning, my dear friends."

They responded, "Good morning, Minister Bottomley."

He opened his Bible and the congregation sat down.

He nodded first at Francis Grover and his wife, sitting proud and erect in their reserved front-row pews. Like always, Grover's wife sat silently, staring straight ahead. To their right sat Henry Grover and Janie Thurston.

In the second row, closest to the pulpit, perched Gertrude, always reflective and ample of bosom. Bottomley struggled not to picture the grotesque face of Gertrude's conjugal mismatch. Even in the abstract, however, Hunker's very existence fortified his unquestioned belief that God indeed works in very unfathomable ways. The man was a great source of vodka, certainly heaven sent.

Bottomley also thought about Gertrude's chicken or meat pies and the chocolate cake she often brought him. Today, he hoped that it was chicken. And maybe he could persuade her to drop to her knees again. He loved watching her bobbing head and running his hand through her wonderful curly hair, speckled with gray. He found himself getting an erection…saved by the pulpit once again.

This pause, this survey of his flock's faces, this delicious moment of near exasperating expectation, was his very own signature.

Bottomley's eyes flickered over the rest of his audience, searching for his quarry. Would Jessica Jackson publicly repent? Would she be wearing a hat?

As of yet, he couldn't find her.

Slightly frustrated, he thought of a poem he had written as a young man—before discovering the pulpit.

He momentarily closed his eyes as though beseeching a higher purpose, while his own verses raced silently through his head:

What am I?
A bad bargain? Someone's guardian?
Always a sinner, never a winner!
Brother to the apes! You can't escape!
A hunk of meat! Always in heat!
We're all the same. Only with a different name.

Reciting that poem at a moment like this was like sipping good bourbon—it warmed his insides, and it actually helped him to cope. Rhyming "meat" with "heat" took balls.

How would his congregation respond if he recited this pastoral epic instead of his sermon?

These thoughts amused him. Then again, maybe someday he'd ask Gertrude or Jessica to spread their legs, and he'd even read his poem to them.

He looked down at his Bible. Written on a sheet of paper, in thick pencil and in proper order, were the key phrases to his sermon. He began: "Dear brethren and sisters, again our town is plagued by these demon rum-runners. The fires of hell hover over this river of sin…" He slammed the dais and looked up at the ceiling. "Smite down these purveyors of sinful liquor—these sons of Satan…"

"Amen!" someone shouted, followed by more Amens.

Bottomley paused for a long moment. His eyes roamed the room. He knew how to use the dramatics of his sermon.

"When vile liquor acts as a means to escape the God-given responsibilities of adulthood and of this beautiful Christian life… I say it is a grave, grave sin…"

As Minister Bottomley's proclamations were bringing another Sunday morning among the good folk of Tiverton to a head, Jessica Jackson entered the church. No hat. That mound of unnaturally wild red hair was impossible to ignore. She had so much of it and, for the minister, it began to evoke more immediate images than the flames of hell.

Bottomley swallowed hard, not believing his eyes, or this feeling of invading lust, or, for that matter, the resurrection of his flagging erection. It's true, he mused, for corn to grow, you must first plant the seeds.

The entire congregation seemed to stop breathing as Jessica sashayed down the aisle. If he, on the pulpit, could smell her perfume, who among them could not? Bottomley knew that some in these pews might fear the building would collapse. A very good chance that could happen, but not necessarily from Jessica Jackson's presence.

Brassy Jessica Jackson made Francis Grover move over so she could sit down. It appeared to the minister that Jessica Jackson knew exactly what she was doing. He watched Grover's pale cheeks turn to the color of ripe cherries. Mrs. Grover, who hadn't been right in the head for quite a while, didn't even know that Jessica was present. How fortunate. *What in heaven's name is going on?* he wondered. *My Lord, how exciting.* He knew now it would be a much longer sermon than usual.

The minister again paused until the waters calmed before him. He waited perhaps longer than he should have, but he was too drunk on the bounty of the moment to proceed with any dispatch. How did Jessica have the nerve to sit next to Francis Grover? Why wasn't she afraid of the scoundrel? Why did Francis Grover seem so nervous? Why? All of these thoughts funneled inspiration from the tip of Bottomley's toes to the roof of his salivating mouth.

Could the immaculate Francis Grover be poking the whore? Mrs. Francis Grover, with perfect decorum, sat with hands in her lap, awaiting Bottomley's next words. Or was she simply falling asleep?

Bottomley's eyes locked onto Janie Thurston, who seemed to be staring him down—almost reading his mind. Janie Thurston made him nervous. She's a tester of men, he thought. For years she sat in the obscure middle of the congregation, but today, at Henry Grover's side, she was front and center. She presented some gnawing threat.

He cleared his throat again. "Before we depart, I must again mention that this building, our church, is becoming very worrisome. During our most recent storm, it trembled and shook so profoundly that I found it impossible to sleep…" He slowly looked out over the congregation, then at Francis Grover, who was glancing around at the structure. "We have discussed forming a building committee who will help us determine how badly this house of God needs attention. We once also discussed the costs and feasibility of either building a new structure or purchasing another existing building. So, we are making progress. I request you visit among yourselves and volunteer to participate in this worthy cause, if the Lord moves you to do so."

He then signaled Arnold Wordell to make the collection.

Bottomley was pleased at the nodding heads among the congregation. Still, he wondered if these cheap Tivertonians who lived on the Heights would really open their knotted pocketbooks.

Bottomley glanced again at Janie Thurston. Her eyes were angrier than before, still latched tightly on his. Take that, you perky little thing, daughter of a sinner. You sit in the front row; you catch my heat of judgment.

Henry Grover seemed oblivious to Janie's discontent. The Grover clan had truly enjoyed his diatribe. It mellowed happily within Bottomley's gassy insides.

"Remember to pray for the success of our brave law enforcement officers whose sacred mission is to save us from the scourge of our age…"

Henry Grover smiled on that one.

Francis Grover began to nod his head. Gradually, it created a chain reaction, and it wasn't long before the entire flock, with the duly noted exceptions of Janie Thurston and Jessica Jackson, followed Francis Grover's lead.

Bottomley continued his golden opportunity; he jabbed his hand towards the ceiling and his voice strengthened. "These murdering, poisoning, money-grubbing rum-runners are rending God's laws asunder."

The outburst from the congregation, "Amen, amen!" filled the hall. Gertrude Moore's high-pitched "AMEN" drowned out all the others. Bottomley smiled, just as Francis Grover smiled.

Janie Thurston turned angrily to Henry Grover, whose lips turned upside down at Janie's reaction.

Bottomley swept his hand grandly in the direction of organist Lucinda Parks. She flexed her fingers, cracked her knuckles, and began to play.

Bottomley led them in dreamy prayer. All heads were bowed except his and those of Janie and Jessica Jackson, whose eyes were now engaged with his in mortal combat.

CHAPTER TWENTY-EIGHT

WHILE MINISTER BOTTOMLEY warned his flock on the evils of rum-running, Gatsby and the men inside his warehouse finished separating Joe's hijacked liquor into various lots for delivery. The former owner had thought of everything. The one-time mill lay in a remote section of south New Bedford, its massive size allowing trucks to enter into the building and remain hidden from view. Herman the German had installed heavy metal doors, so if the law or other hijackers had a mind to raid the warehouse, they'd have to blow the doors off the hinges.

There also was an escape tunnel that led away from the mill, exiting into the basement of the three-decker house Gatsby had bought for his crews. He also had a ship's radio room installed (at some expense) in the attic of the warehouse. It was a Navy-styled, one-kilowatt spark-gap transmitter. He had, like Joe Bucolo, established his own secret code for contacting the offshore mother ships on Rum Row.

The entire liquor load would be distributed in the next few days. Gatsby jotted down everything in a brown leather-bound notebook. He had made it very clear to Kanky and the crews that not one bottle was to disappear in any of the transactions with buyers.

~~~~~~

Later, in the early morning hours, propped up in bed by pillows, Gatsby, wearing wire-rimmed glasses, worked on figures from that same brown notebook. With the successful hijacking, he calculated that he had put a serious dent in Bucolo's working capital…which did raise another question: How much pain could Bucolo withstand?

It was too late now to turn back. He knew he had to continue his offensive. Within a few days or so, he would be running *Diamond Daisy* to Rum Row. He had plenty of buyers for his liquor, and he had made contact with a number of Canadian rummies who were ready to supply him. Of course, some of the offshore boats sold to Joe Bucolo, and he knew that would quickly bring things to a boiling point. He was feeling very confident on how things were proceeding. And he knew then and there that Bucolo and he would soon meet face to face.

In the back of his mind, he worried a little about Kanky getting out of control. If need be, he would put Kanky in his place, here or in the hereafter. Kanky reminded Gatsby of a captain he had in the Army, a brute who always wanted to be the star of the party or the master of conversation. Yet he knew that often it was brutes who got the tough things done. But that wasn't the game he wanted to play. He had witnessed some of that back in Chicago.

He recalled listening earlier to Kanky and his men joking and laughing at what they had done to that Swamp Yankee Hunker Moore and the others at Booker's Wharf. They all agreed that those naked bodies wouldn't soon forget it. He smiled at the images in his mind, and easily recalled some of Collector's ditty on Hunker. What a different world he was living in now.

Chuckling, Gatsby removed his glasses and placed them, with the notebook, on his night table. On the opposite wall from his bed, he stared at a photo of the yacht *Tuolomee,* with owner and captain Dan Cody standing by the helm. The photo couldn't hide Cody's pallid features. His stern, lifeless face always seemed to improve when he was drunk. Cody's appearance reminded Gatsby of his grandfather on his deathbed somehow. These two men had, in so many ways, changed his life. Gatsby nodded, subconsciously affirming this knowledge.

He remembered how, on one California afternoon, wearing beat-up clothes, he had been beachcombing—when suddenly, on the horizon, he saw what looked like a dark-line storm approaching. He could see no one on the deck of a yacht anchored just offshore. It was in a precarious situation; if the boat dragged anchor, it could be wrecked on the rocks. He flipped over a small punt and, with a piece of driftwood, paddled out to the *Tuolomee*. He made fast to the stern and called out. Dan Cody was fast asleep when he heard the warning cries.

By the time Gatsby left the yacht five years later, he had seen the world—all thanks to the generosity of Dan Cody, who proclaimed that young Gatsby had saved his yacht by helping him sail *Tuolomee* to another sheltered cove. Cody also told friends it was quite possible that Gatsby had saved his life.

Without doubt, Gatsby felt his encounter with Dan Cody had to be preordained. Over those few years, his mentoring and deck-handing existence on Cody's yacht was the commencement of all that was about to take place: Gatsby's frequent visits to the Barbary Coast and foreign ports were indeed lessons in survival and prosperity, and what Cody termed life's two-headed serpent. Gatsby learned about the power of money, about men, about the sea, expensive dentists, and most of all, about sex and women, especially with a woman who wasn't afraid of letting loose.

He nodded slightly, reminiscing at the teachings of that old Indian man and the *Kama Sutra*, named for the god of erotic love. Gatsby discovered first-hand that incredible work, which translated into "desire, pleasure, love, and ultimate sex." In this new knowledge, what intrigued him the most was that women were carnally equal, just as sexual as men. The *Kama Sutra* taught how the two sexes were physically designed to provide one another with mind-altering pleasure in the form of lovemaking.

Gatsby never forgot the old man's words: *I will sell you my daughter for a week, and you will learn everything you need to know on how to love a woman that most men do not know, will ever know, or even understand.* At the time, Gatsby couldn't afford it, so Dan Cody paid for those lessons of a lifetime.

Briefly, an image of the old man's daughter circled in his head, but he quickly turned it towards Janie Thurston: how she was so different from many of the other women he had met, and occasionally bedded. Deep down he knew he had to keep it strictly business with Janie. No one could replace Daisy Faye Buchanan—the only woman he ever wanted.

CHAPTER TWENTY-NINE

THE FOLLOWING MORNING, Moran watched Gatsby make his breakfast. It titillated him slightly, as he was only used to seeing people wait on Gatsby for everything.

"Paul, are you sure you don't want something to eat?"

"No, I've already had breakfast. Thanks anyway."

"So, what brings you here so early in the day?"

"I actually debated on whether I should tell you this or not."

Gatsby picked up an egg.

"I'm pretty sure I can handle it, Paul." Oddly, after he said it, he wondered if he could.

"Daisy Buchanan wants to meet with you. She is out East in New York. I guess the letter you had me send to her parents' home in Louisville finally caught up with her."

For a moment, clearly shocked at Paul's words, Gatsby froze.

He broke the two yokes and flipped the eggs over, then turned to Moran. "Do you know what she wants?" The tone of his voice turned weaker. "Do you know what she wants?"

Gatsby placed the eggs between two heavily-buttered slices of toast and sat down. He took a crunchy bite. Chewing, he said, "The timing is off. This is not how I planned it."

"Look, I can tell Daisy you're out of the country, I can't reach you..."

Gatsby sipped at his coffee cup. "You know what, set a meeting up at Frankie's this week with Daisy."

"I'll take care of it. What about the Thurston girl?"

"Yeah, I guess I need to meet with her...set up a dinner."

For a long moment, Gatsby appeared to be someplace else. Finally, he said, "I need to see what I can learn from Janie."

"You'll win her over, Jay. I'm sure of it."

"I'm not trying to win her over. I want to know what makes Bucolo tick."

A look of anger began to seep into his face. He quickly checked it. "One thing is certain: I have to beat-out Joe Bucolo, one way or another, if my goal for Daisy is to succeed."

~~~~~~

That afternoon, before leaving to meet the boys at the wharf, Joe went into Max's bedroom and, from his bookcase, removed fourteen leather-bound fishing logs containing more than thirty years of Max's fishing records.

He sat on the edge of the bed and opened the oldest, dating back to 1888. He reveled in Max's precise, clean handwriting. Each entry was dated and included notes and amounts on what had been caught—fish or shellfish—and where it had been caught, the prices paid, and of course weather conditions, the tides, wind, even the phases of the moon.

As a boy, Joe marveled how well Max could read the weather. Out of the blue, Max would grab Joe's head and point it down into the bloated trawl net. "See the herring, Joe? Spring's here in four days. See the bluefish, Joe? Summer's already here. See those roe-filled flounders...those hungry codfish, Joe? Winter's three weeks away."

Often, when Joe and Max would gut codfish, there were stones in their stomachs. The old fisherman would get serious and say, "Big storm coming, Joe. Those fish are swallowing stones, giving themselves ballast." At first Joe would smile and nod, but when his predictions always came true, Joe began to understand that Max was connected to nature in a special way. Reading the weather was as natural to Max as feeling hungry. How leaves curled, their premature coloring, the shades of the sea, the river, even the way the waves rolled and heaved up on the beach—it all meant something to Max. He showed Joe how to study the skies for those fast-moving scuds, the flowing cumulus clouds, or the unmistakable mackerel sky.

It tickled Joe how Max made a point of matching his predictions against the *Old Farmer's Almanac*. On most occasions, he outdid them. When he was particularly happy with a forecast, he would ink in a fish on that matching log's entry, much like Nantucket whalers did when they had successfully harpooned a whale.

By the time Joe had perused through 1918, he found what he was looking for. There was an eighty percent chance of a wild nor'easter in May, same as in June, especially when preceded by a very wet and stormy fall season. More so if, before winter, wild squirrels went crazy storing chestnuts in the hollows of trees, some even burying them.

~~~~~

When Joe arrived at the clubhouse, Pearly was alone. He had fired up the stove and put on a pot of coffee. He looked up from the *Providence Journal* when Joe entered.

"Did you get in touch with everyone?" Joe asked.

"Everyone except Billy. He didn't answer his phone."

"Did you tell Janie about the hijacking?"

"Can't hide anything from her. She reads me like the Bible she brings to church."

Joe hesitated for a moment, then smiled. "How's she doing?"

Pearly's eyebrow arched slightly. "She's still very excited about that proposal she made to Francis Grover."

Joe appeared nonplussed by the news. "Not only beautiful, but smart. A rare thing nowadays. A good cook, too."

Pearly gave him a questioning look. He mumbled, "A good cook, too?" Pearly fired back, "Janie still seems excited about this Grover project with that investor."

"Really?" Joe turned away slightly. He didn't see Pearly still eyeing him. "What's this investor's name?"

"Not sure, but I sense something. I'm thinking there's a change in the wind with my daughter."

Joe just tossed him a silent look.

Just then, the boys walked in—everyone but Billy Bancock. They engaged in some small talk and made themselves coffees.

Joe slowly looked around at his men. "I don't intend to let Gatsby shut us down. I've decided we have to respond to the hijacking. I figure we're gonna have to play hard...maybe sink his rum boats. But it's more than just my decision. No Rhode Island fisherman worth his salt likes the idea of sinking any boat for any reason. So, I want to open this up to discussion." The formality of his statement bristled Joe's neck and it seemed to tighten his throat. He sat down to listen to the others talk.

Pearly was genuinely enthusiastic. He nodded his head, acting like a proud father who had just seen his offspring do something extraordinary.

Sammy, on the other hand, remained quiet.

Hunker asked, "When we gonna do it?"

"First night we have some good fog cover," Joe answered.

Hunker stomped his feet. "Now ya talking, Joseph."

"I think we should sink only one boat," Pearly added. "One boat is certainly worth more than the liquor he hijacked. I don't think we want to escalate this too much. Do you know what I'm saying?"

"First mistake!" Hunker snapped. "You gotta hit him hard. Give him something to really think about." He glanced around at the men. "You boys will never understand it, but that's what this is about. This isn't just vengeance. This is about fear!"

Joe's eyes drilled into Hunker's face. "Just one boat, and that's the end of that, okay?"

Hunker danced a little jig, lifted his leg, and farted. "That's for Gatsby and Kanky."

Joe grabbed his jacket and walked to the door. He stopped. "Nobody talks about this. I'll see you boys later."

"Where ya going?" Pearly asked.

Joe didn't answer and left.

"What's wrong with him?" Bobby Bancock asked.

Hunker ignited a match on the potbelly, bringing it up to his stogie. "Can't ya tell? He figures Max wouldn't approve of sinking anyone's boat."

Pearly stared at Hunker's flaming match, listening to him suck his stogie. "If Joe's not careful…" He let his words fade away.

Hunker finished Pearly's sentence. "Maybe Joe's balls will be hanging from Gatsby's chandelier."

Finally, Sammy broke his silence. "You boys are a bunch of striped-assed monkeys if you think sinking Kanky's boat is gonna solve any problems. Jesus H. Christ! You should be talking sense to Joe, not some sort of gypsy revenge. Only gonna bring more trouble. Mark my words…you hear?"

Pearly couldn't deny the hint of truth in what Sammy said.

Hunker added, "I'd rather be a striped-ass monkey than let those no-good fucks get away with what they did."

"Hunker," Sammy snapped, "you *are* a striped-ass monkey!"

"Damn good thing ya my friend, Sammy, damn good thing."

~~~~~~

Maggie had just finished giving Billy what he loved most, but he didn't seem to enjoy it as much tonight. Since she arrived at his cottage, he was acting different. She quickly figured that there had to be something on his mind. And it couldn't be good. "I'm waiting, Billy. What's going on?"

"I'm scared! Things are a mess. Somebody is a step ahead of us now. The Coast Guard is shooting cannons at us, the Booker's Wharf hijacking, what they did to us in that truck, and Joe lost around twenty-five thousand dollars' worth of booze..."

Maggie looked at Billy with a guilty expression. Billy caught the change in Maggie's demeanor and for a moment he seemed to think on something. He leaned into her. "You're not telling anybody what we talk about, Maggie."

She didn't respond.

"Maggie, tell me you're not."

Suddenly, from the darkened doorway, Joe's voice struck Maggie and Billy like daggers to their chests. "Yes, Maggie, why don't you tell Billy what you've been up to."

"Oh my God!" they both said together. Billy cried out: "JOE! JOE! I—"

Joe moved slowly into the room. Billy sat on the edge of the bed and yanked up his pants, opposite from where Joe stood in the doorway.

Maggie said, "I'm sorry, Joe. I'm really sorry!"

Billy quickly followed Maggie's plea. "I screwed up, Joe. I wanted Maggie so much; I couldn't think straight."

"I can understand that, Billy, the Jackson women are hard to resist." Joe's voice was calm and even. There appeared to be no real anger in his tone. "Maggie has great abilities..."

Billy's head jerked to Maggie. "You said you never did that to him!"

Maggie whispered, "Shut up, Billy. This is giving me a serious condition of swamp ass."

In the dim light, Joe half-smiled. "You and asses, Maggie."

Billy piped in, "You're right about that, Joe..."

To their surprise and shock, Joe pulled up a chair and moved it closer to the bed. He sat down and looked at the two of them; they were quite a pair. Poor Billy, he let himself be led by his cock, which

Joe surely knew was bigger than his brain. And how could he really be upset with Maggie? While Maggie was smart and possessed a brain, she was never confident enough to use it wisely. Joe's guilt from their complicated relationship had softened him and melted his anger towards Maggie's betrayal. "Relax, both of you."

"Thank you, Joey."

Billy followed. "Thank you, Joe."

Maggie continued, "I didn't want to do it, but there's something serious they're holding over me."

"What is it, Maggie?"

"I can't tell you, but I really regret what I have done."

Joe said, "Well, Maggie, now you're gonna work for me... And Billy, you and I will have a talk. We both know that we can't let the boys know about this. They'll want to use Maggie for lobster bait." His eyes moved from one to the other. Satisfied they were appropriately contrite, he nodded.

"Thank you, Joe, thank you," they said together.

Maggie said, "I promise I'll make it up to you, Joe."

"I know you will."

Chapter Thirty

IT WAS GETTING DARK when Joe pulled into the parking area of the White Horse Inn. He recalled the Seaconnet Grange was holding its annual directors' meeting. He walked around to the side door and started up the back staircase just as Pat Morris was coming down.

"Who's upstairs?"

"Couple of new swell-looking heads," Pat said. He tapped the handrail. "I'll see you later. I've got to check on my tea party."

"Say, did you ask Janie Thurston?"

"Janie said she had to attend the Grange shindig. She's with our esteemed police chief." Pat Morris winked. "She said: Tell Joe to ask me again."

Joe nodded and cocked his thumb at Pat, who returned the gesture.

A round of applause from the Grange meeting grew and subsided. "Talk to you later, Joe."

On the third floor, at the end of the east hall, Joe headed towards the muffled voices and the laughter of a private party. There was something admirable about having the two extremes of Prohibition under one roof, and he thought Pat should be congratulated.

He knocked and Tommy Walsh opened the door. He had his arm around the waist of a young girl with frizzy hair and bright-red lips. "Joe! Come in, come in."

The room was filled with smoke and about twenty people. Joe recognized a couple of faces. Seemed most of the people were from Fall River and New Bedford.

"Hey, everybody," Tommy whispered loudly and the room quieted down. "I want you to meet someone." Tommy put his arm around Joe's shoulders. Everyone turned to the two men. Tommy raised his glass. "This is Joe Bucolo, a very good friend of mine. He's the best fisherman on Narragansett Bay…"

There was a mumble of greetings and salutes as Tommy led Joe over to a makeshift bar.

"Wow," Joe said softly, "liquor right off the boat."

Tommy chuckled and mixed him a drink. "I guess you know what's doing downstairs."

Joe nodded. "Yeah, most of Tiverton's esteemed, except maybe for Janie Thurston."

Tommy said, "Hard to tell how long that's gonna last…before Janie catches their Bible-banging fever."

Joe said, "That would be too bad, wouldn't it? But with Pearly's blood running up and down those long legs, it'll be a while before the bluenoses catch her."

Tommy chuckled. "Nicely put." He led Joe aside. "Say, there's a girl here I want you to meet, Heinrich Schmitz's daughter. She's a real looker. In fact, she said she wants to meet you!"

Joe sipped his drink and said, "I'm always interested to meet friends of yours, Tommy."

Tommy guided Joe over to a sofa where the two women were seated.

Nina Schmitz stood up and smiled. She was wearing a white blouse with a blue pleated skirt that quivered every time she moved. Joe's eyes found real pleasure in her yellow hair, ruby lips, and blue eyes.

"Nina," Tommy said, "I want you to meet my friend Joe Bucolo. Joe, this is Nina Schmitz."

She held out her hand to shake. Joe took it and felt a circular motion of Nina's finger in his palm. He said, "What was that?"

"An offering." She continued to do it.

Joe glanced again at their hands. "Well, I like it, I guess."

The frizzy-haired girl reclaimed Tommy's arm. "We'll be back later," Tommy said. "You two get acquainted."

Smiling, Nina added, "So, Bucolo, have you thought about me?"

"Frankly, I have."

"I knew you would." She looked around. "This place is a joke. You come here often?"

Joe wondered if anyone had heard her. "You don't like it here? What's your pleasure?"

She ignored him.

He lit a cigarette. "How's your father?"

She said, "Oh, my father's very well, thank you, very nice of you to ask."

"What can I get you to drink?"

"Whiskey and water, heavy on the water; I hate feeling drunk."

When he returned with her drink, she said, "My girlfriend is in love with Tommy Walsh."

"Jesus," Joe said, "he's married with seven kids."

"I know. Doesn't it rip your heart apart?"

Joe added, "Mrs. Walsh is a nice lady."

Nina smiled again, sipping her drink, and moved closer. "Nice to see a man with principles." She touched his arm and gave him a quick kiss.

She then ambled over to the windows and looked out over the basin and the Seaconnet River. Joe followed and moved up tight behind her.

Without turning, she said, "I used to love it over here when I was a kid. Tiverton and Little Compton were fun to visit. We had no money during the war. No one would hire Pappy. We'd come over here in my uncle's truck on weekends and pick potatoes to earn a little money. I hate being poor."

She turned around and Joe studied her eyes, her lips, the way she could be shocking, vulnerable, and then seductive in a split moment; it clearly kept him on edge.

Pat Morris and two waitresses brought in a buffet and more people showed up.

"What do you say we leave?"

"Well," Nina said as she looked at the approaching luncheon, "I'm really hungry."

They made sandwiches and filled a bag with assorted fruit. Joe grabbed a bottle of whiskey and, without saying goodbye, they left. In the hallway below, people were leaving the Grange meeting.

"Let's go out the back."

Nina jerked his arm. "Nobody sneaks me out the back door."

"I'm not sneaking," Joe said.

"Well, then…?"

Descending the stairs, Joe saw Henry Grover, in a shirt and tie, escorting Janie.

Grover glanced up and deliberately stopped walking towards the door. "Well, well," he said to Janie loudly. "Look who's here."

"Pretend you're the Queen of England, cuz you look it," Joe mumbled. "This guy's an asshole."

Janie's eyes brightened when she spotted Joe and Nina. She smiled and acted like Joseph Bucolo was some long-lost friend. "Hello, Joe. How are you?" Janie even smooched kisses towards him, and then gave him a very intense gaze, which caught Nina's eye.

Slightly tilted by her look, Joe played along. "It's been a long time, Janie. I'd like you to meet my friend Nina."

Janie gave Nina a quick once-over. Joe marveled how girls did that. He was glad Nina looked so dressed up, as Janie absorbed everything about her.

Nina said, "Pleased to meet you, I'm sure."

Henry Grover started to pull Janie away, but she resisted.

Nina asked, rather loudly, "So, Janie, who's your lover?"

Janie's mouth hung open and her eyes dropped downward. A few who couldn't help but overhear the question turned to stare at Nina.

It may have been Nina's short-clipped blonde hair and white-and-blue outfit or that she looked like Lillian Gish. Maybe it was her romantic accent, not German or French, but certainly European, different enough to catch the ear of every man and woman in the hallway. The corridor fell silent.

"I asked who's—" Nina began again.

"The young lady heard what you said," Henry interrupted. "She does not intend to answer your vulgar—"

"This!" Janie raised her hand. "This is Henry Grover."

Nina nodded. "Pleased to meet you, I'm sure." Turning to Janie, and with a raised voice, she added, "He's a stiff one, isn't he?"

Joe laughed.

Nina took Joe's arm and they walked through the crowd down the hall. The Grange guests cleared a path to the door. Joe closed it behind them.

"That's the kind of exit I like to take," Nina confided out on the porch.

Joe whistled. "I don't think I've ever taken an exit like that."

Nina squeezed his arm. "Looks like it's gonna be a long night."

~~~~~~

When Janie got into the car, she was furious. Henry, however, stared straight ahead, hands tight on the steering wheel. "I wanted to remind you what Bucolo's really like. Did you see that harlot he was with?"

"Don't you ever do that to me again! You may be Tiverton's chief of police and Francis Grover's son, but I'm Janie Thurston. I don't need anyone to remind me of anything! And far from looking like a harlot, she was the most sophisticated woman I've ever seen in Tiverton. Who the hell do you think you are?"

"Please, your language." Henry started the engine.

"Furthermore, Joe Bucolo doesn't have to answer to anyone! And neither do I! Or for that matter, Henry, neither do you. Least of all to me." She folded her arms angrily.

Henry was having a difficult time hiding his anger. He said, almost at a whisper, "I was hoping someday you and I *could* answer to each other…and you wouldn't be answering to any other man." Henry's voice couldn't be any weaker.

Janie replied, "I don't answer to any man, Henry. And I never will. Besides, you're going about it the wrong way. That's your problem, you're too rigid. You take everything so damn serious. You remind me of your father. God, you're so alike."

"Really?"

She could see that he was genuinely surprised by her comparison. She added, "Do yourself a favor, Henry, relax. Life is not all black or white. People are people. You're not responsible for what people do."

Henry scowled…or was it a pout? "I'll try." He started the car and began to drive out of the parking lot. "I must learn to be patient when it comes to you. Thank you, Janie, for showing me my faults."

"You're welcome."

Henry said, "See that, our first fight and we've already solved it."

"Henry, that wasn't a fight!"

Chapter Thirty-One

AN HOUR OR SO LATER, back at her cottage along the Acushnet River, Nina changed her clothes. Removed her bra and promised Joe no *Nocnitsa* grease. She buttoned her paint-splattered work shirt and tied the tails in a knot, then stepped out of her skirt and hung it up carefully.

Joe quickly began to unbutton his shirt.

"Oh, don't rush me…later for making love." She took his hand and led him to the door. "I've never met a fisherman yet who wouldn't rather look at a boat first than make love." She pouted. "Oh, come, come now, I just want to show you something."

Joe sighed and followed her outside. She carried a lantern and followed the path ahead of him. Instead of turning to the boat shed, as he expected, she skipped straight to the water and out to a small pier. She hung the lantern on a piling and climbed down a ladder onto the forward deck of a little speedboat that looked, to Joe, about fourteen feet. Nina took the lantern and held it high.

"Well? Come on down."

He helped her unroll the canvas cover and they sat in the cushioned cockpit and admired the little inboard. Joe's eyes studied the small craft. He marveled at Heinrich's handiwork. Smooth as glass. The fastener holes were carefully bunged and sanded, and Joe could tell there were many layers of varnish protecting the Philippine mahogany. The brass work reflected the lantern's light. She had a sharp bow with a bronze angle iron that, looking down, seemed like a Roman spear. Joe figured she went like the devil.

He said, "This is a beautiful boat."

"Good. I was hoping you'd like it."

"What's her name?"

"*Wolf*," she said. "To ride the *Wolf* on the sea, with a lady of the night, for any man that will function right."

"Is that a poem?"

"No, it's a love book, fisherman. Let's go."

"Hey, what's with you?"

She was climbing back up the ladder. "What's with me? First you want to screw, now you want to talk poetry."

He grabbed her leg. "What's with you?"

The next thing he knew, she jumped. Joe caught her under the armpits. She felt weightless. Maybe a hundred pounds, he figured. He felt like she was floating.

"You're like a feather."

"What do you expect for five-foot-two, eyes of blue, could she, could she, could she screw?" She kissed him hard and dashed her tongue into his mouth like a lizard snacking on insects. In a matter of moments, they were naked, but she suggested and Joe agreed that a bed would be better. Both, carrying their clothes, scampered naked by the light of their lantern up the hill to her shack. Nina had a very pale glow to her skin Joe couldn't quite understand. Once in the house, they began an evening of lovemaking like none Joe had previously known.

In the middle of the night, Nina woke and whispered, not even sure if Joe was sleeping, "I hate your girlfriend."

He wasn't in the mood for chatting. "Who's that?" he asked, his eyes closed, thinking about Maggie and Billy and how he would use them against Gatsby.

Nina said, "Her legs are too long and her hair's too long and she's probably got her legs open right now for that fellow."

"What…who are you talking about?"

Nina pulled him over between her legs, without any resistance. "Your girlfriend, Bucolo. She's in love with you. You might be in love with her. Tell me you don't know that. And I'll call you a liar."

"I don't know what you are talking about."

Joe's thrusts were slow and deep.

"Hey, orphan!" That's when Nina bit his shoulder. "You were thinking about that girl?"

"You're crazy. That's Pearly's daughter. Concentrate on us."

"Slower, Bucolo. No, no, no, she's your girlfriend. Even now, when you're making it with me, she's on your mind. Slower…"

"Who?" he snapped.

She slapped his ass. "Hey, orphan, what's her name?"

"Don't call me orphan!"

"What's her name, Bucolo?"

"Who?"

"Plain Jane."

"Her name is Janie, not Jane. She's my friend's daughter."

"What's her last name?" Joe's thrusts turned faster and faster.

"Thurston! Can't you shut up?" He thought of Maggie and realized she was quiet compared to this German.

After a while, in rhythm with Joe, Nina yanked vigorously on the cheeks of his ass. Joe climaxed like water gushing down the rocks of Sin and Flesh Brook in a drenching gale. When it was over, he was one wasted fisherman, like Captain Durall rattling around in his baggy long johns. It ended with them lying face to face.

Nina whispered clipped German baby talk and kissed him like some little pouting fish in an aquarium, like a young child who wanted to smooch his mommy or daddy at a sunny, grassy picnic.

Joe just held onto her. He was getting a little cold, but he didn't mind at all, except that he kept thinking—she was really one crazy

German who continually confused him—a weird, wild force of nature all her own.

He remembered that Maggie often said the same thing about Janie and him. What did they know that he didn't? Or did he, and he didn't want to admit it?

Am I really that foggy, he wondered, when it comes to women? Way back, even Pearly uttered that to me. Why did he get this strange, protective feeling when Pearly told him about Janie going to lunch with this investor?

He whispered, "Please go to sleep, Nina... I'm tired..."

Nina didn't respond except for her peaceful, light snoring.

He wondered if it was possible to separate love from lust when it came to women. He noticed lately that when he was around Janie, she created a certain amount of chaos within him. Granted, he always noticed her body, and he pictured how they would look together, naked, making love. However, he admitted that there was something else going on, in addition to his strong lusty feelings towards her.

Didn't Janie invite me to lunch, then we went on to Frankie's speakeasy? Didn't we dance, didn't she tell me things that struck a chord? Didn't she say to Pat Morris, "Tell Joe to ask me again"? Not to mention the jealousy he felt when this investor took her to lunch. Who was this investor, anyway? And what about Henry, the asshole he is? Didn't it bother him, in an odd way, that Henry continued to chase Janie? And she let him? Could Nina and Maggie know something that he didn't?

He tried to sleep, but tonight, it didn't come easily—disturbed with images of them being together. Joe whispered, "Why am I so fucking foggy?"

Chapter Thirty-Two

NARRAGANSETT BAY WAS CALM and the night air was cold, adding to the potential for fog building. In the warm fo'c'sle of the *Black Duck*, Pearly poked the banked pea coal, reviving the sleeping embers. Up in the pilot house, Hunker wiped the sleeve of his red-and-black-checkered wool shirt across his lips, farted loudly, and bit into another fried chicken leg.

"Barnyard Hunker," Pearly yelled from down below.

Occasionally, lights from the surrounding shores were visible. They flickered like distant stars through the dark mist. When the *Black Duck* passed the Warwick Neck Beacon, it was after midnight.

Joe throttled down the engines. He flicked on the console light and unfolded the chart. With the flashing beacon on the starboard side, he plotted a compass course to Oakland Beach.

Pearly climbed up from the fo'c'sle. Hunker was still chewing on the chicken bone as he stared silently out the pilot house window. Pearly watched Joe's face closely, attempting to read any weakening of his commitment to the objective.

Hunker tossed the bone down into the fo'c'sle's garbage bin. He wiped his fingers on his pants and said, "Now I know why Sammy didn't come."

Pearly said, "Shit, Sammy's just getting old. You should've heard

him earlier. He started telling the Bancocks about a dead crow hanging from the bowsprit of a death dory. And right at the stroke of midnight, whistling—not talking, not asking—but whistling for the black
souls of the fishermen that sunk their boat. I'm telling you…" Pearly
gave out a rasping chuckle, "the Bancocks believe in that stuff."

"Fuck yes!" Hunker snapped. "Everybody believes in that stuff.
Still gives me the fucking creeps! Sammy was smart to stay home."

Joe glanced at both men. "Jesus Christ! We ain't gonna kill anyone! So stop with that bullshit! I don't like sinking a boat either."

"Damn right!" Hunker said.

"Can't argue that point," Pearly added.

"Are we there yet, Max?" Hunker asked. Pearly and Hunker
laughed and slapped at each other's heads.

"At this speed," Joe said, "about thirty-five-and-a-half minutes."

~~~~~~

It was the building, pale glow that signaled their arrival to Oakland
Beach. Joe slowed the engines and shifted them into neutral. The
Liberties changed cadence. Their muffled rumbles seemed too loud
for the quiet night. Joe shut them off and drifted for a few moments.
Shore lights from Water Street broke slowly through the fog, creating
an eerie atmosphere. Voices and occasional shouts of revelry carried
through the foggy night, sounding as though some drunken men with
babes were sitting on the foredeck.

On shore, to the left of the speakeasy, Gatsby's warehouse hovered
ghostly above the landing, absorbing the mist within its water-logged
timbers.

"We're here, alright," Hunker said. "Just listen to all that goddamn fun." He grabbed his eight-gauge goose gun.

"Put that down!" Joe snapped. "Drop the hook."

Hunker went astern and released a throw-away anchor attached
to a short line. With no wind and not much tide, it didn't take much
to bite the muddy bottom.

Pearly lowered a small skiff into the water. Joe and Hunker got in. "We won't need that," Joe said.

Hunker still had his goose gun slung over his shoulder. "Ya never knows!"

"When the fuck will you ever listen?" Joe glanced at Pearly. "If anything goes wrong, you be ready to move."

"Don't worry 'bout me. You guys just do a good job."

Hunker handled the oars, dipping them quietly into the water. Earlier, he had wrapped the oarlocks with twine so there were no chafing sounds. He rowed for about five minutes before coming into the murky shadows of the buildings.

He stopped rowing and waited for Joe to find some bearings. A soft westerly breeze carried the musty odor of decaying wood. The headlamps of two cars washed across the skeletons of the waterfront pilings and then disappeared. They heard the slamming of car doors and the laughter of both men and women.

"Things sound awful strange in the fog," Hunker whispered. "Like graveyard voices from Hillside cemetery…"

"Shut up!"

Finally, after another car and more muffled chattering, Joe pointed. "Head that way."

Hunker rowed in the direction of Joe's outstretched arm, and within minutes they brushed up alongside the bow of a boat. Joe stared up at the name plate. The vessel's name was *Hobo*. Tied astern was the *Tramp*.

Silently, Joe tied onto a piling and climbed aboard the *Hobo*. He went to the pilot house and tried the door. It was locked. Then he went to the aft hatches that led to the engine room. As he turned, he bumped into Hunker standing behind him. "I told you to stay in the skiff."

"I go where Joseph goes. Besides, someone's gotta watch ya backside."

Joe knew it was no time to argue. They lifted the hatches and leaned them against the port-side gunnel. Joe flicked on Max's old nickel-plated flashlight, and then they climbed down a ladder to the engine room. The light's beam, somewhat weak, reflected off the entrails of a very messy engine room. The air was heavy with gasoline and stale whiskey. One thing was certain: Gatsby's engineer wasn't as fussy as Sammy. Hunker stood by the ladder while Joe crawled between the two large six-cylinder, Model F Sterling engines.

Joe swept the light around the hull. "There," he whispered. The two big brass sea valves were easy to reach, and from them, a two-inch rubber hose connected to each engine. Through those hoses, salt water circulated into the Sterling's cooling systems.

He handed Hunker the flashlight and took out his pocketknife, a gift from Max when Joe began fishing. In his heart, Joe knew that Max would not look kindly on scuttling a boat, except if it was absolutely needed. Aloud, Joe said, "It's needed, Max. I have no choice."

Joe, with some difficulty, started cutting the hoses. "I should have brought a bigger knife."

"This is fun," Hunker said. "Almost better than a woman."

"Say, just what do you do with wingless flies?"

Hunker whispered, "Joseph…Joseph…Joseph. You know I can't tell ya…" Suddenly, he grabbed Joe's shoulder. "I hear somethin'."

"*Nocnitsa*," Joe whispered. "The sea hag."

Hunker asked, "What? What are you talking 'bout"?

Suddenly, from above, voices. "Don't fall in the fucking water." The first man had an Italian accent and sounded drunk. "What a shit night." There was more laughter.

Hunker pointed his hand upward and shut off the flashlight. "Kanky's men…topside."

Joe worked the knife quickly. At first, a little water started to leak, then it erupted into a gusher.

They crept slowly towards the hatch's opening. They looked up into the darkness, waiting for their eyes to adjust.

They heard that same voice, "Don't fall in the fucking water."

Above stood the silhouettes of two men. As Joe and Hunker watched, they could hear the gurgling water from inside the boat.

Another sound of water, accompanied by a strong smell, suddenly hit the deck of the boat. It almost splashed in the faces of Joe and Hunker, who jerked back away from the hatch ladder.

"They're pissing!" Joe whispered.

"Piss on you, Kanky, you cheap asshole!" the first man's voice said.

"Piss on Walter too," the second voice added. "Did you see Kanky hanging over that Chinese pussy? What a fucking greenhorn! Kanky thinks he's a big boss now…"

The first man mumbled, "He *is* a big boss. Don't try telling him he's not. Hey, there's a bottle of whiskey on the boat. I saw Kanky hide it last trip. Gatsby better never find out."

More laughter. "Why, that sneaky Portagee bastard. Let's get it."

Joe nudged Hunker. They climbed out of the hold as the men came down the ladder. Hunker grabbed the first man and slammed his head against a piling and dropped him to the deck.

"Hey! George, you okay?"

Hunker reached up and grabbed the second man's ankle. "George is taking a nap." Hunker threw him onto the deck and banged his head against the gunnel.

Joe grabbed some loose line and they tied the two men together. Beneath their feet, the *Hobo* was already settling deeper into the water.

Hunker said, rather gleefully, "They might drown."

A boom on the dock was equipped with a block and tackle, the kind used for unloading boats at low tide. Hunker climbed up the ladder. Everything was misty, but he heard music from the gin mill. He wished he could go in there, get a nice stiff drink, and beat up a few people. However, the realization of what he was doing drove a sharp rush of excitement through his chest. He whispered, "Fuck Gatsby, the shit."

As he lowered the hook to Joe, a blast of noise came from the club. Through the mist, Hunker could see the shapes of three men standing on the porch.

Joe hooked the block and tackle line to the men's feet. Hunker tossed down the hauling line. As he climbed back down the ladder, he glanced over at the three men, who were now heading in their direction.

"Hurry up! Someone's coming! Pull!" Hunker jumped to the deck and pulled furiously on the line with Joe. As the two unconscious bodies rose into the air, the blocks began to creak.

"Those blocks need oil," Joe said, as if he cared.

"Goddamn," Hunker cracked, "this is good fun!"

The blocks creaked louder as the bodies cleared the boat.

"That's high enough," Joe said.

"No, no, right to the top," Hunker said, laughing. "This is a bonus. Too bad it ain't Kanky."

One of the men, hanging from his ankles upside-down in midair, regained his senses and began moaning.

"We better scram," Joe said.

Hunker secured the hauling line to the bottom rung of the ladder. They got into their skiff and shoved off.

From the speakeasy, one of the approaching men shouted, "What's going on here?"

"Someone's stealing the boat!" yelled one of the hanging men. The man ran down to the warehouse shed and switched on the lights. "Hey! The boat is sinking—get Kanky! Walter!" Then the man dropped to one knee, leaned against the piling, and started shooting his revolver.

Bullets whizzed over Joe and Hunker's heads.

"Row, Hunker—row!"

"Bullshit! Them mugs ain't gonna chase us away with a peashooter." Hunker cocked his goose gun and let loose. The kick almost upset the skiff. The oars fell into the water. "Jesus Christ!" Joe screamed, holding his ringing ears.

The flash, boom, and roar quickly silenced the pistol. Everybody in the well-lit area jumped for cover when the punt gun's pellets shattered the windows and the warehouse's thick siding. Hunker scram-

bled to get the oars back on board and started rowing again. Slowly
the lights disappeared behind the curtain of fog. "That shut them up,
Joseph. Didn't it?"

"Yeah, I guess it did."

~~~~~~

As soon as Pearly heard the gunfire, he started the *Black Duck*'s engines and prepared for the worst. He untied the anchor line, keeping
one turn on the cleat while he watched and waited.

He could hear the splashing of the oars in the fog, but he couldn't
tell from what direction. He gave a low whistle.

"Who the fuck is whistling?" Hunker snapped. "Christ! Sammy
should hear this."

"Shut up! That's Pearly, leading us to the boat."

They heard another low whistle.

"Jesus Christ! I don't fucking believe it!"

Joe pointed.

"Can ya see the boat?" Hunker asked. "Am I headed in the right
direction?"

"You look alright. Keep going. I hear the *Duck*'s engines. There
she is." Hunker pulled up along the portside.

Pearly leaned over the gunnel. "Jesus Christ! You gave me a real
scare."

"So, just for luck, ya start whistling on the boat, did ya?" Hunker
smacked Pearly's ass hard with the butt of his punt gun.

Onboard, he then pulled the skiff onto the deck while Pearly released the anchor line. Joe turned the boat around on a reverse course
for home.

Meanwhile, in the pilot house, Hunker filled Pearly in on what
happened, jumping his conversation around to only the best parts.
Joe puffed on his cigarette and listened. When Hunker got to the part
where Joe cut the hoses to the *Hobo*, Pearly hugged Joe's shoulder and
smiled in the semi-darkness of the pilot house.

"Scuttling a boat is shit work," Pearly commented, which pissed Hunker off.

Finally, Joe said, "I hate superstitions, but...what's a fisherman to do, eh, boys? Gatsby had it coming. We had no choice."

Pearly opened a bottle of King William and handed it to Joe. He took a swallow and shook his head as the liquor slid down his throat. Hunker cracked opened his punt gun. The smell of gunpowder overwhelmed the pilot house.

Pearly took a swig. "Well," he said, "maybe now Kanky and this guy, Gatsby, will think twice before fucking with us again..."

"Goddamn right!" Hunker snapped.

"Maybe, maybe not," Joe said softly.

In the darkness, the three men silently looked at each other.

Chapter Thirty-Three

KANKY DESOUZA LOWERED the two hysterical men down from the boom too quick, letting their heads hit the timbers. They screamed out.

Walter pushed his way through the crowd. His features were unusually strained. Walter didn't like problems. It was his responsibility to keep this part of Gatsby's operation running smoothly. That was the agreement he had made with Gatsby. Beneath the lights, Walter cursed and gazed angrily down at the sunken *Hobo*.

Kanky glared at Walter. "Guess we had-a pay for the hijacking, one way or 'nother."

Walter added, "I wonder how Gatsby will handle it?"

"I guess Joe and his boys are gonna fight us," Kanky added. "I'm-a surprised."

Everyone continued to stare down at the *Hobo*. From out of the bubbling oily water, a corner section of the pilot house roof was all that was visible. As she settled further into the muddy bottom, her lines parted from the heavy strain. The sudden snapping of the manila ropes made the crowd jump. It was as though the *Hobo* was releasing her last moan.

Walter exploded, "Who the fuck does Bucolo think he's fucking with?"

The crowd's attention turned to Walter. They seldom saw or heard the speakeasy manager get really angry.

Kanky said, "Hell, you think-a Joe's gonna come here…shake our goddamn hand?"

Walter replied, "Didn't you just say you were a little surprised?"

Kanky smirked, then looked at the two men with lumps on their heads. "Couldn't you bums stop him?"

"We didn't know what the hell hit us. Look at our heads! You see the size of them lumps?"

"There must have been five of 'em, boss; all carrying guns."

Kanky almost smiled. "Least Bucolo's good enough to hoist them off." He glanced up at the boom. "That-a pretty neat trick, hanging them up there."

On impulse, Walter gave Kanky's shoulder a little shove. "Big fucking deal!"

Kanky's eyes quickly gave Walter a warning.

"Shit, we could've drowned like rats," one of the men said.

"Rats! You are rats!" Walter screamed.

"Need some barge and pretty good crane," Kanky said. "Need some slow lift before put pumps to work. Need to be really gentle… else could-a break boat's back." He nodded. "Pretty good weight inside *Hobo* now."

"You're a genius!" Walter snapped. "Call Beckman's boatyard. They've got all the equipment we'll need."

On the walk back to the Tumble Inn, Kanky said, "Hey-a, Walter, would you-a hoist Bucolo's men off a sinking boat?"

Kanky was surprised when Walter released a nasty laugh. "Are you kidding? I wouldn't have given them a fucking chance."

Inside the speakeasy, amid the excited buzz of the drunken customers as well as Gatsby's anxious men, Walter immediately picked up the phone and called Gatsby.

"Jay, Walter here. I think you need to come to the beach. Bucolo just sank *Hobo*."

"How the fuck did that happen?"

"Simple, we weren't expecting it!"

"I'll be there in an hour. Call Moran as well."

"Okay."

Walter hung up the receiver and turned to Kanky. "He was more relaxed than I thought he would be."

~~~~~~

By the time Gatsby arrived, the speakeasy had settled down some. Paul Moran, who lived in Providence and knew that Gatsby valued promptness, rushed to Oakland Beach. Everyone else on the payroll was very uptight, as no one was sure how Gatsby would react or what would happen next.

Gatsby entered the office. Inside, Kanky, Collector, Moran, and Walter were seated on couches. "Get someone to unload those wooden crates from my car." He motioned to a closet door. "Put the crates in there, and make sure they handle them with care."

Walter left for a few minutes, and three men carried in the crates and placed them carefully inside the closet. Gatsby caught the puzzled looks on Kanky's and Collector's faces. He zeroed in on Kanky. "I think we may need to become more aggressive." He motioned towards the closet. "Let's just say those crates represent another strategy."

Moran chimed in, "Jay, I think Kanky has another interesting idea that I believe is worth pursuing."

Kanky nodded vigorously to Moran's comment. "It could-a be another back-up that-a better than those boxes."

Gatsby mumbled through tight lips, "Bucolo is really getting on my nerves."

Everyone in the room looked silently at Gatsby, who then turned back to Kanky. "Come into the office and we'll discuss."

CHAPTER THIRTY-FOUR

JOE GOT HOME ABOUT THREE-THIRTY, but didn't sleep much. He tossed and turned until sunrise, rehashing his turmoil over sinking the *Hobo*. Deep down, he knew more trouble was certain. Upon their return from Oakland Beach, and after listening to Sammy's rants and concerns about what was coming, the probability of what might happen next filled the clubhouse and everyone's imagination.

It was obvious from Sammy's reaction he'd hoped they wouldn't succeed at sinking the boat. But in the end, there was little disagreement among the gang. They had all given the thumbs-up to what Joe did; something had to be done. Still, everybody agreed with Sammy that they hadn't seen the last of Gatsby and Kanky.

By late morning, Joe had agreed that the wharf required a watchman. Sammy piped up, "I'll take on that responsibility, Joe. I don't mind sleeping here."

"Okay, Sammy." Joe glanced at the Bancocks; his eyes locked on Billy more than his brother. "You boys will have to put in more time on the boats."

Billy nodded rather vigorously.

Pearly asked, "What about the new boat, Joe? Do you think she's safe?"

"That's a serious question," Joe said. "We'll have to worry 'bout that when Gatsby learns about her."

Pearly added, "Wish the prick stayed in Chicago."

~~~~~~

Joe and Pearly parked near Wilcox's winch shed, which housed the engines for the railways. The main building sat between the two tracks on which Cory hauled boats in and out of the water. Cory had a steam shed for bending oak ribs and another for paint and varnish, too. Joe pointed to the fishing dragger *Flo* resting in a cradle. A *For Sale* sign still nailed to the pilot house fluttered in the breeze. From beneath the hull, they heard the methodical clunk of a caulking hammer.

"Gilly Manchester wants to sell, and I've been thinking about buying her for a while."

"Jesus, you are nuts," Pearly said softly, mostly to himself.

Joe just looked at him. "Cory thinks she's one of the best sea boats around, and I'm inclined to agree."

The hammering stopped and old Cory Wilcox worked his way out from under the boat. Cory's skin was white as paper. You could almost see the veins through it. Brown spots, the kind men get from working in the sun, were sprinkled across his face and hands. Yet his eyes were blue and watery and danced with spirit. The shipwright sucked on an unlit pipe.

"Yep, can't stay away from her, can ya, Joe?"

Joe waved.

"Hello, Pearly," Cory called. "Ain't seen you in a dog's age."

"Well, Cory, I can see you're still at it."

"Yep, ya getting a little stout around the middle, Pearly. Yep, must be all that good booze."

Pearly gave Cory a quick finger, which made the old man cackle. Joe bent down and surveyed the vessel's bottom. Reluctantly, Pearly followed suit.

Cory watched them, took out his tobacco pouch, and began to fill his pipe. "Like I've been saying, Joe, she's a good boat. Solid construction, good engine, too."

"I know all that, Cory. I just gotta make up my mind."

Cory mumbled a few words about once knowing some pussies that could never make up their minds. Pearly offered that maybe they both knew the same ones. After all, Tiverton was a small community.

"Okay to go topside?" Joe asked.

Cory lit his pipe and returned to his work. "How many times you gonna go topside, Joe?"

"Many as it takes, Cory." Joe climbed up a ladder to the deck with Pearly following.

Pearly said, "Damn, you'd think *Flo* was Cory's daughter."

Joe paced around the deck. He pulled the handles on the double-drum winch. "Needs rebuilding, but overall, everything is in good condition. Needs some minor woodwork, but it's a damn good boat."

"Sure, it's a good boat," Pearly said. "But it didn't make a living for Gilly."

"I'm a better fisherman than Gilly."

"Yeah, I'd agree with that," Pearly said. "You've had some good luck." He gave Joe a bemused glance. "Just remember that flounder and codfish don't bring in the same money as booze."

Joe cocked his thumb. "Yeah, but at least fishing's got a future."

He waited for Pearly to return the thumb gesture, but he didn't.

Before leaving, both men stood there staring at Minister Bottomley's church. Pearly took a deep breath. "You really believe you can maneuver the *Maria Morso* behind Bottomley's church, and pull this 'bang in' off?"

"I better, or we'll all look like a bunch of damn fools going to jail."

"So, if we do pull it off, this will be our grand finale."

"Probably."

Chapter Thirty-Five

JANIE LOOKED UP FROM HER DESK at Francis Grover's office, surprised to see James Gatz walking through the door.

He gave her a genuine smile, the kind that any girl would feel good about. "Hello, Janie." He immediately put out his hand and they shook. "First, I'm here to ask you out to dinner tonight. Second, I'm here to give Grover a deposit—as earnest money on your project."

Janie appeared really surprised. "I didn't think it would happen this quick."

Gatz gave her a half smile. "Which one, dinner tonight or the deposit?"

"Either one...I guess..."

"I've decided to move quickly. Truth is, I didn't want someone else to latch onto your proposal."

She was taken aback slightly, but managed a smile. "Thank you. But I don't hardly think that would be the case."

"So, dinner?"

Janie took a deep breath and sighed. "Of course."

"It may not be my business, but have you struck any kind of agreement...a deal, if you will, with Grover?"

"Not really. He's never mentioned anything to me along those lines."

Gatz's expression turned guarded. "I find that odd. It *is* your proposal." He looked past Janie and she turned slightly. They both saw Francis Grover standing behind his desk, looking impatient, probably annoyed that they were having a conversation without him.

"Before I give him the check, I want to know—what's really in it for you?"

"I can't answer that, Mister Gatz."

"If you're going to do business, Janie, you've got to learn to protect your interests." He glanced towards Grover and smiled. "Allow me to offer you some advice: trusting Mister Grover would be very poor judgment on your part."

Janie's complexion deepened with her embarrassment. "You're pretty direct, Mister Gatz, as well as astute. However, I believe you're correct."

He chuckled. "If you don't mind, let me handle Grover on your behalf?" Without waiting for an answer, he headed towards the office. "I want you to be in on this negotiation. Come with me."

She reluctantly followed him into the office.

Grover moved out from behind his desk. "Mister Gatz, so nice to see you. Please sit down." He looked at Janie. "Miss Thurston, I'll call you if we need—"

Gatz quickly interrupted, "I'd like Miss Thurston to be part of our conversation, Mister Grover."

Janie said nothing, but gave Gatz a subtle thank-you with her eyes.

Grover hesitated, but he quickly rebounded. "Of course, Mister Gatz…it is Miss Thurston's proposal, and she did work hard on it."

"I have a deposit check for twenty-five thousand dollars, Mister Grover, earnest money sufficient to represent my sincerity towards this endeavor." Gatz gave Grover no opportunity to reply. "I'll get to the point. I believe Paul Moran informed you I would require this to be a fifty-fifty partnership, were we to move forward. Am I correct? He said you had no problem with that."

Grover nodded. "You're correct."

"Good. With that said, we will each turn over seven-and-a-half percent of our interests to Miss Thurston for her work on the proposal, as well as future work in managing the Virginia operation—mainly from here, at your home offices in Tiverton, but with travel to the plant as necessary during peak times in the menhaden season. And Miss Thurston will need her own office—I'm sure you'll see to that straight away."

Grover was having a hard time hiding his surprise and even more so, his discomfort, which was working its way into anger as Gatz's words gradually registered in his mind's eye.

Janie came to his rescue. "More than generous from the both of you, gentlemen. I certainly will do my best to make it a success."

Gatz smiled. "Of that, I am sure, Miss Thurston."

Grover stammered, "Muh...m...my words as well, Miss Thurston."

Gatz, looking more at Janie than at Francis Grover, handed Grover a cashier's check and they shook hands.

Chapter Thirty-Six

FEDERAL AGENTS HAD SET UP a temporary office south of the Providence Farmers Market on the second floor of the Belmont Exchange Building, amongst the commerce of street peddlers, truck farmers, and meat handlers—where the bustling, legit businesses of Market Square ironically provided an excellent outlet for the distribution of illegal booze.

In the corner office, three men sat at a table watching a wrinkled-faced Miss Leonard pour water into tumblers. It was dusk and outside activities were winding down. The evening lights from the loading platforms reflected through the window. A large navigational chart of the coast from Boston to New York hung on the opposite wall.

A thin, scholarly-looking man in a tweed suit, wearing wire-rimmed glasses, said, "Miss Leonard, please turn on the overhead lights." Revenue Agent David Leman had been transferred from headquarters in Washington. He was now in charge of the New England Region. Leman was a tidy fellow with a crisp manner. He appeared to enjoy his work.

Across from Leman sat Dobson McGill, a round-headed Irishman with a red beard and quick smile. He coordinated the newly established Narragansett Bay Operation for Leman. He was the liaison to both the Coast Guard and the Rhode Island authorities.

The third man was Everett Chaffee, Colonel of the Rhode Island State Police. A handsome man, but none too bright, Leman thought.

"First, Colonel, I'd like to thank you for coming on such short notice."

"You're welcome, Mister Leman. Glad to be included in the planning."

"The next time you visit these offices, Colonel, I would ask that you not wear your uniform," Agent Leman said. "I suppose your driver is downstairs with his lights blinking."

"No. No. I sent him on." The colonel got up from the table and looked out the window. "No. He's not down there."

"We're trying to keep a low profile here."

Inspector Leman cleared his throat and looked around the table. "Colonel, as Mister McGill may've told you, the Federal Office is re-directing its efforts away from Boston in order to establish an effective strategy to disrupt the flow of contraband liquor into Rhode Island waterways. Our first step is to coordinate the activities of the Federal Office, the Coast Guard, and Rhode Island State Police. And head-quarters expects us to accomplish that objective in short order."

Colonel Chaffee nodded. "That's a reasonable approach, but still difficult."

"We'll do our best, Inspector Leman," Colonel Chaffee said. "But until Washington blockades Rum Row, cuts off the source, these smugglers will continue to operate."

Leman nodded, impressed with the colonel's assessment.

Colonel Chaffee continued, "You can't expect Rhode Islanders to sympathize with your efforts, especially if the Coast Guard starts blowing local boys out of the water."

McGill turned his red face to Colonel Chaffee. "What exactly do you mean by sympathize?"

Leman quickly interrupted, "Gentlemen, this is why we're having this meeting. Go ahead, Mister McGill."

McGill cleared his throat. "Well, sir, presently the Coast Guard has two 75s and four 36s. Previously, these vessels had to cover an area from Montauk Point, Long Island, clear around Cape Cod and north to Boston. As you can see, the patrols are spread extremely thin…"

Everyone at the table understood the enormous responsibility of the Coast Guard. "Like pissing in the wind," Colonel Chaffee added.

McGill smiled at the colonel's turn of phrase. "But as of tomorrow, all Coast Guard boats will concentrate on the area between Montauk Point, here, and Cape Cod. That means the Coast Guard will definitely have a fighting chance."

Agent Leman said, "In the not-too-distant future, Washington is planning a full-scale blockade of Rum Row."

"That's what we need!" Colonel Chaffee snapped.

"This, of course," Leman added, "will take a certain amount of time to carry out. So, while we're waiting, we must do our part."

"Hell, the sooner they repeal Prohibition, the better," Colonel Chaffee said.

"You could be right," Leman said, "but that's neither here nor there at the moment, and certainly not our responsibility."

"Enforce the unenforceable," Colonel Chaffee mumbled.

"Mister McGill has been gathering information," Leman said. "I'll let him explain what he has learned."

McGill spoke up. "At this moment, we have one organized gang of rummies operating on Narragansett Bay."

"Only one?" Colonel Chaffee's expression was one of bemusement.

"Well, rumor has it another major concern is starting up. And I expect there could be some real trouble over territory. It's this Joe Bucolo, better known as Foggy Joe, who is really supplying the liquor."

McGill took a paper from his pocket. "This outfit from Tiverton manages to keep to themselves; unless, of course, they have a run-in like they did recently and get all kinds of publicity. They supply Newport, Providence, Fall River, and some out-of-state speakeasies. I think we need to shut down Bucolo's gang, leave the mosquito fleet alone. I don't think we should be blowing desperate fishermen out of the water for smuggling in a few cases of whiskey."

"I agree," said the colonel.

McGill nodded. "I visited Tiverton. I have to admit, there's fairly strong sentiment for Bucolo, except obviously from the town's 'dry' element."

"Mister McGill, how did you manage to find this out?" the colonel asked.

McGill stood up and grinned. "I have someone outside who may be of help to us."

"Who could that be?" Chaffee asked.

McGill's expression was one of smug accomplishment. "Henry Grover, police chief from Tiverton. He knows Bucolo very well, and he has a plan to stop him. He's a big admirer of yours, Colonel."

Colonel Chaffee stared at his hands while McGill left the room._

Moments later, McGill returned with Henry Grover in full uniform. Leman emitted a knowing sigh. Tucked under Grover's arm was a rolled-up navigational chart. Leman motioned to an empty chair. Henry Grover nodded, took off his hat, and sat down.

"What's on your mind, Chief Grover?" Leman asked, annoyance still in his voice.

"As Tiverton's police chief, I feel it's my duty to stop rum-running."

"Of course, of course," Leman said, his voice softening.

Colonel Chaffee raised his eyebrows, glanced at his hands again, but said nothing.

"I'm not a seasoned professional, like you all. I'm honored you would call a special meeting just to hear *my* plan. I can't quite believe it. I spent a lot of time figuring out how to finish off Joe Bucolo once and for all."

McGill tapped his pencil on the table. "Chief, just tell Inspector Leman your plan."

Grover unrolled his chart and laid it on the table. He pointed. "This is the Seaconnet River, and here is Mount Hope Bay. I believe you can trap Bucolo right here." Grover jammed his thumb down on the Tiverton railroad trestle marked on the chart.

Colonel Chaffee asked, "And just how can we do that?"

Grover's eyes widened with enthusiasm. "Automobiles travel over the top span, which is permanent. However, the lower train bridge is left open at all times for river traffic. You know? The steamship schedule, fishing vessels, rum boats. It's closed only when the Fall River-to-Newport train has to cross. I'm suggesting you simply have the Coast Guard chase Bucolo and his boats into a closed bridge."

Leman and McGill nodded.

"Sounds interesting," Chaffee said, "but can't they run right under that railroad span?"

"Not enough clearance," Grover said.

Leman looked at McGill. "What do you think? Will the Coast Guard do it?"

"They'll do what we ask." McGill studied the chart. "It could work, as long as we get the right information. We'll need enough time to get ourselves into position." McGill glanced back at the chart and for a moment studied it. "One problem, though. Bucolo can either use the Seaconnet River to return or the East Passage. If he comes back home through the river, he doesn't have to go under the bridge. Correct?"

"I thought of that," Grover said. "After Bucolo leaves Tiverton for Rum Row, the Coast Guard should send a patrol boat to the mouth of the Seaconnet, and you'll force him to use the East Passage."

Leman nodded. Colonel Chaffee remained expressionless.

Leman added, "We have to catch them with the liquor aboard their boats. It's the only way to seize their vessels and send them to jail."

"Sounds good to me," McGill said. "Wish I had thought of it. But we have to get the right information to the Coast Guard ahead of time."

"Don't worry, Mister McGill, you'll get the right information."

Colonel Chaffee said, "Chief Grover, why such a patriotic interest in Mister Bucolo? Most small-town authorities don't like getting involved with the Coast Guard or with government agents, especially with residents of their own community."

Grover said, "Let's just say I don't like lawbreakers, especially if they live in my town."

Grover glanced at Colonel Chaffee. "Sir, I've asked the Tiverton Town Council for money to buy a Tommy gun. They turned me down. Could you, in your capacity, help me acquire one?"

The colonel's eyes tightened. "There's no need for you to have a Thompson machine gun, Chief. No need at all."

Grover stood up and rolled up his chart. Clearly disappointed, he just nodded and squeezed his chart.

Leman looked at McGill. "Do you think the Coast Guard will want to get involved with this?"

McGill stressed his answer. "Absolutely!"

Leman asked, "What makes you so sure?"

"Not long ago, the Coast Guard was chasing Bucolo through the fog, and they ran aground. A young sailor died in that mishap."

Leman nodded. "Oh yes, I was made aware of that incident."

McGill added, "It was a gruesome scene. The Coast Guard wants this Bucolo. They'll do anything we ask if they can blow him out of the water."

Grover blurted out, rather loudly, "Bucolo deserves the hard fist of the law! He needs to be put out of business!"

"This all seems very personal, Chief Grover," interjected Colonel Chaffee, looking at McGill, then Grover. "Don't forget, we're talking about simple fishermen here."

Agent Leman struck a match and lit his cigarette. "Frankly, Colonel, I don't give a rat's ass. Washington wants results, and it's our job to deliver."

"Call us, Chief Grover, when you have the information," McGill said. "Just make sure it's correct…and thanks for your service."

When Grover left the room, Colonel Chaffee looked at McGill. "Now, Mister McGill, tell us the real reason Chief Grover has volunteered his help."

"From what I've heard, this Bucolo fellow is probably poking...or trying to poke Grover's girlfriend."

CHAPTER THIRTY-SEVEN

FROM THE KITCHEN WINDOW, Pearly watched Janie enter James Gatz's Packard. He didn't get a good look at the man, but either way, and for the first time, Pearly had an uncomfortable feeling in his chest. He whispered, "My sweet thing...how things are changing in your life..." His moist eyes then turned upward. "You should be very proud of her, Rosemary. I surely am, but I'm also worried. So, watch out for our daughter."

He waited at the window until the Packard was out of sight. Then he mumbled, "I need a drink."

~~~~~~

As Gatz drove up Riverside Drive to Main Road, the Basin looked especially beautiful. There was no wind, and the sun had dropped below the horizon of Portsmouth, leaving a jagged south-by-north ribbon of a fiery red sky.

"Sailor's delight," Janie whispered. "Tell me that isn't a gorgeous sunset."

Gatz gave Janie a long look. "You're right, but I must say, you look more beautiful than that sunset."

"Why, thank you. Speaking of which, it took until twenty minutes ago for me to decide what to wear."

Gatz laughed. "Well, Janie, that's rather honest, I would say. But it's not the dress."

She gave off a weak smile. "Where are we going?"

"Providence. I understand there's a great restaurant in the Imperial Hotel."

She immediately developed a look of apprehension; Gatz sensed her uneasiness. "I assure you, there is nothing to be concerned about."

"Oh, I know that. Otherwise, I wouldn't be sitting here. Besides, we're 'partners,' aren't we?"

Gatz smiled. "That we are. Have you ever been there?"

"No…although my friend Maggie Jackson said I should go there sometime."

Gatz gave her a glance, but didn't respond.

~~~~~~

Just like Maggie, Janie was in awe of the Imperial's Bacchante dining room. As she and Gatz passed through the bar on the way to their table, she caught the bartender giving Gatz a nod and smile of recognition, yet Gatz seemed to ignore him.

Comfortable now in their booth, Janie still couldn't settle herself, awash as she was with wonderment over the surroundings. She didn't even have a reference point to dream about before tonight. It was unsettling yet intoxicating at the same time. She reminded herself that from their first lunch together, she had set boundaries in her head concerning James Gatz—who appeared to offer more than she ever considered possible from any man. Since that first meeting, she counted out his qualities, which were many, but she didn't want to be swayed by exterior forces she simply wasn't accustomed to. And she kept reminding herself that she didn't really know him.

Gatz seemed to be enjoying watching her reactions, sensing the inner battle she was waging with herself.

Finally, she said, "This is quite the place, James. I'd be lying if I said I wasn't impressed."

Gatz relished her enthusiasm. "I'm happy you approve. There are many places in this country…even the world that outshine this fine establishment. Ambiance and meals prepared by world-class chefs." Gatz chuckled. "Dishes to die for."

"It sounds like you've experienced some of those places."

"Yes, a few…here, there…"

Janie seemed intrigued. "Tell me more."

"In due time, Janie." He laughed. "Soon, my life will be as open as this menu. Shall we order?"

She nodded. "Of course."

~~~~~~

It had been a wonderful dinner. Gatz had asked if she'd like a cocktail or some wine, but she refused, so he didn't have anything either. Surprised by his gesture, Janie said, "Please don't let me stop you from having a drink, James."

He smiled. "It's illegal, Janie."

Through some of their conversations, much of which were trivial, Janie noticed that whenever she asked a question, he tended to think for a bit before giving a firm, well-formed answer.

Gatz said, "Truth is, I've never been a big drinker, even before Prohibition. Frankly, I like to keep my wits about me."

Janie smiled. "Something my father has said from time to time: one survives by doing clever things and even sometimes doing dishonest things…but you still need your wits about you."

Gatz laughed. "Again, Janie, much too honest."

~~~~~~

Later, outside the hotel, they waited for his car. In those moments, Janie suddenly sensed a slight impatience in Gatz. She was about to ask him what the trouble was, but the valet pulled up and took her words away as the doorman opened the passenger door for Janie.

Inside the Packard, Janie turned to Gatz. "It's been a lovely evening, James, thanks."

He nodded. "I suspect you've had many of these."

Not quite an answer, but Janie smiled anyway. "What do you mean?"

"Grover's son, the police chief, seemed quite intrigued with you. The day I was there, I suspect he didn't appreciate me taking you out for a business lunch. He probably wanted to arrest me."

Janie laughed. "Henry has a way about himself that he's yet to even recognize. In some ways, he's still a boy in a man's body."

"So, he's not your type."

"Not really, but my friend thinks Henry Grover is the bee's knees. And she's an authority on men."

"Bee's knees? Not sure what that means."

Janie countered, "First time I ever heard the term, it came from my friend Maggie."

Gatz's expression deepened. "Are there any other suitors I should be worried about?"

Janie said softly, "I take that as a compliment, James, but at the moment, I would say no."

"This Joe…Joe Bucolo…is he a worry?" He tried to make light of the question with his tone.

Janie picked up on it, but after a moment, she chuckled. "Only to the law, especially the Coast Guard." She seemed surprised that Joe's name had come up, and for a moment, her thoughts appeared to be elsewhere. "How do you know him?"

"Waterfront rumors…scuttlebutt…rumors also that he's a ladies' man. He appears to be a legend in some quarters. What do you think?"

"I suppose some of that is true. But to be honest, Joe is really a down-to-earth fisherman. The sea is locked in Joe's soul…" She laughed. "Sometimes I think he would rather be fishing for a living. I do know he loves the water, boats, and…yes…women…"

"In what order?" Gatz asked.

"Off the top of my head, I'd say women were at the end of his list."

Gatz appeared to be put off by that response. Janie detected a slight twitch at her reply.

He stared at her, searching for any hidden meanings. "You almost sound in awe of Mister Bucolo?"

"Mister?" Janie let out a hearty laugh. "Not hardly...not hardly at all. However, most women I know in Tiverton do find him exciting. He's also generous with some townsfolk that have had it tough, but he plays that down. It was also a trait of Max Bucolo, his stepfather. Although I did see Joe get very angry...once."

Gatz picked up on that comment. "What was the cause of that?"

"In sixth grade, he didn't win first place in the flower exhibition with his tulip display because his grades were rather low...only because he was always bunking school, going out shellfishing to earn money. He did get second place, though."

"Sixth grade! Tulips!" Gatz guffawed. "Then I believe he *is* someone to worry about."

Janie smiled but said nothing.

Chapter Thirty-Eight

FRANCIS GROVER'S EYES MOVED between the leather cover of his office Bible, which lay in front of him, and Henry, who had his back to him, staring out through the window at the fleet of seiners that had given the family its wealth and power. Henry turned. "Father, do you remember a man named Kanky who worked for Max Bucolo?"

Francis Grover snapped, "How could anyone forget any of those sinners, a malignant harvest of the Seaconnet—this river of sin."

"Well, Father, I'd be cautious about casting any stones." Henry moved closer to his father's desk. "I received a call from Kanky and he threatened me...and actually, you as well..."

"What are you saying, Son? I don't understand."

"He said he would expose...what he called one fucking dark secret about the Grover family..." Henry shook his head. "It could be a fucking mess!"

Francis Grover recoiled slightly from his son's profanity. But at the same time, a strange curl shaped his lips. "How much money does he want?"

"None...he just wants me to finish off Bucolo and his Swamp Yankee gang for good."

"What are you going to do about it?"

"You would be very proud of me." Henry sat down.

Francis Grover's expression didn't warm to his son's self-compliment. "Go on."

"Kanky wanted to make sure I spoke to the federal agents in Providence, which I already have. I told them about my strategy to stop Bucolo. It's foolproof." A sly smile began to spread on Henry's face. "Furthermore—"

"I don't need to know the details, especially you, scheming with the Portagee!"

Henry gauged his father for a moment. "Had you stayed true to Mother, Kanky wouldn't have anything he could use against us." Henry's expression tightened. "After all, you were a married man, Father, but Jessica Jackson…Maggie's harlot mother!"

"The flesh is weak, son. I was young, younger than you, frustrated, more foolish. You should've seen Jessica Jackson. She was one tempting, ripe woman. The devil's ultimate temptation." Francis began to toy with his pencil, tapping it gently on the ink blotter. Not looking at Henry, he said softly, "Your mother was never interested in the ways of the flesh."

"She had me!"

Francis hesitated, even his lips quivered, but no response.

Henry's tone turned agitated. "Did you give Jessica Jackson money?"

"Yes," Francis Grover admitted. "And I still do. At times I tried to break it off, but that's impossible."

"What do you mean?"

"You saw her in church recently. She was serving a warning to me. She's capable of wreaking havoc in this town."

"What do you mean?" Henry sat frozen, as if movement would certainly worsen the next revelation.

"I've enjoyed spending time with Jessica. She's told me many times, she loves me."

"God Almighty!" Suddenly, Henry's body jerked like he'd received an electrical shock. "Tell me, Father, where does her love for you and this enjoyment take place?"

"In Fall River, at the Hotel Drake. We've been going there every Sunday night for over thirty years."

Henry was visibly shaken. "All those Bottomley gatherings, all those pious sermons? And you lecture me about the thirsty Thurstons...you're a hypocrite!"

"Don't take that holier-than-thou shit so seriously. Hopefully, you will learn from my only mistake."

The plea in Francis Grover's eyes sought to cancel his son's rage. "Being a whore isn't an insult, Son. It's a reality of life. A man pays money and gets what he wants. And that's how Jessica has supported herself and her daughter for twenty-five years."

Henry's face flushed. "Well, get this: Kanky also said your lifelong enemy, Max Bucolo, had his way with Jessica every Saturday night for over ten years, and he never paid her one red cent."

Rage erupted over Francis's features. "Damn that heathen, Swamp Yankee clan!" His eyes burned like some prophet of doom. "Damn them all!" He jammed his pencil down, breaking it into two pieces.

Henry laughed again. "That, Father, is what I intend to do with Bucolo and Kanky. Break them! Break them for good!"

"Will anyone get killed?" Francis asked softly.

"If they do, so what!? They're lawbreakers! They'll pay for their sins!"

Slowly, Francis Grover laid his hand on the Bible and glared hard at Henry. "Join me, Son, join me." Henry placed his hand over his father's, whose eyes turned into razor-like slits. "You do have the law on your side. Destroy this bad breed any way you can, before they destroy our God-fearing family. I'll stand behind you every step of the way."

CHAPTER THIRTY-NINE

DESPITE ALL THE BAD LUCK Joe Bucolo had recently experienced, it didn't stop the first expected run of spring herring—the schools of fish were so thick, you could walk on them. Their arrival was like a welcome guest to the Seaconnet. Within that same week, hungry striped bass, bluefish, and sea trout followed the herring, gorging their bellies like there was no tomorrow.

On some mornings, Joe would carefully check out what was going on in the Tiverton Basin as the community's daylight waterfront became a hub of activity. Chugging exhausts, donkey engines, spinning winches, pump motors, squeaking pulleys, shouts, wooden hammers securing barrel hoops all added to the springtime excitement as boats made two trips a day to their fish traps at Sandy Point Shoals. The local economy was charged. He loved watching the bravado, the shouting, and the cursing. That air of prosperity, though short, was always sweet. For Joe, it was part of his roots, and he loved it all.

In this short seasonal fishery, shore seiners were making incredible catches inside the creeks along the Seaconnet, Seapowet, and Fogland. The river seemed pregnant with fish. Most of the herring catches were packed in salted brine and stored in wooden barrels, in long rows, on Peabody's Wharf, awaiting shipment to New York and Boston markets. The fishing season had truly begun.

Some specialty seafood markets hired fish cutters to remove and pack herring roe—a delicacy, some claimed, that went beyond description. Annoying seagulls invaded Tiverton from miles around. At times, their hungry calling, flapping wings, and messy droppings dominated the waterfront. Occasionally a shotgun blast from an irate fisherman would chase them away, but always they returned.

Swaying in the warm breezes—as though drying out laundry—nets, seines, and twine sections hung from every available boom and tackle in the Basin. Men dressed in black rain gear worked like frantic soldier ants on the landings, and aboard their boats.

New mackerel barrels arrived every day on the *Queen City* and *Islander*, creating work for Rhode Island carpenters. The strong pickling aroma of brine and the fresh salty odor of fish permeated the waterfront. It represented the smell of hard-earned money. For most of the workers, it was the only way to survive until the next season. And so it went for this seaside community, even back to the time of the settlers and Wampanoag tribes.

Seafood dealers congregated, making deals, promising better prices, while some men dressed in suits, brandishing shiny liquor flasks, bluffed the younger fishermen into another season of just holding their own with no real net profit.

This fresh-market business had its own cast of characters; at times, even Francis Grover had Janie Thurston buying fish. She seemed to do better than most. Wholesalers and truck drivers were everywhere, with private cutthroat deals being thrown together as the catches were unloaded. The fresh-market business always brought short spurts of anger and vicious name-calling to a number of unloading wharves, including Grover's fish plant.

This was the time when fishermen tried to keep promises made to their wives, girlfriends, and mothers. Now was the time to buy that new suit, that new stove, or that engagement ring.

— CHAPTER FORTY —

ABOUT A HALF-HOUR BEFORE they were to meet, Frankie-the-Bone led Daisy Buchanan to a private booth. A gangster's girlfriend played through Frankie's mind when he first saw her. He had seen his share of beautiful women, but he quickly surmised that Paul Moran's boss had to be some big-time criminal—mostly because, in order to possess such a woman, it had to be someone who was not afraid to use a gun to keep her.

Frankie was floored when Gatz arrived. He was now trying to piece together who James Gatz really was. Suddenly, Frankie knew Mister Gatz was Jay Gatsby, the man he had warned Joe about. The man Kanky was working for. The man who wanted to put Foggy Joe out of business.

His second thought: Why was Mister Gatz using an alias? What was he hiding and from whom?

"Nice to see you again, sir."

"Likewise, Frankie." Gatz looked around. It wasn't hard to find Daisy; her presence graced the lounge with a level of elegance it didn't deserve. "I see that my sister has already arrived."

As Gatz walked away, Frankie whispered, "Sister?" Gatz must think I'm stupid. What he really wanted to say: get the fuck out of here! But he knew that wouldn't be prudent.

When Gatsby's eyes locked onto Daisy, his former memories of Louisville, Kentucky, came back like the racehorses of their annual May Derby. He quickly noticed that she wasn't wearing a hat. Back in Kentucky, she loved hats, all kinds: lace, sheer, embroidered, even sunhats, some decorated with flowers or, as some couldn't believe—fruit.

As Gatsby approached her booth, he thought she certainly looked different: more mature, even worldly—maybe not as fragile since Louisville. After all, in 1917, she was only an eighteen-year-old debutante and certainly, at that time, the belle of the ball. Now she was dressed rather daringly, and her hairstyle had changed; surely not the same she wore at that autumn Army dance where he first saw her, less than two weeks before he had to leave for the Great War. A war where he escaped injury, except when he returned from Europe, he found that he had lost Daisy Faye's hand in marriage to a wealthy blueblood named Tom Buchanan. He never really got over the loss.

Daisy politely stood and held out her hand. He was surprised by the gesture.

He quickly took hold of it. She leaned over and kissed him on the cheek.

"Hello, Lieutenant Gatsby, you look quite handsome."

His eyebrows rose slightly from her use of Lieutenant.

"Nice to see you, Miss Faye."

Likewise, she seemed surprised by his use of her maiden name. "I'm really Mrs. Buchanan…"

"I know, but I prefer thinking of our past relationship, even though it's almost three years old."

For a quick moment, Daisy appeared tilted by his statement. It caught her somewhat off guard.

"I prefer calling you Miss Faye, if you don't mind?"

She smiled. "Maybe you should call me Mrs. Gatsby?" Her words, whether in jest or real, gave Gatsby a rush of blood to his head. He felt slightly faint. This was what he'd always wanted.

"Well, Jay, I really like the way you look…you have matured, certainly, since Kentucky. You remind me of one of those successful New York stockbrokers."

Gatsby was surprised by her comments, so he didn't stop her. She continued, "Why…oh why, did that terrible war have to take you away from me?"

His brain immediately replayed what he had said many times in his head: Don't you mean Tom Buchanan took you away from me? Why didn't you just wait?

Her voice shook him from his thoughts. "What a delightful time we would have had. My God! I just uttered a proper description of what our lives could have been. And it comes from the bottom of my heart. How truly wonderful…"

"Oh, Daisy, you don't know how much I have longed for those words."

Suddenly, Gatsby recalled them back at her parents' house, dancing alone in the large parlor. That night she had worn a lacy dress, and Gatsby remembered how, at times, he could feel her body against his, and he wondered then if she was leading him on. He hoped so.

He couldn't forget how his heart raced, almost uncontrollably, when Daisy's face closed in on his. He prayed that their kisses would be the beginning of their lives together. How wrong he was. The terrible war and Tom Buchanan took care of that.

Daisy suddenly seemed to be in the moment of happy memories. She raised her hand into the air, as if declaring, pay attention to what I'm about to say. *"Tell me, my dear Lieutenant, what do we intend to do after the dance is over?"*

Gatsby shook his head, almost in total disbelief. "My God! Those were your exact words."

"Of course. How could I, Miss Daisy Faye, forget that night?"

"Incredible. During the war, when I got lonely, I repeated your charming words. I even wondered if I would ever see your beautiful face again."

"How sweet it is, Lieutenant. Why...I'm...I'm frozen with delight... Mister Buchanan never uses words like that on me."

He wanted to immediately lambast her husband, but thought better of it.

She added, "It turned out to be such a wonderful night. I was so happy my parents were away on vacation. You were so gentle and loving with me..."

For a moment, Gatsby wasn't sure how to respond. In a way, he was shocked that she brought up their intimacy. He began to feel lightheaded, and he wanted to tell her that in the morning he actually felt like a married man.

Daisy, suddenly flooded with melancholy, appeared to shift the direction of their conversation.

"I'm very impressed with what your fine lawyer said about your successes. It is indeed something to be proud of."

Gatsby suddenly heard a sense of business and money in her voice. Is that why she's here?

"I'm sure you're not aware that your Chicago background is rather notorious, and it followed you, even right back here in Providence."

"I wasn't aware, Daisy...as I have tried to keep a low profile."

He caught himself in that moment. He wondered if her compliments were artificial or real. He decided to take the helm.

"I'm wondering, Daisy, just why did you request to meet with me?"

"It's slightly embarrassing, but my husband is in a financial bind at the moment. I volunteered to see if I could help him. You were the first person I thought of."

"Does your husband know you're here?"

"No. I thought it would be better if he didn't know."

"It's of your choosing, Daisy. Besides, I don't know him...and I really don't need to."

She softly said, "Tom has the temperament of a tornado...you're so totally opposite of him."

Gatsby felt a smile but capped it. He wanted to tell her that he did know a few details about Tom Buchanan, all supplied by his lawyer, who had a knack for extracting those hidden, often juicy details about someone's life. Moran even had various photos of Buchanan. They came from a maid who was fired for not going to bed with him. According to Moran, Mister Polo Player, as he was known, had a colossal ego, and loved to brag. But in truth, it was only his vast family wealth that had ever earned him those bragging rights.

Tom thought money made him more intelligent than everyone else. He was also a womanizer and had even cheated on Daisy with a Paris maid on their honeymoon. This detail had disturbed Gatsby beyond the pale.

Buchanan called himself an evolutionist, who believed the whites or the Nordics should be the dominant species. All the other races didn't really count. He revealed those feelings to only a few select people.

Gatsby considered Buchanan's philosophy ignorant and dangerous, but it married well with his brute persona. He recalled the front cover of a polo magazine with Buchanan holding the reins to his championship horse.

As he gazed upon Daisy, he visualized Mister Polo Player. his beefy frame hunched forward like a slanted tower of cement. But it was Tom's shiny, black riding boots that seemed to represent high society to Gatsby more than anything else. He had perused that photo more times than he should have. Once, Gatsby had even pictured himself in an eighteenth-century musket duel with Buchanan. Finally, he burned the magazine.

"So, Daisy, what is it you want from me?"

"I almost want you to say no to what I'm asking."

"Why is that?"

"Deep down, it's just not fair to you, especially after all these years."

What caught Gatsby's ears was that she had suddenly lost her "full of money" voice—that voice of privilege. He tried not to show it, but he was stunned by her ability to sashay onto another subject, as if she were on a dance floor and the orchestra had just changed songs. Yet, he wasn't sure if she meant what she said. It didn't matter; she had come to him.

Daisy's features softened, especially her eyes. She took a moment. "I enjoyed your devotion, especially after you left for the war. Truth is, I lived vicariously through your loving attention. Even then, after I married, our secret romance kept me on an even keel, as sailors dearly say, especially at times when Tom misbehaved." Daisy's lips quivered slightly, as though she might cry.

"Misbehaved? That's a rather weak word, Daisy."

"So you do know more, Lieutenant Gatsby. How wise of you." She shook her head and sighed.

For Gatsby, only one thing was certain: Daisy still wanted to protect the life she was used to. No matter how unhappy her marriage. One thing he found odd, as he stood there thinking, Daisy didn't make him anxious at all—nothing like she had in his memories. And he knew why—married or not she was still his Daisy.

"Whatever you need, Daisy, you know how to reach my lawyer. I am happy to help you…and your baby, but your husband should never know."

"I am a fool, Gatsby, but isn't that the privilege of all girls—to be a fool?"

She stood and, without another word, left.

Gatsby watched her walk away, and in his mind he saw Daisy returning to a life he and she would soon share together. His plans were working.

CHAPTER FORTY-ONE

JOE AND PEARLY HAD SPENT the last week at Schmitz's boatyard, helping Sammy install the Liberty engines on *Whispering Winds*. Meanwhile, Joe had told Mary to try to make contact with any offshore vessel carrying high-grade rum. Speakeasies were low on rum, and business was booming. Things were coming together.

Every time Joe entered Heinrich Schmitz's boat shed, his head murmured: *Whispering Winds*. He loved her name and it was still his secret. She was going to be extraordinary. His true nature belonged with the *Flo*, but his adventurous heart still longed for this new rum boat. For him, she evoked the exhilarating freedom of the high seas, just like the buccaneers must have felt. She was beautiful, like a promise nestled in her cradle. If one was going to smuggle booze, she was everything he had hoped for, and beyond that, she was already lucky—protected from the sea hag, *Nocnitsa*.

When the Liberties were set in the engine room, preliminary alignment measurements with the propeller shafts were almost perfect. The final coupling of shafts wouldn't take place until the boat was in the water, allowing the hull to swell and settle. Sammy couldn't stop praising Heinrich Schmitz. Joe was ecstatic.

~~~~~~

On the way home from New Bedford, Joe stopped off at Mary's Diner. Except for a booth of young girls, the lunch crowd had gone, and Mary was cleaning up, getting ready to close. When he sat down at the counter, she nodded quickly. She had something to tell him—something important.

Mary poured him a coffee. "I contacted Captain Maytee."

Joe spoke low. "The *Caprice*?"

"Yes, he's carrying Bacardi rum, Absolut, and tins of Cuban Alky...and something more." Mary's eyes ignited with speculation.

"What?" Joe asked in a whisper.

"Chinese runaways."

Joe shook his head. "Maytee's a real pirate!"

She detected a trace of excitement in Joe's voice.

"Are you sure?" he asked.

She nodded. "When I decoded the message, it read: 'foreign contraband can also accompany booze.' Means only one thing, Joe."

"I don't want any part of that! But I do want his rum."

Joe's attention was drawn to the giggling grade-school girls drinking ice cream sodas, here for their Saturday afternoon treat. "When can I get his rum?" he asked without turning.

"Captain Maytee said anytime will be fine, unless someone else cleans him out. He'll be five miles south of the gully on Coxe's Ledge. He said he can fill your order, and I said okay."

"Good job, Mary. Thanks." Joe got up and headed for the door. "See ya later." Instead, he walked back to the counter. He pointed. "See those young ones? That's how old the girls are on Maytee's schooner."

"You're certainly in a strange mood," Mary said.

"You would be too, if you were buying booze from a slave trader so Frankie-the-Bone can sell rum to the students at Brown."

"You want me to cancel?" Mary felt she was being harassed. "I'll call Maytee and tell him that Foggy Joe has suddenly got religion." Her voice rose. "Is that what you want?"

The girls in the booth turned to Mary's loud voice.

"No," Joe said. "I want you to confirm it. Look, Mary, don't get those teats in an uproar. Okay?"

"I wish they *were* in an uproar, Foggy Joe."

=== Chapter Forty-Two ===

IN THE HIGH-CEILING, blue-painted hallway, Tom Buchanan opened the front door, slightly surprised. "Jordan, come in, welcome to Chicago." Tom was relieved that his home was now back to its former glory for Jordan's first visit. It had only taken a few days for the landscapers and painters to accomplish their work. His relief would have turned to rage had he known Gatsby was the benefactor who had refilled the household coffers during his recent bout of tight money.

Jordan entered the living room, missing Tom's eyes that were locked on her fine ass. For an instant, he had an image of them riding their horses together, her legs spread, her ass moving deliciously up and down.

She asked, "Where is Daisy? I thought she knew I was arriving today."

"She took the little one to the doctor for a checkup." He glanced at his watch. "She'll be gone for a while. Come in, would you like a drink?"

"Sure. I'm no longer in training. Today, I'm actually feeling feral."

Tom said, "I suppose riding your horses doesn't help?"

"True, they do work on a woman's body in different ways. If you know what I mean?"

"Of course," he answered, his brain again ignited with sudden imagery. "Even with a man. Although sometimes it can be painful." He almost laughed but didn't. She stood at his bar, waiting for her drink.

A changing sea breeze blew through the room, fluffing out the curtains. The sounds were like sails searching for a tacking wind. He handed Jordan her drink, then closed a few windows. He came up alongside her, and they both leaned on the bar and nursed their drinks.

He stirred his cocktail with his finger and stared at Jordan. "You look very nice, like always…."

Jordan nodded and her lips fluttered slightly. She moved closer to him and they both set their glasses on the bar.

They kissed, hard and deep into each other's mouths. His big, roaming hand smothered her modest breasts. Then, like some nighttime blood-sucker, he attacked her neck, while at the same time he lifted her tight skirt up to her waist. In slow motion, Jordan turned around and leaned over the bar. Tom dropped his pants and pushed her white panties down over the cheeks of her ass. He penetrated her easily, and Jordan released a gratified moan and whispered, "Don't stop, Tom…"

Then and there, he went at her like he was on his polo horse swinging a mallet, heading for a wild ball. Jordan reciprocated, like she was in a fast gallop on her favorite horse.

Over cries of passion, they both reached their climax. She took his hand and led him to the couch, almost tripping on her panties. He said, "You are feeling wild, Jordan."

"Don't speak, Tom…more effort than words."

He couldn't hide his surprise at yet another command.

For the longest time they again went at it, this time with her riding him—until the phone rang.

Jordan snapped, "Let it ring!" She tried to hold him to her, but he jumped up anyway and headed for the phone on the table, the cheeks of his ass resembling two mounds of vanilla ice cream. Jordan's finger marks were still visible where she tried to pull him in deeper, due to his shortcoming.

"It could be Daisy." He heard Jordan swear something inaudible. Breathless, he answered, "Hello."

Daisy exclaimed loudly, "Our beautiful little girl is very healthy, Tom, really healthy. Isn't that marvelous? I must be a very good mother. Wouldn't you think? And you must be a very good father?"

"Yes, Daisy. That's great news."

"We should celebrate this evening."

Tom turned and watched Jordan hastily fix her clothes and silently walk out.

As she shut the front door to the house, Jordan thought to herself, Well, my friend Daisy, I've done what you asked. If you decide to leave Mister Buchanan, you'll have your legitimate grounds.

Chapter Forty-Three

ABOUT THE TIME HENRY GROVER arrived at Joe's wharf in order to spy and implement *his* plan, Gatsby and his men had already dismantled the phony mast and camouflage on *Diamond Daisy*. Up till now, because of the wharf's secluded area, very few people were aware of his new rum boat in New Bedford. Gatsby had covered all the bases.

An air of excitement surrounded Gatsby, which was difficult to hide. Everything that he had organized was finally coming to fruition. In many ways, it was a milestone for him. This endeavor was all on his shoulders, whether he succeeded or failed, and he was determined not to fail. He wondered what his grandfather would think in a moment like this.

While the crew made ready to depart, Gatsby watched them through the small window in the rear of the pilot house. He had selected Kanky and Collector with three other men for tonight's trip. Gatsby also decided that Collector would be engineer. When he first arrived in New Bedford, Gatsby hired the shipyard's engineer for an extra week so that Collector could educate himself with the rum boat's engines and everything else in the engine room. It was his job to keep *Diamond Daisy* running smoothly.

Standing in the wheelhouse, he knew no matter what happened

from here on in, this was his destiny. It was all about the real James Gatz and not Jay Gatsby. However, he would still keep the Gatsby name, as he had become accustomed to it. He bargained with himself on whether he would eventually ditch the name—it would all depend on how successful he became in his rum-running career, and how things went with Daisy in the future.

He knew the odds of getting blown out of the water or going to jail were quite real—but those dangers went hand in hand with his new trade. He did find it strange that he wondered if Joe Bucolo felt the same way about being blown out of the water or going to jail when he set out for Rum Row.

Gatsby leaned over an open hatch in the pilot house floor and yelled down to Collector, who was on standby, "Start the engines."

"Yes, Captain," responded Collector loudly.

Gatsby chuckled slightly, but more to himself.

All three Liberties whined for a moment, then roared to life. The excitement and the sensations Gatsby felt from those powerful engines were almost unbearable. As he held the mahogany-spoked wheel, Gatsby wiped the sweat from his hands on his pants. He felt his heart beating faster than normal, similar to when he practiced the Kama Sutra. Yet, this was even more exciting.

He ran *Diamond Daisy* away from the wharf at an idle, then passed slowly through Clark's Cove. In Buzzard's Bay, a slight southerly wind threw up beads of salt water, greeting the vessel—acting like a priest baptizing her first trip to Rum Row. Kanky and the crew joined Gatsby in the pilot house, but they spoke in whispers. Since the sinking of the *Hobo*, Gatsby thought they might be contemplating the worst—being blown out of the water.

Kanky moved up alongside Gatsby. "Will-a be any other competition for *Caprice*'s cargo?"

"Shouldn't be. I've got his position. We are closer, going to beat Bucolo and his gang to the ship. Besides, I sent a phony radio message to Captain Maytee, told him Foggy Joe wasn't coming tonight."

"*Caprice?* What-a that name mean anyway?"

Gatsby said, "Unpredictable...like the urges of ladies."

Kanky laughed. "This-a going to be very interesting. What-a happens if-a Joe show up?"

"We'll have to see how that works out, won't we?"

A moment later, Collector bounded up from the engine room. Even in the dim light of the pilot house, it was easy to see he wore an expression of excitement. He then sang his little ditty: "*Diamond Daisy is a lady of the night and she loves what she does for her boys out on Rum Row...and she's gonna take care of her boys and the engines that love her too...cuz Diamond Daisy is a lady of the night...*"

Gatsby smiled. "Rather appropriate, Collector. You have real talent."

"Thank you, Captain...There's more..." Collector continued: "*At the helm, we never see doom or gloom...Gatsby's eyes are razor sharp as a bird of prey...While he makes every day our payday...*"

"Nice of you to say that, Collector," Gatsby said, "I really appreciate it."

Everyone chuckled except Kanky, who mumbled, "You-a pissing me off lately." In the semi-darkness, Kanky eyeballed Collector, who just smiled.

CHAPTER FORTY-FOUR

WHEN HENRY GROVER ARRIVED at Max's Wharf thirty minutes earlier, the engines of Joe's rum boats were already running. Yet they were still tied-up, while the boys loitered inside the clubhouse.

"What are they waiting for?" Grover whispered to himself. He had hidden his car off Main Road and walked through the woods, stationing himself alongside the clubhouse. There was a damp southwesterly breeze, and between the wind and the slapping waves, it was difficult to hear anything at the window that looked into this den of thieves.

Henry watched Bucolo talk to his men. He saw them slowly nod their heads; occasionally they'd laugh. Their laughter warmed Henry, because he knew more than they did about how this evening could end for them—if things turned out the way he hoped.

Hunker opened the gun cabinet and removed his eight-gauge punt gun. Henry reached down and touched his revolver. That crude hulk of a man was capable of anything. When Henry was very young, Hunker was a market hunter, and he often carried that same punt gun over one shoulder while the other held a group of high-flying 'honkers' as he walked down Neck Road near Nonquit Pond, just east of Seapowet Marsh, where he lived. Hunker had always been an exhibitionist.

Henry's eyes were locked onto the mounted pig's head. Truly a symbol that represented the moral code of the men who gathered beneath it.

He studied Pearly, who seemed to be contemplating something very serious. Of all the men, Pearly was probably the closest to Joe. If there was a second-in-command, it was Pearly Thurston. His father hated the Thurstons. But right now, Henry didn't care if Janie's father was Satan himself. One way or another, Janie would be his wife. Besides, being related to a capable man like Pearly Thurston could be an asset.

Suddenly, chairs scraping and boots stomping signaled that it was time. The rum-runners started for the door. He saw Sammy blow out the lanterns, and the building went black. Henry crouched closer. From the corner he heard them talking low, walking down the wharf, then they climbed down the ladder to their respective boats.

When he heard the rum boats' muffled exhausts, Henry's heart raced, and with the smell of gasoline fumes, the clear mission ahead for these lawbreakers aroused feelings close to envy in Henry Grover. As a man, he felt a bite of desperate loneliness. Janie Thurston flashed through his head. He had been thinking hard of late that he needed to turn the tide in his life.

A few minutes later, he watched the rum boats, one by one, idling away from Max's Wharf.

Henry stayed hidden until they disappeared into the shadowy darkness of the Seaconnet, headed south. He had his confirmation. The rest would be up to those federal officers, the Coast Guard, and of course the bridge.

Chapter Forty-Five

IT WAS A PERFECT, COOL, BLACK NIGHT with a southerly breeze. The swish of the rum boats' bows cut through the water while the powerful hum of the Liberties was all that broke the silence. Now and then, irate sea birds would screech in panic and dive under the bows, heads and bodies shaped like daggers, escaping the onslaught of the boats by inches.

At the mouth of the Seaconnet, Joe put the *Black Duck* on a compass course of one hundred seventy degrees. According to Mary's verified radio position that afternoon, the *Caprice* was anchored roughly south of the Scallop Gully on Coxe's Ledge, a location about thirty-two miles off the Rhode Island coast. With no sea running, the trip offshore passed quickly.

About ten miles out, and west of the Mussel Ridge by a good six miles, they crossed astern of a southbound freighter bellowing heavy smoke. Sammy pointed. "Probably heading for New York or Virginia…"

Joe nodded silently.

Less than twenty minutes later, they passed over the twenty-fathom edge and came upon an anchored Grand Banker, the *Highliner*, of Canadian registry. An ex-fishing vessel turned rummy, she had the white warning glow of a lantern hanging from her stern. Joe remembered the *Highliner* from her very first trip; the Nova Scotian captain was one nervous Nelly. Joe was surprised he returned.

He veered his course slightly to the west. Pearly and Hunker also altered their heading. Within twenty minutes, along the thirty-fathom curve, the hundred-foot *Caprice* came into view. She was a square-top-sail schooner with a combination of fore and aft sails, plus small quadrangles. Above the ocean, her furled canvas and masts stood high in a timeless moment, only adding to the illusion of eighteenth-century buccaneers. From her fo'c'sle portholes leaked small beams of light, making the vessel appear warm and inviting.

As they got closer, they could make out the outline of another vessel tied alongside.

"What the hell! We've got company."

"Betcha it's Kanky," Sammy whispered.

"No bet." Joe shifted the *Black Duck*'s engines into neutral. "Give the signal. We'll tie up on the starboard side."

Sammy hemmed and hawed for a split second. "I don't know, Joe. I don't like this...you hear?"

"Damn it! Crack the bell!" Sammy heard the firmness and repressed anger in Joe's tone. He opened the pilot house door, took hold of the leather thong handle, and cracked the bell three times, paused, and cracked it again. Flashing lanterns returned the signal.

Joe gently nudged the *Black Duck* closer. As they passed the stern of the strange rum boat, Joe read, "*Diamond Daisy*. Christ! It looks brand new... Could be Gatsby?"

Reflections from their lanterns revealed that the *Caprice*'s deck was stacked high with liquor crates and tins of Cuban Alky. Sections of meshed netting that held the cargo in place were in the process of being untied.

From out of the shadows, a small Chinese man, holding a lantern, jumped nimbly aboard the *Black Duck*, carrying manila bumpers. On the stern, Sammy tossed a line to another crewman. The lines were drawn tightly and quickly made fast. All was secure.

Sammy pointed to the other boat and asked, "Who the hell is that?"

The Chinese man shook his head, then shrugged.

Within minutes, the *Mallard* and *Wood Duck* pulled up. With only a slight southerly breeze and a smooth-running sea, the Chinese crew had no problem securing the rum boats alongside the *Black Duck*.

Joe and Sammy climbed aboard the *Caprice*. Behind them, they heard Hunker and Pearly complaining about this new competition. Joe turned to Sammy. "Tell them to keep quiet or else."

They now heard Captain Maytee shouting orders in broken English. Another Chinese man, holding a lantern, stood by Captain Maytee.

The captain looked and dressed like a Caribbean pirate. He had the fine features and dark skin of a mixed Jamaican bloodline. His hair was long and curled over his muscular shoulders. His toothy smile was wide and endearing as the two men shook hands vigorously.

"Ah, Monsieur Bucolock. It is very good to see you. It has been some time. But I was not expecting you tonight. I am puzzled. The radio message said you wouldn't be arriving tonight."

"What radio message?" Beneath the glow of the lantern, Maytee saw that Joe appeared confused and getting angry as well. Joe said, "I didn't expect this, Captain. I have two other boats with me. This wasn't part of our agreement…"

Maytee raised his hand to his Chinese deck boss to hold off loading *Diamond Daisy*. He held up three fingers and the deck boss nodded. Almost immediately, three armed Chinese appeared out of the shadows.

"Follow me," Maytee said. "As I said, I am also confused, we must discuss…"

Joe turned to Sammy. "Get Hunker…"

Before they entered the main stateroom, Maytee asked, "What are your needs?"

Joe took a paper from his top pocket and read: "Same as the radio message: Three hundred cases of Bacardi, three hundred cases of Absolut, two hundred cases of Golden Wedding."

He handed the list to Maytee, who nodded. "Is there anything else?"

"How is the Cuban Alky?" Joe asked. "Is it any better?"

Maytee shook his head. "It is the best grade that I can buy."

"Good, I'll take a hundred tins, split them between the three boats."

Joe and the three armed Chinese men followed Maytee. Joe figured the captain wasn't about to take any chances that things could get out of hand.

The large quarters were laid out like a suite at a fine hotel. Sweet incense burned in a dish. "You still enjoy your comforts, Captain."

"Of course," Maytee said. "Why not?"

Seated on a small couch was a young woman wearing a leather strip of beaded rawhide around her neck. Other than the movement of her doe-like eyes, she offered no sign of welcome.

Sammy's jaw dropped at the sight of the girl. He whispered, with real meaning, "I'm in love, Joe. Leave me on this vessel. You hear?"

Joe looked at him, surprised, then said, with a chuckle, "She is pretty, Sammy."

Alongside her sat Jay Gatsby, staring at Joe. Standing on each side of the couch were Kanky and Collector. They each had pistols strapped on their waists, and they showed no emotion at all looking at Joe. Behind them, Maytee's men stood at ready.

Maytee suddenly realized that neither man knew each other personally. He pointed to Gatsby, then Joe. He nodded. "Shall I introduce you two?"

Almost together, Joe and Gatsby said, "We've never met, but we know who we are."

Hunker entered, carrying his punt gun, but said nothing, except that he did size up the Chinese girl. Sammy gave Hunker a jab in the side and whispered, "She belongs to me, Hunker, I intend to marry her."

"Of course, Sammy," Hunker grunted, "I'll even be your best man."

Joe barely smiled at their exchange, but it did tickle him.

Captain Maytee did not like the sight of Hunker's shotgun, nor, earlier, the sidearms on Gatsby's men, so he simply compensated with his own men.

Hunker and Kanky glared at each other like two bulldogs eyeing a meaty bone.

Maytee quickly sensed a clear coolness among them all. He turned to Joe. "I do not know who sent that radio message, but…" he turned to Gatsby, "I believe someone has…" he searched for the word, "how we say in Jamaican: someone *trickify* on Monsieur Bucolock. So, I must *tump down.*"

Hunker whispered to Joe, "What the fuck is he talking about?"

"He's gonna stick to his word—the original arrangement," Joe answered Hunker out of the corner of his mouth.

Hunker smiled.

Gatsby nodded slowly. "I understand Jamaican values, Captain Maytee…and I'm sure you are a man of honor. There is no point in me trying to change your mind."

Maytee nodded. He was relieved, as was Joe, by Gatsby's attitude.

However, Kanky and Collector shifted slightly on their feet, then separated slightly, not sure what Gatsby's or Joe's next move would be. Hunker even shifted the punt gun slightly higher in his arm.

Joe looked at Gatsby, still surprised how easily he had acquiesced, but he said nothing.

Maytee clapped his hands. Two Chinese men appeared. Maytee spoke, and they scurried up the companionway. He looked at Joe, made a slight probing motion: Do you want any women?

Joe made no attempt to hide his feelings. "I smuggle booze, Captain…I don't smuggle people."

A dark shadow crossed the captain's face.

Gatsby followed suit. "I'm passing on the women as well, Captain. Possibly some other time."

Maytee shrugged. "Then let us have a drink." He turned to the girl sitting next to Gatsby and spoke to her in Spanish. She stood and went through a door into another cabin.

Gatsby said, "Captain Maytee, would you mind giving Mister Bucolo and myself a few private minutes?"

Maytee seemed nervous with the request. He glanced at Joe, who nodded. Everyone cleared out of the stateroom.

Gatsby slowly turned to Joe. "Well, Mister Bucolo, I knew we would meet sooner than later. Let's just say I didn't expect I would see you here tonight

"Sorry to disappoint you, Mister Gatsby, but I am well aware of your reputation."

Gatsby almost smiled. "I've done some bad things, old sport, it's rather easy."

Joe nodded. "What's really hard, old sport, is *not* doing bad things. Growing up, I've faced that dilemma a number of times."

Gatsby was nonplussed. "I'll keep that in mind, Mister Bucolo."

"Best you not forget." Joe stared him down.

Gatsby's eyes dropped. "We have something in common, Mister Bucolo."

"Really?"

"When I was young, I dug butter clams on the shores of the Great Lakes…fished for salmon, too. I really enjoyed it."

"Maybe you should have stuck with it. Certainly safer."

Before Gatsby could respond, the girl returned, carrying a tray with glasses and two bottles of wine. Maytee followed, as well as the others who had left.

Captain Maytee poured out three glasses and handed one each to Joe and Gatsby. "To your health, Monsieur Bucolock…Monsieur Gatsby… I hope to do business again with you gentlemen."

Gatsby said, "To your health as well, Captain."

They clinked glasses and each man took a sip. Gatsby said, "I need to get on my way…find another vessel." As Gatsby set down his glass,

Hunker, Kanky, and Collector came back into the captain's quarters.

Joe turned to Hunker. "Start the loading." Without a word, Hunker left.

"Mister Gatsby," Joe added, "I saw a rummy about ten minutes north of this position. She's the *Highliner*, from Nova Scotia. I bought from her two weeks after Prohibition was law."

"Thanks, Mister Bucolo, I'll check her out." Gatsby got up and left the quarters, followed by Collector, then Kanky. Joe's and Captain Maytee's eyes followed their exit. Kanky didn't turn his back until climbing up the fo'c'sle stairs.

There was a long moment of silence. Maytee said, "I was concerned there would be some violence."

"Me too." Joe relaxed somewhat and lit a cigarette. He offered one to Maytee, who refused.

They spent the next twenty minutes negotiating the cost of the liquor. Joe managed to get Maytee to lower the price of the Cuban Alky by a dollar a tin and the Bacardi by two dollars a case. But Maytee knew he was selling to a reasonable man, and the price of loaded merchandise was always less negotiable than cases stacked in the hold. Not to mention there were no bullets flying about.

Within an hour, all boats were loaded. On *Caprice*'s deck, Maytee placed his hand on Joe's shoulder. "A word of warning, my friend. Mister Gatsby showed patience and friendliness tonight…but he has calculation behind the eyes. Beware…"

Joe said, "I'm way ahead of you, Captain. Who do you think sent that message? But I do thank you."

"I hope to see you on my next trip, my friend."

Joe nodded and climbed aboard the *Black Duck*.

Chapter Forty-Six

THE GOOD WEATHER WAS HOLDING, not a cloud in the star-filled sky. They were now on a compass course that would bring them right into the Seaconnet River.

A half-hour later and about five miles from the coast, a slow-sweeping searchlight suddenly crossed the mouth of the Seaconnet River. For a few moments, the light continued to zigzag back and forth.

"Aw, shit!" Sammy snapped. "Trouble!"

Joe eased the *Black Duck* to the northwest as they watched the sweeping light. "Looks like a patrol boat," Joe said, "and they don't care if anyone knows."

Sammy asked, "I wonder if it's that patrol boat 483—looking to settle the score?"

"Wouldn't surprise me," Joe said.

Sammy's voice became shaky. "What are we gonna do, Joe?"

"Relax." Joe took a deep breath. Even with the hum of the engines and the sounds of the ocean against the hull, it seemed unbelievably quiet. Finally, he said, "Go home through the East Passage... no choice."

"Aw, shit!" Sammy took out a cigarette and lit it. "I'm getting a bad feeling 'bout this. You hear?"

Joe changed his course, with Pearly and Hunker following. Joe's mind wouldn't rest on why the Coast Guard had seemingly made their position known. It just wasn't the way they usually operated. Then again, maybe someone on the cutter's bridge thought they had seen something. Maybe luck was on their side, and quite simply an anxious sailor had blown their position.

At one-fifteen, they reached the East Passage entrance, and the warmer temperature of the ocean clashed with the cooler inland waters, creating ghostly ribbons of haze.

Joe eased up on the engines, and the three rum boats moved slowly through the eerie work of nature.

Moments later, they were through the cover and returned to clear visibility and calm water. Even though it was a black night, the stillness of the East Passage made everyone feel conspicuous. Notwithstanding, it was a long way to Tiverton, and at one thirty-five, on their portside, they were approaching the south tip of Prudence Island, where the lighthouse blazed diligently. Like their last run, the boats separated slightly and veered away from the flashing light, edging somewhat towards the east shore of the passage. All eyes strained into the blackness of the Prudence Island shoreline. Seconds later, they were through the flashing beacon.

"Maybe luck's with us," Sammy said quickly.

"Hope so," Joe said as he looked at the beacon already behind them. "Old coot like you doesn't get to see a beautiful girl too often… you hear?"

Sammy cackled for some time, warming Joe.

Joe took out his pocket watch. He held it beneath the panel lights. "One forty-three. We're running a little late tonight." He gave the engines a little more power.

"Who's buying the Alky?" Sammy asked.

"Micky Thompson."

"Old Micky will turn that stuff into real firewater."

With Hog Island on their portside, they passed through the new bridge construction and entered Mount Hope Bay.

Within twenty minutes, the rum boats swung wide around Common Fence Point and headed for the trestle bridge. As they passed by Francis Grover's fleet of moored menhaden vessels, Joe slowed down.

With the *Black Duck* leading, Pearly and Hunker maneuvered their boats into a single-line formation, making their way towards the trestle bridge.

Suddenly, Sammy shouted, "Look!"

A spotlight erupted from the dark shadows of Common Fence Point. It obviously belonged to a Coast Guard patrol vessel.

"Aw, shit!" Sammy yelled. "Aw, shit!" He dropped to his knees and began to lift the engine room hatch.

Straight ahead, another spotlight ignited—it appeared to be coming from the middle of the trestle.

"The bridge!" Joe screamed. "Goddamn it! The train bridge!" Everything fell into place. Now he knew why the Coast Guard had revealed their position at the mouth of the Seaconnet. He cursed himself for not realizing it or, for that matter, ever thinking about it. He was impressed with their plan. Someone had outsmarted him.

Sammy jumped up and peered straight ahead. His head was swiveling. "Jesus Christ! If the bridge is closed, what we gonna do, Joe?"

Joe jammed the throttles forward. The Liberty engines roared to life. Neither Pearly nor Hunker had changed course. They were waiting for Joe's reaction.

"The tide, Sammy! What's the fucking tide?"

Sammy hesitated for a moment. He crossed to the port door of the pilot house. Grover's menhaden vessels were hanging bows north. He yelled, "It's falling! Falling! Maybe, maybe half tide…"

"Get down!" Joe screamed. "Way down!"

"Aw, shit! Joe, we're gonna be killed!"

"Get down, you old coot!"

"Joe! You're crazy!"

~~~~~

On the bridge, Colonel Chaffee and McGill walked up and down the tracks, slapping the backs of the sharpshooters hanging over the railing. McGill called through his megaphone, "Don't fire until I give the command. Repeat. Don't fire until—"

The lawmen watched the lead boat roaring towards the bridge, straight at the spotlight, dead-center into the closed span.

McGill and Chaffee shook their heads in disbelief. "Jesus Christ! They're not going to stop!" Guns at ready, everyone was waiting for his signal to open fire.

~~~~~

With a shattering encounter of glass and wood against a bridge girder, the *Black Duck* was suddenly beneath them. Everything went flying into the air—the pilot house roof was severed clean—carrying with it the stern cases of liquor. Tins of Cuban alcohol erupted, spraying the line of lawmen hanging over the bridge.

Within moments, the other two boats also crashed under the trestle—ripping their pilot houses away. The odor of hard spirits showered the men, not sure whether they should shoot or stand down.

Once the third boat cleared the bridge, a giant beast of a man stood out on the deck, bellowing as he pounded his torso with his fists. The sound was not human and seemed to last forever. It seemed to belong to some wild jungle animal, Agent Leman thought to himself. What the hell is happening here?

~~~~~

From the command position, Chaffee and McGill were mesmerized by the rum-runners' action. They were in utter disbelief of the one thing they had not anticipated. They had waited far too long before yelling, "Fire!"

With the boats already through the bridge, the agents, guardsmen, and state police rushed across the tracks.

They whirled the spotlight around, shining the beam wildly across the empty waters.

By the time the riflemen fell to a kneeling position and opened fire, all three rum boats were lost in the darkness of the Tiverton Basin, heading towards the open Seaconnet River. The shooting continued until McGill screamed for them to stop.

~~~~~~

On the north side of the bridge, Lieutenant Wallace, on Coast Guard 483, focused his patrol light on the splintered and floating remains. Already the fast-moving tide was grabbing the drifting booty and carrying it south into the tangled currents of the Basin. Not only that—Wallace didn't realize his patrol boat was about to be trapped in those fast-moving eddies as well.

He slammed his fist against the console and glared at his men standing silently by. "Swamp Yankee fishermen! Fucking scum of the earth!"

~~~~~~

On Murphy's Wharf, on the east shore of the river, Tommy Walsh and his shore crew saw the dancing beam of light and listened to the distant gunfire with uneasy excitement. Hearing their echoes, Tommy couldn't understand why Joe was returning by way of the East Passage. He had specifically told him they would return north, up the Seaconnet. Why would he use the East Passage?

When the shooting stopped, Tommy ordered everyone into the trucks.

He was still confused, but he knew if Joe had indeed survived, he would be heading for an alternate site. With lights off and spirits low, the five trucks headed south, towards Seapowet Cove.

~~~~~~

Janie Thurston jumped up and about fell out of bed. At first, she thought she was dreaming. But with her eyes opened, she still heard the gunshots, and they were real. Cold terror ripped through her. Pearly, Joe, and his gang were being riddled with bullets. She was certain her greatest fear had finally come true.

Hearing more gunfire, Janie tripped on her nightgown running down the stairs. By the time she reached the sunporch it was quiet, but she could see the beam of the searchlight jerking wildly, illuminating a narrow path back and forth over the Basin.

She dropped to her knees, rested her chin on the windowsill, and cried over the unknown terror she felt. Her father was living on the edge between life and death, and she couldn't understand why. Yet, at the same moment, another sensation passed through her. This one was less familiar, but Janie knew it was something wild in her bones— something about being a Yankee Thurston.

~~~~~~

Along the shoreline of the Tiverton Basin, the sound of the ambush caused cottage lights to snap on. Most residents figured something bad happened, and that it probably involved rum-running and the steel hands of the law.

~~~~~~

Unlike Janie, when Mary Standish heard the gunfire, she knew it was real. She glanced at her clock: two-thirty. It was about the time Joe would be returning from Rum Row.

She ran down to the diner kitchen. She kept her lights off. From the rear windows facing the Basin, she saw a spotlight coming from the bridge. She knew a trap had been set.

With a worried chill settling over her shoulders, Mary pulled her bathrobe tight and stared out towards the light, praying that no one had been hurt.

~~~~~~

Awakened by the melee, Minister Bottomley fell out of bed, moaning. He crawled over to the window of his third-floor bedroom and looked north, towards the sound of the shots and the railroad bridge. Seeing nothing but the swerving spotlight, he figured the man behind it must be as drunk as he felt. He opened his window and sucked in the cool night air.

In his mind, that white illumination seemed like a sword from heaven, chasing those purveyors of the demon rum on this river of sin. He knew he had another good, rousing subject for his next sermon.

Then he heard the most extraordinary primeval bellowing and the roar of the night boats whizzing by in the dark, their wakes splashing heavily against his dock. It was a deep, echoing cry like nothing he had ever heard. Maybe, he thought, he should pray for the agonized victim.

He descended barefoot down the stairs to the pantry and a late snack, an afternoon gift from that voluptuous red-headed whore across the street, after he had brought her Gertrude's peach pie. How he loved this excitement. Munching spicy molasses-and-raisin cookies, his mind returned to Jessica and his favorite observation of mankind: it's impossible to know good without knowing evil.

~~~~~~

The night was only beginning for Coast Guard 483. Underestimating the force of the falling tide, the vessel's rudders and engines proved no match for the powerful outgoing currents. Before Lieutenant Wallace could back down or even turn away, his patrol vessel was repeatedly slammed against the bridge's northern granite abutment. With much confusion and angry yelling, Wallace and his crew finally secured the vessel.

Lieutenant Wallace realized that Coast Guard 483 would have to lie there until the tide slacked or turned. Even if he wanted to pursue the rum-runners, he couldn't. It had not been a good night. In no hurry to face the other lawmen, Wallace slowly climbed up an iron maintenance ladder onto the trestle. Agent Leman walked over and looked down at the patrol vessel's damage and said to Wallace, "Hasn't been a good night for boats, has it?"

"No, sir," the lieutenant responded. "That's just what I was thinking."

Leman added, "I'm sure of one thing, Lieutenant Wallace: we are dealing with rather…unusual men."

"More like crazy!" Wallace snapped back. "Who the fuck in their right mind would attempt that? Sir."

"Crazy is the word!" Colonel Chaffee said as he approached and returned Wallace's salute. He added, "I'd be goddamned if I'd ever do what those boys did. Any of you hear that rum-runner's yell? It chilled my blood. That man belongs in the jungle!"

They stood in silence for a moment.

"It's a wonder no one got killed," Leman said softly.

"Who knows, maybe somebody did!" Henry Grover replied loudly.

"Chief Grover…that sounded like a wish!" Leman said.

Henry Grover ignored Leman and continued walking down the tracks towards Riverside Drive.

Colonel Chaffee spoke softly. "I don't think Mister Bucolo has seen or heard the last of Chief Grover."

McGill stared off into the darkness after Grover. "I'd have to agree with you, Colonel! But after tonight, I wouldn't bet against Bucolo."

Lieutenant Wallace kicked at the bedding stones of the train tracks. He looked at Agent Leman and asked, "What do we do now?"

Agent Leman shook his head. "I don't know. Bucolo may lie low after tonight?"

"Don't count on it," Chaffee said. "This goddamn bridge sure didn't bother him. One thing we know, Bucolo's got balls."

Leman gave a chuckle. "Lieutenant Wallace, at the crack of dawn, you and your crew are to salvage whatever floating booty you can. I'm afraid that's all we're going to get out of this operation."

~~~~~~

About halfway down the river, near Seapowet, Joe eased up on the throttles. With no windshield, his face and eyes were stinging. The shooting and the searchlight were long behind them. He saw no signs of any pursuing Coast Guard. He was worried, however, about the patrol vessel they had seen earlier in the night at the mouth of the river. Could she be waiting in the shadows of the shoreline? With everything else that happened tonight, he knew anything was possible. He figured that Kanky or Gatsby had possibly masterminded the ambush.

While the *Black Duck* sat idling, they could smell the reeking Cuban Alky.

A short distance behind them, Pearly and Hunker were also slowing to a gradual stop.

Joe cupped his hands and called to the others, "Looks like they quit, but keep your eyes open. They could still have some surprises for us."

"Jesus suffering Christ," Sammy's first words since slamming under the bridge. His feet were on the floor of the engine room, his elbows resting on the deck of the pilot house, his head in his hands. "My ears are killing me."

He struggled to climb up over the pilot house's debris. Joe almost stepped on him. "We're all crazy," Sammy said.

Joe glanced at his engineer but said nothing. He shifted the engines into neutral and waited for Pearly and Hunker to maneuver alongside. Joe went out on the deck. A broken case of King William was close by. He grabbed a bottle. His hands were shaking as he took a swig. He handed the bottle to Sammy, who was standing up now, leaning against the console. Sammy had a long draw.

With bottle in hand, Joe jumped aboard the *Mallard* as she came alongside. Pearly was on his knees, hands pressed against his chest. Billy Bancock was holding onto the helm, a raving wreck.

"Everyone okay?"

"Jesus! Those bastards meant business," Pearly said, grabbing the bottle from Joe, then he rolled over on his back. "What a fucking trap!" He sucked on the whiskey.

The *Wood Duck* came alongside, Hunker already swigging on his own bottle.

Bobby Bancock jumped off Hunker's boat and grabbed Joe's arm. "No more for me, Joe!" He snapped the bottle from Pearly's hand. "This business is too much for this country boy. I'd rather shovel cow shit or pick potatoes."

"Goddamn it! I don't blame Bobby," Hunker added. "We almost didn't make it. We got caught in your fucking wakes. Just take a gander at my bow."

Hunker's boat had lost part of her bow stem. The heavy wakes of the *Black Duck* and *Mallard* forced the *Wood Duck* higher up against the roof girders of the bridge.

"A little more on the wash," Hunker added, "and she'd be stuck there on the trestle. Those lawmen would be picking over my bones right now."

Joe shook his head. "Well, boys, just figure if that tide had been higher?"

"You sure took a helluva chance," Pearly said, not altogether kindly spoken.

"It was that or the iron coop," Joe said.

"Fuckin' close call," Hunker added.

"I think we're all nuts," Billy Bancock said, obviously siding with his brother. His remark drew a moan of agreement from Sammy and very weak chuckles from the others.

"Where we gonna unload?" Pearly asked.

"Almy's," Joe said. "I'm sure that's where Tommy will be heading." They returned to their boats and headed southeast to a secluded landing inside Seapowet Cove.

~~~~~~

Tommy Walsh and his crew waited. Much excitement hung in the air as the badly damaged rum boats tied-up. Talk would come later, but right now everybody had to work with the determination of Maytee's Chinese crew to get the boats emptied. There still was no telling if a patrol boat would suddenly show up.

By five a.m., Tommy Walsh and his crew had finished, and Joe promised the shore gang an extra bonus for the quick unloading. The run tonight cost him eighty tins of Cuban Alky and ninety-three cases of liquor. Not too bad overall, considering.

By the time the empty rum boats were tied up at Max's Wharf, the sky in the east was brightening.

~~~~~~

Inside the clubhouse, as they waited on Sammy's coffee, little was said outside of the men's confusing and conflicting opinions, the most commonly verbalized being: "Who the fuck set us up?"

Joe said, "Gatsby or Kanky…I hate to say it…possibly Grover… but I don't think he's that smart…take ya pick."

Hunker asked, "Question is, what are we going to do about it?"

"Well," Sammy added quickly, "sinking his rum boat didn't seem to solve anything."

Pearly said, "You got a point there."

The second most frequently expressed affirmation was from Hunker: "I'm going to kill the pricks."

The morning had the makings of an endless chatter session, the kind that fishermen relish, where the talk jerks back and forth in shouting matches and no one proves shit at the end.

Joe stopped the chatter dead in its tracks with a little humor. "Hey, boys, get this. On Maytee's schooner, Sammy said he was in love with that young Chinese girl…and he wanted me to leave him there."

Hunker piped in, "Yeah, my skinny friend warned me that she belonged to him."

Sammy shouted, "Honest to Christ, I was in love…you hear?"

"Of course, Sammy," Hunker grunted, "I'll even be your best man."

Everyone roared, even the old coot himself.

Chapter Forty-Seven

JANIE WAITED FOR PEARLY by the kitchen door. She waved to Joe but made no effort to leave the house. Pearly could see much of his late wife in Janie's expression. It was unnerving, and his legs weakened; he actually felt cut off at the knees.

In the kitchen, he grabbed a chair and sat down, head in his hands. He said, "Okay, get it over with."

"Oh, Daddy, you had me worried to death."

"I'm sorry, Janie, really…" Pearly's eyes were stinging.

"Well, it's over," she said. "And you're okay, that's all that matters."

Pearly took a deep breath, relieved that she hadn't jumped all over him. He wondered why she hadn't.

"Can I make you some breakfast?"

"No, just coffee. Joe wants us back at the wharf. We've gotta get the boats repaired, and we gotta get over to New Bedford. We've got a lot to do."

Janie nodded. "Do you want to talk about it?"

"We were set up. They were waiting for us at the trestle. They closed the bridge and had us trapped. If it weren't for Joe's quick thinking, we'd be in the coop."

She walked over with the coffeepot and looked at her father. "No one can outrun the law forever. You and the boys have been pressing your luck for some time now. You all should smarten up."

"Now, you sound like Joe." Pearly reached for a bottle of whiskey on the counter. He poured some into his cup, and Janie covered it with coffee. He took a sip and said, "Joe and me, well, we're beginning to see this business as a no-win situation. In fact, it wouldn't surprise me none if he bought a dragger and went back fishing."

She returned the pot to the stove. "Oh?" she asked. "And when did this all happen?"

Pearly shrugged. "I suppose this morning, you know, after slamming into the bridge."

"I'm relieved to hear that."

"You don't have to look so happy," he said.

She decided to push the issue. "Are you saying right now that you're quitting?"

"Whoa! Don't put any words in my mouth. But some things gotta happen first. Besides, there are other considerations."

Suddenly she looked pissed off. "Like what?"

"Well, Joe's in a financial bind. And with everything that's happened lately—the new boat, the hijacking. Even this morning, not much profit there."

Janie nodded. "Daddy, what exactly do you mean?"

"Remember I mentioned last week how Joe and me were working on something?"

She nodded.

"Well, Joe intends to pull off one good score. One huge 'bang in'."

Janie's expression quickly changed to that of aggravated puzzlement. "Isn't that just what the gang needs to do? One big 'bang in.' God Almighty in heaven! A 'bang in'! Whatever that means! Great idea, Pearly!"

Pearly blinked. What was this he was seeing in his daughter? She'd never spoken to him like that. "Yes, it's a wild idea!" Pearly's voice tapered almost to a whisper. "But we think it can work. Joe intends on

landing an entire cargo of booze—thousands and thousands of cases—all at once. End the trade with a big bang!"

Janie shook her head. "When will you ever learn?"

"Probably never."

Janie's expression toughened. "You could've been killed this
morning. Dead. Gone. Not just till the next tide, Pearly. Gone forever.
Done! Me alone! You burning in the fires of hell forever—you—the
instrument of Satan!"

No doubt about it. She was in a strange mood. *Wrong time of the
month?* he wondered. Wouldn't dare say it, though—specially with the
shape she was in this morning. "Listen, just be a little more patient. If
we can pull it off, we're done with the trade."

"Why don't I believe you, Daddy?"

"Beats me."

~~~~~~

By late morning, the banks of the Tiverton Basin and the Seaconnet
shorelines were dotted with searchers. It didn't take long for the word
to spread. Dozens of scavengers prowled the beaches, hoping to cash
in on Joe Bucolo's bad luck.

It had turned into a contest between the Coast Guard and the
local beachcombers, who had already made the biggest dent in the
tide-swept tins of Alky and floating cases of booze. Some of the bur-
lap-and-straw-packed bottles were getting waterlogged and sinking.
This was good news to the more industrious skiff-owners, who began
dragging the bottom with small scallop dredges.

Many of the townsfolk ventured down to Max's Wharf to survey
the damaged boats.

Mary's Diner turned into a beachcombers' headquarters for the
speculators. Talk was some had been injured.

Bridge attendant Eddie Grayson, a fond lover of the hard spirits,
was unusually quiet about the run-in. When he came in for his coffee,
he claimed he had been ordered by the agents to stay inside the trestle

control shack. Because he lived in Tiverton and didn't want any trouble with Chief Grover, Eddie didn't dare open his mouth about what he had seen, heard, or suspected.

Whether you were a wet or a dry, the ambush at Tiverton Basin's bridge was being elevated to legend.

~~~~~~

Minister Bottomley's ears were ringing when he left the rear exit of his church. All morning, he had been receiving calls from his faithful followers, giving him their perspective on the incident.

He walked out onto the long dock. For Bottomley, it was an uncomfortable experience to be standing over the lapping water. He couldn't remember the last time he had been behind the church. His life was inside the sanctuary, and his comings and goings were always by the front door.

The wide, heavy timbers creaked under his weight, and he wondered if was safe. In fact, since moving here, he questioned the safety of the entire building. Over the years, especially during those bad storms, the Basin would rise and the structure seemed to be giving way.

He was heartened that his skinflint congregation was finally responding to his warnings.

Last Sunday, Francis told Bottomley to be patient—and someday soon, he would have his own new church. Praise the Lord.

Bottomley's biggest problem was the smell. The church had a cavernous saltwater cellar that, in its day, kept oysters fresh and succulent until ready for market. Depending on the moon or storms, however, the cellar would flood. The smell could get as putrid as anything he'd ever encountered—even worse than a long July wake when the ice had melted beneath the dearly departed.

Bottomley was thankful he slept on the third floor, away from the stench of low tide. Usually, during summer services, he would keep the church windows open to help disperse the air. On a full-moon tide there was no escape, though, and many of his congregation carried hand fans. If it didn't make him retch so, he'd keep the windows shut tight until just before the service to germinate the putrid smell into a demon's brew—maybe that would move his congregants to generosity for a new house of worship.

Since daybreak, and between the phone calls, he had been watching to see if the Coast Guard or anyone else had been near or around his dock. So far, so good. To the north, near Peabody's Wharf, he saw a couple of men rowing a skiff, obviously hunting for liquor.

Bottomley carried a long-handled dip net. He looked around carefully, trying to make sure no one could see him.

A salty, rotten odor penetrated his nose as he stood at the end of the dock. He associated the stench with those fishermen who never went to his church, who ran rum, who drank booze, and who chased after women—who even had the smell of low tide. He sniffed hard and cleared his throat. What a life. Still—and despite his own penchant for the bottle—he was determined to save them all from the clutches of Satan.

The tide was rising beneath him. The water lapped at the riddled, worm-eaten construction.

With some discomfort, he bent over and peered under the dock. Sure enough, like a cornucopia of delectable sea creatures, he saw the straw-wrapped necks of liquor bottles bobbing up and down, drifting with the tricky currents, some jammed against the support cross-timbers. He also heard the hollow echoes of Alky tins bouncing against the barnacle-encrusted pilings.

Bottomley dragged the crab net through the water. For a long time, he swiped at the elusive bottles.

Occasionally he moved his position, groaning in frustration. Holding tightly onto the edge of the timber with his left hand, he took another drag through the water. This time, despite its straw wrap, the round, iron frame of the net broke the bottle. He heard the glass break. It made a soft plop. All that good booze disappeared. Bottomley's lips twisted and he mimed a silent curse. He shifted his body to the right and continued on with more empty swipes.

But then—glory be—not long after, a bottle of Overholt Rye hung heavy as he slowly lifted it out of the water. Bottomley's eyes twinkled with delight. He had just caught a record fish. When he took the bottle from the net, he wore a grin from ear to ear. He calculated that as the tide rose, his luck might incrementally improve—if all those sinful rummies trawling for his booty didn't get to them first.

Leaving the net behind the church, he carried the bottle inside his coat pocket, mumbling a thankful tune for punishing Joe Bucolo. As he reached for the door, it opened.

In the hall stood the white-legged, barefooted, red-headed trollop from across the street.

~~~~~~

Jessica handed him the empty peach pie pan. "It was delicious. Thank Gertrude for me."

"Oh dear," he whispered. "I can't do that." Bottomley took it from her. "Miss Jackson, I'm honored that you're paying me a visit. Come in."

She nodded towards his coat pocket. "I see that crabbing was good."

His hand slapped to the coat pocket. "Miss Jackson, were you spying on me?"

She laughed. "You've been spying on me and my daughter from the day you moved in here. Why do you think we undress in front of our windows?" She dropped her voice to a whisper. "We know it gives you a thrill, and it gives us something to laugh about." She giggled.

Bottomley simply ignored her comments. "I must say, you being here in my house pleases me beyond words."

"You can skip the sermon, Reverend."

"I'm not a reverend… I'm a minister."

"Sure…and I'm *Jeanne d'Arc*."

Puzzled, he asked, "John…who?"

"Never mind. *Minister* Bottomley, please make me a drink."

"Certainly. I trust you are a lady of tight lips."

"Tighter than Gertrude Moore's, I suspect."

Again he whispered, "Oh dear." He took the bottle of Overholt out of his pocket. "We shall partake of my meager catch. You realize I do suffer from the chill of this awful river of sin."

Jessica nodded her head. "I too suffer from that same chill, dear Minister."

He nodded vigorously. "I'm happy that you understand. I must say, I just couldn't believe my eyes when I saw you at my Sunday service."

"Make me that drink, please?"

Bottomley pointed to his sagging, worn couch. "Get comfortable, Jessica…how's Overholt Rye and water?"

She nodded. "Not too much water." She sat down. While he made her drink, she adjusted her low-cut dress at the top. "What do you want to know, Minister Bottomley?"

"Your attendance at my service this past week had a lot of people…chitchatting—to give you the benefit of the doubt. What made you finally come to my service? Was it solely to harass Francis Grover?"

Her eyes flashed concern. "Why, Minister Bottomley, I'm repenting for all my bad, lusty behavior. I'm going to try and turn over a new leaf."

"Really…are…are you really repenting for all your bad behavior? I hope—"

"Maybe not all. Now, what would you like from me, my dear Minister?"

"You certainly must know, dear Jessica."

"Okay, but first, hand me that drink."

~~~~~~

Cory Wilcox was a good shipwright, but he was also a shrewd businessman. For the longest time, he stood on Max's Wharf, shaking his head, gazing down at the wrecked rum boats. When he knew Pearly was on the verge of pushing him into the water, he climbed down the ladder and boarded the *Black Duck*.

Joe and the others waited. Cory spent a good long time surveying the damage, making notations on the clean side of a cedar shingle. When he finished, he called up to Joe, "Yep, more work than you realize. If you want a true balance, Joe, I've got to start from scratch. But your boats have to be at my yard so the work can go faster."

Joe nodded. "Okay, you'll start with the *Black Duck* first."

"When?"

Joe rolled his eyes impatiently. "Soon as possible. Today, Cory, today."

Cory shrugged. "Didn't know you were in such a hurry."

They watched Cory climb the ladder. Pearly shook his head in exasperation.

On the wharf, Cory turned around and said, "By the way, Joe— that fellow from Bristol, he really liked the *Flo*. Said he was going to bring me a deposit. Said he wanted to buy her."

Joe motioned to Sammy. "Get the engines running." Then he turned back to the shipwright. "I'll be over with the *Duck* shortly."

"Remember, Joe, first one with the deposit..."

"I know, Cory. I know."

Chapter Forty-Eight

IN THE SPEAKEASY LOUNGE of Jay Gatsby, Walter and Kanky listened intently to Collector.

Gatsby snapped, his expression almost violent; so much so, Collector jerked back slightly. "What do you mean, Bucolo will be running liquor soon? His boats are out of commission."

Collector said, "While I was visiting my new girlfriend, I went by a boatyard on the Acushnet River. I saw a new rum boat—stopped and nosed around...got to talking with some workers. Boat belongs to Foggy Joe. From what they tell me, she's expected to be the fastest rummy on the East Coast."

Kanky's eyes exploded with rage. "How-a fuck did Bucolo do that?"

Puzzled, everyone looked at each other.

Gatsby asked, "Is the boat ready?"

Collector nodded. "I'm telling you...she's brand new...a real beauty, too. She's ready to run booze... It's supposed to be a secret, Bucolo calls it *Whispering Winds*. I like the name. Sounds, huh, kind of nice. I might make a song for her. They claim she'll outrun a cannonball."

"Don't get carried away, Collector." Gatsby was clearly irritated by the news. And Collector seemed to appreciate the fact that Bucolo had an ace up his sleeve a little more than he took kindly to.

Kanky's eyes flashed to Collector. "Yeah, shut-a the fuck up!"

Gatsby went over to the closet and carried out a crate and set it on a table. He pried it open and moved aside some thick cotton wraps, exposing sticks of fused dynamite. He grabbed a couple of the charges. "This will take care of Bucolo's rum boats. Forever."

Everyone stared silently at the explosives.

Walter went to say something, but changed his mind.

~~~~~~

Later that afternoon, Kanky was shocked when Henry Grover called to say he was coming to Oakland Beach. When he pressed Henry if there had been any more news on the bridge incident, he got no-where. Deep down, Kanky hoped that maybe something bad had happened to Joe, and Henry just wanted to deliver the good news in person. Still, he wondered if he could trust Henry Grover. After all, Grover was a policeman—and just maybe he was coming here to even the score. Gatsby arranged to have enough men around to see that nothing like that happened.

Then again, Kanky actually looked forward to having Henry Grover at Oakland Beach. It would finally give him the opportunity to flaunt some of his success on this side of the state.

It tickled Kanky to think how Henry's straitlaced principles would hold up inside the shit-laced sins of the Tumble Inn. Kanky made it clear to Bertha, the head madam, that he wanted the best-looking temptations around when Grover arrived. He hoped that the police chief had an affinity for pretty bottoms.

~~~~~~

Henry Grover, dressed casually, studied the exterior of the speakeasy. Somehow, he thought that this monstrosity seemed to fit Kanky. His father was right: bad seeds, bad breeds. On the drive over, he contin-ually reminded himself that dealing with Kanky was like dealing with a deranged animal. Nobody knew the real Kanky.

Just as he reached the top of the stairs, the front door opened. A small Chinese man bowed and stepped aside. Henry was disturbed that this man had been watching for him. The Chinese man rushed by him and opened a second door. Henry looked up at the scrolled *Tumble Inn, Tumble Out* sign.

Inside, the strong odor of whiskey and cigarettes saturated the air. A woman stood at the bar. A number of tables were occupied by a few good-looking girls.

He recognized Kanky sitting at a table with a freckled, red-haired lady. Kanky's backside was against a wall. He had a bottle of vodka in front of him and two glasses.

Four men playing cards at an adjacent table watched Henry approach Kanky's table. "Hello, Henry," Kanky said, almost pleasantly.

Henry nodded and glanced at the woman, who excused herself and walked to the bar.

"Sit-a down, Henry."

Henry pulled out the chair and sat opposite Kanky.

"Would you like-a something to drink?"

"You know I don't drink."

"Of course, but you're a long way from Tiverton. No one will-a know."

"Well, I will!"

Kanky poured himself vodka and leaned forward and smiled. "Would-a you like one of my girls for the afternoon?" He motioned towards them, who were sitting on couches, looking rather appealing, revealing plenty of legs and boobs.

Henry lingered on them momentarily. "No, thanks," he said.

Kanky nodded, noticing a slight weakness in Henry's voice. This pleased him. "Such honor...good-a discipline. It-a impressive."

"Proper upbringing," Henry said, with a seriousness that indicated he clearly believed in such things.

Kanky snapped, "What-a the good news you bring? Anyone killed, or badly a-hurt?"

Henry gave him a smirk. "There is no good news."

"So, what-a the fuck happened?" His words seemed to echo in the room. A spray of Kanky's saliva traveled over the table.

"Oh, my idea worked," Henry said. "They had Bucolo cornered against that closed trestle. I mean he was trapped. Trapped like a rat. I saw it all. But he and the rest of his boys still managed to get away."

"Jesus Christ! How?" Kanky's voice brought his men to attention. They turned and now watched Grover closely.

Henry said, "Bucolo and his boys ran their boats right under the railroad bridge."

Kanky's hand swung out, sending the bottle of vodka skipping and spraying across the floor, finally popping as it hit the brass foot-rail. "That-a slippery no-good fuck!"

Henry added, "Plenty of damage to their boats…lost a substantial amount of liquor."

"What did-a the law do?"

"Nothing! The cutter was trapped against the bridge. Caught by the tide."

Kanky shook his head. "Joe a fucking slippery fucker!"

"Right now, they think Bucolo is pretty tough to beat."

Kanky said, "Looks-a like Foggy Joe made them look-a like-a greenhorn fools."

Henry added, "Frankly, they think he's got plenty of nerve. Coast Guard's keeping the incident quiet."

For a long time Kanky sat there, stewing and contemplating. Finally, eyes zeroed in on Henry, he asked, "Why you come here, Henry? Especially with all this bad news?"

"I wanted to make sure that you're not quitting."

Kanky laughed. It even brought weak grins to his men. He pointed up towards a chandelier. "I won't-a quit until Bucolo's balls a-hanging there."

Henry nodded. "Good! I just wanted to be sure. I also wanted you to know that I'm still here to help."

Kanky's eyes narrowed, as though an alarm sounded in his head. "I didn't realize-a your father's reputation was-a that important."

"It's not! It's for me. It's personal."

Kanky nodded. "Personal? What-a the hell does that mean?"

"Janie Thurston," Henry said softly.

Suddenly Kanky smiled knowingly. "Figures. Joe always got the cream of the crop; always fucked-a the prettiest ones."

Henry's face flushed with anger. "He's not fucking Janie! And he never will fuck her!"

Kanky's head tilted, like some bird listening for a worm. "That's-a nice to hear, Henry, real-a nice. I mean it's-a nice to hear you fucking cursing. Makes me feel-a like you're fucking human, especially with all your fucking proper upbringing."

Henry glared at Kanky. "Just make fucking sure that Joe doesn't get the best of you."

"Don't-a worry, he-a won't. Bucolo always tries to avoid trouble."

"Strange," Henry said, "trouble seems to follow him around."

"Maybe, but I'm going to be-a Joe's biggest trouble."

Kanky signaled one of his men for another bottle. "Are you sure you don't want a drink? Maybe you and I should-a celebrate our continuing alliance."

Henry stood. He appeared to be getting ready to leave.

Kanky poured himself one and raised it in a small salute to Grover.

Henry just watched Kanky down the shot and pour another. Henry asked, "What are you going to do?"

Kanky chuckled. "Simple; you…and me are going to keep-a Joe's good luck running."

As Henry left, his eyes again locked in on the girls sitting on the couch.

A few moments later, Gatsby and Walter, neither looking happy, opened the door to his office.

Kanky asked, "Did-a you hear what-a he said?"

Gatsby nodded. "Every word! Grover's an asshole, but he's a man with a purpose."

Walter added, "Well, it appears that Bucolo is a much more formidable adversary than we thought."

Kanky softly agreed, "Yeah, I think-a you right. He even-a surprised me."

Gatsby said, "I believe that's an understatement, Kanky."

Walter added, "I wouldn't count on Grover being any help at all… unless he just shoots Bucolo."

Kanky's voice turned nasty. "Henry might-a just do that if Bucolo fuck-a Janie Thurston."

CHAPTER FORTY-NINE

JOE AND PEARLY STOPPED BY Wilcox's boatyard. The *For Sale* sign was still hanging on the *Flo*'s pilot house. The gang said nothing.

Cory and three carpenters were already working on the *Black Duck*.

Despite the number of men, the rebuilding job seemed to be progressing slowly, with only the pilot-house framing completed. Cory was measuring out the windows.

The boys surveyed the work. "If Cory was any slower, we'd have to call Doc Peckham," Sammy offered.

That tickled Hunker, who nudged Sammy. "I'll be pissing on ya grave before Cory ever finishes the *Wood Duck*."

"Thanks!" Sammy slapped Hunker's head. "Thanks for that!"

Then Hunker asked what everyone was thinking. "How come ya ain't got more work done, Cory? Jesus Christ, I could have built a fuckin' boat by now."

Cory's right eye squinted, and he sucked life back into his dying pipe.

"If you fellows hadn't lost that booze in the Basin, maybe my men would've come to work instead of going treasure-hunting for two days."

Behind Cory, his men were nodding and grinning. Some appeared to have been hitting the sauce.

289

"Well, Cory," Pearly asked, "did you find any treasure?"

Cory snapped, "Course, you damn fool."

That tickled Sammy.

Joe shook his head and said, "I've got something for you, Cory." He took an envelope out of his pocket.

Cory put down his ruler and approached Joe. He was still cackling as he eyeballed the brown envelope. He said, "Yep, you're in luck. That fellow from Bristol hasn't shown up with the money yet."

"Yep, in luck," Pearly mumbled.

Joe handed the envelope to Cory. "Here's five hundred. It's my down payment. I'm gonna need a little time to come up with the balance."

Pearly's head shifted towards Hunker, then both men turned to Sammy. No one said anything, but neither Pearly nor Hunker could hide their displeasure.

Cory said, "Figured that was going to happen, Joe." He tapped the envelope against his hand. "Come into the office and I'll write you up a receipt."

"Why don't you write it on a shingle!" Pearly snapped.

Cory gave Pearly a bemused look. "Warms my heart, Joe, it just warms my heart that you're gonna own the *Flo*."

Pearly, Hunker, and Sammy stood together on Cory's broken-shell driveway while Joe and Cory walked towards the office.

Pearly said, "Well, boys, it's finally happening."

Hunker grunted, "Jesus Christ, I hate the thought of going back to work."

Sammy said, "Well, we better start thinking about the fishing trade again. You hear?"

Hunker said, "Damn! I never thought the rum trade would come to this."

Sammy glanced at both men. "Joe's been saying it right along. You striped-ass monkeys never wanted to listen."

Hunker took out a fresh stogie and lit it from the old stub. "Hey, Sammy, ya my friend, but shut the hell up!"

Pearly took a deep breath and said softly, "I really wonder if we'll even get a chance to pull off that 'bang in'."

"Don't look good," Sammy added. "Don't look good, you hear?"

CHAPTER FIFTY

OVER THE YEARS, GATSBY FOUND that the best solutions to big problems (as an inebriated Dan Cody counseled) was sleeping on them. As he thought about Daisy, he reassured himself that even though his strategy wasn't progressing as quickly as he hoped, in the end, he would have her.

Though it was still early, he longed to soak in his bathtub and put on his pajamas, accompanied by a few shots with beer chasers before bed.

Later, after a fair amount of whiskey and beer, and failing to sleep, he called Moran.

Moran answered with a deep, sighing hello until he realized it was Gatsby. "Yes, Jay, what's going on?"

"Call a meeting tomorrow morning."

Moran asked, "Anything I should be aware of?"

"I'm through playing around with Bucolo. I'm ending this, one way or another."

Moran was silent, just long enough for Gatsby to ask, "Do you have a problem with that?"

"Of course not, Jay. Like I said in the beginning, bullets for booze. If anyone can pull this off, it's you. I'll call the boys."

~~~~~~

The following morning, there was an air of tension in Tumble Inn, Tumble Out. Earlier, Walter and Kanky had warned the boys that big doings were coming. Up to now, Gatsby hadn't really curtailed Foggy Joe's activities. At times, the men speculated that Gatsby was no one to mess with. Through some of the speakeasy clientele, rumors of Gatsby's past had become solid gossip, especially under the hazy miasma of booze and drugs. Walter and Moran seldom discounted any of the stories that circulated, and as Moran said, it doesn't hurt to let them think you're capable of violence.

Gatsby's connections to the Chicago mobs were history. As to the ones he had rubbed elbows with, most had been gunned down. At one point, rumors circulated that a serious hit had been ordered on Gatsby by Al Capone, who also liked to wear fashionable white flannel suits. It irritated Capone that at the big Chicago parties, Gatsby always looked better than he did. It wasn't long after the Capone-ordered hit that Gatsby quietly moved away.

~~~~~~

Gatsby wasn't through the door when he kicked an all-night patron in the leg, who had fallen asleep on a couch. He motioned to Walter. "Throw that fucking old sport out! You're supposed to be running a high-class place…"

Walter, surprised by the action, nodded quickly.

Moran took note of the return of Gatsby's "old sport" comment but said nothing.

Gatsby added, "Everyone inside."

While the boys piled into the office, Gatsby unlocked his closet door.

Kanky asked, "What's-a we gonna do, boss?"

"Simple…we're going to put Bucolo out of business, once and for all."

Collector said, "I don't think that will be simple." His sing-song voice trailed off, threatening to improvise another ditty.

Gatsby shut him down when he replied, "Listen, Collector—I like you, but maybe you should go work for Bucolo."

Collector laughed. "Well, boss, that would be stupid on my part. You just said you're going to put him out of business."

Gatsby nodded weakly. "Okay, boys, this is what we're going to do."

CHAPTER FIFTY-ONE

JOE AND THE BOYS SPENT the day at Schmitz's boatyard, getting ready for the christening. Away from Tiverton, being out in the fresh air, working on the boat cleared Joe's mind of the recent bridge incident. One thing was certain: wanting to leave the trade didn't guarantee an easy exit. He was like a hooked fish, trying to shake it off; but the harder he tried, the deeper the hook grabbed. Neither the new boat nor competition from Gatsby and Kanky nor the Coast Guard were simple matters. They presented dangerous situations, plus a shrinking cushion that only complicated his financial condition.

At day's end, over glasses of whiskey, they toasted his new boat. She was ready to be launched.

On the way back to Tiverton, Joe decided he wanted to speak with Janie.

~~~~~~

Returning home that evening, Janie saw Joe leaning against his car, smoking, in front of her house. He ran out in the road and waved his arms, signaling her to stop.

She braked and pulled over, almost going half in a ditch to avoid hitting him. He flipped his cigarette away and opened her door.

"I didn't think you were going to stop."

"Joe, I live here." She looked at him, almost cautiously.

He said, "It sure didn't look like you were gonna stop."

He seemed a little nervous, she thought. She became guarded, not sure what he wanted or what she should say.

He lightly cleared his throat. "I know this is going to sound strange, and you may not believe me, but I have been trying to turn some stuff around…"

She suddenly realized that Joe was the only man lately she really was interested in. She had an urge to laugh, but didn't. She calculated that it said a lot about his character—realizing he had to be fairly sure of himself. Her insides flushed with happy confusion.

"I know you don't believe me…but it's true."

She smiled and then laughed. "What does any fisherman's tall tales have to do with me?" Janie surprised herself—the question just popped out of her mouth.

"Why are you being so difficult?" he asked.

She saw her reaction irritated him. "I'm Pearly's daughter, Bucolo. You got something to say to this fisherman's daughter, spit it out."

"Well, I'm changing."

She feigned encouragement. "Good."

"I had a real nice time with you at Frankie's. I hope it was the same for you? I'm changing my life because there's a lot of stuff going on. Some good, some not so good."

She said, "Listen, don't do anything that you don't want to do, especially on my account." She had to say it, but her heart was thumping like a trapped bird. She could hardly control herself. She hated it that she didn't even know her heart would pump that way because of Joseph Bucolo.

He continued, "I'm really thinking that you and I could have a future."

There was a moment of silence. Just then, a fish truck loaded with mackerel barrels rumbled by. The driver honked a few times. Janie waved and smiled.

"Who's that?"

"Oh, just a guy…works for Grover's company."

For a moment, Joe's eyes followed the truck. He turned back to her. "Well, can't you say something?"

"I'm happy that you're trying to change your ways. I'd hate to see the Coast Guard blow you out of the Seaconnet."

"Thanks," he said, sticking his hands into his pants pockets, "that was certainly encouraging."

She said, "I told you before, Joseph Bucolo, I have a tendency to speak my mind."

He smiled. "Joseph…I like the way you say that. Would you like to come to the christening of my new boat?"

"I do. I mean…" Janie thought, What in the wide Seaconnet did I just say? "Of course I'll go. When is it?"

"Tomorrow."

"What about Pearly?"

"What about him?" Joe's voice had a sudden edge to it. He squinted. "If he wants to be at the christening, he can go with the boys."

Janie's head tilted slightly, surprised. "Have you and my father had words?"

"Nothing more than the normal, day-to-day opinions."

She gave him a curious look, but said nothing.

~~~~~~

Pearly had supper on the stove. Janie smelled the simmering beef stew and his homemade biscuits, his specialty when he was trying to apologize for something. She walked through the kitchen and onto the sunporch. He was reading the Fall River *Evening News*. Like many nights, he sat with his chair leaning against the wall, a glass of whiskey in his hand. The chair's two front legs were off the floor. He glanced up at her. "Hello, sweet thing."

"Hi, Daddy. Sure smells good." She leaned over, kissed him on the cheek. "By the way, I just saw Joe."

Pearly asked, "What'd he have to say?"

"He invited me to the boat's christening."

"He did?"

"Is Joe angry at you, Daddy?"

"Who said he's angry?"

She sat down opposite him. "Joe seems different."

"You wouldn't understand," Pearly said. "He's been mixed up lately."

She felt those glad knocks in her chest returning. "What's that supposed to mean?"

Pearly folded the newspaper. "Henry Grover called. Said he'll pick you up tomorrow morning." Pearly took a deep breath. "What the hell is that all 'bout?"

"Don't worry about Henry Grover."

"Is he pushing you to get married?"

"What do you think? He wants to buy the Almy house. He wants me to look at it with him."

"Jesus. I don't like the sound of that."

"I continue to tell Henry I'm in no rush for anything like that…he just doesn't listen. In what way does Joe seem mixed up?"

"When a man is really hung up on a woman, he doesn't see much further than his…his…nose."

She smiled. "I know what you mean, Daddy."

Pearly cleared his throat and added, "Just don't let Henry, Gatz, or any man force you into anything you don't want to do. Remember you're a Thurston first. You call your own shots."

"When the time comes, I will be the one to make that decision."

"Another thing…I think I've been a little too hard on Joe. I mean, I have his interest at heart, but I also have my own. Do you get my drift?"

"No, Daddy. What do you mean?"

"Well, I just want you to know that when this 'bang in' is over, Joe's real serious about settling down. Like I said, it would be nice if

Joe and all of us had a bigger nest egg to fall back on… In fact, he gave Cory Wilcox a deposit on a fishing dragger."

"He did?" Janie's voice revealed more than she wished. "Daddy, are you changing your mind about fishermen in general, or just Joseph Bucolo?"

Pearly looked at her out of the corner of his eye; the other eye seemed focused on the gleaming, mirror-like waters of the Basin. "Hopefully, Henry Grover doesn't become a spoiler in our plans to quit the trade."

Janie's back stiffened. She realized her father was hinting at something more. "Just what are you saying?"

"Bluntly, until the 'bang in' is over, Henry Grover is capable of creating problems for us. I suspect if you decide…of course it's your decision…if you decide that Henry isn't for you, he's liable to turn into a very nasty man."

"Are you suggesting that I string Henry Grover along?"

"I'm just looking out for us. That's all I've ever done. All's fair in love and the rum trade."

Janie's eyes flashed. "Everything is fair when it benefits you."

"What benefits me, benefits us. Joe wants to go back fishing, but I'm telling you, he needs a lot of help. *We* need a lot of help. If keeping Henry Grover happy helps for the time being, well…you gotta make that decision."

For a long moment, she just looked into his eyes. The damn seagulls screeching outside irritated her. She clearly understood his drift.

She got up from the chair and took off her sweater. "You're making it very difficult for me to say no," she said.

"Forget I even asked, sweet thing."

Janie hesitated slightly. "Sure, Daddy, sure." She walked into the kitchen and stood in front of the china cabinet. She saw the reflection of his shit-eating grin in the glass door when she moved just so. "I had a taste of some real good gin at Frankie's speakeasy. I found myself really liking it. What do you think of that, Daddy?"

From the porch, Pearly's heavy chair thudded back onto the floor. "What? You've been to Frankie-the-Bone's?"

"Yes, Daddy, Frankie's speakeasy isn't just for other women. I rather enjoyed it."

CHAPTER FIFTY-TWO

LATER THAT DAY, MAGGIE WALKED slowly across the Thurston yard. Clearly, she was blue. Janie opened the door. She was in a robe and her hair was wet. "Hey, Maggie, what's up?"

"I'm just feeling a little low today."

Janie grabbed her hand. "Come in." She led Maggie out onto the sunporch. "Sit down. You want something to drink?"

"Whiskey? Beer chaser?"

"Beer chaser? I only have whiskey," Janie said. "I'm out of Pearly's gin too."

"Forget the beer. Okay, whiskey with water."

She returned to the sunporch and handed Maggie her drink, then she sat down. She watched Maggie take a long draw of the whiskey.

"Tell me something good, Janie. What's going on with you?"

"Not much. Things have been quiet. I'm not so sure about my proposal anymore. Francis Grover never seems to find the time to continue our discussions. And my investor, James Gatz, has been silent since he took me to dinner at the Imperial Hotel."

"Say that again? Who is your investor? Where did he take you?"

"James Gatz, the Imperial Hotel. Why?"

Maggie jumped up and said, "Your investor, James Gatz…is also Jay Gatsby…he's the one trying to put Joey out of business!"

"What!?" The revelation hit Janie like a rogue wave on a calm beach day. "What the hell are you saying, Maggie? How do you know?"

"His attorney blackmailed me into sharing information about Joe's operation."

"Blackmailed!"

Janie stood up and walked over to the window. She looked out; it took her a moment to absorb Maggie's revelation. Then she said, "Since the day he came into Grover's office, and those few times we were together, I kept saying to myself, something is off with this man. And it appears my intuition was correct."

Maggie drained her glass. "I hope you didn't open your legs to Gatz?"

"Of course not!"

"That's good...because you've been lied to since the beginning. We were both manipulated to get at Joey—to force Joey out of rum-running."

Janie nodded. "Now...I do feel like a damn fool."

"Me too!

"Does Joe know they were blackmailing you?"

"Yes! After Joey lost twenty-five thousand dollars in the hijacking...he showed up at Billy's cottage. He suspected Billy, I guess... He confronted us. I was scared to death...but I told him the truth about how I was forced to help them..."

"Twenty-five thousand dollars?" It quickly registered with Janie. She swore under her breath. "My proposal...Gatz paid Grover's deposit with Joe's hijacked money."

Maggie said, "When I heard about all that money, I became very afraid."

"I can't imagine what Joe wanted to do to you when he found out."

"Strange, he was very calm."

"I'm glad to hear that."

"I can't believe this, Janie… Can I have another whiskey?"

Janie got up and fixed Maggie another drink. She made one for herself as well.

Maggie asked, "What are you going to do?"

"Clearly, it is over with Gatz. And now with this new information, how do we break it to Joe?"

~~~~~~

Henry Grover stood in front of the full-length mirror that hung from the wall of the second-story hallway in his family's home. He adjusted his tie.

With Gatz and Bucolo both chasing Janie, Henry knew he had to make his move—and tonight, at the Almy house, he would ask Janie for her hand in marriage. While he knew he should feel more confident, Henry worried about what Janie's answer would be. On top of that, he still couldn't shake the revelations of his father's affair with Jessica Jackson. He knew now that there would forever be a connection between the Jacksons and the Grovers. It was a rather unsettling thought, and he found himself dwelling on the images of both his father and Joe Bucolo fucking Jessica Jackson. All these sinners worried Henry.

He agonized about the possibility that Janie Thurston would reject his proposal. Throughout the day, thinking on what he would do if Janie actually said no cooked up violent thoughts in Henry. He continually reminded himself that it would be Bucolo's fault if Janie wouldn't marry him. The Lord will provide, Henry thought. Good things come, especially to those who patiently wait.

Henry wondered when Kanky was going to make good on his promise. He hoped it would be soon. Then, rather strangely, he said out loud, "I'm really pleased and confident that Chief Henry Grover is finally taking the law into his own hands."

~~~~~~

The Almy house sat on the west side of Nanaquaket Neck, about three

miles south of Peabody's Wharf. Nanaquaket homes were more elegant than those up on the Heights. The house was a large Victorian
with a prominent widow's-walk tower on the roof, and bordered on
three sides by a porch with two hanging swings. Painted white, it had
two huge brick fireplaces on each end of the house.

Henry unlocked the door and flicked on the hall lights. The parlor furniture was covered with dust sheets. The rooms were bright,
with shiny wood floors and bookcases in every corner. It was airy and
certainly impressive. Janie did her best to check her enthusiasm but
found it very difficult. "Holy cow," she said at least three times.

"It includes all the furnishings," Henry gushed. "The bank gave
me a list. It's quite a lot of stuff." He grabbed her hand and led her
into the dining room.

"It's beautiful, Henry. This is unbelievable."

"I knew you would love it," he said excitedly. "I just knew it."

Janie gave him a fleeting glance but said nothing.

"This is so beautiful, Henry. It's every woman's dream."

She was looking at Henry, but an image of Joe crossed her mind.

"Henry, I don't know what to say."

"Just say you will marry me. Will you be my wife, Janie?"

He still had that impatient look in his eye. Jesus! He's quite not all
there in his head. That thought zipped through her like a bullet.

His hand tightened over hers. She winced and he eased his grip.
"I'm sorry, the excitement; it's what you do to me."

She saw his lips move. "Will you be my wife, Janie?"

He yanked her tightly into his arms and kissed her hard.

Janie pushed him away. "Henry, this is much too fast!" She was
astonished how she could feel so little passion with a man like Henry Grover. While she once considered him a potential match, she
couldn't stomach him any longer. So she was looking up at the ceiling
when she reluctantly snuggled her thigh between his legs, thinking of
keeping Henry from becoming "a very nasty man"—a spoiler of Joe's
hope for the future—and wondering if she were going beyond the call

of duty, even for her father. "I need more time," she finally said. "I'm not going to marry until I'm sure of the man."

"How much more time?" Henry's voice cracked. His eyes turned vacant.

"This is a big commitment, Henry." She raised her voice. "Do you understand?"

"Yes." She could barely hear him.

"But Henry, as far as when and who I marry, that's my decision… Please, I just need some more time…"

"I understand," he said weakly.

As they left the Almy house, Janie recalled what she had said to Gatz: one survives by doing clever things and sometimes even dishonest things…but you still need your wits about you.

She knew then that she was truly her father's daughter.

~~~~~~

The moment Janie had been waiting for and dreaded arrived when she received Gatz's telephone call.

"Hello, Janie. I wanted to make sure you were at the office. I'd like to stop by. Do you have a few minutes to speak with me?"

"Of course, James. But I'd prefer that we meet outside, in the company's parking lot."

"Good, in about an hour?"

"That'll work, it's my lunch hour."

"Thank you," he replied.

~~~~~~

As Gatz approached Janie, she surmised that he didn't look very confident—not like in the past. He extended his hand, but she didn't take it.

Gatz seemed puzzled.

From the upstairs window, Janie noticed that Francis Grover was watching them. It took a few seconds for her to speak. Finally, she said, "You've been trying to ruin Foggy Joe…beat him down…even using Maggie and me…all for your own ambitions—your ventures!"

He attempted to respond, a range of emotion crossed his face. He resigned himself that it would be futile and remained silent.

Janie stared at him, not satisfied by his retreat, "Who the hell are you?"

Gatz turned away, unable to look at her.

He remained speechless and then abruptly got into his car.

Both Janie and Francis Grover watched him race out of the parking lot, the Packard's back tires spewing up bits of crushed clam shells.

Chapter Fifty-Three

JANIE HAD MADE UP HER MIND by the time she slipped out of bed the next morning: She needed to tell Joe about Gatz and now understood that she was being used to get at Joe—help put him out of business. She also knew that her proposal with Francis Grover was dead in the water. It didn't matter anyway; she would be giving her notice as soon as the 'bang in' was over. More importantly, Joe and the boys needed to be careful, as she was certain they were in real danger—now more than ever.

She went downstairs and found Pearly hovering over the kitchen stove, making breakfast. He turned around at her steps on the stairs. It was the time of the year when sun flooded the east windows in the morning. In the bright light, her father appeared majestic, like a prophet from the Bible. But he's still a sinner, she thought—a big sinner—but despite that, I love him dearly.

"Good morning."

She gave him a kiss on the cheek. "Hhhhmmmm, Jonnycakes, bacon...my favorite breakfast."

"It's a special day."

Janie found herself blurting out, "James Gatz is actually Jay Gatsby...the man who wants to put Joe and you out of business."

Pearly's shocked expression alarmed her. "What the...what are you saying, sweet thing?"

"Just that! He's had everyone bamboozled...including me."

He said, "I need to tell Joe immediately."

"No! Let me do it, Daddy. I feel it's my responsibility. I was completely taken in by him."

Pearly's anger fueled his hunger as he helped himself to the pile of Jonnycakes smothered in maple syrup and butter.

Janie poured herself a cup of coffee and sat down. "Henry asked me to marry him last night." She watched him closely, studying his reaction.

Pearly's fork stopped in mid-air. His cut-up Jonnycake just hung there while he waited for her to continue. "So, what happened? I mean, what did you say?"

She took a sip of coffee. "I tried to string him along, but I can't guarantee what he might do. When do you think that 'bang in' will happen?"

He stuffed a piece of Jonnycake into his mouth. "Soon, I hope."

"Sooner, the better," she said firmly.

~~~~~~

The minute Janie was inside Joe's Buick, she turned to him. There was a long moment of silence. He just looked at her and waited. Finally, she said, "I learned that James Gatz is Jay Gatsby, the man who's trying to force you out of business."

"I know." Joe waited a moment. "Maggie tracked me down this morning and told me everything."

She had so many questions, but decided not to ask any of them. After all, it was a day for celebrating—the christening of the *Whispering Winds*. She figured, why should I wreck the day?

~~~~~~

When they arrived at Schmitz's boatyard, everyone was all smiles when they saw Joe and Janie.

Pearly pointed to the rum boat's nameplate: *Whispering Winds.* "You did good, Joe, really good. I couldn't have made a better choice myself."

Janie leaned into Joe and softly said, "The more I think about it, the more I really like it. It's kind of mysterious...just like her captain..."

Joe laughed and gave her an appreciative smile. He looked around and felt everyone's warm camaraderie. It didn't hurt that Max was being honored with the boat's name as well.

Heinrich Schmitz appeared quite the gentleman, in his brown tweed jacket and tie, as he gave orders to his workers to get everything ready.

Joe yelled, "Boys, lend a hand." Sammy, like always, didn't have to be asked twice.

They slid the big doors open, and for the first time, the new boat had a blue, watery background. The Acushnet River was on the rise. Within the hour, she would be at peak tide.

The men began removing the work staging and wooden support blocks. When they were done, the vessel rested on only the four arms of the cradle, waiting for her chance to float free. Heinrich had a man sweep off the tracks while another followed with a spatula and grease bucket. No *Nocnitsa* grease, Joe noticed. He glanced up into the rafters.

Hunker and Sammy rigged a hanging bottle of champagne encased in burlap.

Nina Schmitz joined them, wearing shorts and in bare feet. She took her father's hand and waved to Janie and Joe. Hunker ambled over and said something that made Mister Schmitz and Nina laugh.

Schmitz checked his watch and, together with Hunker, walked down to the edge of the still river. "The tide is almost at its peak." Schmitz pointed to a stake driven into the sand that marked the highest level of the tide.

Joe turned to Janie. "You ready to give her life...to crack the champagne?"

"I'd be honored, Foggy Joe."

Pearly moved alongside his daughter and grabbed the hanging burlap-wrapped bottle. "Just give it a good whack, Janie, just like the doctor who slapped your ass."

"I'll give her a good whack, Pearly."

Behind them, Schmitz's helper had started the cradle's winch engine. The building echoed its noisy patter, like the beating of a heart. An air of excitement and anticipation filled the boat shed.

"Are you ready, Miss Janie?" Schmitz asked.

Joe raised his hand, and everyone calmed down. Janie looked at Joe. He said, "When you're ready."

She moved slightly closer to the boat and raised the bottle like a club. "I christen thee *Whispering Winds*." With a little too much force, the bottle shattered, and Janie's words were lost in the cheers.

Schmitz, with eyes glistening, signaled the workman with his hand. He released the winch brake, and the boat rumbled slowly down the tracks. Joe and the boys followed her, and when the stern dipped into the water, they let out another cheer.

In a matter of seconds, the river swallowed up the boat's bottom. She lifted quickly, freeing herself from the grip of the cradle. It was a touching sight that struck a chord and brought more applause from the men. Sammy, alone on the stern, also wiped tears from his eyes and waved back at them.

Janie released a loud, excited hoot. Nina grabbed Janie's hand, and they ran down to the dock with one of her father's helpers. They got into Nina's speedboat, *Wolf*, and motored over to *Whispering Winds*.

After securing the rum boat, everyone boarded her. Mister Schmitz and Joe joined Sammy below, checking for leaks. They found a few weeps along the starboard keel that Mister Schmitz said would swell up soon enough.

"Isn't enough water in the bilge to make a cocktail," Sammy said.

Back topside, everyone looked very pleased. Hunker and Pearly set up a makeshift bar on the starboard gunnel. Nina and Mister Schmitz provided homemade beer. Joe toasted Mister Schmitz, his workmen, the beautiful day, and of course, his new boat.

Later, carrying two drinks, Joe met up with Janie in the pilot house. He handed her a glass. "Compliments of your father."

"Is it gin?" She took a sip and half-smiled. "I'm starting to like this stuff."

Joe said, "Well, you know, there's more where that came from."

She gave him a sunny look. "I'm glad Nina showed up. I was beginning to feel like this was only a man's party." She touched the console. "But it's obvious there's only one lady here, and we're all standing on her, eh, Foggy Joe?"

"Hey, that's pretty good."

She set the glass down and looked around the pilot house, trailing her fingers over the varnish. She turned her back to him and began toying with the steering wheel.

Joe's arm encircled her waist and he kissed her on the neck. She moved her head in an inviting gesture. He said softly, "I'm really happy you're here. And I'm happy you christened my boat…"

Slowly, she turned around.

Joe's eyes rested on her lips. He waited for a signal, but finally, he kissed her.

The kiss was soft, but she gently pushed him away. "I think for the moment it would be best if you stayed over on the portside."

"Didn't you want me to do that?"

"Yes," she said, "that's the problem." She looked him squarely in the eyes. "Well, Joe, I guess I'm not ready to give myself to you in broad daylight in front of your whole gang." Janie interrupted herself, "I shouldn't have said that!"

"You're confusing me, but that's okay." He touched her arm. "By the way, what are you doing later?"

Janie's eyes ignited. "Why, I hope I'm still with you."

"Good," he said. "You'll enjoy the party."

~~~~~~

Jimmy Sample's speakeasy was a short ride away. In the fading day-light, the working-class neighborhood had a warm, homey feeling—a perfect front for a successful speakeasy. Billy reserved the back lounge for Joe's party. Entering the room, the aroma of fresh steamed clams caught everyone's attention. Two long tables were dressed with breads, cold cuts, cheeses, and chilled oysters. Other tables held small kegs of beer, packed in boxes of ice. Bottles of hard liquor lined a side table. Billy supplied three pretty girls for waitress service.

Pearly beamed. "Boy, it all looks great, and plenty of it." He rubbed his hands together as he approached the table. He helped himself to an oyster.

The three-piece band began to play. Hunker was the first to dance. He grabbed one of the service girls and began his jig. His body bounced back and forth, up and down, like the courting dance of a strutting rooster. Although erratic and comical, everyone clapped at Hunker's barnyard jig. Sammy joined in as well—his head resting against a tall woman's breasts, laughing and spinning.

Pearly yelled, "Come on, shake a leg." He pulled Janie from her seat. For the first time in her life, Janie found herself dancing with her father. She'd had a few drinks by then and was feeling them. She found it amazing that Joe was acting as though Nina weren't even in the room. When the dance was over, Janie collapsed into her chair and sucked on another gin.

"Better go easy on that stuff," Joe said. "Gin has a way of sneaking up on you."

Janie giggled. "I'm a fisherman's daughter, Foggy Joe. Have you forgotten that?"

He shrugged and smiled.

When the band began to play a slow number, Janie pried Joe from his seat.

Pearly said, "Forget it, daughter. Joe doesn't know how to dance."

She said, "Wanna bet?"

Janie and Joe walked smack into the middle of the crowded dance floor. She pulled him close. He didn't resist. After a few moments, Janie said, "Well, your feet are moving the right way." She belched.

Joe laughed. "You sound like Hunker."

She hiccupped.

"Take a deep breath," he said.

Janie saw her father dancing with Nina; both were smiling. She whispered into Joe's ear, "I need some fresh air."

"Yeah, I think you're right."

~~~~~~

Outside, Janie leaned against the building while Joe smoked a cigarette. As they walked to the car, she hugged him.

"Maybe I should take you home," he said.

When they got into the Buick, she leaned over and kissed him hard.

"Jesus, I've wanted a kiss like that since this morning."

"Only since this morning?" she asked, punching him lightly on the shoulder. "I've been waiting longer than that." She slowly ran her hand through his hair. "I don't want to go home, not yet anyway. I feel fine now. Let's go back to *Whispering Winds*."

~~~~~~

At Schmitz's empty boatyard, Janie pushed Joe against the hood of the Buick and kissed him. The pressure of her body against his left no question of where they were going. He led her up the ladder, onto the deck of the boat.

"She needs ballast...lots of liquor," Joe said. "She's riding too high."

"You talking about me, Foggy Joe?" They both laughed.

Topside, they kissed again. Janie's lips turned hot, demanding. Joe was surprised but surely didn't object. He opened the pilot house door and turned on the instrument lights, highlighting Janie's features as she leaned against the helm. The dull glow from the panel was just enough to guide them down the fo'c'sle stairs, where the scent of fresh varnish hung in the air. Joe switched on a small overhead lamp.

"Joe Bucolo," she whispered. "It's been a wonderful day, and I hope it never ends." She hiccupped. "Should we wait...save something...until...?"

He hesitated, as though trying to decipher her words. He leaned down and took hold of the hem of her dress and pulled it clean over her head, as quickly and simply as if he'd snapped a towel.

"Wait!" Janie screamed. But it was too late.

She snatched her dress out of his hands and held it in front of her. "You weren't supposed to do that."

He kissed her, and she pulled back. He noticed she wasn't very steady on her feet, and he ran his hands slowly down her backside. "You are very beautiful."

Softly she breathed, "Oh, Joe," then suddenly pulled away. Janie's hand went to her mouth. She gagged and puked up Jimmy Sample's smorgasbord all over Joe's pants and the deck of the fo'c'sle.

"Oh, Janie," he softly said, "you poor thing. That's awful."

"I'm sorry!" she uttered, still gagging and wiping her mouth on her arm. "You did warn me, Foggy Joe. But I didn't listen."

"Can I get you something? Maybe a glass of water?"

She began to pull the dress over her head, but it got all tangled up—and then she couldn't get it right. It covered her head so she couldn't see anything. She became nauseous and heaved again. The heaves were dry now but, still tangled, Janie grew frantic.

When Joe's hand touched her, she screamed, "No!"

"I'm only trying to help!"

"I'm sorry." She burst into tears. Janie couldn't believe what was happening—this was supposed to be the most romantic moment of her life. "Why didn't I listen to you?"

He whispered, "I'll be out on the deck, if you want me to get you something." She heard the sympathy in his voice.

Alone, Janie cried. When it got quiet, she slowly disentangled herself from the dress. It was a mess. She found her boots. At least they were dry.

Janie rubbed her eyes. She wasn't crying anymore, but feeling drunk and mighty sad. She went out on deck and found Joe sitting on the gunnel, waiting. "Please bring me home, Joe. I feel terrible."

~~~~~~

It was a very quiet ride from the christening.

Back at her house, she pushed open the kitchen door and flicked on the light. Joe followed her into the house, and they just stood there.

Finally, she said, "Can I tell you something?"

He didn't reply.

She reached for his hand and said softly, "I hate myself for behaving the way I did tonight. I wanted to make you happy, myself happy, and it all went wrong." Janie's voice didn't waver. "I hate myself for getting sick like that. I hate gin."

He said softly, "I'm sorry it wasn't a perfect ending to a perfect day. I know it was awkward and confusing…I'm truly sorry you got sick."

"Thank you." She kissed him on the cheek and took hold of his hands. "Oh, Joe, I'm so happy, and so confused."

With a quick squeeze, she let go of his hands. He left the house with her standing in the dark.

Janie closed the door and turned off the kitchen light.

~~~~~~

While Janie sat at her kitchen table, looking very green around the gills, Gatsby was deep into plotting his next move. The shrill ring of the phone interrupted his thoughts. Gatsby answered, "Hello."

"Hello, Jay, Moran here."

"Yes, Paul."

"I have an update from my man in Chicago."

Gatsby, his voice concerned, "What is it?"

"No, not that kind of update. Nothing about your old bootlegging acquaintances. This is about the Buchanan household."

Gatsby, somewhat relieved, "What did your man have to say?"

"He's keeping his eyes on things as you've asked. All seems to be restored to its former glory, a few of the staff are back employed, and Miss Daisy and her child seem well. I thought you would want to know."

"Okay, I appreciate the update. Goodbye, Paul." As Gatsby hung up the telephone, he smiled to himself, knowing that Daisy was comfortable. He then wondered when her ape of a husband would once again fuck up. He promised himself he would be well prepared the next time Tom Buchanan pushed Daisy back into his orbit.

CHAPTER FIFTY-FOUR

JOE AND THE GANG spent the next day on the Acushnet River testing *Whispering Winds*, which proved to be everything they could ever want. The four Liberty engines were a perfect combination for the eighty-foot hull. Likewise, the oversized rudders gave her outstanding turning abilities.

Joe clocked and measured her speed at thirty-five knots. He figured there wasn't a patrol boat on the East Coast fast enough to catch her. Sammy, however, reminded him that there wasn't a rum boat built that could outrace a cannonball, or bullets from a Lewis machine gun.

On one trial run, they stacked her entire deck three high with water-filled mackerel barrels. They calculated the weight to be equivalent to the biggest load of booze they would attempt. *Whispering Winds* lost only about three knots.

With steel bullet sheathing in the engine room and in the pilot house walls, Joe did have problems compensating the compass. Sammy and Joe worked for hours fastening magnets in various positions around the compass binnacle. When everything had been tested and retested, the boat was about as ready as she could be.

Around midnight, with no fanfare, *Whispering Winds* quietly arrived in Tiverton. Joe and Sammy stayed aboard the boat.

~~~~~~

The following day, Joe could tell by the excited blush on Mary's cheeks she finally made contact. She had prepared a bag of sandwiches and a big container of coffee.

She handed Joe a paper. "The *Yankton*'s carrying just what you need. She's anchored on the eastern edge of Coxe's Ledge, between thirty and forty fathoms. In fact, she just arrived. The captain used some of Durall's codes. Must be a friend."

"Good." Joe studied Mary's information on the vessel's cargo.

Mary then handed him a newspaper. "Things are getting dangerous." Joe's features flushed at the headlines of the *Providence Journal*. It read: RUM BOAT 'TRAMP' SUNK! NO SURVIVORS! By mid-morning, the commander of District Four Headquarters in Boston released a radio report of the Buzzard's Bay incident.

The Coast Guard claimed that the heavily loaded vessel, *Tramp*, opened fire with pistols and shotguns at CG-483, forcing the Coast Guard to respond. The article went on to say that the Coast Guard sank the smuggler. They patrolled the icy waters throughout the night into early morning but found no bodies.

Joe headed for the diner's door.

Mary called out, "Good luck."

Joe waved without looking back.

~~~~~~

Darkness hadn't quite settled in, but the rapidly approaching rain-clouds turned the southern sky quite dark. The new moon was obliterated by the heavy overcast sky. The wind was from the southeast and blowing about twenty knots. On the ocean, Joe knew the weather was going to be fairly heavy.

Sammy had the engines running. He was climbing out from behind the console when Joe and Pearly entered the pilot house. Sammy had just made a final adjustment to the throttle and nudged the control. He grinned broadly as all four Liberties responded in equal cadence. They sounded like one powerful tornado.

Joe patted him on the shoulder. "You're the best, Sammy, the best."

Sammy's face crinkled with satisfaction. "Thanks, Joe."

Pearly handed over the bag of sandwiches and the pail of coffee to Hunker to stow away.

Hunker grabbed a sandwich. "I'm hungry."

Joe looked at Sammy. "Are we ready?"

Sammy nodded. "Ready, Joe."

"Cast off."

When they left the lee of the Seaconnet River, a strong, broadside sea greeted the new rummy. Everyone aboard waited to see how she would respond.

Whispering Winds hardly rolled, steered steady, and the helm answered quickly. Joe was having a hard time keeping his enthusiasm under control. He couldn't believe how quiet the hull was, and how she seemed to embrace the swelling Atlantic. Even with four engines, there was less vibration than his other boats with two engines.

In the semi-darkness of the pilot house, everyone just continued to look at each other, gloating over how well she was behaving. Finally Pearly shouted, "She just loves it, loves it like Sally Half-a-Dollar!"

Everyone chuckled. Sammy said, "Pearly, you can have Sally. We'll stick with this lady...you hear?"

Joe gradually nudged the throttle forward. *Whispering Winds* picked up speed, and she continued to run comfortably.

Around ten o'clock, they approached the thirty-fathom edge and sighted their first lights. Drizzle speckled the pilot house windows.

Joe eased up on the throttle and headed slightly west, steaming for another ten minutes, when another set of lights came into view.

As they got closer, Joe could make out the *Yankton*. She was a Grand Banker, smaller than most, simply rigged, with her sails furled and tightly bound. She looked seaworthy enough, snugly riding the swells like a contented seagull.

Two men in oilskins emerged from her stern cabin and waved lanterns.

"Crack the bell, Sammy."

Joe ran the boat to the leeside of the sixty-foot Grand Banker, where bumpers hung from her port gunnels.

The captain of the *Yankton* was waiting. Beside him two men held lanterns. The captain shook Joe's hand as he boarded his vessel.

"Joe Bucolo."

"Name's Blakely," the captain said, "Warren Blakely."

"Do you know Captain Durall?" Joe asked.

"He's my cousin." Blakely glanced past Joe and surveyed *Whispering Winds*. "Fine-looking vessel, looks brand new?"

"She is." Joe noticed that Blakely's words ran close together in short, squeaky blasts.

Blakely nodded. "Business must be good."

Joe got right down to business. "My Sparky said you can fill my order?"

"No problem. In fact, you will clean me out. I'd like to leave for Canada tonight. A fast blow is a-coming." He touched his nose and added, "I can always smell them."

He ordered his crew to start the loading process, then motioned for Joe to follow him. Pearly followed along.

Beneath the fo'c's'le's lights, Blakely's face resembled a worn navigational chart—ravaged by wind, sun, and sea. It was the face of a man who spent the best part of his life tub-trawling codfish on the northern edges of George's Banks. Perched quite conspicuously on the left side of a rather long nose was a brown mole.

The *Yankton*'s quarters were plain but adequate. Blakely was a man of simple taste who obviously knew the rigors of a fisherman's life, certainly nothing like that southern buccaneer Captain Maytee.

Joe felt a kinship with Blakely. He asked, "Where do you hail from?"

"Halifax," Blakely replied.

"Same place as Captain Durall?" Pearly asked.

Blakely nodded. "Durall staked me to this load of liquor. Truth is, this could be my last trip."

Joe said, "You'll be wise to go back fishing."

Blakely said, "Fishing? No, thanks. I've been thinking about raising chickens. Selling eggs. Something peaceful."

"Now there's a smart choice," Pearly piped in.

Joe ignored Pearly and asked, "When will Captain Durall be back?"

"Soon, very soon."

Joe glanced at Pearly. Blakely smiled, revealing the only two teeth he seemed to have left in his mouth. He added, "Durall has the *Maria* well loaded. I think he also intends to get out of this business."

"To raise chickens, no doubt," Joe said, wondering if Durall had told Blakely about the 'bang in.' Even if he had, Blakely didn't appear to be the gossiping type.

Joe took off his belt and counted out Blakely's pay-off, which was tied up in five-hundred-dollar lots. Joe watched Blakely's eyes as the fisherman recounted the ever-growing pile of money.

"More money here than I've seen in my entire life," Blakely said.

Joe had a feeling that Captain Blakely would be returning to Rum Row.

In the short time they were below, the fo'c'sle's white-painted finish wall began creaking as the brewing sou'easter whistled through the Grand Banker's masts and rigging. Now the two vessels were beginning to nudge and rub hard against the bumpers. Joe turned to Pearly. "Get topside and fetch up those spring lines. Check those bumpers. Keep the crews moving."

By eleven o'clock, *Whispering Winds* was loaded and they left the empty *Yankton*, with Captain Blakely wishing Joe good luck and good fishing. Joe thought Blakely didn't believe him when he said he wanted to go back fishing.

With the added weight of the liquor, the boat paid little attention to the building seas. However, Joe was still cautious as he increased her speed, ready for any unknown quirks the boat may possess.

About ten minutes north of the *Yankton*'s position, they passed another Canadian rummy moving to the southwest. They didn't recognize the vessel.

On the return trip to the Seaconnet River, *Whispering Winds* was running on a new course and in different conditions. The weather was now hitting her starboard quarter, yet she continued to prove herself to be an exceptional sea boat.

About five miles off the coast, rain fell so hard there was no visibility, and the ocean began to flatten out from the heavy downpour. Weather permitting, the Seaconnet Lighthouse would mark their heading back to the river, but with the poor visibility, Joe had to hold a very positive course.

It wasn't until they were just off the western bank of the river that the lighthouse beacon flashed dimly into view.

When *Whispering Winds* crossed over Cormorant Shoals, the high, rolling swells began to crest and curl. Even in those harsh conditions, the new boat proved herself. With her wide stern and substantial load, there was still little tendency to broach, and Joe had no trouble keeping her steady in the heavy seas.

"Amazing," Pearly whispered.

After passing over the Shoals, Joe turned to Pearly. "You're absolutely right, she loves it!"

Hunker punched Pearly and added, "Hey, Joe, it's too bad we're not staying in the trade…"

"Yeah," Hunker said. "Too bad we're gonna go back hunting fish and oysters."

Inside the mouth of the river, the sea conditions diminished, but the downpour still continued. Joe pulled back on the throttle and turned the boat into a northeasterly direction, towards Church's Point.

As they approached the east bank of the river, Joe slowed the boat down even more. With the drenching rain, it was still almost impossible to see. Sammy took the wheel while the others put on their oilskins and took up positions on the deck, looking for any patrol boats that might be concealed in the dark shorelines.

To the southeast, they heard the bell buoy clanking away on Old Bull Shoals. Joe knew that the heavy seas were breaking right over the rocks.

He continued to hug the shore, blending in nicely with the dark shadows of the high riverbank. He stuck his head out of the pilot house. "Keep a sharp eye!"

They passed High Hill, and the rain let up some, so Joe decided to make for Mayfield's Wharf.

As they passed the tip of Fogland Point, the rain changed to a fine drizzle. It was like lifting a gloomy veil off the surroundings, and into the northeast they could see a few dim lights.

Joe shifted the engines into neutral. For a few minutes, the boat drifted while all eyes strained into the shadows of the shoreline, looking for anything that seemed out of place. "Everything appears to be clear," Pearly whispered.

Joe nodded. "Give Tommy a fast blink."

Pearly gave a quick flash with the searchlight. A moment later, it was returned.

Joe snapped the engines into gear and moved slowly towards Mayfield's Wharf. Tommy had the trucks backed up and his shore gang was raring to go. As the Bancocks threw lines to Pearly and Hunker, Joe steered the boat against the wharf's bumpers.

Billy Bancock jumped aboard the boat. Tommy Walsh and his crew were right behind him.

Joe shouted, "Get to work, boys!"

By two-thirty, the boat was unloaded, and the rain had practically stopped. Even the wind seemed to have fallen off, and like always, the fast-moving sou'easter had pretty much died. The first half of the liquor was carted up to Mayfield's silage barn while the rest left in trucks.

"Let's go!" Joe shouted. He waved to the Bancocks.

The brothers tossed off the lines and stood side by side as *Whispering Winds* backed away from the wharf. Joe threw it in neutral and called to Pearly, "Get the Bancocks on board. They want to ride this lady, too."

The Bancocks didn't have to be asked twice. As the boat nudged closer, they leaped onto the foredeck. Joe shifted her in reverse and they were underway.

With her deck cleared, all the gang agreed that luck had been on their side, missing any action by the Coast Guard.

As they neared the entrance to the Nanaquaket Channel, everyone was feeling pretty good, even starting to relax.

It was said that rum-runners took their chances. They had to have faster vessels and better equipment. They had to face bad weather, practice good sea sense, have a mix of luck and bigger balls than the next fellow. That is what got' em through. But reading that newspaper account about the Coast Guard sinking the *Tramp* still gave everyone plenty to think about.

Approaching Max's Wharf in *Whispering Winds*, Joe wondered why he felt so good. Then he knew—he was glad to be alive, his relationship with Janie was promising, and he would be returning to fishing for a living.

CHAPTER FIFTY-FIVE

THE PREVIOUS NIGHT'S SOU'EASTER had been replaced with a brisk northwest breeze and clear blue skies. The wind died off in the late afternoon; red streaks of sunlight were slowly turning gray over the Tiverton Basin, and the perfume of late spring laced the twilight air.

Pearly had gone down to the wharf to keep Sammy company. Janie knew he would return late.

Around seven o'clock, Joe's horn surprised her. She rushed outside and jumped into the Buick.

He smiled. "I'm early."

She smiled. "I was ready."

Joe headed south towards Little Compton and Seaconnet Point. The ride was long, dark, and, in places, still bumpy from winter washouts. Janie moved closer and rested her head against his shoulder.

A bit later, the Seaconnet Lighthouse came into view. Its beacon marked Land's End and the beginning of a rolling ocean.

They pulled up to the edge of the cliff overlooking the ocean. The rotating beacon repeatedly splashed a few seconds of brightness inside the car, then left them in blackness. Beneath them, they heard the force of the waves breaking against the rocks.

She said, "I've never been down here at night before. It's kind of scary."

"Even more so when you're out there." Joe motioned towards the ocean. Slowly their faces came together. The kiss was soft and warm.

Suddenly she felt the interior of the car being chilled by the cool ocean air. Janie shivered and snuggled even closer. She sat quietly, looking at him.

He unscrewed the cap off a small silver flask and offered her a drink.

She shook her head and shifted in her seat, angling slightly away from him, as though she wanted a different focus on his face. She asked, "What are you going to do?"

He took a sip. "I've made mistakes," he said, staring out the window. "I should've never let my guard down with Gatsby. I should've listened to Pearly and Hunker. As soon as he started trouble, I should've given Gatsby bigger trouble." He snapped his fingers. "Quick as that! And maybe none of this would've happened."

She ran her fingers down his arm. "The hell with Gatsby, he's not even worth the time for the next tide. You've got to stay with your decision to quit the business. Don't let him change your decision."

"That's what I don't like—being forced. It's one thing quitting because of the law. But another because of some greedy sonofabitch!" He paused, listening to his own words as if they were coming from someone else.

She leaned back and stared at him.

"Truth is, I'm not sure if I want to even chance the 'bang in' now."

She chuckled. "Pearly will be disappointed."

Joe laughed. "Not only him."

After a moment, she asked, "If you pull off the 'bang in,' will you really be done?"

"Yes." He took another sip and handed her the flask. She screwed on the cap without drinking. "For the 'bang in,' a lot of things have to work, and if they do, well, we'll still need a lot of luck—lots of luck."

He shifted in his seat and leaned over the steering wheel. Staring out at the ocean, he added, "I would like to have a little nest egg to fall back on. I'd like the boys to have some, too."

"Couldn't you just sell the boats?"

He smiled at the way her mind seemed to be working. "If my plan doesn't happen, I'll probably try to sell them. But in this business, when you're down and out, people know they've got you in a bind. Rum boats aren't much good except for running liquor…"

She opened the flask and took a sip of whiskey. "I'm happy to be here with you, Joe."

"You know, Janie Thurston, you're really good for me."

She smiled. "I'm really happy we settled that."

They laughed.

Chapter Fifty-Six

PEARLY WAS ON THE SUNPORCH, waiting for Janie's return. "Out here." He was sitting in the dark, smoking a pipe. The porch smelled of tobacco and a tint of whiskey breath.

He asked, "How's Joe doing?"

"Okay, I guess." She looked out the window; the Basin resembled a dark hole.

Pearly said, "Maggie called earlier…"

She opened the window and took a big sniff of fresh air. "Did Maggie say what she wanted?"

"No, only that she may stop by later. Frankly, I think she had a few drinks in her."

"Really?"

"I'm going down to the wharf, keep Sammy company for a while. We're taking turns standing watch on the boats. Joe's sleeping on the *Black Duck* while it is still at Wilcox's boatyard."

"I know, he told me."

"There's a change in the wind, sweet thing." Pearly's voice had a melancholy tone.

"I love Joe, Daddy, and I believe he loves me."

"I kinda figured that out. I think it's been that way for a long time."

She smiled. "You always know more than you say."

"Of course, but sometimes, honey, it doesn't matter. Remember, it's always different for a man. 'Specially someone like Joe."

Janie felt her breath catch in her throat as that sense of insecurity rapidly returned. She asked, "What do you mean, ''specially someone like Joe'?"

Pearly raised his hand. "I'm only making an observation. *Whispering Winds* brought back that old excitement and enthusiasm in Joe, maybe even in all of us. It's strange how a beautiful boat can change a man. Almost like a woman, I suppose."

Janie felt frustrated but managed to keep her control. "Daddy, do you think it would matter how good that rum boat is if she were blown apart?"

Janie watched his head nod. She added, "I'm happy to see you agree. I don't want to be reading about you in the newspaper."

"Did Joe happen to mention the 'bang in'?"

She felt a slight rush of anger with her father. Like all things, he was simply looking down the road of life.

"Actually, Joe seemed to be on the fence. A little bit anyway…"

Pearly, looking disappointed, took a deep breath. "Damn! I was 'fraid of that."

She asked, "Just how much money can be made from this wild endeavor?"

"If everything goes right—plenty."

She asked, "Will it be dangerous?"

"Depends. One thing's certain: we won't be able to outrun any patrol boat. So, we need to be really foxy. We need a very bad storm…a nasty nor'easter, that beast from the east…would be great. And of course, a lot of luck."

Janie shook her head and laughed. "I was thinking…a 'bang in'! Now, isn't that just what you guys would call it?"

Pearly asked, "Well, is it on or not?" Janie heard the frustration in his voice. "Did you try to talk him out of it?"

"Of course not!" She had to fight to control her voice. "Joe said it still could happen, long as everything fell into place."

She heard her father actually give a sigh of relief. "That's good, Janie. You did really good."

Janie almost laughed. "Thanks, Daddy, for turning me into a rum-runner."

"Well, sweet thing, you finally figured that out."

In the darkness, she gave him a puzzled look. It amused her that no matter what she did, Pearly talked about it as though she were on a mission for him. Maybe she was, in a way—after all, she was a Thurston.

"I'm going down to the wharf, check on Sammy. See ya later."

Pearly got up from the chair and headed for the door.

CHAPTER FIFTY-SEVEN

ON MAX'S WHARF, HENRY GROVER was on the north side of the clubhouse again, spying, waiting impatiently to see if Gatsby and Kanky would carry out their promise. Tonight, however, Henry was dressed in his police uniform. He was worried that things might go haywire, and it would be easier to fall back on the law. Henry knew he could always claim that he was just doing his job. That excited him.

For the last hour, he had watched and listened to Pearly and Sammy. When Sammy walked outside and checked on the boats, he was tempted to push the old man into the water. The skinny engineer actually carried a shotgun over his shoulder. Henry snickered softly. "What a strutting, self-important little prick he is." Henry wondered if Sammy had the courage to shoot anyone.

Later, Henry's ears really perked up when Pearly called Chief Grover nothing but a fucking, Bible-banging phony. Sammy added that the chief should mind his own fucking business.

Henry nodded to himself, quickly storing away Pearly and Sammy's remarks for another time. Maybe on judgment day, or when they were going to jail. He wondered how long it would take Pearly—this whiskey-drinking heathen—to mend his ways once he became his father-in-law.

Henry was sorry to see Pearly leave. He really enjoyed eavesdropping on their conversation. As an officer of the law, Henry felt he was gaining insight into what made men evil. In his own mind, he had narrowed it down to money, booze, and sinning women. Now that Pearly left, Sammy was relegated to talking to himself.

Henry studied the mounted head of that cigar-smoking pig, reassuring himself again that it represented the wickedness of Tiverton. Then, he had a strange thought: *Henry, if you wallow with pigs, expect to get dirty.* In any event, he was grateful to be on the right side of the law.

With the falling tide, Henry never did get a good look at *Whispering Winds.* He had no appreciation for rum boats or, for that matter, anything that floated. He even hated his father's menhaden boats. For him, *Whispering Winds* was just another vessel smuggling the demon rum up this river of sin.

The night seemed to pass slowly; he began to doubt that Gatsby would even show up.

~~~~~~

A half-hour later, which seemed an eternity, Henry caught the flash of headlights at the junction of Main Road and the dirt lane that led to Max's Wharf. When the headlights went out, he knew it had to be Kanky—he was hiding his car behind a stand of trees that bordered the road. Henry was glad he hadn't left his car there.

He watched Sammy walk over to the stove and pour himself another cup of coffee. Suddenly Henry saw the engineer turn very attentive, as though he heard something.

Sammy jerked around, spilling his coffee, and disappeared quickly into the darkness of the building.

A moment later, he heard Kanky's accent. Henry's heart pounded.

Sammy had his shotgun pointed at Kanky's temple. He screamed, "Don't move, greenhorn, or I'll blow your fuckin' brains out!"

Kanky dropped his pistol.

"On the floor! On the fuckin' floor—now!" Sammy's voice had

turned to a high pitch of fright and excitement. "What are you doing here? Are you alone? What the fuck do you want?"

"Old man," Kanky snapped, "you talk-a too much!"

Behind them, Gatsby stood in the doorway with a pistol in hand. It was pointed at Sammy's head.

~~~~~~

Henry's eyes ignited with surprise. He almost blurted out: Gatz is Gatsby! Gatz even shaved his beard. He remembered meeting him briefly at his father's office with Janie and her fucking proposal. What the fuck is going on here? His throat went dry; his hands turned clammy; his heart raced.

Now he saw everything unfolding before his eyes. He whispered, "By God, I am going to use this information to my advantage. When the time is right, I will tell Janie and my father that her big investor is a gangster!" Henry couldn't pull his eyes away from Gatsby.

Yes, he thought, this is even more exciting than the ambush at the trestle bridge. It's exciting doing God's work.

Gatsby cocked his pistol.

Sammy dropped the shotgun and turned around. "You! *Diamond Daisy!*"

"You know who I am."

Sammy blurted out. "Jesus Christ! Gatsby! You shouldn't be here! You're asking for real big trouble."

"Shut-a up!" Kanky picked up the double-barrel shotgun and cracked it open, letting the shells fall to the floor.

Kanky glanced up at the mounted pig's head. "Hey, when did-a Hunker die?"

"Aw shit, Kanky, you know that's not Hunker. That's Gertie's pet pig. Hunker had its head stuffed after he ate it."

Kanky laughed.

Just then, Collector entered the clubhouse. "Hey, boss, there's only two boats…no pilot houses, but the brand new one is here. What a beauty! Like I said, I could sing a great song about *Whispering Winds*…"

"Some other time!" Gatsby snapped.

Kanky turned to Sammy. "Where the other-a one?"

"Fuck you!"

Kanky thought for a moment. "Sure. Wilcox's boatyard, being-a repaired."

"You're asking for big trouble, Gatsby. You better leave. It's Joe's turn to stand watch. He'll be showing up here anytime…"

Gatsby stared at Sammy. "No matter, these will do, especially *Whispering Winds*." He motioned to Collector and the other man. "Get moving! Set the dynamite!"

Sammy's eyes widened. "Are you fucking crazy?"

Kanky picked up a bottle of Sammy's whiskey, uncorked it, and vigorously wiped its neck. "You'll see-a soon enough how crazy we are." He took a drink from the bottle.

"Why you doing this, Kanky? It's only going to make bigger problems between you and Joe."

"That's what I'm counting on, asshole."

Sammy shook his head. "Joe has always treated you good. Even when you didn't deserve it. Even after you stole all that money from Max…"

Sammy's comment tilted Gatsby slightly.

Kanky shoved Sammy towards the door. "What-a the hell do you know?" He grabbed Sammy in a headlock and forced him out the door. Gatsby followed.

Sammy yelled, "You no-good bastards! You're gonna all be in big trouble!"

Kanky looked at Gatsby. "What-a you want to do with him?"

"Remember what they did the night they sank *Hobo*? Let's give him a good view, so he can tell Bucolo all about it."

Kanky laughed, grabbed a section of netting, and dragged Sammy down the wharf towards a work boom hanging over the water. He threw Sammy down onto the wharf and, like making a Portuguese sausage, wrapped him inside the net.

Kanky untied the block and tackle, gathered up the netting around Sammy's shoulders, and passed the boom hook through it. They hoisted Sammy high into the air.

Hanging there, Sammy watched the men place the dynamite on the *Mallard* and the *Wood Duck*. He wiggled hopelessly inside the net. As they set the charges on *Whispering Winds*, he screamed, "You lousy bastards! That's Joe's new boat!"

Gatsby yelled, "That's the idea, Sammy! Now shut the fuck up!"

Sammy heard them laugh. He watched them connect the triple fuses. He watched them run the long main fuse well back onto the wharf. Sammy yelled, "You no-good bastards!"

"Shut-a fuck up!" Kanky snapped. "Be-a thankful you're not on the boats."

Sammy still wouldn't shut up. "You ain't any fucking good! You're not fit to piss on. You won't get away with it, Gatsby! You won't!"

"Enjoy the fireworks, Sammy... Tell-a Joe how-a pretty the boats looked being blown sky-high..."

"Fuck you, Kanky! And it's true: your mother shit you out the wrong hole."

Kanky grabbed an oar from alongside the overturned oyster skiff and whacked Sammy on his ass.

Gatsby picked up the fuse and Kanky lit a match. As the fuse sparkled, they all ran down the lane towards the car.

Sammy continued to wiggle helplessly, watching the fuse slowly burn. "Aw shit! Aw shit!"

Moments later, Henry Grover walked out from the north side of the building and quickly snuffed out the fuse with his boot.

Sammy's expression was one of pure relief. "By Je–golly, Chief Grover, never thought I'd be so happy to see the law."

Henry ignored Sammy and instead looked towards Main Road.

Moments later, through the trees, he saw the headlights from Gatsby's car speeding away.

"Please get me down, Chief, please… This is mighty uncomfortable."

Henry walked over to the boom's halyard line. He touched the rope and then looked out over the boats.

Sammy was puzzled. He asked, "How did you happen to be here, Chief?"

Henry untied the boom's halyard line. Finally, he said, "Oh, I've been coming here regular, Sammy. Hell, who do you think has been telling the Coast Guard about Joe's schedule? Who do you think set up the ambush at the trestle bridge?"

"Fuck!" Sammy's eyes turned angry. "Why?"

Grover just smiled.

Suddenly Sammy felt scared, even more scared than before. "Please, Chief, just get me down."

Instead, Henry slowly released the halyard line, allowing the boom to swing out over the water and the rum boats.

Sammy yelled, "No, not that way! Just lower me down onto the wharf!"

Henry continued to pay out the rope. The boom and Sammy were now hanging out over the boats. Sammy quickly realized what the chief was doing. Fear knotted in his throat. For a moment, he couldn't speak. Sammy snapped, "Chief Grover! You're fucking crazy!"

"Maybe, but Joe's going to know Gatsby did this. If I'm lucky, maybe Joe will kill Gatsby. Or maybe they'll kill each other. Either way, I win."

Henry's hand went to his shirt pockets, then into his pants, looking for something.

Sammy's eyes brightened. Henry had no matches. Of course, Henry didn't smoke. He almost started to laugh, until he watched Henry dash into the building and return with matches.

Sammy watched in horror as Henry relit the fuse. Grinning, he looked up at Sammy and said, "About time you went to hell! And don't worry, someday all your friends will be joining you." Henry glanced at the burning fuse and bolted towards the north side of the building.

Behind him, Sammy screamed, "You bastard! You crazy, Bible-banging bastard!"

Sammy watched the burning fuse travel over the timbers, down onto the boats, veering off now in three directions—leading towards the set charges.

A few seconds later, Sammy's screams were lost in the violent explosions of the rum boats. At the same time, the force that killed Sammy hurled the boom and his netted body into Nanaquaket Channel.

CHAPTER FIFTY-EIGHT

THE EXPLOSION SHOOK the *Black Duck* like an earthquake. Joe's head jerked up as a brilliant orange glow flashed instantaneously through the fo'c'sle hatchway. For a moment, he was shocked by the bright, disintegrating glow. He knew instantly what had happened.

He yelled, "Sammy!" His voice sounded like a screech. Hopping on one leg, banging against the wall, he managed to put on his pants and climbed out of the fo'c'sle.

~~~~~~

Janie was just falling off to sleep when she heard the muffled boom and felt the slight shock to the house.

She sat up, wondering what had happened.

From his bedroom, Pearly yelled, "Janie!"

She jumped from her bed, her heart racing, not understanding what could have happened but fearful just the same. She ran down the stairs as Pearly left the house, throwing on a shirt. He yelled, "Call Hunker! Call the Bancock brothers!"

"What's wrong, Daddy?"

Without stopping or turning around, he shouted, "Max's Wharf! Explosion!"

She grabbed the stair's handrail and steadied herself for a moment.

In the kitchen, she grabbed the receiver and, at the same time, looked at the list of telephone numbers. At the top was Hunker. Janie said, "Operator, please get me Spring 0755… Hurry!"

~~~~~~

By the time Joe left the boatyard and reached Main Road, he could see car headlamps barreling south. Lights had gone on in many of the cottages dotting the river. He noticed that the firehouse doors were open and the truck was about to leave.

As he turned down the lane leading to the wharf, a thick cloud of smoke was still bellowing. He jumped from the Buick and his eyes took in the destruction.

The explosion and gasoline quickly turned the wharf into a fiery inferno. Balls of burning debris rained into the water, onto the landing, setting a blaze on a net shed and Max's old, overturned oyster skiff. The roof of the clubhouse was littered with small patches of glowing embers, hungrily trying to gain a foothold through the thick tarpaper and into the dry wood.

Joe ran to the end of the wharf and looked down into the smoking, debris-littered water. He knew Sammy was dead and his boats were destroyed.

His eyes quickly locked onto the floating boom and the body wrapped in a net. He screamed and, without hesitating, jumped off the wharf into the debris. It took only a few strokes to reach Sammy.

He grabbed the netting and tried to shake it from the boom. He saw the iron hook that held all the twine together. He worked it free and began to tow Sammy back towards the wharf. Above him, he heard voices yelling offers of help.

Arms were reaching down, but with low tide, it made it difficult for the volunteers to pull them both from the water.

On the wharf, Harry Manchester, the volunteer fire chief, knelt over Sammy's body. He felt Sammy's neck and listened to his chest. He shook his head. "He's gone."

Joe nodded slowly, staring down at his dead friend. Someone put a blanket over Sammy's body and another over Joe's shoulders. He glanced around and saw that everyone had a look of horror on their faces. He could hear their whispers, yet he didn't understand what was being said.

Fishermen tell stories how, when in the throes of drowning and death, their lives usually pass before them. Joe wondered if Sammy had those visions.

In a silent rage, Joe's insides churned in turmoil. He wanted everyone to leave. They have no business here, he thought. Yet, they really did. When Pearly and Hunker pushed through the crowd, he felt ready to explode.

Pearly looked at Joe, then down at the covered body. "Oh, sweet Jesus!"

When Hunker bent over and lifted the blanket, the crowd immediately turned silent. He ran his big hand over Sammy's matted white hair. "Sammy," he whispered. "Sammy…" Hunker glanced up at Joe and Pearly. Hunker's expression was one of confusion hidden within his rage.

Tears ran down Bobby Bancock's cheek. He sat on the ground at Sammy's feet. He glanced up and found Billy and Maggie, their lips quivering, staring down at him. Silent tears rolled down their cheeks.

A few minutes later, Henry Grover walked through the crowd. He stopped and gave Joe a hard stare. He then leaned over and lifted the blanket from Sammy's face. He fingered the netting and stood up. He glanced at the floating debris and turned to the onlookers. "Okay, folks, time to go home."

Janie moved up alongside her father. He put his arm around her shoulders and pulled her close. She stared in horror at the blanketed body. Tears in her eyes, she said, "Sammy wouldn't hurt anyone." She glanced at Henry and then at Joe. She turned to her father and whispered, "Oh, Daddy, why would anybody hurt Sammy?"

Pearly gave her a squeeze but said nothing.

"Let's go home, folks," Henry ordered. "I don't want to say it again. There's police business here…"

The crowd, still voicing their own opinions, reluctantly began to disperse.

Joe motioned to the Bancock brothers to stay.

Before leaving, Harry Manchester approached Joe. "Nothing for us to do here, Joe. Do you want me to call Wareham's Funeral Home?"

"Thanks, Harry, I'd appreciate that."

When Manchester walked away, Henry looked at Joe. "Appears someone doesn't like you, Bucolo…"

Joe said nothing. Janie reacted slightly. Pearly's hand slipped from her shoulder. Hunker stood up.

Henry added, "Someone like Kanky?"

Joe glared at Henry. "What makes you think it was Kanky?"

"Come on, Joe, everyone knows about the bad blood between you two." With Janie there, Henry wanted to scream out that Gatz is Gatsby. God! He couldn't wait to tell Janie. Tell his father how Gatz hoodwinked everyone.

"If it was Kanky, what are you gonna do 'bout it?"

"There's nothing the law can do…especially when lawbreakers fight amongst themselves. You know the law never has sympathy for outlaws, and that's what you are."

Pearly stepped forward. "You mean if you're a lawbreaker, it doesn't matter if you kill someone? Well then, Henry, this really doesn't concern you."

"Yes, it does." Henry took out a pencil and opened his pad. "I'm investigating an explosion of suspicious nature and the death of Sammy Turner."

Janie moved closer to her father, glanced at Maggie, and attentively watched Henry.

"Why was Sammy Turner here tonight, Joe?"

Joe looked at Janie and their eyes met for a moment. "Sammy practically lived here. You knew he was my engineer."

"For the rum boats? Correct?"

Henry turned to Janie and then back to Joe.

Joe didn't reply.

Henry turned to Pearly and Hunker. "Where were you when this happened?"

Pearly said, "Home, in bed…"

"Can you prove that?"

"Of course, Janie was home…"

Henry looked at Janie, and she nodded. He glanced at Hunker.

Hunker shook his head. "Home…taking a pleasant bath… Ask my Gertie. She always tells the truth. I think."

Henry turned back to Joe. "And where were you?"

Joe glared hard at Henry. Hesitating slightly, he asked, "What's the point of all this, Henry? We didn't blow up the boats."

"It's police business, nothing more… Now, where were you?"

"Sleeping…on the *Black Duck*."

"Can you prove that?"

"No!"

Henry glanced at Maggie and almost smiled. "Anyone sleeping with you?"

Janie and Maggie's expressions turned angry, protective.

Henry's mouth hardened at their reaction. Instead, he looked down at Sammy's body. "See what running booze has cost? Another life. You know, Bucolo, dead bodies are really starting to pile up."

Pearly said, "You know this isn't Joe's fault."

"Sure. Just like the death of that poor sailor at Sandy Point Shoals. He's just an innocent bystander. Nothing is ever his fault."

Joe threw a fist into Henry, catching him on the jaw. Pearly and Hunker stepped between them. Hunker's big hands locked onto Joe's arms. With one finger, he gently patted Joe's wrist, trying to soothe him.

Henry had a trickle of blood in the corner of his mouth. He glared at Joe. "You're going to regret that, Bucolo…"

"Get off my property! You sonofabitch!"

Janie lashed out. "Look at you! All of you! A man's dead here, and you're carrying on like…like children…better yet, like wild animals…"

Henry's head silently jerked at her response.

"Ya," Hunker added, slowly releasing Joe's arms.

Henry gave Janie a strange look and started back to his car.

Janie continued to shout after him. "There's no difference, Henry, between you or Kanky or anyone else." She glanced quickly at Joe, at Hunker, and at her father, who all listened silently. "Damn it! You're all the same!"

Henry got into his car and drove off. Joe walked towards the building and Janie followed him. Pearly and Hunker stood there, standing over Sammy's body.

"Damn, ya Janie sure is a hothead."

"Yeah, just like her mother. But hell, she called it."

"Ya." Hunker looked down at Sammy, then at Pearly. "No matter, we gotta do something 'bout Kanky and Gatsby. We gotta 'venge Sammy."

Pearly said, "Don't worry; we ain't gonna let Gatsby get away with this."

Their attention shifted to the approaching headlights. The hearse from Wareham's Funeral Home pulled onto the wharf. It stopped and two men got out. They opened the back door and removed a wooden stretcher. Pearly and Hunker helped them lift the body into the hearse.

From the doorway of the building, Joe and Janie watched. Maggie and Billy moved back into the building's shadows. They were clearly beside themselves.

"We'll be over in the morning," Pearly said, "to make arrangements."

Mister Wareham nodded and got into the driver's side and the vehicle pulled away.

Hunker took out a stogie. Pearly sat down on the wharf and leaned against a piling. Bobby stayed sitting on the shell-packed ground, watching Joe and Janie at the door of the clubhouse.

Billy and Maggie looked at each other after they saw Janie give Joe a hug.

CHAPTER FIFTY-NINE

NONE OF THE GANG SLEPT THAT NIGHT. They hung around Max's Wharf for an hour or so and agreed to meet up at Joe's house. Hunker and Bobby went by Mayfield's barn and picked up some booze. Pearly got food from Mary's. Billy and Maggie quietly disappeared.

Joe stayed at the clubhouse with Janie, gathering Sammy's stuff together. Janie started getting emotional, so Joe drove her home. When he got back to the Heights, the gang, except for Billy, who had taken Maggie home, was waiting on the porch for him.

They sat in the kitchen and talked until dawn, mostly about Sammy and the times they had shared.

After everything had been said, and everyone had cried and laughed, and all the toasts were over, the talk turned vindictive.

Hunker said loudly, "We gotta do something! I'm tired of all this talk, it makes my brain ache."

Joe smiled on that one. Pearly and Bobby Bancock turned their heads to make sure Hunker didn't see them smile as well.

Hunker added, "Do we kill Gatsby together? Or do I kill him myself?"

Hearing those words, Joe took out a cigarette. He tried to light it, but the match and cigarette wouldn't come together. Pearly reached over and steadied his hand.

Joe inhaled deeply, nodding in a boozy way, now looking at Hunker. "No one else is gonna die! No one! Not if I can help it. And I won't let you boys do anything, either. And nobody's going to change my mind! Gatsby will get his one of these days. His kind always does!"

Pearly asked, "What about the 'bang in'? Is that still on?"

Joe was silent for a moment. Hunker was the only one nodding. "If Captain Durall agrees, and we get the bad weather, and if we're all in it together…one last up-your-ass to the Volstead Act, I say we do it."

The boys broke into enthusiastic agreement. Toasts were made.

Hunker said, "Ya, that would make Sammy happy. Mighty happy…"

Everyone laughed, a bit.

~~~~~~

The next morning, the boys, all hung over, wobbled single-file into Wareham's Funeral Home to make Sammy's arrangements. The congenial funeral director had already received inquiries on where and when services would be held. Gertrude Moore asked Minister Bottomley to officiate over a gravesite service, and he agreed.

When Pearly heard that, he said, "Bottomley's presence might just bring Sammy back to life."

Hunker speculated on how the friendly minister was doing more than just saving Gertie's soul; he knew there would be booze flowing freely at Sammy's funeral, and that Bible-banging midnight drunk surely wouldn't want to pass up that opportunity.

Mister Wareham interrupted the boys and reminded them that the time for a decision was at hand. He had things to get to. It was resolved that Sammy's farewell would be private, and there would be no wake. He would be buried in Hillside Cemetery, not far from the plot of Max Bucolo.

CHAPTER SIXTY

EVER SINCE BLOWING UP JOE'S BOATS, Gatsby and his gang had been worried, but they felt fairly certain they had finally put Bucolo out of business.

Kanky figured Joe wouldn't lift a little finger against him, and he would be done with rum-running for good. Rarely does a man feel such frightened and feigned happiness. On the other hand, if anyone wanted to listen to Collector's refrain, *"Whispering Winds was a beautiful lady. I'm telling you, don't be surprised if she comes after us…cuz beautiful ladies done wrong…always get their way…always get their way…"*

Gatsby finally shut Collector down.

But a short while later, when Walter answered the telephone, everything changed again. "Hey, Kanky, it's for you. Henry Grover."

Kanky held his hands up. "Shut up!" He pressed the receiver to his ear. "Yeah?"

"Sammy Turner's dead," Grover said.

Kanky yelled, "What-a hell are you talking about?"

"Turner's dead! He was killed in the explosion," Grover repeated loudly. The tone of his voice signaled that he was actually happy giving Kanky the news.

"Turner's-a dead? How could that have happened?"

Gatsby came out of the office and looked at Kanky, who kept shaking his head.

Collector did the same. "It can't be."

"I don't know, but I think you went too far," Grover said. "Blowing up the boats would have been enough."

Puzzled, Kanky said, "I can't-a figure it out. No way Sammy shoulda died."

Grover said loudly, "Well, he did! And you better be prepared for big trouble! Bucolo went crazy. Swore revenge—claimed he's going to kill every one of you!"

Kanky, still in disbelief, mumbled to himself, "Sammy should-a still be alive."

"Hey, you still there?" Grover shouted. "Hey!"

"Yeah, I'm-a here." Kanky didn't like the way Grover sounded so cocky on the phone. He slammed the receiver back into place and turned around to face Gatsby, Moran, and Walter. "Sammy's-a dead for sure!"

Collector said, "I still don't believe it. Grover could be playing us. He might want a gun battle? Hoping we just kill each other...especially Bucolo... Remember, Grover has it bad for the Thurston girl."

Moran and Walter caught the strange expression that crossed Gatsby's face.

Kanky added, "There's-a something about Grover, he's beginning to spook me."

Gatsby stared at Moran. "Call Maggie. Find out for sure."

Moran went into Gatsby's office. A few minutes later, he came out and nodded his head.

Kanky continued, "Sammy shoulda been okay. I smell a fish, I think. Sure, maybe tossed around a little," he described the action with his big hands, "but Sammy shoulda been okay."

Gatsby glared at Kanky. "Well, he's not."

Walter added, "Maybe you used too much fucking dynamite!"

Gatsby replied, "Either way, we should expect some trouble from Bucolo."

Kanky said, "If-a Bucolo doesn't finally smarten up now, he'll be joining Sammy."

Gatsby glared at Kanky. "I'm the boss. I'll give the orders."

Collector whispered, "Besides, nobody is gonna convince Bucolo to quit the trade. Bucolo's a Swamper to the bone."

CHAPTER SIXTY-ONE

NINA AND JOE WALKED SLOWLY towards her speedboat. "Last night," he said, "I lost three boats, including *Whispering Winds*."

"Yes, Papa is very upset."

Joe nodded. "My mechanic, Sammy, was killed. Do you remember him?"

She shook her head. It didn't seem to affect her. Joe was struck by her blasé demeanor—she either couldn't comprehend what he had just said, or she really didn't care.

"I can see that you are very sad, Bucolo. More than you should be." She held onto his arm and they sat down, overlooking her runabout.

Joe kept his arm around her as the light chop lapped against the *Wolf*'s bow.

Out of the blue, she asked, "Who killed your Sammy, Joe?"

"Gatsby from Chicago."

"My brother sold his business to that Jew. He's regretted it ever since."

"I was set up," Joe added. "It was deliberate. In cold blood. Poor Sammy must have watched the whole thing." He rubbed his eyes and cleared his throat.

She stroked his hair and whispered, "Let's go up to the cave house. I'll pretend to be a whore."

"I don't want that. I want to do something clean and simple. Look at you. You think you have nothing, but at least you can work. Building boats is good, and honorable. I'm getting outta rum-running. I'm going back fishing."

They sat next to each other, smoking cigarettes, listening to the water. Then Nina said, "You're lucky to be a man, orphan. I wish I could be so independent."

Joe sat and thought for a moment. "Can you get some trucks, Nina?"

"I have a friend with four trucks. They're not great but they go."

"I'm planning one big run before getting out. More booze in one spot than has ever been seen in Rhode Island. I'll pay you to get your four trucks to my shore crew, and I can give you a good deal on a load of booze. Help feather your nest. Do you have anyone you could sell to? You know what I'm saying?"

She nodded like a five-year-old getting candy.

Joe added, "I'll let you know when."

Nina kept staring out over the river. "Are you going to marry Pearly's daughter?"

"I hope so."

"I'm jealous," she whispered. "Come, let's have a drink to your friend Sammy."

CHAPTER SIXTY-TWO

AFTER SAMMY'S DEATH, Maggie was still devastated. The night it happened, Billy and she had a discussion, lamenting on what she had done to Joey and the gang and, of course, Sammy. When Moran called her for more information on the explosion, she wanted to tell him and Gatsby off, but she didn't. She was still waiting on Joe to give her a chance to redeem herself. But she wasn't sure when that would happen.

Later, she telephoned Janie, asking her to come over immediately. The tone of her voice worried Janie. She wondered if it had anything to do with Joe, or Sammy's death? All manner of questions filled her mind.

She parked in front of Brown's Provender. Usually, Maggie preferred to go out and get away from her mother.

Janie glanced up at the apartment windows above the store. Walking slowly up the stairs, she thought, this has to be about Joe. She primed herself for the worst. She had to be strong; Maggie was still her friend.

The door swung open. Maggie had a strange, hysterical expression on her face, almost like someone who might have escaped from a mental institution. The house was a mess, with dirty dishes and clogged ashtrays everywhere. It didn't smell very nice, either.

"I'm glad you came," Maggie said.

"Is everything okay?"

Wearing a pink bathrobe, Maggie shook her head and took Janie's hand, leading her into the parlor. "I'm feeling terrible about Sammy's death. Joey losing his boats… My God!"

Janie glanced around. "Where's your mom?"

"I don't know." Maggie looked hard at Janie. "She's probably in bed with my father."

Janie was puzzled. "What?"

"You heard me…my father!" Maggie pointed to the couch, where a diary with a faded leather cover lay open.

When Janie realized this had nothing to do with Joe, she felt relieved. "Your father died at sea, on a fishing boat, during a bad storm, Maggie. What are you talking about?"

"That's what I thought." Maggie and Janie sat on the couch, the diary between them. Maggie pointed to the book. "This is a record of my mother's fucking wicked life. And I do mean wicked!"

"Maggie, you shouldn't read your mother's private diary."

She shook her head. "I found the key a couple of days ago. It was hidden behind a mirror. I knew it had to belong to her diary."

"Maggie. It's just not right."

Maggie snickered, "Right? This is *my father* we're talking about. Don't make me laugh." Maggie's eyes ignited with contempt as she uttered his name. "Francis Grover!"

Janie didn't understand. "Francis Grover?"

"He's my fucking father. I was born on the fucking wrong side of the blanket. It's all there, and plenty more."

"My God!" Janie snapped. "Francis Grover!"

Maggie jumped up. She was turning into a stark raving lunatic. It gave Janie a rush. She swayed and rubbed her hands as she stared at Janie, then released a hysterical laugh. "Oh, yes, that phony has been doing my mother for twenty-four years. Well," she pointed to the diary, "that is, when he feels the need for sin." Maggie stormed back to the couch and glared into Janie's eyes. "The need for sin!" she screamed. "Jessica…my mother fucked a lot of men in Tiverton. She even had a fling with that fucking asshole Kanky. Can you believe that?"

"My God!" Janie whispered. Everything seemed to freeze while they each tried to read the other's eyes. It was clear that Jessica was one busy lady. But Kanky, that was pretty low on the tree of men.

Janie tried to give Maggie a sympathetic look but was unable to respond.

"That's not the worst of it," Maggie said. "My mother, Jessica Louise Jackson, is a fucking murderer! Now I know the actual crime Moran used to blackmail me! I knew it wouldn't be good. But I never imagined it would be murder!"

"Maggie, you can't be serious?"

"Get this, Francis Grover even helped my mother hide the body."

"Why would Francis Grover do that?"

"One of Jessica's boyfriends found out that Francis was my father and threatened to reveal it to the town. They fought, and Francis and my mother got the best of him…she stabbed him dead!"

Janie shook her head, at a loss on what to say, just staring silently at Maggie.

"Well, say something…anything!" Maggie screamed.

"What can I say? I'm surprised that she would even divulge all these secrets in her diary. Seems risky. No?"

"She said that it made her feel better writing about it. She claimed that if she had a chance, she would confess it on her deathbed. If not, the diary would tell the story."

Janie was dumbfounded and a worried look crossed her face.

Maggie just shook her head. "Besides, I have a right to know these things. My mother would never tell me anything. My father dying in a storm! What shit! She made him seem like a hero. When I was little, I wanted to believe it. But when I got older, I questioned her story. She continued to lie. Now my hero is a fucking phony, and I'm the fruit of his sin! The need for his sin runs through me, just like my mother—a murderer!" Again she laughed hysterically. "Now I know that Francis Grover is an accessory to murder with my mother. My God! Their blood runs through my body!"

"I'm really sorry for your hurt, Maggie. I don't know what else to say." What could she say? Oh, Maggie, you always said apples don't fall far from the tree…

Maggie's gaze turned glassy, and her expression contorted. Janie saw nastiness transform her friend right before her eyes. "Guess who else is in that diary?"

Janie's eyes widened. Pearly, she thought quickly. "Maggie, I'd just as soon not know about other people's private business."

"You never seemed to mind listening to my private business before!"

Janie's voice froze in her throat.

Maggie continued, "You think I don't realize your game? I see through your innocent…pretense. Frankly, it was fun seeing what it did to you. I loved it."

"Maggie, those discussions were—"

"At Joey's expense."

Janie stood up. "I'm sorry you're going through this, but it's not doing you any good retelling this to me. Maybe it's best I go."

Maggie continued, ignoring Janie, her voice foreboding, "Every time I talked about Joey, I watched your eyes turn lusty. Tell me it ain't so?"

Janie's composure was undone by Maggie's stark remark. She started for the door.

Maggie grabbed the diary. "Wait! Maybe you'd like to read 'bout Joey and what my mother did for him on his sixteenth birthday. A present from Max Bucolo! 'Magine that?"

Janie stopped and turned around. Her expression changed from anger to surprise, then outright curiosity.

Maggie tried to force the diary into Janie's hands, but she refused to take it. Maggie said, "I'm sure it'll interest you."

"Please, Maggie..." Janie backed away from Maggie and held up her hands. "I don't want to hear any of this!" She bolted for the door with Maggie following.

"Get this!" Maggie yelled. "She was Joey's first woman. My mother taught him everything."

Janie's hand reached for the doorknob, but she hesitated slightly, repelled yet drawn to the reality of Maggie's revelations.

Then Maggie said in a lower voice, "My mother claimed Joey was a great learner. He's great at everything. Boy, can I vouch for that. Imagine how lucky I am, Janie." Maggie was screaming. "My mother taught Joey everything he knows! There are other secrets as well..."

Janie rushed out. Tears blurred her vision as she opened the apartment door and started down the stairs.

Maggie yelled, "And guess who else fucked my mother? Your father, Janie, your father fucked my mother, too!"

Janie hesitated slightly, then slammed the door, shattering the window pane. Outside, her thoughts were racing, her head was pounding like a stormy sea. Then it surfaced, something rather ugly—sex, lies, and murder; what Maggie shared with her was surreal. Just then, Janie had a strange thought: Where did Grover and Jessica actually hide the body?

~~~~~~

The following morning, just as dawn broke over the Heights, Janie got out of bed. She smelled coffee and something frying. Probably Jonnycakes. She propped up her pillows and stared out at the flowing, incoming tide of the Seaconnet River. Across the Basin, she watched yellow sunbeams welcome the day along Portsmouth's rocky shoreline.

Yesterday's diary revelations made for a restless sleep. She wished that Maggie had never told her anything.

Putting the murder aside for the moment, simply because it seemed so unreal, she wondered why she was more upset about Joe screwing Jessica than her father. She found herself trying to rationalize their past sexual indiscretions. Joe was simply too young to be held accountable. She felt that Jessica was of Pearly's generation. At least that was what she wanted to believe.

She thought about the night at Frankie-the-Bone's, trying to be like the girls who were having all the fun. What did that say about her? What did she really want? Her mother always said she was her father's daughter.

They argued from time to time about the fishing business, yet she couldn't remember, or didn't want to remember, if her mother ever complained about Pearly's whoring. Had her father been with Jessica before or after her mother died? Before or after Joe? Before or after Francis Grover? Before or after Maggie was born? Before or after Jessica murdered her husband? That diary revealed more than she cared to know. Why couldn't Maggie have kept all those secrets to herself? But that wasn't Maggie's way.

As Janie stared out at the water, she felt maybe Minister Bottomly was right: She was indeed living alongside a river of sin. Everything seemed so complicated, yet suddenly, so clear.

~~~~~~

Determination filled Janie's heart, such that it didn't faze her when she saw Henry's car outside the Grover factory.

She walked into her office and saw Henry standing in his rigid, pompous way, looking out the window towards the fleet of his father's anchored menhaden boats. He appeared to be contemplating his future fortune.

She smiled. "Hello, Chief."

Henry brightened immediately. "How are you, Janie?"

"I'm good. I'm here to give your father my notice."

"Really? Why?"

"I know now that there is no future for me here or down in Virginia."

"So, you found out that Gatz was Gatsby…"

"You knew?"

Henry ignored her question. "What about us?"

Enraged, Janie leaped out of her chair and leaned into Henry, "There is no us!" as she slapped him across the face.

Stunned, his face flushed with anger and embarrassment. "You can't mean that!"

"You of all people, Henry Grover, aren't about to tell me what I can and can't do!"

"What about the Almy house?"

"I'd paint it another color." Janie waxed sarcastic at Henry's obvious attempt to reel her back in.

Henry looked at her and shook his head. "You were fooled by Gatz...just like Bucolo will fool you."

Janie wasn't surprised by his vindictive turn. He truly was a small man...if he was any kind of man at all. "So far, Henry, Joe's the only one who's been honest."

Henry's eyes flashed anger, but Janie didn't flinch. He snorted, "With Bucolo, you're going to end up just like Maggie Jackson and all the other women in his worthless life."

"That's a risk I'm willing to take."

"You're actually going to marry him?"

"You have marriage on the brain, Henry. You want to get married, so you think everyone wants to get married."

Frustrated, Henry stormed out of the office, slamming the door behind him.

From the corner of her eye, Janie saw Francis Grover staring at her through the glass partition. In that moment, she wanted to yell out to the Mister Holier-than-thou Bible-banging phony: You're a murderer by association. I know all the secrets in Jessica's diary. Instead, she just shrugged, and Grover immediately glanced back at his papers.

She smiled. God, despite all the recent sadness, bad luck, and breaking her promise to her father to string Henry along until the 'bang in,' Janie couldn't quite remember ever feeling this good.

~~~~~~

Jessica was sitting on the couch reading the *Providence Journal*. Maggie said, "Mom, there's something you should know."

Jessica didn't look up. "You're pregnant?"

Maggie took a deep breath. "No, Mom, I'm not *pregnant!*"

Jessica put down the paper. "Well, you've certainly been acting like it. Why are you so moody?"

"Jesus, Mom, I've got good reason."

"One way or 'nother, we've all got reasons."

Maggie saw the potential here for an argument. "I don't want to fight."

"Life's a fight, Maggie. A constant battle. When will you ever realize that? Look at me."

Maggie shook her head. "This isn't about you. This is about my father. You've been lying to me!"

"What the hell are you talking about? Your father? Your father died at sea—"

"Mom! My father did *not* die at sea! Please, no more bullshit! I read your diary!"

Jessica lunged from the couch in a rage, almost tripping on the hem of her nightgown. She charged around the room, searching. "Who do you think you are? Where is it?! God damn it! That diary is my private business. What right do you have?"

"The right to know who my father is, that's what's right!"

Jessica sat back down and fumbled a cigarette out of her case. "How much did you read?"

Maggie said, "I read it all, Mom, some of it twice. I even shared it with Janie. She needed to know because I've been lying to her all my life about my father dying at sea."

Jessica's hand shook as she lit her cigarette. She quickly sucked in the smoke. "I'll never forgive you, Maggie, never. That diary was my personal life." She stood up.

"Maybe it was, Mom, but it's not anymore." Maggie snatched the cigarette out of her mother's hand and pushed her back down onto the couch. "I don't intend to see you going to jail for murder, so there's nothing for you to worry about."

"For years, Maggie, I really wanted you to know. That's why I wrote it all down in my diary. Damn that Francis Grover!"

"Listen, Mom, for me, that diary has the ability to get us both outta this miserable life."

Jessica countered, "It's not that miserable."

Maggie said, "I'm happy you were so precise. Your list of every man you've fucked for the last thirty years is going to get us a wad of money. I'm going to be knocking on some Tiverton doors. And don't worry, I'll take care of you."

Jessica asked, "Where's my diary?"

"Safe and sound," Maggie answered sweetly, smiling to herself. She finally had her mother's complete attention.

— CHAPTER SIXTY-THREE —

FIVE CARS FOLLOWED WAREHAM'S funeral hearse, Joe with the Bancocks, Pearly with Hunker and his wife, Gertrude, Janie, Mary Standish, Maggie, Jessica Jackson (much to the annoyance of Minister Bottomley), Cory Wilcox with Edmund Palmer, Doctor Peckham (quite drunk), and a few local fishermen.

Hillside Cemetery was in south Tiverton on a rolling knoll, framed by evergreens and stone walls. Gray headstones of varying age and shapes sloped gently westward towards Seapowet Marsh, offering a sweeping view of the Seaconnet River.

The men carried the coffin from the hearse to the gravesite under the bright midday sun, with a calm blue river off to the west. The plot was perfect for Sammy. Joe and the boys had paid for Sammy's plot and extra to rush the headstone. Mary suggested Sammy should have the outline of a boat carved into the marble marker. The gang thought it a great idea. Hunker, in a moment of reflection, found the words: *For Sammy's long, long journey*. One large floral arrangement, in the shape of an anchor, read: *Sammy, You Will Be Missed. Your loving friends.*

Janie, Mary Standish, and Gertrude Moore stood on the right side of the grave while the men wavered together on the left. Bottomley stood at the head with his open Bible, his fat pink lips and pudgy cheeks poised for action.

Bottomley cleared his throat. "Friends of Samuel Aurel Turner, please bow your heads and contemplate with me life's true meaning."

"Amen," Gertrude Moore said loudly.

Hunker looked askance at his wife.

"And I saw a great white throne and the one who sat upon it; from his face the earth and heaven fled away, and there was found no place for them. And the dead were judged out of those things that were written in the scrolls, according to their works. And the sea gave up the dead…"

Joe's eyes drifted towards Janie. She was looking at him.

"Amen," Gertrude Moore said again, even before Bottomley's prayer was over.

"…this is the second death, the pool of fire. And if anyone was not found written in the book of life, he was cast into the pool of fire…"

Bottomley raised his head from the Bible and looked out towards the Seaconnet River. "Oh, Lord, have mercy on the soul of Samuel Aurel Turner, this harvester of thy mighty river, thy mighty ocean, he who reaped her benefits. Oh, merciful Jesus, grant Samuel eternal rest. Amen."

Hunker nudged Pearly, who just nodded.

"Amen!" all in assembly said together.

Bottomley closed his Bible. For a long moment, no one moved. Mister Wareham nodded to Bottomley, who then turned to leave.

Hunker slurred, "Thank you, Minister, for your beautiful words."

Bottomley nodded. Gertrude nodded. Bottomley and the women walked together towards the cars. Cory Wilcox and Edmund Palmer put on their caps and gave Joe and the boys a nod. Then they left.

Mister Wareham approached Joe. "Soon as you leave, Mister Bucolo, my men will finish up here."

Joe said slowly, "Me and the boys would like a minute alone."

"Ya," Hunker said, "we wanna say one last goodbye to Sammy."

"Certainly," Mister Wareham said. "We'll go have a smoke." He motioned to his helpers and they walked, shovels over their shoulders, to the hearse.

Joe watched the women get into the cars. Gertrude Moore returned to town with Bottomley. As soon as the cars disappeared behind a cloud of dust, Hunker retrieved five bottles of whiskey from Joe's Buick and gave one to each man.

Joe nodded towards the coffin. "Say a few words, Hunker. I think you should be the one."

Hunker was honored. He looked at the coffin and then at the boys. "Oh, give Sammy beans when he's hungry, whiskey when he's dry…"

"Jesus, Hunker, have some respect," Pearly said.

Hunker just continued, "A tight kitty for Sammy's stiff cock, and old heaven when he dies, when he dies. 'Specially now that he's dead."

Joe said, "Damnit, Hunker, have some respect."

"Bullshit!" Hunker said. "That song is heaven to me, and it was heaven to Sammy. Let's not forget that. Now boys, before we drink, we need to pour one for Sammy on his coffin." Five bottles were tipped down and saturated the pine. Next, they all took a drink.

After that, Pearly nodded, Hunker, then the Bancock brothers, and finally Joe. Then they all broke into a quiet, rumbling laugh that had the men looking from one to the other, eye to eye. It was a laugh that could morph into a sob with the turn of a thought.

Hunker raised his bottle and took a drink to tamp down the rising emotion. Everyone again followed suit. Then, before starting for their cars, Hunker tucked the bottle under his arm and began to unbutton his fly. Pearly turned around just as Hunker took out his cock.

Pearly yelled, "Hunker, you're not really going to do it?! Hunker, you're not?!"

Hunker, who had already started to pee, glanced at Pearly, and said, "A promise is a promise."

CHAPTER SIXTY-FOUR

THE PHONE RANG A LONG TIME, until Joe finally picked up the receiver. "Hello."

Janie asked, "What are you doing?"

"I'm cleaning Max's house. Later, I have to go down to the boatyard. I'm still bunking on the *Black Duck* these days."

There was a slight pause on her end. "Did you have any supper?"

"Not yet."

"Suppose I bring you something to eat?"

"At the boat?"

"Sure."

~~~~~~

The warm fo'c'sle of the *Black Duck* was cozy. Joe banked the small coal stove and placed a kettle of water on top. That was something Sammy usually did to add a little moisture to the tight, dry, heated quarters.

Even though the *Black Duck* was tied up at Wilcox's boatyard, Joe was still sleeping aboard with his double-barreled shotgun by his side. Gatsby just might be thinking of finishing what he started. Joe had decided to wait until after the 'bang in' to avenge Sammy. He would act alone, and he would act appropriately. Without having to say anything, he believed the boys understood what he would do.

He heard Janie's car driving up over the crushed-shell lot. He climbed the stairs into the pilot house and watched her get out of the car. She walked beneath the *Flo*, which was still on the railway.

He went out on the deck to help her board. The Basin was choppy and under a brisk, westerly wind, it made for a very cool night. She was carrying a plate over a bowl covered with a towel. Food was the furthest thing from Joe's mind.

"Hello," she whispered, almost as though she didn't want anyone to hear her. "I brought you a ham sandwich and a bowl of soup."

"I'm glad you're here," he said. "I'm hungry." He latched the pilot house door and placed the food on the console.

"Can you make coffee here?" she asked.

Joe chuckled. "Can fishermen swim?"

She said, rather seriously, "I'm not sure."

"Well, Pearly can't swim. None of the boys can. I'm not the best swimmer either."

"Oh, Joe, no talk about my father, the boys, or rum-running. Okay? I'm here for the night. By the way, I gave my two-week notice to Francis Grover and to Chief Grover."

Suddenly the meaning of her words made his mouth dry. Nothing outside the *Black Duck* mattered. He kissed her and found her mouth hot and sweet-tasting. Janie's body pressed into his.

He took her hand and led her down into the dimly-lit fo'c'sle. Steam drifted up from the kettle's spout. On the portside, against the bulkhead, they could hear the soft, burning crackle of hot coals inside the stove.

"Don't bump into that. It'll give you a nice blister."

Without saying a word, Janie turned around and lifted the back of her hair. Joe gently kissed her neck and began to unbutton her dress. She moved her head pleasurably. The dress fell from her body.

She turned around and, with her right hand, grabbed the fo'c'sle's overhead beam for balance. He took in her flawless white skin. Her breasts lifted and flattened out like swells on the ocean, her nipples erect and eager. She made no move towards him or to cover herself.

He continued to absorb her body. "Beautiful," he whispered, "just beautiful."

She smiled.

He exhaled like he was blowing out a candle. "I'm crazy about you, Janie."

He undid his belt, stepped out of his pants, and slipped off his shirt. They were both naked except for their boots. Janie continued to look at him, breathing harder now, her right hand still clutching the foredeck's beam.

"I never saw a man naked before," she said softly. She thought of the silver dollar in Pearly's cash box. "You've got a strong body, Joe. Guess you'd call them fisherman muscles."

He smiled and said, "Before we go any further, I've gotta tell you something."

"You haven't got anything to tell me that I don't already know. You know how to fish these waters better than me." Her voice had a snap to it, an edge of firmness.

He nodded. "Okay."

"Would you either stoke that fire or put a blanket over me? I'm getting a little chill."

"I'll do both," he said. He threw a blanket over her and added some fresh coal to the stove.

Janie sat down on the bunk, and behind him, he heard her boots fall to the fo'c'sle's deck. She was now stretched out in the berth beneath the blanket, her toes pointed overhead. Joe unlaced his boots and placed them next to hers, then slipped under the blanket up against her warm skin and eager hands.

CHAPTER SIXTY-FIVE

SHORTLY AFTER SAMMY'S FUNERAL, Maggie commandeered a used car from Joel Bancock. She got a good deal, a black little Ford coupe for twenty-five bucks. Joel was another occasional customer of Jessica's. Maggie knew how to negotiate, and it was just a matter of a discussion with Mister Bancock. My God, she thought. What freedom.

She parked in front of Palmer's Barber Shop and waited. Cory Wilcox and Edmund Palmer had gone to Doctor Peckham's house after the funeral for a few drinks. Later, Cory dropped Palmer off, and she followed him inside.

Palmer, watching himself and Maggie through the shop's mirror, said, "How do I know you'll keep your mouth shut?" He was clearly drunk.

"I'm not going to damage your good name, Mister Palmer. You have the word of an old whore's daughter on that," she said matter-of-factly.

He went into the back room of the shop and returned with an envelope. "That's half my life savings."

"Half-a-loaf is better than none." She grabbed his hand and shook it like any businessperson would do. "Thank you, Mister Palmer."

She was pleased with the way it was working. She already had a car and four thousand dollars appropriated by her mother's kitty. She chuckled on that one.

~~~~~~

The next day, Maggie called Janie and apologized for the night she'd gone mad after she'd read her mother's diary. Temporary insanity, she called it, and the two old friends quickly agreed to let bygones be bygones. Then Maggie got down to business and asked Janie to connect her with Francis Grover, who readily agreed to an eleven o'clock emergency appointment. A meeting on family matters, for which Maggie was well prepared.

She was now walking up the steps to the office of Francis Grover.

Janie smiled and stood when Maggie opened the door. She gave her a big wink. "We've been expecting you, Miss Jackson." Janie tapped on Francis Grover's door jamb. "Miss Jackson's here for her appointment, Mister Grover."

"Thank you, Miss Thurston. Would you please close the door?"

Maggie stuck out her hand, which seemed to surprise Francis Grover. He jumped up, shook it, and gestured to one of two chairs opposite his desk. "Now, what can I do for you, Miss Jackson?" They both sat down.

"Well, Dad, I'll make it short. My mother entertained you, sexually speaking, one thousand, two hundred and fifty-six times between 1899 and last week. Almost twenty-five years' worth."

Francis Grover's mouth slowly formed an O, and he stared at Maggie for a moment, speechless.

"I have a list of the time and place of each of your meetings, including that very first time—behind the Odd Fellows Hall up on Pocasset Hill when you conceived me."

Still speechless, Francis Grover, somewhat dazed and looking on with sad eyes at Maggie Jackson, sat rigid, like a corpse. His black shirt was buttoned tight at the wrists. His hands were folded, and they rested motionless on the green blotter of his desk.

"Actually, you being my dear father is the lesser of our family problem."

"Family?" he mumbled.

Francis Grover's normally pale skin blushed like his face was on fire. His lips moved, but nothing else. Finally, he was able to find the words. "And now, Miss Jackson, you're going to ask me for money. Am I right? And if I don't pay, you'll smear the good name of Francis Grover all over this community. Is that where this is going?"

"No, Dad." Maggie stood and hiked her skirt over her hip.

Francis Grover's eyes finally moved and his voice turned sharp. "Are you going to do something vulgar?"

Maggie ignored his stupidity. She moved behind Francis Grover's desk, next to his chair, and pointed to the bowling-pin-shaped birthmark on her upper left thigh.

"Henry has one of these too, on his neck. You know, Dad, I guess we are all cut from the same hunk of baloney."

Maggie dropped her skirt, and as she returned to her chair, she saw Janie, with her mouth wide open, watching through the office windows. "If you don't give me what I want, Dad, I'm going to tell Henry that Jessica Jackson has a bowling-pin-shaped birthmark just like the one I showed you on her poor old body."

"What do you want?"

"One thousand, two hundred and fifty-six *fucks*, times twelve, ya know, for the apostles, equals fifteen thousand seventy-two dollars… give or take. Jessica claimed there were times when you were really horny—so it was two, three times a night. 'Magine that." She looked at him doubtfully. "Anyways, I'm not charging you for those bonuses, or being an accomplice to you-know-what. I've got my car downstairs. We'll drive to your bank in Fall River."

— Chapter Sixty-Six —

WITH MONEY, MAGGIE LOOKED quite charming in her bob haircut and new clothes. It added an air of sophistication; so much so, she could've easily attended any society party. When Janie opened the door at Joe's house, she exclaimed, "You look so wonderful! The new Maggie Jackson. Joe, come here, take a gander."

Joe entered the parlor. "Well, well…very nice, Maggie."

Maggie beamed, clearly happy with their response.

"I'm glad you came, Maggie. Take a seat in the kitchen."

She sat down and smiled at Janie. "I feel like a new woman."

Janie said, "I'm really happy for you, Maggie."

Joe joined them and placed a paper with notes on the table. "This is what I want you to say. Study it…then you're gonna pass this information on to Gatsby."

"Of course, Joey. I appreciate the chance to make it up to you." She glanced at Janie, a look of remorse on her face. Janie patted Maggie's hand.

"Do you have Moran's number?"

She nodded. "When do I make the call?"

Joe handed her the notes. "Soon, but you can't make any mistakes, Maggie. Study these notes. Then you'll speak with Gatsby…"

A half-hour later, with Joe and Janie by her side, Maggie made the call.

~~~~~~

At Gatsby's New Bedford office, Moran, Kanky, and Collector were in discussion on *Diamond Daisy*'s next trip to Rum Row. Gatsby answered the phone.

"Um…Hi, Jay, this is Maggie. I'm surprised to hear your voice, I was expecting Mister Moran."

"Hello, Maggie, we're glad to hear from you. Mister Moran thought you may be going back on your deal?"

Moran and Kanky leaned forward in an effort to listen.

"No. I'm calling with important news."

"What is it, Maggie?"

"Joey called a meeting with his men. They're planning this big deal. They call it a 'bang in.' I thought this was important enough to call you right away."

"That was wise, Maggie."

"Joey has a deal with a Canadian captain to bring in his entire ship…loaded with liquor. Could be around thirty to forty thousand cases…maybe more. The ship will be landing under the cover of a major storm."

"Thirty to forty thousand cases, you say?"

Gatsby's men were eyeballing each other, clearly impressed.

"Interesting." Gatsby's left foot tapped nervously at his fast-thinking assessment. "Where will this ship land, Maggie?"

"According to Billy Bancock, Joey has a deal with the owner of a large facility called Melville's Landing in the West Passage of Narragansett Bay."

Gatsby placed the receiver against his chest and looked at Kanky. "Do you know Melville's Landing?"

With an expression of surprise, Kanky nodded, "It's-a huge…former shipbuilding company for the Navy. Went-a bankrupt. Out of the way, too. Pretty smart location."

"Good job, Maggie. I won't forget this. Now, Maggie, call me if anything else comes up."

"I will."

Gatsby hesitated slightly and added, "We'll talk soon."

Maggie glanced at Janie, who had also heard him; their expressions bordered on laughter.

"We'll talk soon, Maggie, goodbye."

Maggie hung up the receiver and looked at Janie and then Joe.

"You did good, Maggie."

"Thanks, Joey."

"There's one more thing I need you to do...it's about Henry Grover."

~~~~~~

Gatsby looked at Kanky, Moran, and Collector. They had thin smiles on their faces.

Gatsby stood up. "Have the entire crew ready. Moment's notice! Line up as many extra trucks and men as you can find. That's a lot of booze. We need to be prepared. Get on it, now!"

Collector mumbled, "Fucking Bucolo...you can't put a good man down."

Gatsby gave him a look. "Write him a ditty, Collector. We'll all sing it when we're spending his money."

~~~~~~

Later, alone, sitting in his office, Gatsby appeared to be somewhere else in his thoughts. He wondered where Daisy was. Was she still thinking about him? His thoughts shifted to the Imperial Hotel as he recalled his conversation with Maggie: "I'm about to embark on a major enterprise. I intend to take over and control the smuggling of liquor into Rhode Island waters."

He remembered vividly that it took her a while to respond. Finally, with a worried expression, she whispered weakly, "Like…Joe, err…like Joey's been doing?" Realizing Gatsby's eyes were on her, "I've heard whispers about his success… It's all quite secretive…"

To Gatsby's sensitivities and recall, Maggie's words sounded painful—as if she were trying to justify her revelation and pending guilt.

Janie Thurston suddenly overlapped Maggie in his head. He had said to Janie, "You almost sound in awe of Mister Bucolo?"

"Mister?" He remembered how she laughed, rather vigorously. "Not hardly…not hardly at all. However, most women I know in Tiverton find him exciting. He's also generous with some townsfolk who have had it tough, but he does play that down. It was also a trait of Max Bucolo, his stepfather…" He still couldn't forget her eyes when she made that statement. Yes, he reluctantly thought, Bucolo's a lucky fellow.

Again, he recalled Janie's words: "Something my father has said from time to time: one survives by doing clever things and sometimes even dishonest things…but you still need your wits about you."

Gatsby's left foot again tapped rapidly against the floor. He said aloud, "Swamp Yankee mentality! It just runs too deep. Yes, their real strategy is to *trickify* Jay Gatsby…" He released a chuckle that turned into a soft laugh.

CHAPTER SIXTY-SEVEN

LESS THAN A WEEK AFTER Sammy's funeral, Mary Standish, monitoring her radio, finally received a message from Captain Durall. The *Maria Morso* was fifty or so miles off the coast, loaded with prime liquor and waiting on Joe. He would stay there until Joe gave him the word.

Joe suggested to Captain Durall that he anchor well south of the thirty-fathom edge until they had suitable bad weather.

Captain Durall agreed, though he did inform Joe that he had no Louisa aboard to pass the time away. Joe promised the captain a pleasant surprise if he was patient.

Mary asked Joe if Durall was a good catch. Joe insisted Durall wasn't her type, and he mentioned it to Pearly, who hit the roof. Joe wondered if Mary had made the remark on purpose.

Joe contacted Frankie-the-Bone to confirm his role as the banker. Despite Joe's latest problems, Frankie hadn't changed his mind. He was going to get fifty percent of the load at a time when nobody had booze, as well as anticipating things would get hotter on Rum Row. He also promised to supply a good-time gal for Durall. Sally Half-a-Dollar, Frankie added, loved Canucks for their ability to make love with their lips and tongue.

In the meantime, Joe kept Pearly busy on the *Flo*, getting the dragger ready for fishing. Joe wanted the steering mechanism rebuilt, and a new double-drum Hathaway winch installed. That should keep Pearly out of the way.

Down at Max's Wharf, he had Hunker and the Bancocks assembling trawl nets. Hunker had always been a good twine-and-needle man, but he didn't much like those long, monotonous hours anymore. By starting the twine work now, Joe figured, the nets would be ready when the *Flo* was.

Cory Wilcox had finished repairing the *Black Duck*'s pilot house. Except for priming and painting the new woodwork, which Joe and Janie had started, the boat was again ready to carry booze.

With the turn of events, Janie and Joe had gone over the money side of the rum trade, only to find that Joe hadn't been the best businessman around. A few successful liquor runs had produced profits, but they calculated that between the hijacking losses, vessel repairs, expenses, crew, and captain shares, plus the shore gang's wages, there hadn't been a lot left over for Foggy Joe.

The final payment on *Whispering Winds* had put a big dent in Joe's cushion, so much so that between the *Black Duck*'s new pilot house and buying the *Flo*, Joe was on the cuff to Cory Wilcox for about sixteen thousand dollars.

~~~~~~

Over the next week, much to Joe's annoyance, gentle weather continued. He and Janie kept busy working on the *Black Duck*.

On Saturday, Janie was wrapping their paintbrushes in oilcloth when she caught Joe up on the forward deck looking at the bright sun and blue sky. They had just finished applying the last coat of paint to the roof of the pilot house. Joe shook his head and didn't look very pleased.

Janie said, "Painters are supposed to be happy in nice weather."

"Normally, I am. But nice weather isn't what this rum-runner needs right now."

She smiled. "Maybe the weather gods are trying to tell you something."

"They're telling Captain Durall I'm an asshole. That's what they're telling him."

"Be patient, Foggy Joe, be patient." She spread a quilt on the deck and sat down against the port gunnel, facing the warm sun. She opened a picnic basket.

"Why are you smiling?" he asked.

She handed him a sandwich. "Sitting here on this deck brought back a pleasant memory," she said.

Joe took a bite of his sandwich.

"I think I remember the moment I fell in love with you," Janie said.

"That's hard to believe," he said.

She gave him a soft punch. "You were working with Max," she said, "and one day Pearly took me down to Seaconnet Point. You were unloading fish piled high on the deck. You were standing in the middle of the fish like some conquering hero. You seemed so proud, so successful. Yet when I looked at you…you seemed shy." She raised her finger. "But…you did smile at me, only once. When I smiled back, you turned away."

"That's funny, I don't remember that."

She punched him again. "I bet."

They had just finished eating when Joe noticed a plume of black smoke from somewhere around Fogland Point, and it was steaming up the river. It had to be CG-483.

Janie asked, "Who's that?"

Joe lit a cigarette and inhaled deeply. "Coast Guard. They're probably wondering where we've been."

Janie smiled. "Safe at home with me, and that's where I like it."

As the cutter approached the Basin, he said, without looking at her, "They're just reminding us that they're still around."

Janie watched the cutter enter the Basin, heading for the train trestle bridge.

Joe started to whistle.

Janie, with a look of disbelief on her face, said, "You never whistle on a boat."

Knowing well what she meant, he asked, "Why?"

"You know what they say, it brings on the gales."

"So, what's the problem, Legs?"

Janie hooted. "I get it!"

Between hoots and short bursts of laughter, the two of them continued to whistle as they watched the cutter pass through the open railroad bridge.

CHAPTER SIXTY-EIGHT

AFTER THREE DAYS, THEIR WHISTLING finally worked. The storm really went wild at daybreak. The howling wind and driving rain aroused Joe from a restless sleep aboard the *Black Duck*. He knew in a second, he had his nor'easter, and it was acting like the beast usually did. He immediately headed for home. Along Highland Road, he watched the high maples and heavy-limbed evergreens bending and jerking unmercifully under the blow of the wind. In the distance, the river was a boiling mass of white water.

Inside the house, the walls were creaking and there was a raw chill in the room. The cold air was an excellent telltale sign. This beast has plenty of strength, he thought. That's good, really good.

Joe mentally charted Captain Durall's last position, which was about forty miles south of Rhode Island. As the storm intensified, the *Maria Morso*, steaming north, would be riding in the wild canyons of curling waves. Not a comfortable ride, for sure. He hoped they had packed the liquor tightly and securely.

In the kitchen, he tapped the barometer and nodded his head. "Jesus! It's dropping to hell!" He grabbed the telephone receiver, screamed at the operator: "Spring 0485."

~~~~~~

Pearly knew who was on the other end. He didn't even say hello. "Yeah, Joe? I know. She's a beauty. Sky's black as bunker oil. It's real cold, too. You should see the Basin. The tide's horsing in every direction, and the wind…well, we've got a damn good nor'easterly brewing with plenty more life to it."

Joe smiled at Pearly's weather report.

Joe said, "You can thank Max for his great records. I'll pick you up in a few minutes. Call Hunker and the Bancocks."

"Already have," Pearly said. "But hey, Joe—Francis Grover's menhaden boats are anchoring-up in the Basin. They must be figuring it's gonna get really bad."

"Shit, how many?" Joe asked.

"Two, so far: the *Saint Peter* and the *Saint Paul.*"

"Jesus, I hope they don't move them all. Could make the Basin pretty crowded. Damn!"

Pearly released a *hhhhmmmm*. "Maybe you should call Francis Grover and tell him to leave you some room for the *Maria*. Listen, Joe, just keep your wits about ya."

Joe didn't smile. Grover's boats moored in the Basin could make it difficult getting the *Maria* into Bottomley's dock. All the other things that could possibly go wrong tumbled through his head. They always had been there, but it took the storm and the kickoff of the 'bang in' to finally bring them to the surface.

Strange that this was what his time in running booze came down to, or rather how it would end. A grand finale. A wild plan with haunting liabilities. Like this new problem: the Tiverton Basin full of moored menhaden boats seeking shelter from the very storm that was the linchpin of this very risky operation.

Max always warned him to be prudent. Think things out. Sleep on it, dwell on it, and ponder every quadrant. Always know what you're getting yourself into. Max also said: No matter how difficult it is to achieve, success is the best kind of revenge. You often had to take big risks to kiss success. This was the absolute truth. The 'bang in' seemed like a good idea at the time. Yes, it was a big gamble, but it was also a chance to kiss victory smack on the mouth. It was on, and Joe had to believe everything was going to work out fine.

~~~~~~

With the onset of a violent nor'easter, nearly the whole state was in shutdown mode. Most Rhode Islanders were well acquainted with the "beast from the east"—usually because of winter blizzards or storms like this one: a very windy and rainy nor'easter. Radio warnings were broadcast every fifteen minutes, and by suppertime, cities and towns were practically in blackout conditions. Again, most residents had learned it was best to stay off the thoroughfares—and that included the ocean.

Joe had told Maggie to call Gatsby at five o'clock sharp and tell him that the 'bang in' was on—and the ship was scheduled to arrive around ten o'clock at the Melville Landing facility.

Gatsby had to explain repeatedly to Moran and Kanky why he decided Maggie was lying and trying to pull a fast one on them—his intuition was in play here, based on the knowledge he gained from both Maggie and Janie in the past.

It was hard for them to grasp his reasoning, and they had no choice but to go along. Yes, it was a hunch, but he felt that he was correct. Besides, Gatsby was in charge.

Gatsby and his boys were now rolling towards Tiverton.

On top of that, Kanky called Chief Grover and told him to meet him tonight because he was going to deliver Joe Bucolo to him—dead or alive.

Henry suggested meeting at his father's business office.

~~~~~~

After picking up Pearly, Joe stopped off at Mary's Diner. She'd been up early, monitoring the radio. She received one very garbled transmission: "*Maria* moving. Terrible sea conditions." For Joe, that information was good enough. Pearly agreed.

When they arrived at Max's Wharf, the river had the appearance of high mountain rapids. The wind was ripping off the peaks of the waves and hurling them against the wharf.

"By Jesus," Pearly said, "we ain't had a storm like this in a helluva long time."

Inside the building, seated around the crackling potbelly, Hunker, Tommy Walsh, and the Bancocks were drinking coffee and waiting anxiously. "Weather sure is goddamn mean," Hunker said. "I hope the *Maria* hasn't been blown down to the Carolinas."

Joe shook out his slicker. "She's already on her way in. We've got about four or so hours, I figure. We better be ready!"

After Joe went over everything, the Bancock brothers looked at each other as though everyone else was nuts. "Wait a minute, Joe." Bobby Bancock stood up. "Is this a joke?" He swiveled around, looking at everyone. "It better be, cuz it's one fucking nutty idea."

Hunker gave Bobby a stern look, and he quickly shut up.

"The first half of the load is going into Frankie's trucks," Joe said, as if that answered questions on the stupidity of the 'bang in.' "The other half we're gonna hide in the church's wet cellar…sell it later on… Some of it will also be loaded onto four trucks from New Bedford."

"Wait a minute," Hunker said. "What about Bottomley?"

Joe smiled. "He's gonna be your responsibility."

"Jesus H. Christ! Ya mean I have to shoot him?"

"Course not!" Pearly snapped, missing Hunker's joke.

"You're gonna get him out of the church and keep him busy for the night," Joe said. "At least long enough until we're done with our work."

Hunker nodded. "For how long?"

Joe said, "As long as it takes."

"How in hell am I supposed to do that?"

"You should be able to think of something." Joe turned a bit to hide his smirk. "Whatever happens, we have to keep Bottomley in our good graces until we've emptied out his cellar and sold off all the booze."

"Jesus, but that's asking a lot," Hunker said.

Joe nodded. "Not really. Bottomley ain't gonna want his congregation to know what we used his church for...besides, a few cases will guarantee he keeps his mouth shut."

There was general agreement on that subject.

Hunker thought about it for a moment, then grinned widely. He walked over to the liquor cabinet, took out two bottles of Overholt, and uncorked one. Clearly, he was already looking forward to his challenge. Smiling at the gang, he said, "Yeah, ya right. Besides that, Bottomley ain't gonna want his congregation to know what him and me are gonna do. Yessiree, this is gonna be fun." Hunker started to chuckle at his private thoughts.

Curious, Pearly asked, "Just what are you thinking, Hunker?"

Hunker drained his mug and raised it towards the mounted pig. *"Oh, give me beans when I'm hungry, whiskey when I'm dry. And tonight, I's gonna die!"*

Despite their puzzlement, the boys laughed with him.

Joe shook his head. "I kinda feel sorry for Bottomley."

Again, everyone nodded in agreement.

After they all settled down, Billy Bancock spoke up. "Okay, if we're all gonna die, what's our job?"

"First, you drive us down to Mayfield's and make sure Pearly and I actually get on the *Maria*. Then you come back up here and make sure the trestle bridge stays closed. Or we could have the Coast Guard cutter helpin' us unload."

Bobby developed a very concerned expression. "Do you have any suggestions on how we do that, Joe?"

"I've already talked to Eddie Grayson. He's gonna close the bridge for us and keep it closed until morning. But you have to let him know when to close the bridge. You gotta bring him two cases of booze."

"Two cases!" Hunker said. "I'd do it for one!"

"By the way," Joe said slowly, surveying the gang, "Eddie Grayson swore me to secrecy, but yesterday he told me that Henry Grover was behind the bridge ambush."

"I'll be a sonofabitch!" Pearly said.

Hunker said, "Makes me wonder how much more he's been involved in."

"That'll give us something to ponder when this is all over and we get bored tonight," Joe said.

They all laughed.

"For the moment," Joe added, "we have to forget about Henry Grover."

Billy Bancock asked, "What else can we do?"

"After you secure the bridge, stop by the diner, and let Mary know it's on. Then go down to the church and wait for us behind Bottomley's church."

The brothers nodded together.

Hunker said, "Jesus, if we pull this off, we really can quit the business."

"That's the general idea," Joe said.

Bobby Bancock shook his head. "I can't believe the captain of the *Maria* agreed to it. 'Specially something as risky as this. He must be as nuts as us."

Pearly smiled. "Actually, Durall's coming in for the tootsie Joe promised him."

"Tootsie?" Hunker asked, slamming the door to the stove.

Joe said, "Sally Half-a-Dollar," and winked. "She's coming in Frankie's trucks."

Hunker curtsied to the mounted pig. "Sally Half-a-Dollar, pleased to meet ya."

"Jesus, Hunker," Pearly said, "stop thinking 'bout you."

"What do ya mean?"

Pearly said, "Mention a woman who'll drop her drawers for quarters, and you're all ears…"

"All pecker, ya mean!" Hunker threw some punches at Pearly's shoulder, who returned a few, and everyone cheered them on.

Finally, Joe raised his hand and pointed to Bobby Bancock. "One more thing: when you're done at the bridge, put Henry Grover's car out of commission."

Bobby Bancock stopped smiling and rolled his eyes. "Jeez, Joe."

"Just do it. And don't get caught."

The brothers nodded and started to put on their oil slickers.

Hunker asked, "What's Pearly gonna be doing?"

"He'll be with me. I'll need extra eyes getting the *Maria* through the Basin and into Bottomley's dock."

"It's going to be a tight kitty," Pearly said.

Hunker shook his head. "Jesus! I hope this works…"

Pearly quickly added, "It's gonna work. If everybody does their job, everything will work out fine."

Joe gave Pearly a silent, worried look.

Hunker then removed his eight-gauge punt gun from the cabinet. "What do you want that for?" Joe asked.

"In case the holy minister gives me a hard time."

~~~~~~

Within the hour, Joe sent Hunker and the brothers to bring the dory down to High Hill. They would need it to get out to the *Maria Morso*.

Joe and Pearly met Frankie-the-Bone in Fall River. It took a large satchel to carry Durall's entire payment, including Joe's bank for Captain Durall.

~~~~~~

Meanwhile, Hunker fell under a powerful sickness. He left his car and crawled on his elbows through the mud, up the steps to his house.

Hearing his cries, Gertrude Moore came running out of the entryway to help him. They slipped and fell back down the stairs. They were both covered in mud and soaked to the bone. Gertrude became hysterical when she realized Hunker wasn't drunk, but sicker than she'd ever seen him.

"Gertie, get the minister. I need Bottomley. Go! Go! Now!"

~~~~~~

Mary Standish closed the diner at noon. She monitored the radio but told Joe she didn't think they would hear from Durall until he was close to Seaconnet Point or possibly right in the river. At exactly seven o'clock, Mary finally received the coded word from Captain Durall: "Bring the clams and butter."

CHAPTER SIXTY-NINE

HIGH HILL WAS ABOUT A HALF-MILE south of Fogland Point, also part of the Mayfields' cow pastures. It had one right-of-way, and the hill provided a perfect and secure overlook for viewing the river. The winding, bumpy road led directly to the east bank of the Seaconnet and to the hidden dory.

The gale winds screamed through the scrub oak and berry bushes, sounding like a thousand unseen creatures howling in the dark. The cars swayed in the wind; their doors snapped open, nearly breaking off their hinges.

"Ain't fit for man nor beast!" Pearly shouted.

"That's why we're here!" Joe shouted back.

The Bancocks led the way down the embankment towards the dory, followed by Pearly and Joe. Pearly carried the burning but shuttered lantern. The overhang of the cliff helped to kill the wind somewhat, but it was still very difficult to see, and they had to move slowly over the slippery, rocky shoreline.

Bobby shouted, "A light! I see a light!" Everyone stopped walking. He pointed out into the darkness, slightly upriver. "To the north'ard. I'm positive it was a light."

Peering into the blackness, they all saw the light flicker through the wind-driven rain.

Joe quickly climbed up onto a large rock. "It's gotta be Durall!" Pearly handed Joe the lantern. He braced himself against the wind and opened the shutter. The wind blew out the flame. "Sonofabitch!" Joe snapped. He dug into his pants pocket for Max's flashlight, blinked it, twice. After about twenty seconds, he was answered.

"It's Durall!" Joe shouted. "Get the dory!"

Tipping the dory to empty it, they dragged it to the water's edge. Joe and Pearly got in, but the heavy surf made it difficult. Finally, both Bancocks had to wade out up to their armpits to set the dory free of the beach.

With some hard rowing, the dory finally broke through the heaving, rolling surge and was caught by the offshore wind. Every minute or so, a flicker of light came from the ship. It took almost fifteen minutes for them to reach the vessel.

As they came up on the starboard side, Pearly turned and screamed, "Christ! She seems too big for the river!"

Joe jerked around and saw the large, dark outline. At anchor, they rowed astern, around to the portside. In the lee of the vessel, they could make out some figures scrambling about the deck.

Someone on the ship threw over a rope ladder. "Here!" a voice yelled. "Here!" Suddenly a lantern flashed, marking the spot. Joe and Pearly made quick time climbing up the ladder.

Durall and his very nervous crew were waiting at the rail. Meanwhile, they swung out two stern davits and, with a block-and-tackle sling, hoisted the dory up. Durall shouted, "Where the hell have you been? Didn't you get our messages? We've been transmitting for hours."

Joe noticed Captain Durall's voice was loud and shaky, and even in the wind, he reeked of whiskey. "How long have you been here?" Joe yelled.

"Two hours!" First Mate Peter screamed. He, too, spoke with excitement in his voice. Everyone aboard the *Maria* was excited. It was clear the crew was in a big hurry to shed their contraband. There was much at stake. They ran for the shelter of the bridge's overhang on the portside. Here, the storm seemed to momentarily fade.

"Jesus!" Joe said. "We only picked you up at six o'clock and then only once."

"This storm," Durall said, "bad as a hurricane."

"Then you were glad to come in?" Pearly said.

Durall said, "I still do not like being in American waters…"

"You'll like it soon enough," Pearly said. "'Specially when you get that tootsie in your bunk."

Durall nodded without a smile. "Maybe yes, maybe no. Of course, that and the money will help to change my mind." He glanced at Joe. "Do you have all the money?"

Joe lifted the satchel. "All here!"

Joe's eyes swept the cluttered deck. Except for paths leading fore and aft, they had well-secured cases of booze jammed into every open space.

"Why didn't you put this liquor in the holds?" Joe asked.

"The holds are chock full," Durall said proudly.

Joe glanced at Pearly, realizing something for the first time.

Joe turned to Captain Durall. "Jesus…how many cases you carrying?"

"Well, if they counted right in St. Pierre…I should have around forty-five thousand, of mixed brands, give or take a few."

Joe hesitated slightly, as though Durall's figures had to penetrate his skull. Then, "Jesus Christ…that much?" Joe saw the look of genuine surprise on Pearly's face.

Durall caught their expressions. "Joe, you told me to bring in all the *Maria* could carry. I did. And you're getting a very good wholesale price for such a large shipment. Did you not realize how large my cargo would be?" Durall's voice hinted of annoyance. "Are you complaining?"

"No, of course not! I should've paid more attention to the numbers."

"We just were thinking about other things," Pearly mumbled, thinking the same thing.

Durall, clearly peeved, turned to Peter. "Hoist anchor." Without looking at Joe, he said, "Captain Bucolo, follow me."

Inside the pilot house, Durall flicked on a small red light that illuminated the compass. The steering wheel, made of polished oak and heavy brass, was gigantic. The coal boilers were running. The decking beneath them vibrated to their rhythm. A bitter smell, like smoke and liquor, saturated the pilot house air. Alongside the steering wheel was a long brass handle that controlled the engine's forward and reverse.

"Is this river deep enough?" Durall asked. "My *Maria* sits heavy in the water with this load."

"Yes," Joe said. For a moment he had to reassure himself, mostly because the *Maria* suddenly seemed so large. He added, "And the tide is still rising, at least till midnight."

They heard the windlass turning, slowly lifting the chain. When it broke water, the heavy anchor swung against the portside of the boat, causing a deafening impact.

Durall said, "She's yours, Captain Bucolo. You are now in command."

Joe took the helm and threw the control into forward. "Not too fast," Joe said.

Durall shouted into a tube that connected to the engine room, "Ahead, one-third."

The *Maria Morso* answered slowly. She seemed to be vibrating more than she should. Joe spun the helm hard to starboard. "Jesus! How many turns does it take?"

"Many," Durall replied loudly.

"Great," Joe muttered. Maneuvering through the Basin jammed with moored menhaden boats should be interesting, but he smiled weakly and nodded to Durall.

When the *Maria*'s bow finally swung into position, Joe steadied the wheel until he had the northerly heading he wanted.

Durall said, "She's off about six degrees on true north…"

Joe nodded. "No problem here. We should be seeing the shoreline real soon."

"America," Durall said, mostly to himself.

"Pearly, keep your eyes open for Fogland Point."

He cracked open the pilot house door into the weather and kept watch. Between the whipping wind and rain, the visibility was almost zero. "Nothing yet," Pearly called.

Even though the *Maria* moved slowly up the river, she devoured the distance. It wasn't long before he made out the shadows of the Seapowet shoreline north of Fogland.

"How long?" Durall asked.

"Maybe a half-hour…maybe less," Joe said.

Durall shook his head. A moment later, in the pilot house's darkness, Joe heard the pop of a bottle being uncorked. Joe noticed Captain Durall's voice was loud and shaky.

"Might be a good idea to start your crew unlacing those deck loads. Get the holds ready, too," Joe said. "It'll make things go faster when we land…" He heard the gurgle of Durall taking a swig, the smell of whiskey, and then the smack of his lips.

Durall said, "There isn't much room on deck. But I'll tell them."

When he left the pilot house, Pearly looked at Joe and asked, "Well, what do you think?"

"Ask me later. One thing's for certain: the *Maria* is way too big for this river. And she's carrying a helluva lot more than I figured."

Pearly said, "Sure seemed like a good idea at the time."

"Doesn't it always." Joe suddenly wondered if he had locked himself into an unrealistic, dangerous situation—a bravado commitment to Captain Durall that couldn't possibly work. His 'bang in' was moving down the Seaconnet River, and he realized then that it was finally something more than speculation.

CHAPTER SEVENTY

IN THE TIVERTON BASIN, the storm continued to raise havoc with the Grover factory. The fish plant's high sides caught the full power of the gale. The relentless wind beat against the east factory wall like drums.

Inside his father's office, Henry Grover, in uniform, sat on the corner of the desk, toying with a scrimshaw letter opener. He stared at Gatsby and Kanky, dressed in oils and boots, standing by the window separating Janie's office from Francis Grover's. All the men had pistols strapped to their hips. Kanky and Collector each had an extra one tucked in their pants belts.

With his eyes on their pistols, Henry asked, "What makes you think this so-called 'bang in' will happen tonight?"

Gatsby said, "I've got my ways, Chief. Never doubt that. It's going to be tonight, and it's going to be more fucking booze in one spot than has ever been landed in Rhode Island...and for that matter... anywhere else in this country. Quite an achievement, if it succeeds."

Collector added, "Truth is, Bucolo has proven to be quite an adversary."

Gatsby tossed Collector a warning look. Henry glanced at Collector, but surprisingly gave him an agreeable soft nod.

Kanky said, "Yeah, we can't-a believe Bucolo could get any off-shore rummy to come in... Plenty-a dangerous."

Henry snickered. "If you think Bucolo can bring an offshore rummy into Tiverton in this storm, you're as crazy as he is." Outside, the storm's furious soundscape seemed to back Henry's comment.

Henry's eyes shifted from Kanky to Gatsby. "What do you want me for? Are you forgetting about the law...the Coast Guard?"

Gatsby moved closer to Henry. "We've arranged for the Coast Guard to be off Long Island, searching for a sinking fishing boat. The State Police, tonight, do not exist. You've already helped the Feds with the bridge trap...so if any show up, send them on a wild goose chase...send them to Melville's Landing on the west shore..."

Kanky added, "Inform them you got it from a good source...Maggie Jackson's body. Yeah, just like her-a mama." Everyone laughed.

"Maggie!" Henry's eyes glared at Gatsby. "Why would she give you that information? What does she have to do with this?"

Gatsby shook his head and said, "Everything. Maggie and the rest of these Swamp Yankees think we've been had. I figured that out, first hand. Don't worry, you'll still get Bucolo...one way or another. Let him do the dirty work, and we'll take his booze."

Henry snapped back, "If you had just finished off Bucolo, it would've ended all our problems!"

Gatsby banged the desk. "Why didn't you just shoot him yourself?"

Kanky chimed in, "Yeah! Be a fucking man! Don't be-a 'fraid of the dirty work, ya fuckin' pussy!"

Henry scoffed. "You call *me* a pussy, Kanky? I've already beaten you to some dirty work!"

Gatsby and his men appeared puzzled.

Kanky snapped, "That's a fucking laugh!"

Henry moved closer to Gatsby, almost in a threatening manner. He whispered something. Gatsby and Kanky immediately pulled back in surprise. Kanky's hand went to his sidearm.

Kanky and Henry were now face to face. Kanky screamed, "What-a the fuck you sayin'!?"

"You heard me! I was there that night. After you left, I released the boom with Sammy still hanging over the boats and dynamite. Then I relit the fuse."

Kanky spun around to look at Gatsby, who was more surprised than shocked. "Of course, so that's how-a Sammy died. I knew we didn't-a do it. You were hoping Bucolo would blame us—maybe even-a kill us all."

With a look of glee on his face, Henry smiled as though he were proud of the murder.

Kanky tapped his chest with a ruler from Henry's father's desk. "By killing Sammy, you figured-a Joe and I would kill each other?" Gatsby and his mugs nodded. They were all impressed, surprised by Henry's ruthlessness.

"If you were in my shoes," Henry said, snatching the ruler from Kanky's hand, "you would've done the same thing. Here's my deal. You finish off Bucolo tonight. You get the booze. You get Bucolo's operation. Then get the hell out of my town for good."

Kanky grinned. Then, loudly, he taunted Henry. "What? And leave you with-a the girls? From what I-a hear, Janie don't want you, and you can't have-a Maggie, that's incest, Chief!"

Collector added, "That's even against the law, right, Chief?"

"What the hell are you talking about?" Henry snapped back.

"Didn't your holier-than-thou father, the almighty Francis Grover, ever tell you who your mother-a was?" Kanky roared. "The town whore—Jessica Jackson!"

Grover was shriveling into a prune, gazing vacantly down at the floor, a strange curl on his lips. He now had his hand edged towards the service revolver on his hip.

Kanky was in his glory. He turned to his men, who were enjoying the spectacle, palms up—as if Kanky had just pulled a rabbit out of a hat or made something disappear.

In utter disbelief, Henry mumbled incoherently; his eyes rolled slowly up at the men as his hand moved even closer to the grip of his revolver.

Kanky, in response, made a move for his own gun—just as Henry unholstered his.

With one deft move, Kanky slammed Henry's arm with his massive hand, and the gun discharged into the floor. Collector joined the scuffle. The gun went off again, shattering the glass partition.

Gatsby's men jumped behind the filing cabinets for cover.

Collector, Henry, and Kanky fell to the floor, fighting. Henry was snorting and bellowing like a sick calf. The gun went off once more, slightly muffled this time. Henry's body fell limp.

Slowly, Collector and Kanky got up. They stared down at Henry, who was motionless. Blood oozed from his neck, flooding the hardwood of the office floor.

Kanky glanced at Gatsby and said, "Jesus Christ, boss, I think he-a shot himself."

Kanky rolled Henry over. His eyes were wide open in a frozen stare as blood flowed like lava from the bullet hole. "He's-a dead!"

Kanky stared down at Henry, then looked at his men. Finally, he said, "Throw him into the Seaconnet. Francis Grover's menhaden can-a eat him. Kinda fitting."

CHAPTER SEVENTY-ONE

SINCE NIGHTFALL, JANIE, quite nervous, had been sitting on the sunporch, watching the storm whip through the Basin. She still couldn't believe what Joe was trying to do. She was hoping she would catch a glimpse of the *Maria Morso*, but so far, the wind-driven rain had provided very little visibility.

Occasionally, on Main Road, she saw a car's headlights, but that was all. For almost an hour now, most of Tiverton had been without power. "Perfect," she said aloud, "just like Joe had hoped."

She thought that a glass of gin and tonic water would help her nerves. It did, so she was on her second one.

Over the sound of the storm, she was startled by a pounding on the kitchen door. She got up from the chair and walked through the darkness slowly towards the kitchen. A lantern was burning on the kitchen table.

"Janie! Janie! It's me, Maggie!"

She rushed to the door and opened it—finding Maggie there, hugging her elbows, drenched to the bone. "Come in, come in!"

Janie had to throw herself against the door to close it. She looked at Maggie. "You want a drink?"

Maggie glanced nervously around. The glow of the lantern made shadows on the kitchen walls. "Is your father home?"

"No, why?"

"I'd take some dry clothes."

Janie handed Maggie a towel and pulled some things from a laundry basket in the corner. While Maggie changed clothes, Janie poured her a shot of gin.

"One of Moran's men just paid me a visit, asking questions about Melville's Landing. I think they are suspicious."

Janie said, "Suspicious, how?"

Maggie stared questioningly at Janie. "I'm not sure they bought the story Joe had me tell them."

Janie nodded. "Why?"

Maggie grabbed Janie's hand. "I don't know. But I think something bad is going to happen to Joey tonight. We've got to warn him!"

A look of panic crossed Janie's face. "Okay. I'll get my rain slicker. Yes, we've got to warn Joey."

"Joey?" Maggie smiled knowingly.

Chapter Seventy-Two

GERTRUDE MOORE VIGOROUSLY worked her rocker, knitting a sweater faster than usual, waiting anxiously for Minister Bottomley and Doctor Peckham. Suddenly she heard, "Gertie! Gertie! Come here!" She glanced towards the ceiling, threw down her needles, and ran up the stairs. She stopped outside of Hunker's door and listened for a moment. Hearing nothing, she knocked.

"Come in! For Chrissake!"

Gertie entered the darkened bedroom. She moved warily.

Hunker was holding his chest as though in great pain. "Where is Minister Bottomley?"

"He's coming, Benjamin."

"I'm dying, Gertie, I'm dying. I could even be having a heart stoppage. I pain so much, Gertie, I hope the minister gets here soon."

She said, "Are you sure you just don't need a big burp or need to pass gas?"

"No, damn it! I must make peace with my Maker…"

Gertrude's eyes brightened as she moved closer to the bed. Despite her anxiety, she almost seemed pleased with Hunker's wishes.

"Yes, yes, Benjamin. He'll be here soon…" She turned and hurried out of the room, stopping at the door. "Doc Peckham will be here, too."

"Naw, it's hopeless, Gertie. My heart's shaking like a willow in this storm. I just want to make my peace. I need the holy minister."

~~~~~~

When Minister Isaac Bottomley arrived at Hunker's farmhouse, he saw Doc Peckham's car. Earlier, Gertrude had told Bottomley her husband wanted to make amends for all his sins. For the minister, the thought of saving this heathen from the clutches of Satan truly excited him. Gertrude also told him she thought her husband was going to die. Bottomley didn't know what to expect.

He actually assessed the condition of the property—wondered if the value of the farmhouse and land was enough of an enticement to marry the widowed Moore. It wasn't a serious analysis, he told himself, but it did cross his mind. Maybe then she would open her legs on their conjugal bed?

Gertrude hung his wet coat in the mud room. With the power out, she lit a lantern and guided Bottomley into the parlor. She whispered, "Oh, Minister Bottomley, I am distraught that Benjamin is so ill, but elated that he wants to make peace with his Maker. This has been my most solemn prayer."

Minister Bottomley nodded. "Yes, he is a brave, brave man."

"You must save his soul," Gertrude said. "You must! You must draw him up from the depths of hell. I dread the thought of my Benjamin in hell while I'm in heaven. He has been a good provider."

Bottomley took hold of her hands. "Yes, Gertrude, we shall do God's work for Benjamin." Upstairs, they heard him coughing.

In a struggling voice, Hunker cried out, "GERTIE, GERTIE!"

"Upstairs," Gertrude said, "in his bedroom."

Bottomley looked up and clutched his Bible. "Give me strength, dear Lord. Help me drive the evil from his soul."

"Amen! Amen!" Gertrude said. "For my Benjamin is stuffed with much evil."

Bottomley bowed his head and began to walk slowly up the flight of steps, the staircase creaking with his weight. My God, he thought, how this heathen needs saving. I can smell the devil within him from here.

Doc Peckham, with a heavy expression on his face, clumped down the wide, oaken steps. Bottomley quickly backed down.

"Oh, good evening, Minister."

Gertie asked, "Oh, Doctor, how is Benjamin?"

Doc Peckham waved his hand, as if searching for fresh air. "Did you hear him calling you, Gertie? He's been calling your name."

"Oh, yes, Doctor." She blew her nose. "Is it bad?"

"I'm sorry to say." Doc Peckham nodded. He took Bottomley aside. "I wouldn't give the old buffalo till the rooster crows five. His innards are already fermenting."

"I understand," Bottomley said and headed back upstairs with his Bible held out in front of him like a shield.

Hunker heard Bottomley's footsteps now, so he took another long drink, farted rather loudly, and shut his eyes.

Bottomley stood in the doorway and, beneath the glow of a lantern, gazed at Hunker, whose massive head was partially hidden by a quilted blanket.

He slowly approached the bed, his nose twitching, his lips shaking, engulfing himself in Hunker's lingering gas. "My God," he whispered, "how this man needs saving. He smells of evil." Bottomley cleared his throat. "Mister Moore, I'm here. It is I, Minister Bottomley."

Hunker slowly opened his eyes, grimacing as though in extreme pain. "I'm glad you came...mighty glad." Hunker forced an outrageous cough.

"It is my duty," Bottomley said. "I am here to help you meet your Maker."

Hunker nodded, his words spaced between coughs and gurgles. "Good—it is surely...what I...want." He pulled himself up, propped his pillows, disturbing the blanket and allowing his clouds of gas to escape.

"You still seem quite…quite strong, Mister Moore," Bottomley said, crinkling his nose. He dragged a chair up to the bed and sat down. He opened his Bible. "I am ready; you may begin to confess your sins…and then we will pray."

"First," Hunker said, "I need a little medicine."

"Of course," Bottomley said, looking about.

Hunker leaned over the side of the bed and picked up a bottle of Overholt, one of many.

On seeing the whiskey, Minister Bottomley became uneasy. "Do you really need that, Mister Moore?"

"I'm the one dying…" Hunker emitted a cough that was sure to spray whiskey-tainted saliva over the minister. "…ain't I?"

Bottomley blinked. "Yes, that is true." He produced a handkerchief and, almost wistfully, wiped the droplets from his face.

"Then I need it." Hunker took a big swallow. "One more thing: my name is Hunker. That's what's gonna be whittled on my tombstone."

"As you wish," Bottomley agreed, nodding solemnly. He eyed the Overholt.

Hunker now had his two hands clasped around the bottle of liquor. "Would you give a dying man a last request?"

"Why certainly, anything to help you achieve peace."

"Join me in a drink," Hunker said.

"When are you going to confess your sins?"

"First we drink, and then I'll tell you everything."

"If you insist." Bottomley took the bottle and, much to Hunker's annoyance, vigorously wiped off the neck and took a swig. Hunker thought he handled the booze like a true wet.

Bottomley smacked his lips and leaned closer. "This shall be our secret," he said, handing the bottle back to Hunker.

"It shall die with me," Hunker promised.

"In that case," Bottomley said, turning to make certain the door was closed, "I wouldn't mind to have another."

Hunker leaned over the bed and produced a second bottle. "Now we each got one."

Bottomley hesitated for a moment, shrugged, and took the bottle. He uncorked it like a bartender and swigged another drink. Savoring the liquor, he said, "Now let us begin."

"What do you want me to confess?" Hunker asked.

"Everything."

"You mean how I jollied all those women, even though I was married to my Gertie?"

"Yes."

"You mean how I drank, swore, and ran rum?"

"Well, not exactly," Bottomley said. "More importantly, your infidelities, especially with all those tainted, innocent women."

"They weren't innocent, not by a long shot," Hunker said as he had another drink.

Bottomley followed suit.

"Say, Minister, are you really a bluenose?"

Bottomley smiled, felt his nose, and chuckled. "Will it be our secret?"

"It shall die with me," Hunker said.

"I do have a weakness for hard spirits. The cold, damp nights by that river of sin is my cross." Bottomley picked up the Bible. "But now…it is time to confess. Remember, you're not a well man."

"It's hard for me to begin," Hunker said. "I've done a lotta sinnin'."

"Let your mind soar with the angels, Hunker. Cleanse yourself. Go ahead…"

"Well, I have been a very lustful man," Hunker said. "Why, when I think 'bout it, I was a downright pig."

"Were they…local women?" Bottomley asked.

"Many of them were," Hunker said.

"Did they give you pleasure?"

"Of course, 'specially the ugly ones," Hunker said.

"Why them?" Bottomley asked, with a very curious expression on his face.

Hunker smiled. "They try harder. Nobody wants them, and they just try harder. By golly," Hunker held his throat and coughed, "they sure gave me some good times."

"They were the work of the devil," Bottomley said.

"You're right, they were wicked. I just couldn't help myself. I had no willpower."

"Didn't you try to fight it?"

Hunker took another drink and farted loudly. "No, not 'specially."

"You were weak," Bottomley added, trying to hold his breath as he had another drink. "Were these women lustful?" Bottomley closed the Bible and set it on the bureau.

"Say," Hunker asked, "what the hell does their lust have to do with my soul?"

"Maybe it wasn't all your fault," Bottomley said.

"I never thought of that, Minister. Say, maybe it's all their fault that I was a pig," Hunker said. "I *had* to be a pig."

"You are no pig, Hunker. No, it was the devil controlling you and those women. The devil made you act like a pig."

"Why did I enjoy it, Minister?" Hunker asked, shaking his head remorsefully.

"The body is weak," Bottomley replied. "Very weak, but now you must hide nothing. You must drive Satan from your soul. Expose yourself to salvation."

Hunker lifted his blanket. His nightshirt was rolled up above his thighs and he was naked. At first glance, Bottomley jerked back. But soon, Bottomley was, in fact, leaning over the bed, spellbound by Hunker's gnarled, wart-laden, twisted, hair-covered appendage.

Hunker continued to hold the blanket high.

Bottomley took another long drink and then stole another peek. "Please, please, Mister Moore, cover yourself."

Hunker dropped the blanket back over his body. "Can a man with a cock like that be saved?"

Bottomley shook his head and had another drink. "No sinner is beyond the power of salvation, but I must confess you have a very unique…" he hesitated and sat back stiffly, "you have a very unique *condition*."

Hunker leaned forward, speaking quietly. "To be honest, my Gertie doesn't think it's very unique. She told me that my private parts belong out in the pasture."

Bottomley's face flushed. He tried to clear his throat and about choked on his phlegm. "Mister Moore, Hunker, we are becoming much too personal." Bottomley rested his elbow on his knee.

"Forgive me. I thought that's what ya needed," Hunker said. "Confess everything. Say, can I tell ya 'bout my wingless flies?"

Bottomley's face sparked with interest. "Wingless flies? God's pesky little creatures? Of course."

Hunker uttered a weak moan. "Well, it's this way. When I take a bath, I sit in the tub and the tip of my private part sticks out of the water, sorta like a turtle's head."

Bottomley nodded hesitantly. Hunker knew the minister's curiosity had him trapped. Bottomley took another drink and nodded vigorously. "Please go on."

Hunker coughed lightly. "Before I take a bath, I catch me a half-dozen or so flies. Then, with Gertie's tweezers, I take off their wings so they can't fly. Then I put them on the very top of my floating private."

"I'm sorry, Hunker, I don't understand."

Hunker coughed again, this time vigorously. "Well, those flies go absolutely crazy. With their little legs they keep on running round, round, and round. Six or so make for a crowd of them. They can't swim and they can't fly. My cock is all that's between them and the soapy deep blue sea. But let me tell ya, it feels mighty superior."

"Oh, dear, that sounds so..." Bottomley began to stand up, but the whiskey had taken hold and his legs didn't work so well. He slid back into the chair. "My goodness," he said, "it appears I've had too much to drink." He waved his hands in the air, perhaps as if he were shooing away flies. "Dear Hunker, you might as well continue your sins."

"Don't worry, Minister, I intend to. Come on now, let's have a little fun..."

"Ooooooh, what kind of fun?"

Hunker smiled and tossed off the blanket. "You'll see."

CHAPTER SEVENTY-THREE

BOBBY BANCOCK'S VOICE CRACKED. He glanced at Billy, who just shook his head and picked up the two cases of booze. "What do you mean, you can't close the bridge? What do you mean?"

Eddie Grayson's eyes were locked hungrily on the two cases of Overholt in Billy's arms. "Not my fault!" Eddie said. "It's this damn storm. After I opened it for Francis Grover's last menhaden boat…I couldn't shut the bridge! Main power is out! Aquidneck Island is in total darkness."

"What the hell does that mean?" Billy yelled.

"Ain't enough power to close the bridge. It happens sometimes, especially when you get a storm like this."

Bobby shook his head. "Damn! What do we do now?"

Eddie Grayson shrugged.

Billy Bancock asked, "What if a train comes?"

Grayson smiled. "Lucky thing. None due tonight."

"Yeah, real lucky," Bobby said.

Billy looked at the bridge in disbelief and shook his head. "Let's get out of here!"

Eddie Grayson looked over his glasses at Billy. "Can I still keep the liquor, boys?"

Billy leaned over and left one case.

The bridge attendant nodded weakly. "Well, I guess one's better than none."

~~~~~~

The *Maria Morso* continued to steam slowly north past Ghoul Island, and the wind and rain still hadn't let up. However, the steady downpour had flattened the white-capped waves. The crew had untied the cargo nets that held the huge piles of liquor in place. Two men started unbolting the heavy wooden hatches to the hold.

Pearly ducked his head in from the driving rain and said, "Can't see much at all, Joe. I think the power may be out. Tiverton's black. Portsmouth's black. Aquidneck Island's black."

"Just keep looking!" Joe snapped, his eyes not leaving the glow of the compass. "We should be close…"

"How much longer?" Durall asked.

"Not long!" Joe said. "Not long at all!"

Durall shook his head. "I'm beginning to think I made a foolish mistake." He uncorked his bottle again and took another pull.

"Don't worry, Captain," Pearly said, "you won't feel that way when you're spreading tootsie's legs."

Durall hesitated momentarily and laughed. "That is true. A man can be on his deathbed and a pair of open legs will detour his last thoughts."

Joe said, "Will you two shut up?"

Durall took another swig and tossed the empty bottle out the door. "Yankee land," he mumbled. "I hope I don't end up in jail."

The rain subsided and they could make out the high, dark eastern shoreline. From outside the pilot house, Pearly tapped on the window. "I can see the Basin!"

Joe nodded. "I see it, too. Okay now, get ready." Joe glanced at Durall. "Dead slow!"

Durall slurred the order into the tube.

As the ship entered the lee of the Basin, the wind and the waves abated. Without reflecting shore lights, it appeared like they were entering a cave. High above, the whirling black-gray clouds were racing to the west-southwest. Joe stuck his head out the portside door and looked north towards the railroad trestle but was unable to tell if it was open or closed.

"Is the bridge closed?" Joe shouted.

"Can't see!" Pearly yelled.

"Where the hell is it?" Durall asked.

"To the east'ard!" Joe snapped.

As the *Maria* entered the Basin, she suddenly seemed much too large to maneuver. Joe bit his cheek and tightened his grip on the sloppy helm.

"I see a menhaden boat," Pearly called, "'bout a hundred feet to starboard. There's another to portside. More room to starboard."

"I see them!" Joe quickly spun the wheel to the starboard. "Enough room?"

"Jesus Christ! It's going to be close! Be careful! The tide's running strong…"

"Which way?" Joe shouted.

"Tide's pulling to the east! Hard! Hard!"

Behind Joe, Durall was cursing in French.

The *Maria* slid past the stern of that portside menhaden boat, but the horsing tide pushed the *Maria* starboard.

"Shit!" Joe spun the steering wheel and pulled the control handle into reverse, trying to slow the *Maria* down. Both vessels were closing fast.

Pearly yelled.

Durall threw up his hands and cursed loudly, "I am surely the biggest asshole!"

"Shut up!" Joe shouted.

Even without propeller power, the tide-driven *Maria* slammed hard into the menhaden boat, her bow climbing up and over the low stern of the seiner. Just before they hit, Joe saw its name: *Saint Peter*, Francis Grover's very first menhaden seiner.

The *Maria*'s barnacle-encrusted bottom ran easily over the *Saint Peter*, iron to iron, screeching and moaning, as though the vessels were joined in agony. The *Maria*'s keel split the *Saint Peter* in two, sinking her like lead ballast.

"Jesus Christ!" Joe said.

"What was I thinking?" Durall shouted. "I shall surely die in Yankee prison!"

Pearly was so excited that he was having trouble thinking or speaking. Finally, he said, "Fuck it! Francis Grover deserved it!"

Joe could only shake his head.

Chapter Seventy-Four

FRANKIE'S TRUCKS ARRIVED at Riverside Drive like a wartime caravan. Fallen trees and washed-out roads in Swansea had held them up a bit. For some reason, Sally Half-a-Dollar had jumped out in Fall River, but no one would really care, except probably Hunker and Captain Durall.

Behind the church, the Bancocks heard the *Saint Peter* collision. But what they heard only lasted a few seconds, as most of the thud was blown down the river by the howling wind.

"What the hell was that?" Bobby yelled.

Billy hesitated, his backside to the wind and rain, eyes straining out into the dark Basin. "Probably something Joe was worried about."

Bobby cupped his hand and spoke directly into his brother's ear. "I'm beginning to get a real bad feeling about all of this."

Minutes later, the rusty bow of the *Maria Morso* pierced the black curtain of rain, looming thirty feet above them, moving effortlessly and faster than the Bancocks thought prudent, especially at its dangerous starboard angle approach.

"Jesus Christ!" Bobby Bancock shouted. Some of the men, cowed by the hull's incredible size, started to move backward. Billy, Tommy, and a few of the shore crew dashed into the wet cellar's doorway.

On the bow, First Mate Peter had a hawser in his hand. Alongside the starboard gunnel, Durall's crewmen were anxiously waving coiled lines.

From the *Maria*, they heard Pearly yell to Joe, "Slow her down! Damnit! Slow her down!"

Pearly continued to shout. The vessel, despite being in hard reverse, was still moving much too fast, and at the wrong angle for a safe landing.

The *Maria* crunched into the timber-built dock with an impact so tremendous that Billy Bancock and Frankie's truck drivers were tossed on their asses. The hull slid tightly against the heavy timbers, and the men could see and smell the smoke from the friction of iron against the wooden pilings. By the time the vessel was secured, the entire dock had lifted into a rim-racked tilted position, while some of the more worm-eaten struts snapped like kindling.

Tommy lifted his lantern. "Everybody outside! Joe will be looking for us."

On the landing, the men scrambled to their feet as the crew began tossing lines to secure the ship.

Billy and Tommy ran towards the vessel. "What do you think?"

Tommy shouted, "Damn fine landing, considering."

Despite the mayhem, the *Maria Morso* at rest was an impressive sight. For Joe, it already was a success of sorts. Just getting the ship into the Basin had been a minor miracle. He didn't want to think about the *Saint Peter* or getting the *Maria* back out. The crew of the ship fought the wind and the rain as they swung over a gangway to set up the sluice run to unload the liquor. Tommy Walsh and his crew adjusted the staging on the dock.

The Bancocks came aboard. Bobby cocked his thumb and slapped Joe's back. "You did it, Joe, you did it," he yelled. "This storm is great!"

Pearly returned the thumb gesture. "Poor *Saint Peter*," he yelled back.

Billy called through cupped hands. "We heard…"

Joe also returned the cocked thumb. "Everything set at the trestle?"

Bobby shook his head. "Power's out. Eddie couldn't close the bridge."

Joe glanced at Pearly.

Durall heard Joe's curse. "What is wrong?"

"Nothing wrong," Joe yelled. "Electricity is out in the area."

"What does that mean?" Durall asked, throwing his arms into the air.

"We've got good darkness! Now get your crew moving!"

"Where is my tootsie?"

Joe ignored Durall and glanced at Bobby. "Henry Grover's car?"

Bobby nodded with enthusiasm. "We found it at the fish factory... cut his wires, but we didn't see him anywhere."

Billy added, "I cut the wires in his personal car at the police station. But he wasn't there either."

Joe looked past the Bancocks towards the driveway alongside the church.

Frankie's trucks were already backing down to the ship. "Good work, boys! Now get moving...get Frankie's trucks loaded and outta here!"

"Where is my tootsie?" Durall asked again.

"She'll be here soon!" Joe looked at First Mate Peter. "Start your crew!"

The first mate yelled, "Double down, men! Remember, we're in America! And we don't belong here!"

The 'bang in' was on!

~~~~~~

Gatsby's Packard and the other car pulled over on Main Road, north of Mary's Diner. Except for the occasional dull glow of candles and lanterns in windows, the entire riverside community was pretty much in darkness.

Kanky was very anxious since Chief Grover's shooting. "Where do we-a wanna go now, boss?"

Gatsby took a deep breath. "We'll sit here a while. I don't want to spook anybody. If they actually do come in, they're gonna need trucks. If we see trucks, we'll just follow them."

In the lee of the driving rain, Kanky rolled down the window and saw the reflection of a lantern coming from Mary Standish's apartment.

Kanky took out a cigarette. "You know-a, boss, I be surprised if this-a really happens."

"It's going to happen," Gatsby said. "One thing's certain, they got the night for it."

About ten minutes later, they saw headlights approaching from the south on Main Road. As the car got closer, they slouched low and watched it pass, and then it stopped in front of Mary's Diner. Someone in a rain slicker got out.

"Interesting," Gatsby said. He rolled down his window and smiled. "Well, well, Janie Thurston. I bet that's Maggie behind the wheel. Interesting, real fucking interesting. I told you; something is happening here."

~~~~~~

Janie ran up the flight of stairs on the north side of the building and banged on the door. Mary opened it. Behind her, a lantern's flame danced in the dark. Janie stepped inside. "What's going on?"

"According to the Bancocks, your father and Joe are aboard the *Maria*. If everything is on schedule, they should be already here or arriving anytime."

"Where?"

Mary nodded. "Behind Bottomley's church."

Janie's expression erupted in amusement. She laughed. "And to think Joe was worried."

Mary smiled. "Just be careful. Stay with the Bancocks. Tommy and his crew should be there, too."

Janie hugged Mary. "I'll see you later."

"Let me know if there's anything I can do," Mary added.

~~~~~~

Janie bucked the wind back to Maggie's car. As she got in, she noticed the Packard and the other car parked across the street. Janie asked, "That car looks familiar to me. I think they're watching us…"

Maggie turned and looked. "That's one of Gatsby's cars. I remember it."

"Maybe, but we can't lead them to Joe. Let's take them for a ride. One way or another, we're now part of Joe's gang…"

Maggie's expression tightened. "Okay, I guess."

"Don't worry, Maggie. Take off like you're going to New Bedford."

She jerked away from the diner. Maggie drove as fast as she dared towards Bulgarmarsh Road.

Gatsby's Packard followed at a distance.

"It's working!"

"Joey will be proud of us," Maggie said.

They turned up Bulgarmarsh Road. Janie looked through the rear window. "Damn it, Gatsby stopped. He's turning around." She nudged Maggie. "Go back! We gotta warn Joe and the boys."

Maggie asked, "Where are they?"

"Getting religion!"

CHAPTER SEVENTY-FIVE

GERTRUDE MOORE HAD BEEN KNEELING in prayer beside her rocking chair, afraid to think of the future. Yet she couldn't understand why Hunker's bed had been making such a ruckus. The squeaking mattress sounded like a pack of hungry mice. Extremely nervous, she climbed the stairs, stopping occasionally to listen.

Suddenly, all was dead quiet. They must be in a silent prayer, she thought. Or is it possible my Benjamin has passed on? Slowly, she opened the door. Gertrude's mouth dropped open, and she gasped in utter shock. Minister Bottomley was sprawled over the bed, naked as a plump newborn.

Spellbound, Gertrude whispered, "My God!" She turned to Hunker, who was up and dressed. He was pouring whiskey over Bottomley's clothes.

"Benjamin? I thought you were dying," she said.

"Not tonight, Gertie! Not tonight! The minister saved me from dying!"

Gertrude's hand went to her mouth. She was astonished. "Benjamin? What happened to Minister Bottomley?"

Hunker shook his head. "Now, Gertie, ya let the minister sleep it off. He's swamp't, stew'd, soak'd. And ya wouldn't want any of his congregation to see him this way…would ya?"

"Benjamin! What in heaven's name have you done to him?"

Hunker started for the door. "Why, I showed the minister a good time is all. And I'm feeling better. Aren't you happy?" He kissed her forehead.

Gertrude had trouble keeping her eyes off Bottomley's broad, flour-colored ass.

Hunker stomped down the stairs two at a time. Gertrude ran behind him. "Benjamin, what am I to do with the minister?"

Hunker shouted, "Bake him a pie, Gertie. Or better yet, jump in the sack with him, keep him warm."

"Benjamin!" There was a slight change in Gertrude's voice. "Are you serious?"

Hunker opened the mud-room door. He grabbed his oilskins from their hooks. "Yes, Gertie, I'm serious. Besides, tonight I learned it's getting pretty hard to beat my wingless flies."

CHAPTER SEVENTY-SIX

OUTSIDE OF JESSICA'S APARTMENT, directly across from Bottomley's church, two Packards pulled up behind Maggie's new car.

No one wasted time getting out of the cars. Kanky, however, went to the rear of the car and opened the trunk. Collector joined him. Cushioned in canvas, Kanky unwrapped two Thompson machine guns. He handed one to Collector.

As soon as Gatsby saw the guns, he shook his head. "Where the hell did you get them?"

Kanky smiled. "Bought them from my cousin in New York."

Gatsby's angry eyes zeroed in on both men. "This isn't part of *my* plan. This isn't Chicago! I didn't want anyone dead tonight!"

Surprised, Kanky didn't like Gatsby's response. "Boss, Henry Grover was-a accident! He deserved it. He killed-a Sammy." He lifted the Tommy gun slightly higher. "This-a only to scare Bucolo and his boys."

Collector could see that Gatsby clearly didn't appreciate the firepower. He added, "It'll stop a gunfight, Mister Gatsby, before it even starts… These boys aren't used to this kind of weapon."

Kanky nodded. "Collector-a right. They gonna shit-a in their pants."

Gatsby again stared down Kanky. "Remember what I said! Else I'll use it on you!"

~~~~~~

Captain Durall was first to see Janie and Maggie running towards the ship. He and Joe were on either side of the gangway, counting and unloading cases leaving the *Maria*. Even with oilskins on, they were obviously women. Perhaps Durall saw them first because he was the only one looking for a tootsie. "Two tootsies!" Durall cried out. He was quite excited.

Joe glanced at Durall and thought, you'd think they didn't have any women in Canada by the looks of him.

At the same time, Pearly spotted Janie and Maggie walking towards him. He knew immediately something had to be wrong.

He called out, "Janie! This is no place for you!" His tone of voice tilted them slightly, especially Janie. Her feelings of being part of the gang suddenly vanished.

Clearly surprised and angry, Joe yelled, "What the hell are you doing here?"

The two women glanced at Durall, then back at Joe. Suddenly they knew it might be best not to say anything in front of the captain.

Smiling, Captain Durall said, "Hello, tootsies!"

They tossed him a weak nod, but it was clear by their expressions they were reluctant to say anything in front of Captain Durall.

Joe glared at Maggie. "Spill it! It's too late to hide anything now."

Durall's smile disappeared.

Janie blurted, "We just saw Gatsby, he tried to follow us but we think we gave him the slip. We came to warn you! He knows the 'bang in' is here in Tiverton.

Pearly asked, "How the hell did Gatsby find out?"

Joe said, "He somehow figured it out."

Captain Durall interrupted, "What's going on here?"

Joe said, "Nothing to worry about, Captain."

"Well then, please introduce me to my tootsies."

Maggie pointed to Janie. "She's taken. I'm Maggie. I'm your tootsie."

Durall's smile returned. "You have the captain's permission to come aboard."

Before Maggie could walk up the gangway, Kanky walked out of the building's shadows, spraying a burst of Tommy gun fire into the air. "Don't move! Don't anyone move!"

Gatsby and Collector were behind him. At the same time, Gatsby's other men, their pistols drawn, rushed into the wet cellar and covered the crew inside.

Captain Durall cursed loudly in French. Maggie stood silently by his side, looking very nervous.

Gatsby's eyes shifted quickly to the ship, then back to Joe. "I'm impressed, Mister Bucolo. It's an ingenious scheme. Just can't stop trying to outdo me, can you? But I've fixed that now, haven't I?"

"I congratulate you as well, Mister Gatsby, for figuring it out."

"You can thank your Yankee friend Maggie here, Mister Bucolo. I read her like an open book."

Joe gave him a puzzled look, then it clicked. Still, he didn't respond.

Maggie left Durall's side and joined Janie. They glanced at each other, but remained quiet.

Kanky laughed. "What a fucking joke...the minister's church! Gotta a hand it to you, Bucolo..."

"Yeah," Collector added. "Pretty damn smart...pretty damn smart... That's worth a real song..."

"Shut-a up!" Kanky yelled. He reached inside Joe's oilskin and searched for a pistol. "Well, well, still no-a gun. Ain't changed, have you, Joe?"

Collector frisked the other men for firearms.

Joe moved into Kanky's face. From his tight lips, he said, "You couldn't leave it alone, could you, Kanky? Even killing Sammy! For what?"

Kanky waved the machine gun at Joe. "We didn't kill-a Sammy!"

Gatsby turned to Joe, then Janie. "Chief Grover murdered Sammy!"

Everyone was beyond shocked. Janie's hand went to her mouth as tears filled her eyes.

Gatsby added, "Grover bragged about it tonight before he shot himself. Grover wanted me to kill you, Mister Bucolo. He was obsessed, hated you!"

Kanky nodded. "We got into a fight; rolling around on-a the floor…it was accident… Chief Grover pulled out a gun…damn asshole shot-a himself."

Gatsby continued, "We made sure Sammy was away from the explosion, but Grover released the boom and swung Sammy out over the dynamite."

Maggie and Janie traded looks.

Joe snapped, "You expect us to believe that?" However, for a brief moment, his features appeared to be filled with doubt.

Kanky snarled, "Who gives a fuck what you think!"

Janie stared so hard at Gatsby, he couldn't hold her look.

Kanky motioned to his machine gun. "Pretty impressive…isn't it?"

Joe said, "Yeah, especially in the wrong hands."

Captain Durall, blurry-eyed, mumbled, "To think I was worried about your Coast Guard."

Gatsby said, "You should have made this deal with me, Captain."

Joe shook his head. "Where are your trucks? Did you expect me to supply you with trucks?"

"My trucks are on their way. I'll also make your minister a better deal for the use of his church."

"What are you going to do with us?" Durall asked.

Gatsby chuckled. "I'm going to let you take your vessel back to Canada… 'Course, it'll be empty…including the money Mister Bucolo was going to pay you…"

Durall seemed to sober up really quick. He screamed out in French: "*T'es une raclure de bidet!* [You're a bidet scumbag!]"

Joe made an angry movement towards Gatsby, but First Mate Peter reached for Kanky's Tommy gun. A burst from the gun caught Peter square in the chest, tossing him backwards against the gangway.

Maggie and Janie screamed. They both moved slightly backwards, Maggie even closer to Captain Durall.

"Why the hell did he do that?" Kanky shouted. "He made-a my finger twitch."

Gatsby snapped, "I warned you, Kanky!"

Pearly knelt down and unbuttoned Peter's oilskin. In the light of the lantern, they saw blood flowing from his chest, mixing with the rain. He checked Peter's neck for a pulse, and looked up at Joe and then at Kanky, shaking his head. "He's dead."

Kanky's eyes drifted to the others. "Jesus Christ! I didn't-a want to shoot him!"

Joe's fists tightened. "Then why the fuck you holding that gun!?"

Gatsby gave Kanky a look that could have executed him on the spot. So much so, that Kanky turned away from him.

"You are fucking gangsters!" Durall shouted, pointing down at his first mate. "Murderers!"

Beneath the screeching wind and beating rain, there was a pause of silence while everyone stared down at Peter's body. Durall pulled Maggie closer in order to block his movement. He pulled out his horse pistol from beneath his jacket and shot Kanky—removing a good part of his head. Janie and Maggie screamed.

~~~~~~

When Hunker exited his car in front of the church, he saw the line of trucks, the Bancocks' jalopy, Maggie's Ford coupe, and across the street, in front of the Provender, two big Packards. He knew it had to be Kanky and Gatsby. He grabbed his eight-gauge and headed down the shelled driveway towards the rear of the church.

On the north side of the building, pounded by the wind and rain, he hid alongside the trucks, facing the storm's force. Most of Frankie's drivers and helpers were huddled together in the lee of the building, not sure what to do. Hunker couldn't hear much of what was happening, but he could see.

When Kanky's machine gun went off, Hunker shook with violent rage. He heard Janie and Maggie scream. It was all he could do not to squeeze off both barrels into Kanky's backside. But it wasn't a time to be foolish. He had to act carefully or more would die. He waited and watched. He couldn't hear Captain Durall's words, but he heard the crack of Durall's horse pistol. He watched Kanky's body fall to the dock. He actually breathed relief and mumbled something that was carried off by the wind.

Hunker stood opposite the sluice run and the vessel's gangway, calculating that he could not be seen by the men inside the cellar doorway until he was out in the open. Besides, there was no other way to approach Gatsby. It was a chance he had to take. Without any more thought, he headed towards the ship, screaming ferociously like the devil himself was coming.

Everyone jumped at Hunker's yelling. It even checkmated the noise of the storm. By the time Gatsby's men in the cellar realized what was happening, Hunker had jammed his shotgun into Gatsby's back. "Hold it! Drop ya guns—now!"

Gatsby turned slightly, but he didn't drop his pistol.

Hunker glared at Gatsby. "Tell ya men, Gatsby, tell'm, else I will split you in two! You'll be dead, just like your asshole Kanky. Just give me an excuse! Drop ya pistol!" He jammed the gun into Gatsby's back. "I ain't fucking around!" he roared. He then pushed harder with the punt's barrels.

Collector dropped his machine gun and shouted, "Do what he said! Everybody…do what he said! He's crazy!"

Hunker's big head snapped to Collector. "Hold it! Who told you I was crazy?"

Collector silently shook his head.

Gatsby finally dropped his pistol.

In the cellar doorway, Gatsby's men also dropped their guns.

"Tommy!" Hunker yelled, without taking his eyes off Gatsby.

"Right here, Hunker," Tommy Walsh boomed.

"Did they drop their guns back there?"

"We got 'em, Hunker. We're taking care of the bums now."

Pearly kicked Kanky and Collector's machine guns into the drink. Joe reached down for Gatsby's pistol, cocked it, and pointed it at Gatsby. The action drew a smirk from Gatsby.

Janie shouted, "Don't, Joe! Please, please don't!"

Gatsby glanced at Janie, then back at Joe. He grinned. "Don't worry, Janie, Mister Bucolo won't shoot me!"

Joe stared coldly at Gatsby, but Hunker's big head moved right into Gatsby's face. "It won't be him; it'll be me! I'll do it for Sammy! Now down on your stomachs. All of you!"

Gatsby didn't move. Hunker jammed the stock of his punt gun into Gatsby's belly, forcing him down on his knees. He was about to crack the barrel of his gun against Gatsby's head, but he quickly dropped, facedown.

Gatsby turned his head up and stared up at Hunker. "We didn't kill Sammy! Grover did! Kanky was telling the truth!"

Joe motioned to Pearly. "Tie 'em all up. Put'm aboard the *Maria*. We'll deal with all this later!" He turned to Hunker. "Stay here with me!"

Captain Durall's crew carried the first mate's body onto the *Maria*.

Joe said to Janie, "You better leave."

Janie said, "No! I'm staying. I want to help!"

Joe moved closer to Janie and whispered, "Strange, I believe Gatsby's story about Sammy."

Janie nodded. "So do I."

As soon as Frankie's trucks were loaded and on their way, Joe,

Hunker, and Janie worked together in the cellar, packing the wooden cases, leaving some room at the top for the still-rising tide.

Since the killing of the first mate, Joe felt sick to his stomach. He knew any one of them could've been the victim of Kanky's twitching finger, and he couldn't stop thinking about it.

Since they began packing the liquor, the water had risen rapidly above the cellar floor. He checked his pocket watch. The tide still had better than two hours to go.

Joe occasionally lifted the lantern over his head and observed the structure. He wasn't pleased with what he saw, nor did he like the sounds the building made every time it was hit with a major gust of wind.

Hunker took interest in Joe's concerns. "What's bothering ya, Joseph?"

Joe pointed up to the sagging ceiling. "I think the storm and the *Maria* have put a lot of strain on this place. It just doesn't look very stable."

Hunker laughed. "Maybe we'll have to donate to the minister's building fund."

Joe's expression didn't need any words.

Janie cut in. "On occasion," she said loudly, "Bottomley mentioned it to the congregation. He didn't think the church was that safe, especially during storms."

"He was right," Joe said. "Wish I had known that."

"Well, my Gertie never told me," Hunker added.

Janie glanced at Joe. "If you had gone to church, maybe you would've known."

"If I went to church, I sure as hell wouldn't come here!" Joe said. He looked at Hunker. "By the way, how's our minister?"

"Sleeping peacefully, I'm sure. Or eating pies with Gertie, I think. We owe Doc Peckham some booze for his die-a-nosis." Hunker released a crazy laugh, drawing the first smiles from the others since the shooting. The tension of the 'bang in' eased a bit, but everyone kept packing cases in the church's cellar.

Once it was filled, they had trouble closing the doors due to the building's southwest sag. Tommy yanked off a few boards from the bottom of the doors and nailed them shut.

Chapter Seventy-Seven

THE *MARIA*'S CREW, IN A BIG HURRY to shove off, kept sliding cases down the sluice run. Tommy's crew did a double step for almost two hours to get the ship unloaded.

Joe decided on using Almy's turkey farm for storage, as it was close by and made the most sense. They ran three trips to the farm while the rest of the booze had been stacked behind the church for Nina. Within an hour, the wall of wooden liquor cases grew to about six feet high, ten feet wide, and fifty feet long.

Finally, the ship was empty.

Tommy yelled to Joe, "We gotta get this booze outta here, pronto."

"Where the hell is Nina?" Joe said, mostly to himself.

By midnight the rain had slackened, but there still had been no letup in the wind. The tide was still rising, and it was extraordinarily high.

Joe couldn't remember a storm this bad. He did know that when the tide changed, the weather could worsen. At this point, he was certain that the Coast Guard wouldn't be a threat for the remainder of the night, but he was still anxious to get the ship heading back down the Seaconnet.

He smiled at the thought of Max's historical and promised nor'easters that had given him more cover than he needed. With Frankie's trucks headed for Providence, he had repaid Frankie's bank. What was in the cellar and behind the church, plus the turkey farm, represented the gang's profit. The only issue now: Nina hadn't shown up yet.

~~~~~~

Not long after, Janie, very excited, came running over to Joe. "Guess who's here? Nina and her trucks."

"Where the hell's she been?" Joe asked.

Janie took in a deep breath. "She took a wrong turn…got lost in Little Compton."

Tommy yelled to his shore gang, "Get those trucks loaded!"

As soon as Nina's trucks were in position, Tommy's shore crew worked like Maytee's Chinese crew. Everybody was all business, barking orders, counting and stacking cases, moving from truck to truck.

Tommy and Janie approached Joe. "Nina's covered her load as agreed. But we have a problem; she didn't expect those extra cases…"

"Run them up to the turkey farm!" Hunker blurted. "There's about two hundred cases."

Tommy shook his head. "I've already sent my shore gang home with my trucks."

Joe checked his pocket watch and looked at Janie. "It's getting late. Listen, Nina lost her brother. Heinrich built me a great boat. I think they deserve the bonus. In fact, I think we owe them at least that. They've had a lot of bad luck…"

Janie yelled, "We've got another problem. Nina's having trouble with her truck's engine."

Joe glanced at Billy. "You go with Nina…keep her engine running."

Billy cracked a big grin. "I'll do more than that."

Everyone glanced around at each other, expressions of agreement on all their faces.

Joe yelled to Billy, "Tell Nina the extras are a gift from me and the boys!"

"Don't forget Max," Pearly yelled, wearing a big grin. Joe shot Pearly a look and nodded.

Janie gave Joe a quick hug.

With Billy driving, they left, the flapping canvas covers on Nina's overloaded stake-body trucks on the verge of ripping apart.

~~~~~~

True to form, when the tide turned, the nor'easter intensified. The *Maria*'s crew had wasted no time in breaking down the sluice run. They carried Kanky's body onto the vessel and decided on dumping him offshore, without ceremony. They placed a tied Gatsby in a stateroom and locked it.

From the open pilot house door, Captain Durall yelled a number of times down to Joe that he wanted to leave.

Joe and Janie found Durall and Maggie in the pilot house. Maggie had on a dry seaman's shirt and a pair of pants rolled up to her knees. They had been drinking. Durall smiled at Joe and nodded to Maggie. "Captain Bucolo, my tootsie and I have enjoyed these last few hours. We have much in common."

"That's good to hear," Joe said.

A crewman stuck his head into the pilot house. "We're ready to shove off, Captain."

"Good!"

Joe glanced at Maggie. "What are you gonna do?"

"I'm returning to Canada with the captain. He has some fine French attributes…"

Joe did a double-take. "Don't kid me, Maggie."

"I've never been there, Joey. The captain promised me a good time. It's my chance to see another part of the world."

Joe nodded. "It's your decision, Maggie. But I don't know this man other than in business. You know that?"

"Are you sure, Maggie?" Janie pleaded. "Really sure?"

"Time to say goodbye to this fish town, Janie. Keys are in the coupe. Give them to my mom. Tell her I'll write." Maggie put her arm around Durall's waist and winked.

Janie threw her hands up in the air and—not knowing what else to say—hooted, "Hallelujah!" Maggie and Janie had a good, long hug.

Hunker looked at Durall. "Didn't take ya long."

Durall smiled. "I have my ways."

"Come on, let's get out of here!" Joe ordered.

Joe left Janie with Pearly, Tommy, and Bobby Bancock. Hunker was staying with him. He would be needed to help row through the heavy surf to the beach in the dory.

Durall walked to the door of the pilot house and shouted, "All hatches secured?"

"Yes, Captain, all secured."

Durall turned back to Joe. "It's your ship, Captain Bucolo."

Hunker asked, "How do you want to do this?"

Joe shrugged. "I'm worried about the tide. It's horsing hard. Tell them to throw off the lines. Let's hope the wind will just blow us off the landing."

Hunker went to the starboard stern side and shouted to release the lines.

Maggie waved from the pilot house. Janie returned it with a mix of emotions.

Even with the lines released, the *Maria* hung there, the tide holding her against the landing.

Joe yelled, "Rig up a double stern spring-line! Tell them to wrap some pilings. I'm gonna try to spring the bow away from the pilings."

Hunker passed the orders to the crew. As soon as the line was made fast, Joe shifted the engine into reverse. "Slow as possible," Joe said.

Durall repeated the order into the tube. It took a few moments, but with the *Maria* shaking violently, her bow slowly fell away. With the weight of the ship and the force of her propeller, the tremendous strain on the lines and the pilings caused everything to creak and moan.

Pearly, Janie, Tommy, and Bobby quickly backed away from the dangerously stretched hawsers.

Joe shouted, "Get ready to release it!"

Just as he gave the order, there was a sudden loud crunch of ripping timber; oak planking and carrying beams.

Pearly screamed a warning, "Everybody back! Get back!"

The *Maria* lurched backward, her stern slamming against the pilings. The vessel jammed that section against the southwest corner of the building, shifting supports beneath, and even in the cellar.

Back in the church's storage basement, two main carrying beams cracked, triggering the south corner to sag and drop about a foot. Above, on the first floor, pews and Lucinda Parks' organ slid and crashed against the west wall of the building.

Pearly grabbed Janie while everyone else ran up onto the driveway to solid land.

Finally, the *Maria* drifted away from the church's landing. Joe snapped the control into forward, turned the vessel south, and steamed slowly out through the Tiverton Basin.

"You got it made, Joe," Hunker said. He laughed. "Just watch out for the *Saint Peter*."

Durall popped another bottle. No real harm was done to his ship. And this beautiful young girl was more than just a tootsie. He smiled at Maggie. "I got my money, I got you, and we're going home. I'm a very happy man."

"Me too," Maggie said, "me too."

~~~~~~

As soon as the *Maria Morso* disappeared into the raging storm, the First Riverside House of Worship began to tremble violently. It sounded like a herd of stampeding cattle inside the cellar.

Pearly, Janie, Tommy, and Bobby Bancock looked at each other, trying to figure out the frightening noise.

Following that, they heard another loud creaking noise from the support timbers snapping like wooden matches.

"What do ya think, Daddy?" Janie yelled.

"Well, sweet thing, I hope it's nothing…" For a minute, the disturbance came to a standstill. Everybody walked a few feet and stopped.

Bobby cocked his head like he was listening to a pocket watch. Beneath their feet the ground felt like it was quaking.

Pearly and Tommy yelled together, "Move! RUN!"

Everybody rushed towards the front of the church on Main Road and, breathing heavily, just stood there.

Across the street, Jessica Jackson stood in her doorway. She yelled, "Is everything okay, Janie?"

"Everything's fine, Jessica. You can go back to sleep now."

"Where's the minister?"

"He's on a house call, Jessica. Everything is—"

"Where's Maggie?"

Janie was about to answer when suddenly a loud, jarring roar came from the structure.

"Look!" Bobby pointed to the building. "Holy shit!"

Jessica Jackson stood awestruck in the frame of the doorway—her hand clamped across her mouth.

In horror, they all watched the three-story building collapsing like a dead accordion—plunging into the Basin—hurling up spumes of water and whirls of debris. The force exploded the cellar's cases of liquor out into the Basin. The roaring wind muffled most of the noise. Thousands of cases, like bobbing corks, began to drift out into the turbulent, tide-swept waters.

Pearly, Tommy, Janie, and Bobby Bancock ran back down the driveway and watched.

"The liquor!" Bobby shouted. "My God! The liquor!"

Janie burst into tears.

Pearly and Tommy could only silently shake their heads.

Bobby Bancock grabbed Tommy by the shoulder. "I can't believe it," he yelled. "Will ya look at all that fucking money floating away!"

Janie just continued to cry.

~~~~~~

By the time the *Maria* passed Ghoul Island traveling south, the rain had let up considerably and visibility improved, but the wind had increased. Joe ran the ship a little harder going back down the river. He turned to Hunker and said, "Take over. Hold her on one hundred eighty degrees. The captain and I have to count the money."

In Durall's quarters, Joe placed all the money on the table. Maggie's eyes looked like they might just pop out of her head.

"You remember our deal?" Durall asked.

"Of course. I have no intention of trying to pay you less."

"Most men would try. My ship is empty and heading for home. You actually have more of a bargaining chip than I. You are an honorable man, Joe."

"Joey is surely that, Captain," Maggie added. "Now, under the circumstances, don't you think Joey deserves a dollar off each case?"

Joe smiled. "I appreciate the gesture, Maggie, but the captain and I agreed to the price some time back. A deal is a deal."

"My tootsie is correct. I will discount you twenty-five cents per case." He pulled Maggie close and hugged her. "My new business partner."

Maggie said, rather quickly, "I don't want to be in business with anyone. Thank you very much."

She smiled and glanced at Joe, almost looking for approval.

"Except for the unfortunate death of my first mate," Durall added, "this operation went very well. When Prohibition is over, they will all talk of this with great respect."

"Tell you what, Captain: see that your discount goes to the first mate's wife or his family."

Captain Durall gave Joe a long, touching look. "I will do that. Peter has a young wife. Thank you."

"Good. I now have one more thing to take care of." Joe grabbed Durall's arm. "What are you thinking about Gatsby and his men?"

"My first mate is dead, and that makes Gatsby an accomplice to murder. My crew and I have no qualms about throwing him and his men overboard."

Maggie mumbled, "Oh, dear…"

Hunker grunted. "Mighty long swim! If they make it, they're innocent."

Joe glanced at Hunker and back to Durall. "You're the law on this ship, Captain. But it was Kanky who killed your man. And you served justice on him."

Hunker and Joe exchanged looks. "So, the way I see it, that's the end of that! It's really in your hands, Captain." There was a slight nod from Hunker and Durall, but no more was said.

Durall's men were standing outside the cabin. Now, free from American soil and steaming for home, Joe could see anger on the crew's faces. Clearly, they had revenge on their minds.

Gatsby and his men were strapped to the lower berths, their hands tied behind their backs. Joe's eyes brushed over Louisa's red corset and red garter belt that were hanging from a porthole bolt. No card-playing tonight, he thought.

"What…what the…fu…fuck you going to do with us?" Collector uttered.

"It's out of my hands! When Sammy and the first mate died, you broke any hook with me."

Gatsby said, "You know I didn't do it?"

"Well, Jesus Christ! First Sammy, then Henry Grover, then First Mate Peter. You claim they were all victims of circumstance."

"They were!"

Joe shook his head. "Maybe, maybe not. But you're all here right now because your man killed the first mate."

Gatsby snapped, "You saw it happen! I didn't want to kill anybody. I was against Kanky and those Tommy guns. It was too late to argue about it."

Collector nodded. "Mister Gatsby is telling the truth, Joe."

Joe was silent for a few moments, trying to decipher the way things had gone and exactly what Gatsby claimed. He softly replied, "You still brought all this on yourself, Gatsby, as soon as you allowed them to put those fucking Tommy guns in their hands."

Collector shouted, "Mister Gatsby was against those guns. It was all Kanky's idea!"

"Throw them overboard!" one of Durall's crewmen shouted.

Gatsby's face turned white. "You can't let them do it! You can't! Collector's telling the truth!"

"Durall is the law on this ship," Joe said. "It's all up to him."

Pearly's expression revealed complete agreement.

~~~~~~

Off Fogland Point, Captain Durall slowed the ship and put the engine into neutral. Drifting south from the stern wind, the crew lowered the dory into the water. Everyone, including Maggie, was at the rail. Hunker and Joe climbed down the ladder and got into the skiff.

Durall and Joe shook hands. "I am terribly sorry about your first mate."

Durall shrugged. "In life, how can one ever know?"

Joe turned to Maggie. "You take care."

"You too, Joey." She gave him a kiss on the cheek. "And take care of our Janie."

Joe gave her hand a squeeze and climbed over the rail to the ladder. He motioned to Durall to get closer. He whispered, "Captain, Gatsby's men are just like your crew. They obeyed orders."

A look of surprise slowly crossed Durall's face. "You think I am a primitive? I already decided that I will give Gatsby's men a choice: either they toss Gatsby overboard or we toss them all overboard."

Joe accorded him a small salute. "Good luck, Captain."

From the dory, Joe and Hunker silently watched the *Maria* move slowly down the river. When the ship disappeared into the stormy night, Joe said, "Well, that's the end of that! I do hope Maggie makes out okay."

"She'll make out fine," Hunker grunted.

"Row, Hunker, row. We've got liquor to sell. Then we're going fishing."

~~~~~~

Everybody was waiting on the beach. They each had a bottle, and they were drinking. At first Joe thought they were just celebrating. Bottles were lined up on the hood of Joe's Buick. Bobby handed Joe a bottle without a smile, then he gave one to Hunker.

Pearly and Hunker each took a swig, and Joe raised his bottle for a toast. "To success!"

"Not really," Pearly said. "Not really," he repeated.

Joe asked, "What's wrong?"

Janie shook her head. "Well, there's no cellar. There's no church. And there's no liquor."

For a long moment nothing was said; the wind continued to blow.

Finally, Pearly said, "Joe, the whole damn building fell into the water. That's all there is to it."

"You weren't even out of the Basin when it happened," Janie added. "Swallowed up by the Seaconnet...like fish bait."

Joe stared at Janie in disbelief. All she could do was silently nod her head.

"There'll be liquor," Pearly added, "drifting up and down the Seaconnet River and eventually all over the bottom of Narragansett Bay, probably for years to come."

Joe made a nervous little noise, like a deep clearing at the throat. "Jesus." The wind pressed his oilskin against his chest. "The whole damn church and all the fucking liquor?"

Hunker moaned. "Oh, good God!" He leaned against the car and started to slide down to the ground. "If I were superstitious, I'd be thinking the good Lord is punishing Bottomley and we got mixed up in the funeral wake."

"Now that's something a Seaconnet fisherman would say," Janie exclaimed. There was no joy in her voice. She glanced down at Hunker, who had retired to sitting on the muddy ground, sucking vodka from his bottle.

There was another long silence. The only sounds were the gurgling of vodka and the storm.

Out of nowhere, Joe started to laugh. He grabbed his ribcage with both arms and hugged his sides and kept on laughing. "Oh, it hurts," he said, "but it's so fucking funny." He broke into full laughter, his shoulders shaking like crazy.

The others looked at each other and slowly joined in, all but Janie. Above them, even the dying, howling Beast from the East seemed to be having a say. There wasn't a light to be seen on either side of the river. Still, Joe and the others saw, or pretended to see, thousands of cases of booze bobbing down the Seaconnet, headed for points south and eventually sinking to a watery grave… Another potential harvest for another day.

~~~~~~

On George's Bank, Captain Durall decided to bury First Mate Peter. His family were hook fishermen from Chapel Cove, Nova Scotia. Peter's father and brother, while tub-hooking for halibut, had been lost in a storm. The crew felt it was appropriate that Peter join his family.

Captain Durall allowed Gatsby and his men to attend the service. Collector, temporarily released from his bondage, even sang a small rendition of "Amazing Grace," which made Maggie break into tears.

Right after the burial, Maggie and Captain Durall were in bed. Maggie had a determined look on her face. Durall said, "I'm listening, my tootsie. Explain it slowly. Don't get so excited."

"It's simple, my sweet captain: Gatsby and his crew are worth more alive than dead. You cut him a deal...it's either over the side, or ransom money..."

"How will we accomplish this?"

"First, we see if Gatsby is agreeable. That shouldn't be a problem. I'm sure he wants to live. We settle on an amount. Gatsby's rich. This I know. I'll call his lawyer, his money-man."

"You are indeed a businesswoman, my tootsie."

When the *Maria* arrived at her home port, Paul Moran, following orders, had chartered a plane and was standing on the wharf with a briefcase. Gatsby and his men waited while Captain Durall and Maggie counted the money twice that Moran had brought with him.

When the tally was done, Durall and Maggie actually shook hands with Gatsby.

Later, at Miquelon's small airport, Gatsby said to Moran, "I've had time to think, Paul. These Swamp Yankees got the best of me... I certainly underestimated Mister Bucolo. He has qualities that I wish I possessed."

Paul shook his head. "Don't be too hard on yourself, Jay. You're alive, and what you just went through now gives you the ability to do anything you want."

He quickly thought of Daisy and their time together in Louisville. He had let her believe that he was a person from the same class as herself—that he was fully able to take care of her. That had not been true then, but it was now. He would continue to pursue her—win her over—no matter the cost.

"By God! You're right, old sport, I still have my fortune...and I will win back my Daisy Faye."

Moran nodded, but he didn't respond. Inside his head, he was confused and fascinated that a man so rich, so sharp, and so worldly could revolve his existence on the pursuit of this married woman. Again he wondered how Gatsby's obsession for this elusive diamond girl would end. Paul Moran wasn't a betting man.

EPILOGUE

NOT LONG AFTER, GATSBY'S PURSUIT of Daisy Buchanan persisted. He scanned the Chicago newspapers daily, hoping to catch even the slightest mention or glimpse of Daisy, a ritual he performed with religious devotion. Ironically, Tom Buchanan unwittingly presented Gatsby with an opportunity when his affair with another woman prompted the Buchanan family's move from Chicago to Long Island. Gatsby settled into a lavish estate across the bay from the Buchanan residence, where he entertained on a grand scale, hoping for an encounter with Daisy.

Eventually, Daisy did come to him, and for a fleeting time, it was the realization of all Gatsby's dreams. But today, as he reclined alone in his pool, he reflected on how swiftly it all disintegrated in a single evening. Fatal mistakes, both in words and deeds, were committed. They should never have all gathered together in the city on that suffocating night.

Gatsby realized now that he and Tom's verbal duel in the stifling Plaza Hotel room had produced only misery. While Buchanan sought to diminish him, armed with accusations of the source of Gatsby's wealth, Gatsby had been convinced it was his chance to openly secure Daisy's affection forever. He had boldly urged her to publicly renounce any love she had ever felt for her husband. As the men clashed over her, Daisy erupted, reproaching both with her frustration and making it clear to Gatsby that his desires and expectations of her were excessive.

Unlike the water that cooled his body, Gatsby's brain couldn't stop reacting like a fiery inferno as the evening's events played over and over.

In hindsight, he recognized that Tom had only dispatched Daisy to return to Long Island alone with Gatsby because he felt victorious. He also revisited the folly of agreeing to let the shaken woman take the wheel of his car. Now, Myrtle Wilson lay dead, and Gatsby was ready to shoulder the blame to shield Daisy from harm.

He stretched out his arms, and both hands dropped into the pool. The rivulets of water traveled up his arm like a gentle massage.

Feeling a slight breeze, he paddled the floater towards the setting sun—and it made his face and chest feel good. He positioned himself even closer as the sun's pending farewell gave him an unexpected feeling of acceptance.

The air floater sagged near his head, and oddly, his wet hair made him think of a Catholic Baptism that he once attended. Then he recalled what his grandfather had said to him: "James… she'll never be yours…" His whisper was barely audible. "Not in any real sense. She's no longer the girl of your youth."

A small flock of noisy seagulls soared above and interrupted his grandfather's wisdom as he was suddenly transported back to Rhode Island and its waterfronts. It had been a while since he thought about Joe Bucolo and his gang. Smiling up at the sun, he also realized now that those Swampers were the true winners with their deep connection and loyalty to each other.

Back then, he had convinced himself that he could outmaneuver Foggy Joe—but he couldn't—just like he couldn't climb the old-money ladder of East Egg, which he hoped would move him closer to Daisy Faye.

Suddenly, the vengeful voice of a man, shouting like some moralizing bizarre mystic, interrupted Gatsby's thoughts.

Gatsby lifted his head just enough…, and then he heard… "You may have fooled me, but you can't fool God!" George Wilson cried out before he pulled the trigger.

Gatsby only heard the crack of the gun—immediately, the bullet slammed into him—and in less than a fraction of a second, everything turned into a silent, white calm while the pool water spiraled into thin circles of red.

~~~~~~

In Tiverton, the sun sparkled brightly along the Main Road. It was decorated with American flags; celebrating its 1922 Founder's Day Parade. Unknown to Joe and his men, in that same week of excellent weather, Jay Gatsby lost his life.

The marchers, in high spirits, had just passed by Brown's Provender. Across the street, the large hole in the embankment where the First Riverside House of Worship once stood was in the process of being filled in. Minister Bottomley, had so far been unable to find a new building for his congregation. Oddly, his flock of stingy Tivertonians appeared to have flown the coup.

The Basin was dotted with moored sailboats and various motor vessels; Francis Grover's entire menhaden fleet, minus the sunken Saint Peter, were chasing menhaden off the coast of Norfolk, Virginia.

Behind the parade, caught in traffic, blowing their horns, were at least a dozen vehicles. Joe's white Buick was dragging tin cans and old shoes. Along the road, onlookers were shouting congratulations to the newly married couple.

With their horns still blaring, the cars turned onto Riverside Drive and pulled into Wilcox's boatyard. A small army-surplus tent was erected near the railway. Inside, people gathered around benches and chairs, with refreshments set up on a long table.

Everyone close to Joe was present. Mary Standish standing with Pearly, Hunker, even Gertrude, Bobby Bancock (minus his brother, Billy, who married Nina and settled in California), Edmund Palmer, Frankie-the-Bone, Cory Wilcox, Tommy Walsh, Pat Morris, Doc Peckham, Ernest Turner, even Captain Durall and Maggie had made the trip down from Canada.

Durall had no choice because Janie had asked Maggie to be her maid of honor. When Maggie got out of Durall's car, she was tilted when she saw her mother and Minister Bottemley standing together. It appeared that Jessica Louise Jackson was receptive to the Minister trying to tend to his flock. Maggie whispered "Hallelujah! My mother has found religion."

Captain Durall heard Maggie, and asked, "My tootsie, what was that about?"

"I think my mother has finally seen the light."

On Cory Wilcox's railway, Joe's fishing dragger rested in its cradle, colorful pennants strung along the mast. The vessel was painted Nantucket green, with a white pilot house. Draped over the dragger's bow was a big blue banner hiding her name. Behind the railway, the *Black Duck* was tied to Wilcox's dock.

Joe never thought the day would come, as it happened, on the *Flo's* maiden voyage, even before her nets got wet, the *Flo's* engine blew up. At that point, Joe's boys were mumbling that the boat had turned into a Jonah. Hunker, feeling no pain, and seldom lost for words said, "'Joe and the *Flo* should've never got married.'"

Without the ability to go fishing, too much time and expenses began to take a toll on Joe's finances. Much to the Swamp Yankee's delight, as well as Janie's silent chagrin, Joe was forced to make a few trips to Rum-Row. Despite the continued pressure from the Coast Guard and the Feds, he still managed under dirty weather conditions to evade the law.

Janie was all smiles when Maggie approached. They hugged. Janie stared at Maggie, with true affection in her eyes. "I'm so happy you're here. My wedding and this celebration would have never been right without you."

Maggie beamed. "How could I not be here, Janie. You were always my best friend. Besides, you and Joe belong together. Everything now, is the way it should be." They both had tears sliding down their faces. They hugged again. Janie said, "I love you, Maggie…"

"I love you, Janie…"

Janie and Maggie glanced over at Joe, who was with Captain Durall and the boys. Joe pointed out towards the Tiverton Basin. Durall just shook his head, almost in disbelief. He said something that made everyone laugh.

Suddenly, Pearly yelled, "Hey, everybody, before we start this here celebration, we must launch this overdue fishing boat…"

There was a loud cheer and a clap of hands.

Pearly smiled. "We've got to do that first because Cory needs high tide…and we all know what high tide can do…" He quickly pointed towards the railroad bridge.

Mumbles from the rum-runners were drowned out by another loud cheer.

Joe glanced over at Cory by the winch engine and signaled he was ready.

Janie gave Maggie her flowers, and climbed up onto a small platform. She took the wrapped bottle of champagne from Joe. "You know how to do this…don't you?"

"Yes, Foggy Joe, I'm getting to be an expert."

She raised the bottle and at the same time, Pearly pulled off the banner, revealing the boat's new name: *Janie's Venture*

Pearly shouted, "Give it a good whack, sweet thing…"

Without hesitation, she smashed it vigorously against the bow. "I christen thee *Janie's Venture,*" she said with an air of puzzled delight.

Shouts and cheers erupted. Joe helped her off the platform, and over the din of noise, he said loudly, "I was beginning to think *Flo*'s name was cursed."

She laughed. "My superstitious fisherman."

Joe smiled and handed her the varnished shingle bill of sale.

She gave him an inquisitive look. "I'm a little confused…"

"It's the beginning of your new company. You're the boss now. You've got the ability…it runs through your blood, like the river you grew up on…"

She began to tear up, just as Cory released the winch brake. Slowly, *Janie's Venture* rumbled down the ways to even more cheers. Cory's men quickly tied her up alongside the *Black Duck*.

Among the crowd, Janie's tears were not alone. After a few dabs of handkerchiefs, the celebration started.

It didn't take Hunker long to bring out the liquor.

Janie and Joe stood inside the tent and looked at the boats, and the boys chatting. Cory Wilcox came over and asked, "What are you gonna do with the *Black Duck*?"

"Well, Cory, with this past year's bad luck, she saved my ass. Joe glanced at the rum boat. "I think I'll keep her for a while… You never can tell if the wind gets to whispering…"

Janie looked at Joe and smiled. "Yep, figured you'd say that."

Pearly shouted, "We knew it boys…didn't we?"

Hunker and Bobby Bancock cocked their thumbs at Joe.

Hunker slapped his thigh and, in a low voice, started to sing. "*Oh give me beans when I'm hungry…whiskey when I'm dry…*" They all laughed and raised their glasses into the air and took a drink in unison. "*Good old whiskey when I'm dry…*"

Pearly quickly raised his finger to his lips and pointed towards the tent and the ladies who were listening and watching them.

Hunker nodded and politely skipped his favorite line and went right to the ending. "*And old heaven when I die…old heaven when I die… when I die…*"

Made in the USA
Middletown, DE
03 September 2024

60196739R10267